REDBELLY CROSSING

ALSO AVAILABLE BY CANDICE FOX

High Wire
Devil's Kitchen
Fire With Fire
The Chase
Gathering Dark
The Ted Conkaffey series
Crimson Lake
Redemption Point
Gone by Midnight
The Bennett/Archer series
Hades
Eden
Fall

WRITING WITH JAMES PATTERSON

Never Never
Fifty Fifty
Liar Liar
Hush Hush
The Inn
The Murder Inn
2 Sisters Detective Agency
2 Sisters Murder Investigations
Black & Blue (BookShot novella)

REDBELLY CROSSING

A NOVEL

Candice Fox

CROOKED LANE

NEW YORK

Books should be disposed of and recycled according to local requirements. All paper materials used are FSC compliant.

This is a work of fiction. All of the names, characters, organizations, places and events portrayed in this novel are either products of the author's imagination or are used fictitiously. Any resemblance to real or actual events, locales, or persons, living or dead, is entirely coincidental.

Published in the United States by Crooked Lane Books, an imprint of The Quick Brown Fox & Company LLC.

Crooked Lane Books and its logo are trademarks of The Quick Brown Fox & Company LLC.

Library of Congress Catalog-in-Publication data available upon request.

ISBN (hardcover): 979-8-89242-564-3
ISBN (paperback): 979-8-89242-565-0
ISBN (ebook): 979-8-89242-566-7

Cover design by Crooked Lane Books

Printed in the United States.

www.crookedlanebooks.com

Crooked Lane Books
34 West 27th St., 10th Floor
New York, NY 10001

First Edition: April 2026

The authorized representative in the EU for product safety and compliance is eucomply OÜPärnu mnt 139b-14, 11317 Tallinn, Estonia, hello@eucompliancepartner.com, +33757690241

10 9 8 7 6 5 4 3 2 1

For Lynette and Maria.

ROB

It was the blood on the doorknob that caught his eye.

There wasn't an all-body plunging sensation, his animal instincts alerting him to the horrors that lay in wait beyond the door to room number four; the smell of death in the air and the darkness within didn't yet make all the hairs on his body stand on end and his stomach swan dive to the pit of his bowels. All that would come later. For now, Rob Winter, publican of the Redbelly Inn, simply stopped and looked at the smear of red and knew his morning routine had been disrupted.

It was a strict routine. At a march, Rob exited his car at precisely seven o'clock every morning, leaving it in the gravel space by the keg room door understood by locals to be his spot. He went directly to the beer garden, where he lifted the lid off a steel bin and scooped out a half-litre of birdseed and poultry pellets, using a cut-down plastic milk bottle that lived in the bin. If he didn't feed the peacocks first, they followed him from room to room issuing their ear-splitting cries, now and then tapping at the windows with their beaks, waking the guests at the inn. One had even come into the office once. Annoying, bossy birds. Rob didn't know who had originally owned the peacocks. Two had simply shown up in the beer garden, and before he could settle on whether to have them carted off by the council or scour the internet for someone who might adopt them, there were six. Not a simple task, getting rid of six peacocks.

After turning on the coffee machine, starting the pumps, clearing the keg lines and opening the basement doors to clear out the stink of spilt and ancient beer—some of it had first seeped into the sandstone one hundred and fifty years ago—Rob made his coffee and sat down to emails. Having completed that infuriating technological kerfuffle and being well into his walk-through of the inn's accommodation floor now, he was on his way to the blessed terminal step of the morning routine—sitting for a quiet moment in the front window of the empty bar and watching the river across the street, whispering to himself his daily prayers.

Now that goalpost had shifted into the distance. Was invisible, almost. Rob stared at the blood on the doorknob, then noticed more beneath it, splashed on the bottom of the door. He scratched at his thinning orange hair and sighed.

This wasn't the first time there'd been blood in the hallway outside the guest rooms. Punch-ups and drunken accidents were as ubiquitous in rural pubs as Akubras, high-vis and oversized schnitzels. Rob raised a fist and knocked on the door of room four, gently, so as not to wake the guests in other rooms. There came no answer. The second, third and fourth rounds of rapping produced no movement, no sound.

Rob went out of the hallway, down the stairwell between the accommodation building and the pub proper, and into the office beneath the guest rooms. He wrangled the computer into displaying the account for room number four, and instantly remembered the ponytailed young woman with the laptop and the polite if aloof demeanour who had checked in the previous afternoon. He took out his phone and dialled the phone number listed for the account. The call went straight to voicemail. As he dialled twice more and got the same result, thoughts occurred to him about the internet problems he'd had that morning. About the valley in which the pub sat, with its temperamental allowances and denials of contact with the outside world. Rob took the spare key card for room four that was attached to a lanyard and hung on the rack on the wall just inside the office. It was his instinctual noting of the time on the clock above the door, and the hard rectangle of the key card in his palm, which issued to Rob the first murmur of warning from deep inside his soul.

On legs made slightly unsteady by nerves, the small, bespeckled publican went back up the stairs and again to the door of room four. He knocked, louder this time, the noise drawing out the man staying in the first room along the hall. The scruffy guy in his thirties was already dressed in high-vis gear and yawning, offering no greeting as he stood outside room one, just staring in curiosity at Rob's activities. The publican rapped his loudest, then put his mouth close to the crack of the door.

'Ms Lutz?' he called.

No answer.

He swiped the key card against the panel and knocked once more, before turning the knob and opening the door as he called out, 'Ms Lutz, are you awake?'

Rob pushed the door fully open.

He stared at the blood on the floor, and felt the plunge.

EVAN

I was loading dishes smeared with maple syrup into the sink when the knock came at the front door of the house. The sound sent a bolt of dread through me. *Dad's here.* My father always knocked. Thumped, rather. The doorbell was right there. Eye height. Dad knocked, because a man knocks.

I walked through the kitchen, stiff, edgy. Glanced out at the gaggle of kids that had arrived not long ago, eager to spend the day with my son, Chris. They were clustered on the back verandah now, some of them still tucking in to the pancakes I'd carefully laboured over only to be issued with a painfully awkward 'Thanks' from about half of the ten kids present. I tried not to take it personally. These were kids for whom all social interactions were hard. Shy, pimpled, greasy nerds who felt at home in the library, who loved their teachers, who still had sleepovers. Chris's tribe. Some of the boys were wearing eyeliner, and one of the girls showed up wearing a velvet corset. She was going to go *paintballing* in a *velvet corset.* Jesus.

The old man was standing there with his hands in the pockets of his filthy jeans when I opened the door. He didn't say hello. Just locked his dead-fish eyes on me and said, 'We need to talk.'

Cancer, I thought.

Because I'm a piece-of-shit son, I always thought that when Dad turned up or called unannounced. *Come ooooon, lung cancer!*

'Can it wait?' I asked. 'It's Chrissy's birthday.'

'That was yesterday.'

'No.' I sighed. 'It's today.'

'It can't wait,' Arthur grunted, pushing past me into the hall. 'Your office. Now.'

I shut the door, turned and got ahead of him in the hall, wanting to cut him off before he had one of his classic interactions with Delle or one of the kids. Delle came into the hall, a doe hearing the footfall of hunters. 'Oh, hi, Arthur. We weren't expec—'

Arthur grunted as he turned into the home office. I gave Delle my best placating wave before closing the door.

'This'd better be quick,' I said. We arrived in a room the family shared, shelves crammed with Chris's PlayStation games and werewolf novels, boxes of Delle's art supplies, some police files I had printed and brought home. 'What's the problem?'

'There's been a murder in Redbelly overnight,' Arthur said. 'And you're going to get yourself on it.'

I felt a tingle of energy in the centre of my chest, reached for the phone in my back pocket. Dad wasn't a cop anymore. Hadn't been active in more than two decades. But somehow he always had his finger on the pulse of the region, knew when there'd been a drink-driving arrest, an assault, a drug raid, long before the jobs showed up on official police channels. Sure enough, I opened the New South Wales Police Active Incident app and found a listing that was only seventeen minutes old, for a town on the other side of my region: *REDBELLY CROSSING, CRITICAL INCIDENT, 1 DECEASED.* 'Right. Jesus. Okay. Technically it'll be Louis Dodge and his crew on that, from Wisemans.'

'You think I give a rat's arse whose case it is *technically*?' Arthur widened his eyes. 'It's a *murder*, Evan. It needs to be yours. The body's not cold yet. There's still time. And I need you to get assigned to it, because—'

'Yes.' I put a hand up. 'Yes, I know, you don't have to—'

'—I'm tired of living under the shadow of your colossal fuck-up.'

You don't have to say it, I thought. But he did. Of course he did. Because Dad was like that. He'd be talking about how I'd screwed up on the job, and what it had done to my loved ones' lives, what it had done to the Powder family's reputation, for decades to come, whether I did anything to clear the shadow of shame or not. Sure, he pretended it wasn't, but what I'd done to disgrace myself was the best thing that had ever happened to my father. It had almost got me fired, and meant Arthur had to come in swinging for me. It put a leash around my neck.

'Who told you it's a murder?' I asked. 'Where'd you hear about it?'

'It's all over town already. The publican found her about an hour ago.'

I rubbed the back of my neck, where a ball of stress was already knotting. 'But it's Chrissy's birthday.'

'What did you just say?' Dad narrowed his eyes, freezing mid-action as he slid a packet of cigarettes from the breast pocket of his flanno.

'I said, it's my child's birthday. I've got eleven kids out there that Delle and I are supposed to take paintballing.'

'You're taking them *where*?'

'Paintballing. It's a game.'

'Evan, listen to me very carefully.' Arthur licked his thin, sun-ravaged lips. 'I am trying real hard, *real hard*, not to leap over this desk between us and put your head through that window behind you. The restraint that I am showing is frankly mind-boggling, even to me.'

'Dad.'

'As if I should have to sell you on the idea *at all*...' Arthur drew out a cigarette, his mean, disgusted eyes still on me. 'This isn't going to be some three-day slapped-together paperwork-heavy piss-in. It's a girl stabbed to death in the pub.'

'Jesus, really?'

'Your reluctance to start making moves to get yourself assigned to this case, because it's your *child's fucking birthday* and you're taking him and his merry band of retards "paintballing", is making me want to weep for you, Evan, and for myself,' Dad said. 'You owe me my reputation back.'

'I get it.' I put my head in my hands. 'I get it.'

'A nice, juicy murder is just about the only thing that's going to bleach the stain of what you did out of public memory, my son.' He jammed the cigarette between his jaws and lit up, right there in my family's office. 'And if you're smart, you'll not only solve this murder but you'll get yourself wounded badly in the process. You could make a lot of people happy doing that, getting med-catted out of the job.'

I kept my face passive. 'I'll talk to Delle.'

'You'll *talk* to *Delle*?'

'I'll tell her what—'

'Saints preserve us.' Dad covered his eyes.

'—what's going on. I'll call Twitcher.'

'Yes, yes, go and beg for permission from the women in your life.' Dad got out of his chair with difficulty, favouring his damaged shoulder, and exited the office, shaking his head. 'I'm going to go chuck myself off the nearest bridge.'

I went out of the office and down the hall, hearing the front door slam closed behind my father and knowing the nausea his visit had left me with wouldn't settle for the rest of the day. The kids were all gathered around Chris at the table on the back deck. Terrible postures. Unwashed hair. Chrissy was licking the inside of his lip where a silver stud was embedded, making the bobble at the end jut out from his face in a way that made me want to gag. The youngest Powder male held up a box wrapped in black paper for a photo, made the sign of the horns with his other hand. Then he started unwrapping it. Delle took my elbow. I couldn't look at her. Wasn't ready yet for my second roasting of the day.

'What was that all that about?'

'Nothing. Work.'

'Is he gone?'

'Yes.'

'Did it occur to your father to come out here and say happy birthday to his grandson?' Delle asked. Like she actually wanted my father anywhere near her or her child. 'Would that have taken more than a few seconds?'

'Delle, on my sixteenth birthday, Dad threw a shoe at my head for making him feel old,' I told her. 'Can you drop it?'

'What did he want?'

'I have to go to Redbelly.' I drew a breath that hitched in my chest. 'And I need you to—'

'Evan!'

'—I need you to *not start with me*, Delle.' I lowered my voice. Some of Chris's friends had taken their eyes off the gift unwrapping and were watching us. 'It's exactly what we need. It's a murder.'

Turmoil in her eyes. The long-held desire to lift us out of the shame of our scandal with a good, solid case, something that might bring my rank back up, get me a posting somewhere out of Mangrove Mountain. She swallowed her anger so hard her throat constricted. A little came out anyway. 'I'm going to be stuck with these weird-ass teenagers all day, alone.'

'You want to go solve the murder instead?' I asked. 'We can swap.'

Chris dropped the wrapping paper on the table and turned over the gift.

'Oh ho ho!' He lifted up a box. Posed with it for another photo. 'Shit! Aw, this is fucking *sick*! Thanks so much, guys!'

Chris leapt out of his chair and came over to show the gift to us. The voices in the room were bumbling and tumbling around in my brain, coming in and out of sharpness as I tried to figure out what the hell I was going to tell Hayley Twitcher. I glanced at the design on the front of the box. Couldn't bring myself to read the words.

'Oh, fun.' Delle smirked. She was never angry for long, Delle. More than half the reason I'd married her. 'It's one of those ancestry kits.'

'A what?' I asked.

I felt Chrissy bump into my shoulder as he huddled in. 'A DNA swab kit. To find out your genealogy. Marty did one.' He pushed the box into my hands. I knew he was searching my distant eyes for validation. 'He found out he's seven per cent Norwegian.'

A sinking feeling hit my already churning stomach.

'You spit in a test tube and, like, send it off to the company,' Chrissy insisted. 'And they give you, uh, an assessment of your genetic ancestry. You know? Dad?'

'It's awesome, isn't it, Evan?' Delle poked me.

You want to know more about our family line? I thought. *Are you insane?*

'Yes,' I lied. 'It's really awesome.'

Chris took the box back and the kids returned to their huddle. Delle went into the kitchen. I stood alone in the corner of the verandah, trying to make sense of the strangely heavy blanket of dread that had wrapped itself around me in the wake of Dad's visit. On the face of it, I should have been happy. A murder in the region was a morbid kind of win for me. Okay, so Dad would have his hand clamped on the back of my neck for the next few days, pushing me to not screw this up like I did everything else. And Delle was going to be exhausted and resentful by nightfall, run ragged by Chris and his friends, and she wouldn't be subtle about letting me know it. But even accounting for these things, the feeling wouldn't lift that I'd just taken a first step down the wrong path.

As I packed a bag, said my goodbyes and stepped out the front door, already dialling my boss, I had the growing sense that these were the waking moments of what was to be a living nightmare.

RUSSELL

There was a woman in the men's locker room at Maroubra Police Station. I heard a thrilled whooping coming from the direction of the showers, some generalised dickheadery I couldn't quite make out, then the horse-clop of those awful court shoes Superintendent Gail Caplan wore everywhere ringing between the rows of lockers and the concrete walls. I pulled off my stinking white business shirt and tossed it into my locker, a problem for Future Russell. I was slipping on a black T-shirt as the short, sharp-edged woman in her sixties came around the corner of my row.

'I heard you were still here.' Gail looked me up and down. She was always looking people up and down. 'Rus, we need to talk.'

'Uh-huh. I know the drill,' I said. 'Your office, Monday morning.'

'No, not Monday. Now. We're talking about this now.'

'I know you're pissed at me, but we can sort it out later. I need to get out of here.'

'Russell—'

'The home invasion on the waterfront. Two bludgeoned to death. I just heard about it. That'll be Paddo's case. I'm leaving before he pins me down, wanting to know a strategy for it. I don't have five hours to teach the guy how to run a crime scene.'

'The waterfront situation isn't the only murder case we took in overnight.'

I pulled on my shoes. 'Huh?'

'I just got off the phone with central command. They're assigning us an out-of-area job,' she said. 'A girl in her twenties, killed out in the sticks. Place called Redbelly Crossing. It's up past Wisemans Ferry.'

'That's miles away.'

'Yes, and we've been landed with it.'

'Why?'

'Because the victim's got an apartment down on Maroubra Road, so she lives full time in our area command. It'll be a joint thing. One team here, one team out there. There are no local coppers in Redbelly Crossing who are detective rank or higher.'

I rose to my feet. 'Okay, look, before you go any further, Gail, it's a no. I'm not doing it.'

'Yes, you are.'

'Gail—'

'Let me remind you of two things, Russell. First: it's "Superintendent Caplan" while we're at work. And second: you don't get to pick your gigs; I do. And I've picked this gig for you, because less than twelve hours ago, you assaulted a member of the public.'

'I've got Bridie this week! You know that!'

'Yes, and you should have thought about that before you started swinging fists, shouldn't you?' Gail barked. 'You punch-happy sack of shit!'

'You're telling me you're gonna send me on an out-of-area homicide'—my voice was rising, echoing across the locker room—'on my *scheduled week off*, just because—'

'Because you punched a drug dealer in the mouth?' Gail put her hands on her hips. Her voice was as loud as mine. 'Yes, Russell. *Hell* yes. And I'm well within my rights to do so! You need to be seen being held accountable for your actions! You can't go around socking low-lifes in front of witnesses whenever the hell you feel like it!'

'Listen—'

'No!'

'Listen, please.' I lowered my voice, told myself not to grab her by the shoulders. 'I'm on leave. I asked for it months ago. And I don't want to go out there. I'm serious. Gail, I'm serious! I'm *from* there, okay?'

'No, you're not. You're from Maroota. That's an hour from here, and Redbelly Crossing is, what—half an hour further again? Don't try to give me that, Russell. I'm a Hawkesbury girl too, you know. I need you out there by midday.'

'But my dad's out there, and my brother's out there, and I don't want to run into either of them,' I said.

'Too bad.'

'But Bridie—'

'Too bad, Russell!' Gail snapped.

We watched each other, fuming. It was starkly silent in the locker room now. Gail Caplan and I were the two biggest, scariest motherfuckers in our command area, and we didn't go toe to toe on much, because whenever we did it had the effect it was having now. Earth-shaking. Our disagreements not only rattled people but news of them spread like wildfire, and inevitably the stories being told about the conflict needed to pick a winner. Gail had me in a corner. Her eyes were telling me there'd be biblical levels of pain in my future if I kept on. Punishments that far exceeded disappointing my already overwhelmingly disappointed child and possibly running into my estranged brother and father.

Gail walked off, so I lost by default. I slammed my locker and kicked over a bin to let the eavesdroppers know I wasn't happy about it.

* * *

I don't like delivering bad news to my teenage daughter. Because over the past ten years, that's all she's got from me. Towards the end of my marriage to her mother, as I started withdrawing from my family life and hiding in my work, I was the father too busy to come see her receive an award at school. Too distracted to listen to tales of her friendship dramas. Too tired to stay up late watching a new Netflix series with her. I was retreating into myself, yes, but I was also using tiredness and busyness as an excuse to avoid being with her. Because a part of me knew the end was coming, and I needed to soften the loss of her father for her somehow. Just after Bridie turned thirteen, I delivered the news to her. That while I loved her mother as a person, I didn't want to be her husband anymore.

I was gay.

And I was leaving.

The five years since had been rocky. At eighteen years old, Bridie had spent almost a third of her life watching her mother grapple with the idea that I'd been lying to her for our entire relationship. There was nowhere in the house to hide from Georgia while she weathered the surprise and humiliation and grief of being abandoned by a man who apparently had discovered all of a sudden, at the ripe old age of 48, that he was a homosexual. It wasn't fair, what I did to Bridie. Or Georgia. But I did it anyway.

I'd moved out of the house immediately but stuck near enough to my wife and child to witness their pain and explain what I could. I tried to balance that with giving them space to recover from what I'd done. No matter how close I lingered, a great crevasse opened up between us. Them on one side, me on the other. Bridie and I were like strangers now, and Georgia and I were down to texts only. This week had been planned as a radical bonding session between me and my kid—suggested to Bridie by her therapist. I'd been thrilled by the idea when she told me. We'd organised for her to come and stay at my apartment in Newtown. I was weirdly excited for her to see my place. We were going to eat Thai food and go to the movies and make fucking eye contact for once. Start trying to piece back together this utterly pulverised thing.

Now I arrived on the doorstep of my former family home in Eastwood, in Sydney's north west, and stared at the welcome mat, preparing to tell my child that this week wasn't going to be the end of the awkwardness, sadness and disappointment that characterised our relationship. The door opened. Bridie was there, taller and older and more shockingly beautiful than she'd seemed when I last saw her, six months earlier. She'd done something new with her hair, but I didn't know if saying something about it would be odd, so I just said, 'Hey.'

'Hey,' she said to my shoes. She pulled the door open and backed away apologetically, like I was a plumber there to remove a dead rat from the laundry drain. 'Mum's not here.'

'Oh.' I braced against the dual waves of guilt and relief. 'She's not?'

'She caught a gang rape case last night.'

'Big weekend,' I said, for some reason known only to god. I followed Bridie to the kitchen, looking around the house for changes to torture myself with. The kettle was new. I liked the old kettle. There was still a picture of Georgia in her police uniform in the hallway bookcase, but the one of me had disappeared since my last visit.

'We've got two murder cases,' I said. 'Three dead overall.'

'Jeez.'

'Yeah.'

There was a duffel bag on a chair at the fucking dining room table. I wanted to cry. My daughter and I continued to stare at our shoes, then started to speak at the same time. Had it always been this hard?

'Should we—'

'Listen—'

'Oh . . . you go ahead.'

I sighed. 'I actually got assigned one of the murders, Bridie. And it's out of town. Well, it'll be half there and half here, because the victim's got an apartment in Maroubra. But I'll be in charge of the half that's out there, in the country. So—'

'So you can't have me for the week?' Bridie asked. I searched her tone too hard for relief, trying to decide if my child hated me as much as I feared she did. For the first time, our eyes met. Electric pain shot right down my throat and into my chest, coming from those unreadable grey orbs.

'No,' I said. But I couldn't stand the pain for more than a second or two. Other words came bubbling up. 'Uh, I mean, no, that's not what I'm saying . . . exactly . . . I'm just trying to see whether—'

'Whether I'm okay to go out there with you?'

'Uhhh . . .'

Bridie was thinking. I should have stopped her but didn't, because I'm a coward. 'Yeah. I don't mind, I guess. Where is it?'

'A place called Redbelly Crossing.'

'*Where?*'

'It's about an hour's drive. Past Maroota. Past Wisemans,' I said, watching the train hurtle down the mountain, brakes off, the only way to stop it to throw my body on the tracks.

'That's not too far.'

'It's not,' I conceded. 'But I'll be working, Bridie. I'll be running around conducting interviews. Making calls. A case like this, it'll be a thousand and a half phone calls, you watch. You won't see much of me.'

She thought. I drew a deep breath. Again, we started speaking at the same time.

'If you think—'

'You've g—'

'Sorry.' I gestured to her, my face burning.

Bridie gave another shrug, slow this time, only one shoulder lifting. 'I was just going to say . . . You've got to eat and sleep some time.'

'I do.'

'I could see you then.'

'Mmm-hmm.'

'Is it bushy out there?'

'Yes.'

'I could bring my rescue cage. Transfer my branch with the volunteer group. What region is that?'

'The Hawkesbury.'

'Right. Maybe if you have a minute now and then between, like, investigation stuff, you could drive me to some wrangles.'

We both looked out the dining room doors to the yard, across the lawn I used to mow, to the spot where Bridie kept her animal rescue cage. It was by the hose reel, where she'd dumped it after washing it last. It was never more than a couple of days between rescues, from what Georgia had told me. Bridie and Georgia had been deep into animal rescue for a wildlife group when the kid was small and Georgia was a constable working swing shifts. The teen got back into wrangling injured animals when she started high school, seeking a distraction from the chaos of our divorce.

'That could work,' I said. She smiled. *Actually* smiled.

Bridie headed for the doors. 'So let's go then.'

EVAN

I was taking corners too fast, the Kia Sportage grinding on the gravel on the unsealed roads, kicking up dust. My mind ticked away as I drove. Thinking about the crime. About cameras. The properties I was passing were few and far between, marked only by the occasional milk-urn letterbox standing sentinel beside a gum tree, or a sign hanging from a wire fence: *Trespassers will be shot*.

I was twenty minutes out of Redbelly and coming in hot. My stomach kept plummeting. Without warning, it just fell, a sickening dive that almost made me double over. I told myself it was guilt about landing Delle with Chris and his crew for the day. Or Dad's reminder of my great shame. We were coming up on one year since the incident. Wiping sweat from my brow, I applauded myself for almost having forgotten it. My phone buzzed. Hayley Twitcher, my chief superintendent out of Gosford, calling me back.

'Isn't it your day off?' Hayley asked in greeting.

'Ah, yes. Technically. There's been a murder in Redbelly Crossing. Have you heard about it?'

'I saw sooomething on the readouuut . . .' I could hear Hayley's leather chair creaking as she adjusted her position. A computer mouse clicking. 'Mmm. Oh, yep. One deceased. What is it?'

'I'm hearing a stabbing.'

'What are you going there for? Don't tell me Dodge and his crew have called you in directly. He knows he has to go through me if he wants extra staff.'

'No, he hasn't. I just decided to head there.'

'Why?'

'Listen . . .' My mind was whirring. I forced myself to slow down. 'Boss, I'm hoping to pitch something to you.'

'Oh, Evan, no.'

'I *know*, Hayley, I know,' I pressed. 'But opportunities for me to make good after what happened are slim. Okay? You *know* that. The last murder we had was a year ago and it was all wrapped up before it even appeared on the readout. And the one before that was a fucking accident. If I could just take a look at this thing and see whether—'

'You do not assign yourself to cases, Evan. Especially when they're out of area. Redbelly Crossing is Dodge's turf. He probably has big dreams of making detective too, you know.'

'Yes, but—'

'Like I've told you a hundred times: if I were you, mate? I wouldn't even *think* about applying for a rank upgrade consideration until the current command team has cleared out. You don't want anybody on the decision team who will remember what happened. If you go up and you fail, it'll be another few years before you can try again.'

I chewed my lip, wrung the steering wheel. 'Yep.'

'You know what I mean?' Hayley asked.

'I do.' I gasped for air. Thinking about Delle, and Chrissy, and the almost imperceptible tightening I saw in their shoulders every time they left the house. Like they were walking into a hard, cold wind. Delle hadn't run into the Sanderson family in town for a while. And things had been quiet at school between Chris and the Sanderson boy, as far as I knew. But this was my chance to make it all go away. 'Boss, I just need this. I *need* this. I would owe you. I mean, I know I already do. But I would owe you more. To the end of the world and back.'

'I get it,' Hayley said.

'Can I go?'

She gave a heavy sigh. 'Okay. Go. Stick your nose in.'

'Thank you.' I sighed. 'Thanks, Hayley.'

'Who's the victim?'

'Girl in her twenties, apparently. Stabbed at the pub.'

'Hmm.' Hayley snorted a rueful, one note-laugh. 'Which one of Redbelly's slithering slimebags has gone and done that, then?'

'Dunno yet.'

'Plenty out there to choose from,' Hayley said.

RUSSELL

We got almost all the way to Glenorie in silence so thick and loud it thrummed in my brain; heavier than the roar of my Mustang. And it's an old Mustang, with a throaty growl and a loose alternator belt. Bridie is tall, like me, so she curled up in her seat in a jumble of legs, like a greyhound on an undersized dog bed, and watched the suburbs become steadily bushier until the horizon had disappeared and we were surrounded by tall, pale gums.

When I couldn't stand it anymore, I said, 'I'm really sorry about this.'

She probably thought I just meant the past hour, when really I meant the past ten years, so she said, 'It's not your fault. It's work.'

'It kind of is my fault, though.'

'How?'

I cleared my throat. 'I might have given a drug dealer a little love tap yesterday. This case is my punishment.'

'You hit a guy?'

'Yeah.'

'Why?' Bridie turned slightly in her seat. I felt her eyes on my face, gripped the steering wheel hard, told myself this week was about being completely honest.

'Um. Well. I'd been called in to take a look at his apartment in Hillsdale. There were bullet holes all over it. The guy's girlfriend had called the cops because they'd been robbed for a bunch of electronics. And she shouldn't have done that, because, you know . . . It was an obvious dealer house.' I shifted in my seat. 'So her boyfriend, he was pissed already. Then the girlfriend starts telling me that there's not only electronics missing from the apartment but cash, too. Lots of it. And I ask why there's so much cash lying around. And the boyfriend grabs her to shut her up.'

'He grabbed her?'

'Yeah. Hard. So, I . . . you know . . .'

'You smacked him one.'

'I did.' I looked over at Bridie.

We both fell silent. Bridie's face was unreadable. I'd punched someone in front of her once, and the guilt about that was like a splinter in my brain. We settled back into the swampy, suffocating silence. My phone was buzzing in my pocket. I rounded a curve and the small township of Glenorie opened up in front of us, a big Woolworths car park and a cluster of shops hugging a little road leading into the suburb. There was a giant fibreglass meat pie sitting on top of a trailer off to the side of the road, big as a kiddie pool.

'I need coffee.' I started pulling over. 'I was up all night filling in reports and stuff for clipping the junkie. Do you, uh . . . do you drink coffee?'

'I do.'

I slipped my wallet from my pocket and handed it to her. 'Maybe you could go grab us some supplies while I get started on those thousands of phone calls.'

She took the wallet wordlessly and got out. The relief her absence brought made me break out in a sweat. This was like the worst date I'd ever been on in my life. I finally answered the unknown number. 'Yeah?'

'Gunther Powder?'

'It's Russell. Who's this?'

'Oh. Right. It's Senior Sergeant Louis Dodge here, from Wisemans Ferry Area Command. I'm calling because—'

'Okay, so for you it's "Detective Inspector Powder", then. Or "Sir".'

There was silence on Dodge's end of the line, a beat while the rural cop switched gears and started pedalling hard to catch up.

'Right. Of course. *Detective Inspector* . . . I was just checking on your ETA. I've got the scene held down, but . . . I don't know if you want a sitrep now, or when you get here, or . . . ?'

'What do you mean you've got it "held down"?' I let my voice, which was already tight, tighten further. 'Get it through your head now, Dodge, that cop speak terms like "sitrep" and "held down" annoy the shit out of me. What's the scene?'

'It's a hotel room, sir. Girl in her twenties killed in her room at the pub here in town. Chloe Lutz is her name.'

'And who's been inside that hotel room?'

'Ah, well, I've got four patrollies from Wisemans Ferry station assisting me. They're my staff. And we've been sent a snapper—uh, a photographer—from Sydney. She got here ahead of you, so I let her in to do her thing.'

'Jesus fucking Christ.' I held my head. 'Dodge, get the photographer out of there until I've done my walk-through. Get *everyone* out of there. Have the four patrollies been in the room?'

'No, sir, they've been in the hall, but—'

'*Get everyone out of the fucking building, Dodge. For fuck's sake!*'

'You've got it, sir. I'm sorry, sir.'

'Don't be sorry; do your job and establish a cordon. Have you got the names of the paramedics?'

'The ones who took the body away, you mean?'

'The body's gone?'

'Uh, yes. It's—'

'*Why is the fucking body gone?*'

'If you'll give me a second to explain.' Dodge drew a strangled breath. 'It wasn't immediately clear to the paramedics on scene how long Ms Lutz had been deceased. The body was limp, and the heating was cranked in the room, so she was warm and she appeared to have been, uh, just recently injured. There was a decision made to get her out of there and continue CPR on the off chance she might be helped.'

'Jeeez.'

'The deceased is now at the local medical centre, until we're instructed by you to transport her Sydney for forensic testing. I've got the staff from the pub trying to drum up a list of names of everyone who was here last night.'

'What? Everyone who was where?'

'The hotel rooms are above a pub. It's looking to me like someone's followed the victim to her room from the crowd downstairs, maybe went berserk when she wouldn't let him in.'

'Listen to me carefully, Dodge. Because I'm only going to say this once.'

'Okay?'

'I need your half-baked theories about what happened during this homicide like I need to contract a flesh-eating disease of the eyeballs,' I said. 'Offer me another one and we're going to have serious problems.'

'Got it, sir.'

I hung up. Bridie had climbed back into the car so quietly I hadn't noticed. She was sitting there beside me with my wallet in her lap and her eyes just slightly too wide. I could feel the pulse in my neck ticking like a bomb.

'I've ordered.' She held the wallet up, eyes on the dashboard. 'I didn't know what card to use, though.'

'Oh, right. Sorry.' I took the wallet from her, pulled out my Visa. She tucked her lips in, nodded, did a little shuffle in her seat like she was trying to decide whether to get back out of the car or not.

'Listen,' I said. 'Bridie.'

'Yeah?'

'When I'm at work . . .' I struggled, my pulse slowing, sweat beading at my brow. 'I'm . . . I'm a complete fucking arsehole, okay? To everyone. It . . . it doesn't matter who they are or whether they're doing a good job or not. It's just how I operate.'

'The Prick Switch.' She nodded.

'Huh?'

'Mum calls it your Prick Switch.' Bridie's eyes darted to mine and then away, quick as a flash. 'Like, you sort of . . . flip the switch on and become a total prick. She said you do it because it keeps people away from you.'

I watched my daughter and felt sad and embarrassed, and yet more understood by my ex-wife than I had in the course of our entire marriage. 'That's right. You two have talked about this?'

'Yes.'

'About me being a prick?'

'Only to say, like, she wishes she had one,' Bridie said. 'A Prick Switch. Like, if she had one, people would leave her alone about what happened in . . . in the marriage.'

I mulled over a question I didn't want to ask, a question I already knew the answer to. The answer had been riding in the back seat of my heart for half a decade. 'People give her shit about the divorce, do they?'

'Yeah.'

'Still?'

'Yeah.'

'What kind of shit?'

'Um, like, they call her "The Beard",' Bridie said. 'Or whatever.'

I looked out the windscreen so I didn't have to look at my child. 'I'm sorry, Bridie.'

'I know.' She popped the car door. 'I'll go get the coffee.'

EVAN

A stretch of farmland, where an old iron clothesline stood crookedly on a hill, festooned with sun-faded socks. A group of Shetland ponies grazing in the shade of a pear tree. Hand-painted signs urging drivers to slow down and watch for wildlife. The bridge to Redbelly Crossing township wasn't visible through the tree line until I was almost on it, white-painted wood and steel frame, bare boards that drummed under the car. I looked across the river and saw the pub, with its striped corrugated-iron awnings and high sandstone chimneys. There was a pair of squad cars and a forensics van parked at the roadside. The entire outdoor seating area was closed off with police tape.

I came down onto the main road and spotted Louis Dodge pacing in front of the police tape, tapping out a message on his phone. I parked across the street from the pub and walked over. The portly, round-faced sergeant from Wisemans glanced up when he heard my footfall in the gravel, seemed relieved to see a familiar face.

'Oh, Evan. Hey.'

'How bad is it?'

'Pretty bad.'

'Who was she?'

'Chloe Lutz. From Sydney.'

'What was she doing here?'

'Dunno. But because she's from the big smoke, they're sending me a detective from there. Guy should arrive any second.' Dodge looked at me, paused the texting. 'Happened last night, we think. They found her this morning. Are you just passing through town, or . . . ?'

'Hayley asked me to come on to it as lead of the local team.'

Dodge dropped his hands by his sides. 'Why would that be?'

'Why do you think?' I said. 'She's trying to get rid of me, and this is the only way she sees how.'

Dodge's meaty face twitched with conflicting emotions. Anger, frustration, nervousness at the idea that whatever he said now might make it back to Hayley, our shared superior. He was a rule-follower, Louis Dodge. A respecter of rank. It was part of the reason he'd come up to sergeant as fast as he had, in a region where nothing happened and there was no opportunity to prove your skills and get promoted out. 'Seems almost like—'

'Like what?' I asked. *Like a reward for bad behaviour*, I thought. Dodge could read the words in my eyes. He turned and eased a sigh. 'Nothing.'

'You'll still be needed. Everyone will. I'll make sure the detective knows you're number three when he gets here,' I said.

'Uh-huh. Thanks.'

'No worries.'

'Speaking of which . . .' Dodge wiped his brow on his hairy forearm. 'Did you say to me once that your dad's a cop?'

I ignored the question, having had more than enough talk of my father for the day and wanting to get a jump on the case. 'I'm gonna go take a look.'

'Because the name I have for the guy who—'

'The hotel rooms are up top, yeah?'

'Ah, well—' Dodge put a hand on my arm. 'It's a closed scene, Evan.'

'Not for me, it's not.' I walked off.

RUSSELL

Tight bends in the road. Hints of the river, brown and sandy and flecked with painter's brush-stroke reeds. I rode the brake as clouds of tiny brown birds erupted from the grass at the side of the road every few kilometres, seeming to waft by only inches from the windscreen, cheating death. Bridie sat up in her seat to take in the township as we came onto the bridge. The pub on the left. The playground. A sign indicating a cafe down the street.

'This is it?' she asked.

'It used to be just the pub,' I said. 'When I was a kid.'

'Oh, that's right.' Bridie glanced at me. 'You grew up out here.'

'Back at Maroota.'

'We passed it? Pop's farm?'

'We passed the road leading to it, yeah.'

'Why didn't you point it out?' she said. 'I always wanted to know where it was.'

I stared ahead, didn't answer the question, because there was no way of answering it. Not without opening all those closed doors in my mind, doors I'd spent decades steadfastly bolting. There was police tape visible outside the pub but no gawkers lined up along it. I parked under a sprawling fig tree and got out, and a beer-bellied sergeant emerged from under an awning. He had to step sideways to avoid a peacock in full rainbow regalia that was pecking around under a picnic table. Bridie got out and gave a little cry of delight at the bird while I went to greet Louis Dodge, who looked like he wanted to smile but didn't dare.

'Sir.' Dodge offered a sweaty hand. I shook it but made a face. 'Forensics arrived about ten minutes ago. And there's one officer up there now, who's been assigned ground team leader, who's getting his first look. I've held everyone else back so you can do your walk-through. They're in the beer garden. I didn't realise you were bringing your, uh, your . . . ?'

'Daughter.' My eyes met Bridie's. 'She's going to make herself scarce until I wrap up here.' The kid didn't need to be told twice and went off after the peacock. 'Show me the room.'

We walked around the back of the pub. Lush gardens hopping with bowerbirds, picnic tables under prehistorically large camphor laurel trees, their branches meeting, blocking out the sun. Four patrol cops were eyeing me as they smoked, leaning against one of the tables, while two women were slipping into protective forensics suits behind the open-doored van. I scowled at everyone, took in the layout of the place. The pub was divided into two separate buildings, an external wooden stairwell between them, leading up to a landing. On the left, the hotel rooms. On the right, an unmarked blue door. I walked up the wooden stairs, taking in the scene behind me, of the beer garden, and in front of me, of the strip of land before the road, the distant playground, the river. Louis Dodge swiped a card to unlock the door to the accommodation area. It opened onto a musty, dimly lit hallway.

'So, everyone has been cleared out,' he said, taking a pair of forensics booties from a fold-out table just inside the door and handing them to me. 'The pub owner, the guests who were here last night, everyone. I confirmed the IDs of all the guests and took initial statements, and they've been informed they will likely be required for formal interviews. Happily, we haven't had any looky-loos gathering outside. We've had a few slow drive-bys, but that's it.'

'Have you got an officer there noting down all the drive-by plates?'

'Uh, no.'

'Why not?' I snapped. 'Your patrol cops are inactive. That's a problem. I saw four idiots lounging around downstairs, smoking. You should have one watching the traffic and two out door-knocking.'

'Of course, of course.' Dodge slipped a phone from his pocket and fired off a text. 'It's just . . . Look, this is our first homicide here in a while, sir. It's certainly the first one I've ever had where it wasn't immediately obvious who the killer was.'

'Good! I sure as shit hope homicides are rare around here,' I said. 'If you were dropping balls like this every other week, Redbelly Crossing would be as popular with serial killers as Los Angeles was in the seventies. There's a few people I'd like to knock off myself; maybe I'll do it here.'

'I get it, sir.' Dodge nodded.

'Who's the arsehole who's in my scene?' I raged, marching up the hall. 'One of your cronies, Dodge?'

'Well, I actually wondered if—'

'Never mind, I'll get him out myself,' I barked.

EVAN

There was a blood smear on the outside doorknob. I stepped over the threshold, glanced at the chain on the lock as I went through, which was intact. I looked at the walls in the short hallway into the room. Both walls told me something. On the left, a new dent in the plasterboard at about the five-foot-five mark, just inside the door itself and beside a framed print of a chicken. Plaster dust on the floor. On the right, on both the wall and the open door itself, medium-impact cast-off patterns in blood. I stood there and tried to visualise what had happened. Saw the victim, Chloe Lutz, being grabbed by the throat or the face as she opened the door, being shoved hard into the wall, making a dent in the gyprock with the back of her head. Being held there while she was stabbed, probably two or three times, in the abdomen, judging from the height and amount of cast-off on the wall. I looked down at the mess of handprints and smears on the bloodstained carpet, stepped over it all, followed the smears as they went up the hall past the wardrobe and the bathroom and arrived at the foot of the bed. The bed wasn't made but wasn't messed up, either. No struggle. The coverlet and top sheet were flipped back on the left-hand side, closest to the bathroom and the front door. I walked over and saw there was no blood on the sheets, or on the walls. Just a couple of big pools in the carpet where Chloe had crawled, rested, dragged herself on, and then finally arrived at the place where she bled out and died under the window to the beer garden. The curtain was still drawn, blocking out the view. I looked up, saw that there were circular oyster-style lights in the ceiling, which were switched off. Saw another blood smear on the light switch.

I went to the spot where Chloe had died, crouched down, looked hard at the shape of the blood in the carpet. She'd been lying on her side, facing the bed. I could see the imprint of her upper arm. Her thigh. I took some deep breaths, rubbed my throat, got the sudden urge to vomit. This wasn't me. I didn't gag at crime scenes like a fucking rookie. What was this whole-body dread, this sense that a storm was about to hit and I was going to be caught in it, swept away?

I rose, looked at the bed again, preparing to do another lap of the room. Voices in the hallway outside made me jolt.

'Who's the arsehole who's in my scene? One of your cronies, Dodge?'

'Well, I actually wondered if—'

My brother, Russell, was there. The sight of him made me freeze. The moment seemed to collapse in on itself. It was like realising I was inside a dream but not being able to wake from it. Nothing made sense. Russell seemed somehow larger and more menacing than the last time I had seen him, five years ago. He'd been puffed up then, the way that he was now, standing in the doorway, mean-eyed and raising an enormous finger to point it at my chest like a gun.

'*You!*' Russell's grey eyes narrowed. 'What the *hell* are you doing here? Don't tell me you're on this.'

'I am,' I said. Dodge was hovering in the hallway behind Russell, a bare sliver of him visible past Russell's broad shoulder: a single eye. 'My chief super put me on it.'

'Forget that,' Russell spat. 'I'm the assigned detective, and I'm not working with you.'

'*You're* the assigned detective?' I fumbled, trying to get a grip on reality. 'How?'

'Doesn't matter how. I'm on this. Which means you're out. Hit the road.'

'Russell, wait—'

'I'm not working with you.'

'You have to,' I said. 'My chief—'

'Tell her I sacked you.' Russell jerked a thumb towards the hall. 'You're redundant. Your services aren't required. *Scram*, Evan, before I create another crime scene right here on top of this one.'

'Are you guys . . .' Dodge's words were again ventured carefully, a mouse trying to talk his way out of a lion's den while two beasts snarled at each other. 'You two are related, are you?'

I nodded. 'Russell is my brother.'

'Huh! Small world.'

'*Get out, Evan!*'

'I thought there must be a family connection.' Dodge folded his arms, curious now. 'Odd name, "Powder". So you're both from—'

'Just give us a minute, Dodge, will you?' I widened my eyes at him, and the sergeant turned and left. Russell remained in the doorway to Chloe's room. I walked over, my hands up in surrender. 'Russell, lis—'

Russell seized a handful of my T-shirt, got chest hairs as well, making me yowl with pain. Water welled in the corners of my eyes. 'No, *you* listen,' Russell snarled.

'Rus!'

'I've had a real prick of a morning, okay?' Russell said, squeezing hard as my hands closed around his fingers. He was almost lifting me off my feet. 'Bridie is downstairs. She's supposed to be staying with me this week in the city. Instead, I've been shafted out here to Fucksville against my will. When Georgia finds out I've dragged our child along on whatever the hell this is, she's going to feed my balls into a paper shredder. The last thing I need to add to this delicious turd sandwich of a day is *your* sorry mug. I'm here to clear this thing up and get back home. Okay? So get a move on. Now, Evan. Go.'

Russell yanked me into the hallway, shoved me hard. I found myself suddenly released. Stood with my face burning and smoothed down my crumpled shirt.

'I can't, Russell.'

'Why not?'

'Because I just finished begging my way onto this job.' I swiped at a tear that had fallen free of my eye. 'I need it. For the detective's exam. If I don't get my stripes and get the fuck out of Mangrove Mountain in the next couple of years, Delle is going to leave me.' I drew a ragged breath. 'You must have heard about my . . . my . . .'

'I heard.'

'Right.' I nodded hard. 'So, you know, then, that I was supposed to be out of here by now. But I fucked up. And this might be my last shot at getting out for a long, long while.'

Russell shook his head, walked away, into the room, stood looking at the scene. 'The mess you've made of your life is not my problem, Evan.'

'Mate, please—'

'No.'

'Ple—'

'It's your son's birthday, for Christ's sake. If you cared that much about him, you'd be doing something with the kid.'

'You remembered.'

'He's still my nephew, even if his dad's a traitorous piece of garbage.'

'Thanks.'

'Yep.'

'Russell, I would love to be out right now with my kid,' I continued. 'And I'm . . . I've been fighting with Delle for a good long while about being stuck out here. It's not so bad for me, because I'm always working. But she's . . . you know . . . She's got to see people in the town. And Chris has got to go to school. So, regardless of what you think of me, and what happened between us—their futures are riding on this.'

Russell said nothing. All the fire had gone out of him. He was like that, I remembered. Like a volcano. Explosive, then worryingly calm.

'I'd appreciate it if you at least left me on the books for this. I don't have to be in your face the whole time. I can be off doing sideline stuff.'

I stood behind him, watching Russell's profile as my brother surveyed the room. I saw him walk further in, turn in a slow circle, taking it all in. The blood on the floor. The hole in the wall. The window to the beer garden. On the bench beside the little television set, Chloe Lutz's duffel bag was upturned, clothes scattered along its length. I took a step back into the room. We were both here now. Two brothers, steeped in the raw, electric awfulness of a fresh and violent death.

'Walk me through the scene,' Russell said. 'And then you can get the fuck out of my sight.'

* * *

He didn't need to be walked through the scene. It had been pretty clear to me before he'd even joined the police at age eighteen that Russell was going to be a better cop than I was. Because Russell was just made that way. Better. He was older, taller, faster, stronger and smarter. He had our father's face, had been named by him: the ridiculously puerile Gunther 'Gun' Powder, a nod to Arthur's alleged German heritage and a ham-fisted attempt to position Russell as he grew up as a dangerous, masculine weapon of a person, his father's dream child. Me, on the other hand: I looked like our mother. I was leaner, reedy when I was stressed and forgot to eat, with eyesight that had almost disqualified me from joining the jacks at all. From pictures I had of her, I knew I had my mother's dark, deep, emotive eyes. Russell would have seen everything critical in the room already, even before I walked in and gestured to it, and it wasn't because he'd been a cop for four years longer than I had, or that he'd sat and passed his detective's exam with flying colours. Russell was good enough. And I had never been good enough, as a son, or a husband, or a father, or a cop.

I shifted past my brother, walked around the side of the bed closest to the window. Russell moved naturally back to the doorway, so he was as far away from me as he could physically get. He stood there for a good minute or so after I'd finished my debrief: silent, thinking, staring at the hole in the wall beside him.

'Dodge is thinking it's a punter from downstairs,' I said.

'Wrong,' Russell said.

I waited.

'It wasn't someone from the pub.' My brother took out his phone and fired off a text, typing with two thumbs. 'At least, not a random admirer who came up here wanting to beg his way into her room, failed and got violent.'

'No?'

'The killer knocked on the door. Said something. It wasn't a come-on, or she wouldn't have taken the chain off. Whatever it was, it disarmed her. She dropped the chain and opened the door fully. As soon as she did, he shoved her into the wall, stabbed her in the diaphragm two or three times so she couldn't scream.'

I nodded.

'There was no interest in rape,' Russell continued. 'He didn't put her on the bed. Didn't fight with her on the floor. Once she was incapacitated, he forgot all about her. She tried to drag herself to the window, unimpeded, while he went on with his business.'

'What business?'

'She's been robbed,' Russell said. He pointed. 'Two chargers, still plugged in. Both on this side of the bed. One for a phone, one for something bigger. A laptop or an iPad.'

'Spur of the moment thing.' I shrugged, feeling stupid even as I said it but having no choice but to plough on. 'Must have been. He's come up here to confront her about . . . about something. He's lost it. Stabbed her. Panicked at the sight of what he's done. Grabbed the electronics on his way out.'

'Wrong again.' Russell sniffed. 'He wasn't panicked at all. This was completely organised.'

'How do you know that?'

'He searched. He didn't just grab the valuables that were on display. He went looking in the bags. The make-up bag, here, in the bathroom. It's been emptied into the sink.'

Russell went into the bathroom. I listened to him rattling around in there.

'He's walked around the far side of the bed.' Russell came out, pointing. 'You can tell that by the footprint in the blood.'

'What footprint?'

'Partial heel print. Open your eyes, you idiot. Look down. You might learn something.' I looked as he continued. 'It's at the edge of the last stain there. Shaped like a crescent moon.'

I saw it, felt stupider still, cursing myself.

'How do you know that's not the paramedic's footprint? Or whoever found her?'

'Because there's only one.' Russell eased out an exhausted breath. 'If the blood was still wet when the finder and the medics got here, there'd be shoeprints all over the damn floor.'

'Right.'

'The fact that you didn't see that footprint or recognise its significance makes me want to jump out that window there, Evan,' Russell said. 'That footprint is the key piece of evidence in this whole room.'

'Oh, just ease up, would you?' I snapped.

'It's critical.' Russell ignored the warning. 'That changes the whole scene. Why go around that side of the bed at all? She had both her major valuables sitting on *this* side of the bed. The phone and the laptop right there, on display. And yet he searched further. *Much* further. *Around the other side of the bed* further.'

'Unless she had something on that side on display and it's gone now. A nice piece of jewellery? Maybe we're looking for the local junkie.'

'Look at the clothes. They're cheap,' Russell said. 'Anko. That's Kmart. She's not wearing a diamond tennis bracelet and Kmart jeans. He wasn't just looking for valuables. He was calmly searching for something specific. He came in calm and he left calm. He even flicked the lights off on the way out. You notice that? Notice the lights are off?'

'I did, actually.'

'She'd have turned them on to see who was at the door. He'd have needed them on while he searched the room. He flicked them off on his way out. Speaks to his presence of mind.'

'Why did he turn them off?'

'Probably so her light wouldn't stay on all night, so nobody would get curious about why she wasn't going to sleep. The publican. Another guest. He wanted to make sure she wasn't found until morning.'

'It might have been shame,' I ventured. 'Couldn't it have been that? Shame at what he'd done?'

'No,' Russell said.

'So what was he looking for, then?'

'A notebook,' Russell said.

'What?'

'There's a pen on the bedside table. A good pen. No notebook. You don't remember to bring your fancy pen and forget to bring anything to use it on.'

I noticed the pen sitting there by the lamp for the first time. It was gold. Embossed. How the hell hadn't I seen it? Russell walked to the bed, lifted each pillow carefully, looked beneath it, let the pillows fall back where they'd been. He lifted the coverlet and peered into the bed.

'Check down the back of the headboard, will you?'

I did. Nothing.

'Is there a handbag?' Russell asked.

I glanced around. 'I'm not seeing one.'

'I'm not blind, Evan. I can look around this bloody room as well as you can. I mean, is there a handbag with the body? Did you ask Dodge?'

'Why would there be a handbag with the body?'

I couldn't believe I said that. The number of times I'd worked an active crime scene and watched a paramedic toss a wallet or handbag onto the victim's lap as they wheeled them out the door on a stretcher. There was nothing more frustrating for an emergency room doctor or nurse than having no idea who the person they were working on was. Russell was looking at me now like I might be having a brain aneurysm, wondering if he was going to have to call a second set of paramedics for me. 'The paramedics who took her out,' he said slowly. 'They'd have—'

'Grabbed it while they were wheeling her away.' I put a hand up. 'I know.'

'I'd bet my bottom dollar there was a handbag,' Russell said. 'If the killer doesn't have it, it'll be with the body. If we're lucky enough, it'll have the notebook in it.'

'Right,' I said, cringing at how impressed I sounded.

'So what's with the laptop and notebook, then? What is she?' Russell asked, staring at me. 'A writer? A journalist? A researcher?'

'How would I know?'

'You were here before me, Evan.'

'I was here *thirty seconds* before you, Russell.'

'How long did you want, exactly?' my brother asked. 'How long would it have taken for you to look at this situation and figure out that whoever this girl is, she's been carefully and deliberately targeted for her electronics and her notebook? How long would it have taken for that hard-won epiphany to percolate in your thick skull, gradually brewing into the miraculous realisation that your very next move should be to google who the hell the victim actually is and what she does for a living?'

'More than thirty seconds.' I pinched the bridge of my nose. He was so much like Dad it was shocking. The way he spoke. The facial expressions. I wanted to say it, knowing how angry it would make him. 'I'll google her now.'

'Forget it. I'll do it. I wouldn't want you to sprain a neuron. Try to pass this intelligence test instead: where's the nearest coffee?'

'Ah, I reckon Dodge and his team would be using the cafe on the corner there,' I said miserably. 'Aside from the pub, that's the only option in town.'

'Go get them to set up an urn and put it in the beer garden. We'll create a base of operations out there, where everyone in town can see us working.' Russell went back into the room's small bathroom.

'You're not honestly putting me on *coffee* duties?' I asked the empty room. 'I'm the second in charge by rank.'

'Are you still here?' Russell barked.

RUSSELL

I needed air. There was a time when I could walk into a crime scene and put everything together into a nice complex story, vacuuming up all the details, stirring them around in my brain and spitting out an initial theory, and then I could move straight onto the next step of the investigation without taking a breath. But the mental effort required to look with hard eyes at the room where Chloe Lutz had been murdered and put together some undercooked ideas about what had happened, all while confronting my brother for the first time in five years, left me numb and jittery. I walked back out to the landing at the top of the stairs and came upon the crime scene photographer, who was hovering at the railing, fiddling with the knobs on her tripod and trying to look anywhere but at me. Word was obviously getting around that I was a world-class arsehole, which gave me some comfort. But I'd blown out all Prick Energy at Dodge and Evan, so I told her gently and politely what I wanted from the scene shoot and then went down the stairs and out to the front of the pub.

Bridie was sitting on a low sandstone wall across the street, messing with her phone. I came and sat beside her.

'Your uncle Evan is here,' I said.

She put her phone down. 'Oh . . . wow.'

'Yeah.'

'I thought he was further out.'

'He is.'

Bridie chewed her lips and looked at me. I was trying not to remember the last time I had seen Evan. We'd been sparring with each other in a doorway then, too. The doorway of my house in Eastwood. The crime scene of my murdered marriage. 'You guys aren't going to work together on this, are you?'

'No,' I said firmly.

'You'd better not. You'll strangle him, and then there'll be another murder to investigate.'

I wanted to smile at the joke but didn't have the strength. 'He'll be hanging around, though.'

'So should I, uh . . .' Bridie picked up her phone again. Just held it to her chest, the teenager's comfort teddy. 'If I see him, should I not talk to him?'

'You're an adult, Bridie. You can decide who you talk to.'

She looked surprised. 'Oh. Okay.'

'I'm not trying to come back into your life and start making rules in the first five minutes,' I said. 'Have you been speaking to him? You know . . . since.'

'No.'

I nodded. The girl was struggling to reconnect with me, her own father, after what I'd done. I was sad but unsurprised to know that contact with my side of the family had fallen away as well. I sat and tortured myself for a minute or two with memories of Bridie and her aunty Delle, the girl sitting on Delle's lap when she was little, eating fairy bread, drawing, laughing. Chrissy and Bridie squealing and splashing in the pool.

'I see Chris on TikTok and I see Aunty Delle on Instagram, but we don't really talk.'

'Mmm.'

'Mum, uh . . .' Bridie struggled. 'She told me. About what Uncle Evan did at work. Sort of. She heard about it through her colleagues.'

'That's not why I don't talk to him.'

'Oh, I know. I'm just saying that I know about that, also.'

'It was incredibly stupid,' I said.

'Yeah, but, like, cops do stupid things sometimes.' Bridie glanced at my grazed knuckles.

'We sure do.'

'Mum said Pop swooped in and saved him from getting fired.'

'Arthur has got a lot of pull around here,' I said. 'But that was stupid move number two. If Evan had taken some time and thought hard enough about it, he might have been able to get himself out of the mess he was in. But he panicked and called his daddy. And now he's up shit creek. That's what Evan does. It's what he's always done. He gets backed into a corner and acts before he thinks. He doesn't wait. Doesn't strategise. He gets in a spot and snaps and does something dumb.'

Bridie was gazing at the river now. She smiled sadly. 'Funny.'

'What?'

'That's how you catch an injured bird.'

'Is it?'

'Yeah. You back it into a corner,' she said. 'Don't give it time to think. Then you just lash out and grab it. I've done it a thousand times. You move too slowly, the bird looks around and finds an escape route. Runs between your legs or flies up and over your head. You've got to move as fast as you can, so they don't have time to strategise. Ambush predator tactics.'

I nodded, trying not to think about Chloe Lutz pinned up against a wall by her killer.

'I'd better go back in,' I told her, and stood. I didn't know whether to put my hand on her shoulder, or hug her, or tell her that I loved her, so I did none of those things and just walked away.

* * *

I found Dodge at the entrance to the pub, standing under a wrought-iron sign bolted into the sandstone that said *Please Tie Horses at Rail.* He slipped his phone into his pocket when he saw me and came over. 'I've got one on traffic.' He pointed to an officer across the street, standing with a clipboard and watching the empty road. 'Three door-knocking.'

'Tell me what you know about the entry,' I said. 'How did this guy get to Chloe? What was she doing here? Everything.'

Dodge adjusted his stance, cocked a leg out, probably relishing being able to tell me something I didn't already know.

'So, Chloe checked into her room at about four p.m. Rob Winter, the pub owner and manager, processed the check-in at the counter in the bar area. She parked in the spot he directed her to, last on the row, and then went straight up to her room with her bags. She wasn't seen again until seven p.m., when she came down for dinner.'

'Where did she go in between those times?' I asked. 'Was she in the room or did she drive somewhere?'

'We don't know yet.'

'What does the CCTV say?'

'Not much,' Dodge said. 'There's a camera over the bar and a camera over the parking area, and that's it for the whole establishment.'

'No cameras on the stairwell? None in the hallway outside the guest rooms?'

'Nope.'

'An impenetrable fortress, this.'

'But busy,' Dodge said. 'On a Friday night, it's pretty loose around here. You've got the beer garden, where a lot of people drink and have dinner, but there are only a few tables out there to sit at. So people who aren't eating wander around, spread out. They go right to the edges of the road. Out there, into the trees. Sometimes people cross the road at the front and go stand drinking and looking at the river. A lot of eyes out here. I have a couple of people saying they saw Chloe come down for dinner. And we've got her on camera ordering at the bar.'

'She speak to anyone? Sit with anyone?'

'We're working on that. So far the word is she was on her laptop while she ate, which was a bit of an unusual sight, it being mostly tradies and locals and people on holiday out here. We don't know yet if she had interactions with anyone.'

'When did she leave the bar?'

'Around 8 p.m.' Dodge heaved a sigh that lifted and dropped his shoulders by about four inches. The sigh of a man who hadn't been this stressed, this busy, in many years. 'She was seen going back upstairs by one of the other guests who was coming down at the same time. Now, when Chloe went back to her room, she was the only person on the floor. All the other guests were out.'

'How do we know that?'

'We're going off their accounts,' Dodge said. 'There are only four rooms total up there. It was a full house last night. We've got a guy travelling alone for work, a young couple on a dirty weekend, a pair of grey nomads making their way around Australia, and then there was Chloe in the furthest room along the hall. The lone guy and the young couple were at the pub downstairs until about one a.m., and the grey nomads were at a local friend's place for dinner. They don't know when they got back but it was at least midnight. They're going to give me their car's sat nav to confirm an exact time.'

'Why was everybody out so late?'

'It was a Friday night.' Dodge shrugged. 'And, look, there's really no point in going to bed at this place until the crowd downstairs has cleared out. The exterior of the pub is sandstone, but it was gutted by a fire in the fifties and renovated cheaply on the inside. The floors are pine.' He looked at the floor through the doorway beside us. 'They're like paper. You can hear people sneeze. My wife, Patsy, and I stayed here once for our anniversary and we could follow individual conversations as we lay there in bed. We weren't trying too hard to sleep, though.'

Dodge braved a grin. I looked at him the way I look at the stuff I scrape out of my ear canals every couple of months. He dropped the smile and continued. 'That's why I'm thinking that by the time all the other guests arrived home, midnight and beyond, Chloe was already dead.'

'Why?'

'Because the grey nomads were in the room next door to hers, and the wife apparently can't sleep unless it's pristine silence. She'd have heard the knock on Chloe's door. She'd have heard Chloe's head hitting the wall. And her falling to the floor, and the guy rumbling around her room. The wife is telling us she heard diddly squat from the room next door from the moment she got home until Rob the publican started knocking on Chloe's door the next morning.'

'I don't believe her.'

'Why not?'

'Because I shouldn't.' I narrowed my eyes at Dodge. 'And neither should you. We've got nothing to back up her assertions. Maybe she thinks she's got Superman's hearing abilities. She thinks she can hear a cockroach jerking off two suburbs over. Whoop-de-fucking-do, lady. Until I can back up her claims with evidence, they're useless.'

'She was able to confirm for us what time the lone guy and the young couple came home,' Dodge said. 'Without consulting them.'

'We put it in the maybe pile,' I said. 'Tell me about the lone guy. The one who passed Chloe on the stairs at eight p.m.'

'He's an electrician. He's out here for work, doing something with the phone lines. Or the NBN, I don't know which. But I've got eyes on him basically the whole time he was down here at the pub, because one of the bartenders was mad about him, trying to get up the courage to ask for his phone number. All three bartender girls made a game of it.'

'I still want all his clothes, all his possessions from the duration of his stay. I want the forensics team to hit his room, and the other rooms too. I want their DNA and their criminal histories.'

'Done.'

I thought for a while, staring at the distant river. Bridie had disappeared from her spot on the sandstone wall. 'How'd the killer know Chloe was up there on her own?' I asked. 'And how'd he know which room was hers?'

'The simple answer is it's someone she knows. She texted or called to say she was up there alone, and what room she was in. We'll know when we have her phone records.'

'Too easy. What's the alternative?'

'He was watching,' Dodge said. 'Looking at the lights in the windows, maybe? Seeing which ones are turned on and which ones are off?'

'Okay, so he finds out which room she's in from watching.' I said. 'Then what? How does he get to her? When does he do it? He's gone up there and killed her while there were still people in the beer garden, if Superman Hearing Lady is correct about the murder not occurring after midnight. Our guy would have had to watch to see who was coming and going on the stairs, so he could be sure the other rooms and the hallway were empty when he went in for the kill. So, what, he's sitting there, watching, not even knowing if he's going to *get* that moment he's waiting for, when all the other guests are out and only Chloe is here? That's a lot of watching. A lot of hoping. A lot of time standing around. A man standing alone in the beer garden watching the hotel windows for hours on end? With nobody noticing that's what he's doing? I don't buy it.'

'Maybe it was one of the punters. Standing there with his mates. Watching the windows for his moment but sort of . . . doing it casually.' Dodge shrugged.

'And then he comes down covered in her blood? He'd have had back-splatter on his pants legs, at least.'

'It was dark. Maybe he was wearing dark clothing.'

'Nope. Not convinced.'

'So what's the alternative?'

'The publican—this Rob character. He's the one who found her, right? He'd know which room she was in without having to watch, and he wouldn't have been out of place hanging around the stairwell and the hall and the rooms. Was he here last night? Working?'

'Yeah.'

'If we find out in due course that it wasn't the publican, and it wasn't a punter, then we've got a vantage point problem,' I said. 'Because where's his vantage point? The roadside out there?' I pointed to the back of the pub, towards the beer garden.

'I don't think so.' Dodge searched the ground at his feet, his eyes restless as they moved over the surrounding landscape in his mind. 'Past the beer garden there's the road, and beyond that there's houses. Just about everyone in town's got a dog, including the people in those houses. He's not setting up camp to watch from someone's property without getting barked at.'

'What about from the front, here?'

'Well, you can't see the hotel room windows from the front of the building. No windows in the hallway.'

'So where did he watch from, then?'

'I don't know, sir.'

'Find out.'

'I will.'

'Back to Rob.'

'Look, sir. I really think that one's a dead end. It wasn't him.'

'Oh.' I stepped back and appraised Dodge where he stood, which made him flinch. 'I didn't realise you were there when the murder happened. Please. Go ahead and stop me from wasting my fucking time, and just tell me who the killer was, Dodge.'

'Sir'—Dodge put his hands up in surrender—'I just *know* Rob Winter. Okay? Everybody does. This is the only pub between here and Wisemans. Rob is a good bloke. We've been close since I started in the area, on account of me driving the odd drunk home for him or clearing out the louts. He's not someone who's gone and stabbed a young girl to death.'

'Can you do me a favour, Dodge? Can you spare me your completely biased assessments of the criminal potential of everyone in town, please?' I asked. 'I'm trying to run an investigation with some integrity here. You clearly bribed someone to get you through the police academy, but even watching a couple of episodes of *Miss Marple* would arm you with the knowledge that nine times out of ten when someone's murdered, the person who found the body is the culprit. And *another* nine times out of ten, the kinds of people who stab young women to death do an all-right job of appearing like "good blokes".'

'I'm more of a *Law & Order* guy,' Dodge said.

'If it's not one of the other guests, or Rob, how's the killer got past the swipe card access to the rooms?'

'If you lose your swipe card, you can punch in a code to override the swipe system, and—'

'—and let me guess. The code is one-two-three-four.'

'It is.'

I gave a rueful smile. 'Where's Chloe's swipe card?'

'We haven't found it yet.'

'And was she given one when she checked in, or two?'

'Rob says that unless someone asks for two, he just gives out one per room,' Dodge said. 'People lose them all the time. Put them in their bags and take them home. He's constantly replacing them.

But, you're right, sir. Rob had access to this upper floor without having to guess the code. He has his own swipe cards. He'd have known which room was hers. He also could have been up there, across the landing, past the blue door, where they have the pub's storage space. He could have made an excuse to go up, and watched for a while until he saw his chance. It's just a short hop across the landing from the blue door to the hotel door. You could make it in a few seconds, without anyone down in the beer garden noticing you.'

'I want his criminal history,' I said. 'I also want to call up everyone who's slept at the hotel in the past six months. Start with the female guests. Get them to tell you about his behaviour.'

'You got it.' Dodge gave a little salute, clicked his boot heels and took out his phone to send the necessary commands via text. I liked all that behaviour. The doing what he was told without asking questions, the salute, the immediate actioning of my directions. But I sure wasn't going to let him know it.

One of the officers I'd seen standing around in the beer garden smoking approached us from inside the pub, having come from the counter where patrons ordered food. The cop was carrying an open laptop on one palm, like a waiter with a tray. He passed the device to his other hand and put his mitt out to shake mine. His grip was firm and he was covered in colourful Japanese koi fish tattoos that reached to the very end of each wrist, exactly where policing regulations allowed them to exist and no further. He was moustached and his name badge read *N. Fry*. I dropped eye contact and backed up immediately, because tattoos and moustaches are a few of my favourite things. 'Sir, glad to meet you,' he said.

'This is Nathan Fry.' Dodge gestured to him. 'One of my staff from Wisemans.'

'What is it, Fry?' I demanded.

'We've identified a couple of key things on the CCTV so far.' Fry gestured inside, to the bar. Dodge and I followed, me at a distance, staying well back, as the cop set the laptop on the bar runner. 'Just keeping you updated, detective. We've only done a quick sweep through.'

Dodge and I crowded in around the laptop with Fry. Evan was suddenly at my shoulder, which boiled my blood instantly. 'I told you to get coffee and stay out of my sight!'

'They've got to actually have time to *make* the coffee, *sir.*' Evan glanced at Dodge and Fry for solidarity, like I was a lunatic who had wandered in from the street and tried robbing the place with a banana in my hand. 'It'll be here in a minute. One of the locals is going to round up a marquee for us to put out there.'

'We should ask for some of their pistachio croissants.' Dodge stroked his chin. 'I bet they'd do a batch up for us. Gotta keep the troops fed.'

'Would you show me this fucking footage, Fry?' I said. 'I haven't wanted to get out of a bar this badly since the time I stumbled into a speed-dating event run by the Vegans Who Love Jesus.'

Fry pulled up a clip from a selection minimised on the screen. The image showed an overview of the bar we were standing at, the angle encompassing both the cash register and the space that might be taken up by the first two or three customers waiting to order. I glanced up at the discreet black dome camera where it was mounted above me and to my left, above some shelves of wine glasses. I knew from my time as a patrol officer working in Sydney's Inner West that the camera was in a prime position for capturing sticky-fingered staff, patrons getting into scuffles over their spot in the queue, and those who snapped when they were refused service for being drunk, maybe threw something over the taps at the bar staff. These were the top three concerns for pub owners, staples of the Saturday night shift.

On one side of the image, a small, fluffy-haired guy was fiddling with the till's touch screen when a petite woman with a blonde ponytail walked into view. The woman who must have been Chloe Lutz put her phone on the counter, and the two exchanged a soundless conversation while Rob Winter checked her in. I watched Rob as carefully as the slightly grainy footage would allow, trying to decide if the publican was looking at Chloe's face or her breasts or her hands while she fished around in her phone wallet for an ID card. Fry pointed to the edge of the screen. 'Check-in at 4.18 p.m., just as Mr Winter stated.'

I didn't comment. Evan stepped closer, his arms folded, elbow to elbow with me. The anger at him for existing was like a rock in my throat. Fry pulled up footage of Chloe edging a small blue hatchback Toyota into a spot beneath a row of camphor laurel and getting out. 'Here she is parking her car in the assigned space seven minutes later.'

I cocked my head as I watched, looked closely at the bags she was lugging in. A duffel bag, the one I'd seen upturned in her room, slung over one shoulder. There was also a sizeable black handbag tucked under her other arm.

'Handbag.' Evan pointed. I ignored him.

'Here's Chloe ordering her dinner,' Fry said, bringing up another video. 'Time stamp says 8.07 p.m. Lines up with what the electrician told us about when she came down.'

'Wrong,' I said. They all looked at me. I kept my eyes on the screen as a lanky figure loomed behind Chloe at the counter. 'The camera shows us Chloe ordering her dinner at 8.07. Doesn't do squat for the witness's account of what time she came down from her room. For all we know, the electrician's lying or mistaken, and she came down at six and skipped around the streets picking dandelions for two hours.'

The men around me considered this. I was hardly aware of them. The tall, lean man standing behind Chloe was rocking back and forth on his heels almost imperceptibly, his angular arms folded, staring directly down from his considerably greater height at the back of her neck. A neck that would, only a few hours later, be seized by a hand and used to smash her head into a wall. Chloe's ponytail was swishing before the tall man as she talked and pointed to the laminated menu on the bar. A dark-coloured ball cap obscured the man's face from the camera. It swivelled sharply like the beak of a big black bird as Chloe walked away from the bar with her drink. His gaze seemed to follow her right to the door, causing him to turn 180 degrees to face the staff member at the till.

'Okay.' I squinted at the screen. 'So, who's the creep?'

EVAN

I stared at the image of my son on the screen, my breath caught in my throat and my brain trying to compute the information it was receiving. The experience was the same as when I had first laid eyes on my own image in the newspaper, the first time I'd made it into the local rag for running into a burning house and coming out with the owner's golden retriever in my arms. There was an unreality to it. An absurdity. That was me, but it couldn't be me. This was my son, but it couldn't be my son. And yet, an all-consuming certainty and dread fell over me, made it impossible to take my eyes off the screen.

'Okay. So, who's the creep?' Russell asked.

No one spoke at first. I couldn't. Dodge and Fry were still taking a moment to examine the image of the tall, lean man behind Chloe. Fry ran the video back and we all watched it again. The turn. The stare. 'No one in particular is leaping to mind,' Dodge said finally.

'It's not Catherine's son, is it?' Dodge squinted at Fry.

'Who's Catherine?'

'The writer's festival lady. Runs the book club, "The Book Feast". My wife's in it.'

'Oh, her. Dunno. Didn't know she had a son.'

'I'll ask her.' Dodge paused the footage, used his phone to take a photo of the image on the screen. I felt sweat beginning to bead at my temples. 'You recognise him, Evan?'

I wanted to scream. I looked at Russell, who had cast his eyes to the floor, thinking, listening, probably trying to pick up intonations in the voices of Dodge or Fry that might reveal they're trying to cover for one of their local mates. Russell trusted no one. The pressure to pass his audio exam now was making my heart hammer in my chest. Because that was Chris. I was sure of it. And there was no part of me that was brave enough to reveal to this group of men, in this moment, that it was my son who'd examined Chloe Lutz in a decidedly 'creepy' fashion in the hours and minutes before she was brutally stabbed to death. Maybe soon I'd be able to get there. But not now. So I said, 'No idea.'

Russell looked at me for the first time in a solid ten minutes. I braced for a torching. It had been five years since my brother saw my son, and in that time Chris had shot up in height a good foot and a half, lost a considerable amount of puppy fat and grown his hair to his ears. I was confident he was unrecognisable to Russell. But could he see the anguish in my face? Russell turned away, flicked his hand at the screen and said, 'Hunt him down.'

The words sent a crackle of terror through me. The meeting terminated, and I walked out the door of the pub and around the corner, right to the edge of the beer garden. I dialled Chris. He declined the first call, sent me to voicemail. Grinding my teeth, I dialled again. He picked up after an agonising eight rings. 'Yeah?'

'Were you in Redbelly Crossing last night?'

'Me?'

I told myself to be calm. 'Yes, you, Chris. Did you go to the pub here?'

'Nooooo, Daaaaad.' Chris drew out the words, like he was speaking to someone for whom plain English was impossibly hard. 'What are you, high? I'm sixteen years old. I can't go to the bloody pub.'

'Where were you? Who were you with?'

'Actually, yesterday, I was fifteen. It's my birthday. I forgot.' Inane sniggering in the background of the call.

'Chris, where *were* you? You went out. Where did you go?'

'What are you asking me all this shit for?' the kid baulked. 'Aren't you there working a fucking *murder* right now?'

'Yes, I am.'

'And you're blowing up my phone asking me if I was there?' His voice was rising steadily. He was as fast to anger as all the Powder men who had come before him. The voices in the background had fallen away. 'Are you for real?'

'There's a person on the CCTV who looks just like you.'

'Jesus, man,' Chris sighed. 'Whoever you've got on CCTV, like, *murdering someone*, it isn't me. And it's kind of wild that you would ask me that at all, you know. Especially today.'

'Okay, look, I've come at this wrong,' I said. 'I'm not saying you did it, but maybe you're a wit—'

My son hung up on me. I stood there staring at the peacocks on the roof of the pub, two of them, wandering along the slanted corrugated iron awning over the extension at the back. They were hunting for frogs, I supposed, in the guttering. As I watched, one of them plucked something out, a slithering, wriggling thing that twisted and writhed before it was swallowed whole. Russell's words came back to me. *Hunt him down.*

I told myself it was the pressure of my first real homicide since the incident. All that was weighing on my performance. That it couldn't have been my son there at the pub—like he'd said, he was fifteen the night before, a hair over sixteen now. The girl behind the counter hadn't carded him for his drink. Guilt swept through me at the idea that I had just called Chris and asked him what I had, in the way that I had. My strange but harmless little boy. My misunderstood creature. I'd bruised him on his birthday, in front of his friends.

The unsettled feeling in my chest wouldn't go away, though. The immediate, instinctive notion that I'd just been looking at my child, exactly where he shouldn't have been, exactly when he shouldn't have been there. I'd started to tell Chris that I was enquiring about it because he might have witnessed something useful to police. But the guilt that was roiling in me now was the knowledge that I hadn't been assessing Chris's usefulness as a witness in the first instance; I'd been assessing whether or not he'd done it.

RUSSELL

I went into the beer garden, stood under a tree, making and taking phone calls. My phone was running out of battery, and I reminded myself to plug it in next time I was in a car. When I went back into the pub, the owner was there. Rob Winter was a small, bespectacled man with wispy orange curls crowning his skull. I found him sitting at the gloomy little bar on a padded leather stool, a notepad spread out on the stainless steel bar top, covered in handwriting that looked like rows and rows of dead and mangled mosquitos. When I entered, Rob stood and took me in. I didn't know if anybody had warned him what I was like, or if the fact that he had found a murdered girl that morning was enough to unnerve him, but he tried to say hello and then thought better of it halfway through the word, so what came out was a strangled 'Hek'.

'Rob Winter.'

'That's me, yes.'

'I'm Detective Inspector Russell Powder.' I looked at him the way I look at the wriggling things I invariably find at the bottom of my street garbage bin when I manage to convince myself to hose it out. 'I want you to run me through this morning's events.'

'Right.' He nodded, putting his hands on the paper in front of him. 'I, uh. I took Dodge through it. And he's got me to start writing my statement.'

'Congratulations,' I said. 'I don't care. I need to hear it all again.'

Rob licked his thin lips. 'That's fine. I can say it as many times as you like.'

I put my hands on the bar. He studied them, the grazed knuckles.

'You don't want to record it?' he asked. I narrowed my eyes at him. 'Because Dodge recorded it. On his phone.'

'I don't want to record it,' I said.

'Why not?'

'Because I don't need there to be any evidence of what I'll do to you if I catch you in a lie, Mr Winter,' I said.

Rob Winter stared at me. A fan came on in the beer fridges behind him, and the bottles tinkled.

'I'm here to find out who murdered that young woman up there.' I raised a finger and pointed up and to my left, towards the hotel rooms. 'And time is of the essence. If you delay me in what I'm trying to do here, even for a second, by not telling me the complete and unfiltered truth, I'm going to have to get creative with some of the objects you have back there.'

Rob's little green eyes dropped to the bar top in front of him. To the muddling stick and the paring knives sitting by a glass canister of lemons and limes. They travelled across the rows of heavy pint glasses to the wall beside him, where all the spirit bottles stood in rows. He glanced the other way, at the glass racks and chopping boards. His eyes finally landed back on me, and he braved a tiny laugh. 'Are you kidding?'

'Do I look like it?'

Rob plucked at the front of his shirt. 'What do you want to know?'

'Think very carefully,' I said. 'Dodge is telling me that you saw to Chloe's check-in. Here. Behind the bar. Four o'clock in the afternoon. You gave her one key card to her room, because that was standard procedure. All correct?'

Rob was silent for a good ten seconds, thinking. Then he said, 'Yes.'

'You didn't see her again until she came down for dinner.'

Rob's tongue unstuck from the roof of his mouth loudly. 'I don't think I saw her when she came down. I was in the office.

Our internet was out. It was later that I saw her. She was already having dinner out the back.'

'Did you speak to her?'

'No.'

'Not at all? Think carefully.' I put my hand on a heavy glass jar, half-full of coins, that was sitting on the counter beside me.

'No. I don't think I did. I *really* don't think I did, and if anyone is saying I did, then . . . I-I-I was grumpy about the internet being down. And the girls in the bar were being chatty and slacking off. So, I don't think I'd have been very talkative with the punters.'

'So you're telling me that you were in an agitated state last night?' I said.

'What?'

'Grumpy. You used the word "grumpy". Just now.'

'Oh, I mean, I was annoyed. About the internet, not about . . . Internet out here in the valley is rubbish, it's in and out all the time. That's part of the reason one of the other guests is here, I think. The guy, uh—'

'The girls. You were also annoyed at them.'

'Yes.'

'Have you noted that in your statement?'

'Excuse me?'

'Your agitated state.' I glanced at the notepad in front of him. 'On the night of the murder. In the hours immediately preceding the murder, in fact.'

'No.' Rob touched the notepad. His hands were trembling hard. 'I mean, I will, though.'

'Yes, you will,' I said. 'Now.'

Rob started writing. He was left-handed, which set off a cooling energy in my chest, a thing that fanned out down my shoulders and arms: the Prick Switch threatening to flip back off. From the blood spatter on Chloe's hotel room door, the angle of the little droplets and arcs, I was pretty sure the killer was right-handed. But I didn't let my switch flip all the way off. The reason Rob Winter's handwriting was so appalling might have been because he was faking the left-handedness. Anything was possible. The silence and awkwardness while I stood there and watched him write made Rob actually drip sweat onto the page in front of him. 'I didn't see her go back up.'

'Why were you the one to find her?'

'I went up there,' Rob said, taking a tea towel from a stack on the shelf to his left and wiping his face with it. 'Every morning I do a round of the whole property. I park and go feed the peacocks. Then I go do the lines and pumps. I unlock the office and answer any emails that have come through overnight. The internet was still down, so that didn't take very long. Then I always do a walk-through of the accommodation hallway.' He pointed upwards.

'Why do you do a walk-through of the hall?'

'Because sometimes the guests leave little surprises,' Rob said. 'So I want to take a look before any of the other guests wake up and find them. Nobody's usually awake before seven, and that's when I would have gone up. Seven-fifteen or so.'

'What kinds of "little surprises" are you talking about?'

'Look, it's a hotel above a pub.' Rob shrugged. 'People don't quite make it to their rooms and they vomit or piss in the hallway. A couple has a fight and the guy gets locked out by his missus and he sleeps outside her door. Once a year or so somebody has a birthday party and they book out all the rooms, and everybody gets wrecked, and somebody takes a shit in the hallway.'

'Once a year that happens?'

'For the past five, at least,' the publican sighed. 'Or they bring home weird things. I found a sheep up there once.'

'A sheep?'

'In the hallway, yeah,' Rob said. 'So, I just always go up and make sure I find the surprises before other guests do. This morning I went up and I saw the blood on the doorknob. I knocked, and she didn't answer. That got me worried. I came back down here to get her phone number from the computer, and I called her. Nothing. I stood there at her door, calling her, knocking. I didn't like how much blood there was, you know? Because there was a bit, the more I looked. Splattered on the door. More than she'd have if she just fell and bonked her head or something.'

'When you got no answer, you went in?'

'I went in and I found her.' He nodded, dropping his eyes to the paper before him. He smoothed out the pages with his palms, chewing on his bottom lip. 'Yep.'

'You performed CPR?' I said, unmoved by the tears springing to his eyes, having watched literally hundreds of suspects across my policing career crying crocodile tears. 'And you called an ambulance?'

'And the police, yep.'

'What did the other guests do?'

'The guy, the electrician'—Rob drew a long breath—'he'd heard the knocking. He came and saw briefly what was going on, but then he left. Think it was all a bit much for him. The smell of the blood was really powerful. You could taste it in the air. The young couple, they just went out when they got up. The old couple got up, but they cleared out pretty quickly as well. They never came and looked in. They saw there was some kind of drama, I think, and stayed away.'

'You were the only person on the floor that morning who went into the room between discovering the body and seeing the paramedics in?'

'Yes.'

'The blood in the carpet,' I said. 'Was it wet or was it dry?'

Rob looked at me. The emotion fell from his face as he tried to remember. 'Dry, I guess.'

'You guess?'

'I suppose you could find out for sure,' Rob said. 'I mean, I was kneeling down beside her. If it was wet, it would be on the knees of my pants. And on my shoes and stuff.'

I stood looking at the little publican, waiting for him to fill the agonising silence with more, but he was so tangled up in the memory of what had happened that he just sat there looking right through the centre of my chest, as though he could see out the other side. I snapped him out of it by saying, 'You're going to open the pub tonight.'

He squinted up at me. 'I am?'

'Yes.'

'Won't that seem sort of . . . insensitive?'

'I care as much about how it seems, Mr Winter, as I do about what cat litter costs in Kazakhstan. I want a big crowd of locals down here mingling and talking about the crime. Spreading rumours and innuendo, pointing fingers and getting loose lipped. Call it a vigil, if you want. Say you'll give every dollar of the takings to Chloe's family. I don't care. Just don't say it was me asking you to open the place up.'

'Why not?'

'Because then it'll look like what it is,' I said. 'A fishing expedition.'

Rob put his hands in his pockets, took them out again, rubbed his mouth. 'This is a small town, detective. A person's standing is important around here. I don't want people thinking I've used a girl's murder as . . . as a promotional activity for my business.'

'Get over yourself, Mr Winter,' I said. 'How good can your reputation around here be if you're not the sort of person who'd sacrifice it in a heartbeat to aid police in catching a killer?'

Rob thought about that. Thought hard, trying to unpick the tangled logic, to figure out if doing a seemingly terrible but actually good thing made him a good or bad person. I left him to work on giving himself a headache and went out into the day.

* * *

I knew Bridie was at my elbow by the smell of her: watermelon shampoo and freshly washed linen. I struggled again not to put an arm around her neck and draw her near to me, instead finishing off my update to Gail Caplan while she waited patiently nearby. My watch said 2 p.m.

'Sorry to bother you.'

'You couldn't bother me if you tried, Birds.' I put the phone away. 'What's up?'

'Do you know where we're staying tonight?'

'No idea.' I rubbed my forehead. 'I haven't thought that far ahead.'

'That's cool.'

'You're probably bored out of your mind,' I said. 'And you've got nowhere to chill out. You're supposed to be getting yourself settled into the room I made for you at my apartment.'

'I have my own room?'

'It was a surprise, which I've just ruined.' I felt tired and flustered, needed coffee. We both fell into the awful thrumming strangeness of that concept: of me setting up a room for Bridie at my place, something only a father who was fairly certain his daughter would visit regularly and use that room often would do. The type of father I had no right at all being, at this stage in our Great Relationship Repair Experiment.

'It's a really nice room.'

'I can't wait to see it.'

'I'm sorry, Birds.'

'Well, since you're feeling sorry . . .' Her mouth moved with a repressed smile. Hope and mischief. 'How would you feel about me borrowing the 'Stang?'

A voice inside my brain started screaming hysterically. I kept my face neutral, which wasn't an easy thing to do. 'The 'Stang?'

'I think I just snagged my first rescue in the region,' Bridie said. 'Eastern water dragon with a busted leg lounging by someone's pool. It's ten minutes from here.'

'I would like nothing more than for you to borrow the 'Stang,' I outright lied, fishing my keys out of my pocket and tossing them to her. 'Tell me how it goes.'

I was smiling as she jogged excitedly away to drive my immaculately restored classic car to an unknown rural location and use it to transport a mangled reptile. The smile plummeted as Evan came around the corner in his Kia, pulling up in the dirt right in front of me, his window open.

'Shouldn't you be under a rock somewhere?' I asked.

'You going to see the body?'

'Not with you I'm not.'

'Well, I just spoke to Dodge. He was heading out to check on his door-knockers. And my eyesight isn't great, but I thought I just saw you toss your car keys to Bridie.' He glanced at his rear-view.

At Bridie, across the road and down the street a little, putting P plates on the back of the 'Stang. 'That was Bridie, wasn't it?'

I stood there, fuming.

'She's so tall,' Evan said.

'Get out of the driver's seat,' I barked, walking towards the car.

EVAN

I endured the silence for as long as I could. The road rumbled underneath us and Russell made back-to-back phone calls, one hand on the wheel and the other on his phone, elbow on the sill. I had time to get a proper look at him, now that he wasn't focused on me. He'd put on weight since the marriage break-up, muscle around the shoulders, a thickness in the torso. The beard was still there, and he still couldn't figure out what he was supposed to do with his hair, but the harder I looked the more I discerned an attention to detail he might not have felt he could get away with as a gay man masquerading as a straight guy—the shirt was ironed to within an inch of its life, and wasn't some off-the-rack department store job but something more expensive. He'd stopped biting his nails and his skin was better. I was glad for him, that he'd managed to shrug off the culture of physical appearance that we'd grown up with: that a man spends $5 or less on his shampoo, doesn't use conditioner, throws all his clothes in the dryer regardless of fabric type, and shaves his beard and nothing else. I still couldn't floss my teeth without hearing my father's voice growling in my brain about what a pansy I was being.

Russell was getting a scene debrief from the investigators working on Chloe's apartment in Maroubra. From what I could tell, there'd been nothing of obvious importance found in Chloe's living space. The girl didn't appear to have a boyfriend, and her things were neat and orderly. The apartment sounded small, with a shared laundry, a 1950s brick place with security cameras at the front and back doors and nothing else. A hot, intimidating presence, filling all the available air in the car with his barking commands and heavy nose-breathing, Russell moved straight on to a phone call with Gail Caplan. Caplan talked so loudly on the phone I could clearly hear her end, which was helpful, because the previous calls had me leaning over and trying to put together clues from Russell's responses.

'What have you got?'

'You first,' my brother said. 'Tell me that the geeks are into Chloe's accounts.'

'Got her bank account, no trouble at all,' Gail said. 'The banks are always quick to pony up. Someone's going to send you a couple of years' worth of statements. But the social media and the email are proving difficult. They've got to go through the security centres for each individual company, and they're all on US time.'

'Have you briefed the press?'

'Yeah. Kept it vague. There's interest, but the journos are absolutely flocking to Paddo's double-bludgeoning on the Esplanade, so hopefully you won't have too many vultures pecking at you. Did you speak to the family?'

'Not yet. Going to see the body first.'

'Then what?'

'I'll hold a briefing with the gormless nincompoops I've been saddled with as investigative staff here in about an hour.' Russell glanced at me. 'But I'm looking at it as being targeted. A silencing.' He explained the crime scene to Gail in detail, talked about the potential missing notebook.

'So, what did she know that she shouldn't have known?' Gail asked. 'What was she working on? Was she out there for work?'

'We need her call list. Her emails. Yesterday, Gail.'

'Yes, yes. Don't get your knickers in a knot.'

'I'm going to set up a public thing for tonight, a fishing expedition.'

'What, like, a vigil?'

'Nothing as formal as that. I'm just going to let it evolve naturally and see what it turns into. Maybe I'll get lucky and they'll drag out the local sicko, he'll confess and the mob will stone him to death, and I'll be home by lunchtime tomorrow.'

'If only,' Gail said. 'What are you going to do? Open the pub?'

'Yep.'

'Will the pub owner go along with that?'

'The pub owner will do what he's told,' Russell said. 'And I'll have divers set to go in the morning looking for the knife or the laptop and phone in the river. But without access to those accounts—'

'Without that access, you'll just have to hang tight.' Gail's voice was singsongy, like she was soothing a tantrumming child. 'What ended up happening with Bridie? Is she at home?'

'She's here.'

I heard a laugh on the other end of the line. 'Oh, wow. Someone likes to live dangerously.'

'Yeah.'

'Georgia finds out you took your kid on a murder, she's going to wear your skin as a party dress.'

'It's a delightful weekend of family fun. Just what I always wished for.' Again, I felt Russell's eyes on me. 'The accounts, Gail.'

Russell hung up and started dialling someone else. I reached over and pushed the phone down. 'Don't make another call.'

'Touch me again and I'll snap your fingers like bread sticks, Evan.'

'We need to talk.'

'No, we don't.'

'Russell,' I said. 'That day—'

'Are you deaf? I *said*—'

'What did you want me to do?' I shouted over the top of him. We were rolling through fields of tall trees towards the ferry stop. Sunshine through the leaves. 'Huh? What was the correct course of action that day, Rus? I got a call from you saying you'd just slugged our father so hard he was unconscious on your doorstep and bleeding everywhere. You told me I could go and find him at the local hospital.'

'Right.'

'That's *exactly what I did.* And suddenly *I'm* the bad guy?'

'You became the bad guy when you left the hospital, came to my home and admonished me for hitting him,' Russell snapped. 'You stood there looking down from your ridiculously high horse, taking the time to tell me that *I* was the one in the wrong for hitting him. After what he said to my child, Evan.'

'Can I ask you something?'

'What?'

'Has smacking someone in the head *ever* worked out for you as a life strategy, Rus?' I kept my tone cheerfully patronising. 'You keep doing it. You look like you've done it just recently. Has it *ever* made your personal circumstances better than they were?'

'I'm thinking about how it might improve my personal circumstances right now, actually.'

'Just try.'

'You're doing it again. You realise that, don't you? You're up on that horse.'

'Russell.'

'While you're over there, prancing around on your self-righteous, peace-loving pony, you might like to take a moment to reflect on all the times you came running to me, needing me to jump in and save your hide after *you* started brawls with kids at school who were too big for you.'

'Oh, here we go.'

'You remember that, right?'

'Yes, let's all keep doing the things we did as teenagers and pretend they're okay to do in our mid-forties. I'll go jerk off into a sock and you can go tipping cows.'

He wasn't even listening. '*Then* you have the gall to go and bring cigarettes and books and outside food and fucking clothes to Arthur when he's laid up in hospital.' Russell shook his head, his lip curled in repulsion. '*Daddy, can I spoon-feed your raspberry jelly to you? Daddy, can I rub your tootsies for you? I'm a good little boy, aren't I, Daddy?'*

I laughed. I couldn't help it. Despite it all, the baby voice was so absurd coming out of this huge hairy beast of a man, with his scars and his mean eyes and his enormous scabbed knuckles on the steering wheel. And Russell's fury got to a place like that sometimes—a place beyond sanity, into darkly comic levels of vitriol. Now I was thinking of all the fights we'd ever had. All of them over stupid shit. 'You really are something else, you know that?'

My brother didn't answer. He was staring at the river, the houses that lined it as we approached the ferry. Hamptons style, two storey, all white trims and boats rocking gently in their moorings. When we were kids we'd walked these houses in the summer, going door to door selling oranges from the farm. Each of us holding the handle of a laundry basket heavy with fruit.

'You know, I don't think any of this is about how I treated Dad after you slugged him,' I said.

'What's it about then, Dr Phil?'

'I think it's about you not knowing how to tell me that you're gay.'

The humour in the car evaporated, snatched from the very air, replaced by a hateful energy that clouded out from the other side of the car. Russell slowed at the lineup for the ferry, watching the big vessel beyond the boom gate making its way towards us. 'Be very careful what you say next, Evan,' he said.

'You didn't even try to tell me.' I shrugged. 'You told Georgia, and Georgia told her family, and they told people, and *they* told people, and it gradually drifted over to Dad and me. But you never called me up and actually told me. Do I get to be pissed off about that? After everything you and I have been through together, I had to hear about what happened on the fucking grapevine?'

'No.' He glared at me. 'You don't get to be pissed off about that.'

'I think you didn't tell me because you were afraid of what I'd say.'

Russell said nothing. He was squinting at swallows twisting and spinning around the ferry, landing on its lines and railings, hurling themselves headfirst into the wind.

I went on. 'By the time Dad had gone and pulled his bullshit at your front door, you must have been terrified about what kind of bullshit *I* was going to come out with. So, you found a way to be angry at me, so I'd never have the chance to tell you what I think.'

'Let me explain something to you, Evan,' Russell said. He pointed at himself, at me, the car around us, the ferry, and the boats beyond. 'This? This whole weekend? This is not that chance. In case you were thinking that it is.'

'Oh, it isn't?'

'No,' he said. His voice was low, rumbling, the growl of a male lion warning a potential rival not to come close to the pride. Eyes full of dark experience. 'It isn't. You want to give me an exhaustive breakdown of what you think about it all? You want to list it all out? Whether you think I was faking it with Georgia. Whether you *knew*, when we were growing up. You go right ahead and do that, Evan. Write it all down. And when you're done, take the paper, fold it neatly and shove it up your own arse.'

I nodded. 'This is what he always wanted, you know,' I said. 'Dad. He always wanted us to hate each other. You're sitting there fulfilling his dream.'

'I guess I really am the better son, then.' Russell gave an icy smile.

The boom gate lifted, and Russell drove us onto the vessel.

RUSSELL

Wisemans Ferry Medical Centre was on a hill across the wide street from a Bottlemart. The liquor store was already parked out with the vehicles of local tradesmen enjoying their Saturdays. They'd be preloading for a big night on the farms and wooded lots around town. I could already smell woodsmoke on the wind as I stepped out beside a long wheelchair ramp. I got a text from Bridie and opened it to find a selfie, her smile wide and an enormous lizard clutched against her side. The thing was as thick around the middle as a pool noodle, its chest and midsection lying along Bridie's forearm, its eyes indignant and looking right at the camera. I could see the back leg was twisted and swollen. Being a middle-aged male and a father, I texted the thumbs up emoji.

Evan ended a phone call and tapped out a text to someone with another of those stressed sighs that everybody around me seemed to be giving every fifteen minutes or so, like the man was a walking pressure cooker with a faulty release valve.

'So, Dodge is telling me Chloe's body was brought here rather than to Gosford,' he said, coming around the bonnet and standing near me. 'After the paras arrived and took her out of the hotel and tried CPR. Once they'd realised she was definitely dead, their thinking was that they needed to get her somewhere sterile, and this is on the route back to the city, at least. She's been kept at room temperature, he says, so that forensics can look into a proper time of death once she's transported to the lab.'

This was good. I didn't say so, but I'd been hoping Chloe hadn't been put on ice before I saw her. That would fuck up time of death calculations even worse than they already had been.

'Do you know these lot?'

'Vaguely.' Evan said. 'I've never brought a body here.'

There was an ambulance parked in a bay marked out for the head GP of the clinic, and a handwritten sign on the door of the centre stated that the surgery was closed until further notice. A red-haired woman in navy-blue scrubs opened the door as Evan arrived ahead of me, smiling at him sadly and giving me a wary look. There was some chatter back and forth between the local cop and the people of his region, so I stood at the window with my best expression of impatience, because the last thing I wanted was to make friends. After I'd cleared my throat at least twice I was offered a set of gloves from a box and directed to a door at the back of the empty centre.

Chloe was still zipped into the body bag, lying on a gurney in a room that looked like it was prepped for minor surgeries. Steel benches, a huge overhead light, privacy curtains. I went over and unzipped the bag all the way, pushed the flap back, and looked at her.

The first thing you get hit with is the smell. An overwhelming wave of copper, then the sour, fetid smell that comes with a body having lost bladder and bowel control in death. The little elastic hair tie that had pulled Chloe's platinum-blonde hair into a high ponytail was hanging on for dear life down towards the last inch of her shoulder-length hair. The hair was resting on her shoulder, sticking to her cheek, matted with blood. Her whole body was coated with dried blood in a dozen different colours—reds, browns, yellow, black. There was no telling what colour her T-shirt had originally been. She was braless. Her eyes were half open and focused on the wall behind me, her face turned my way, like she'd been waiting for us to meet.

Evan came and looked at Chloe from head to foot. I guessed this wasn't his usual fare. He'd probably seen plenty of car accidents and drownings out here, teens wrapping four-wheel drives around trees and speedboats hitting submerged logs at 80 kilometres per hour. The occasional drunken idiot who tried to jump over a bonfire.

I carefully pushed up the folds of fabric around Chloe's already bloating midsection and found exactly what I knew would be there: two gaping, eye-shaped stab wounds, almost exactly vertical and at least two inches long. Evan went around the other side of the table so he could lean in closer to inspect the wounds.

'Big kitchen knife,' he guessed.

'Wrong. Hunting knife.' I pointed to the uppermost wound. 'Bottom of the wound is frayed. Top is neat and trim. The knife had a pointed tip, sharp upper edge and an at least partially serrated lower edge. We've got bruising from a hilt here and here. We're looking for a big-arse bowie knife, like you'd use to kill a pig.'

Evan leant in closer still.

'He's right-handed,' I went on. 'The wounds are slanted that way. Soft diagonal tilt. See?'

'You talked about divers in the car.' Evan stood upright. 'You going to send them in looking for the knife?'

'We won't find it.' I shifted Chloe's T-shirt back into place. 'He's not so smart that he's pulled all this off just to dump the knife off a bridge a hundred metres from the crime scene. But a dive will be good for appearances.'

'So he thinks we're working hard.' Evan nodded. 'We're coming after him.'

'No,' I said. 'So he thinks we're underestimating him. So he thinks that *we* think he's that dumb.'

The two of us stood over Chloe Lutz's body, gazing at her face, at the awful wastefulness of seized and destroyed youth. I didn't know what Evan was thinking, but I was in familiar and sadly comfortable territory. Because I've been angry all my life. The anger simmered sometimes, lowered to a dull, warm flame, but it was never really gone, and all it took was a gentle manipulation of some over-sensitive dials in me to bring it flaming on again. Combusting. Burning everyone around me. Mine was a brain that knew the viciousness on display here like an old friend. It was a viciousness I saw in the eyes of my own father as I lay squabbling in a crib, a newborn already knowing of the badness in the world, already having heard it through the walls of my mother's womb. It was just inevitable to me. I shrugged on the anger at whoever had done this to Chloe Lutz now like I was pulling on a coat I'd owned forever. Felt its comforting weight on my shoulders.

I'm gonna get this prick, I told myself. Evan was looking at the steel bench at the side of the room. Two items were laid on sterile blue-and-white pads there, awaiting handling by forensic techs, who would also come and take Chloe's clothes into evidence. A large black handbag waited there beside a thin silver watch.

'Bingo,' Evan said, taking a pair of gloves from a box beside the items. He opened the handbag and looked inside. 'Damn. No notebook.'

'What's there?'

'Tampons. More pens. A protein bar.' He drew a handful of fabric from the bag, kept pulling, stretching the thing out. 'A . . . cardigan.'

I straightened and zipped Chloe back into her body bag, then pulled my gloves off, dumped them in a bin by the door. 'I'm going to go out and call Dodge for a ride.'

'Why wouldn't you just ride back with me?'

'Because you'll be getting your arse to Sydney.'

'Sydney?'

'Yeah.' I washed the glove powder off my hands in a nearby sink. 'The forensics team at the pub should be wrapped up there within an hour. They'll swing by here to process this stuff. I want you to supervise the extraction of the fingernail scrapings, vaginal swab, skin exam, hair combings, everything. Make sure they swab her neck. We know he grabbed her there.'

'But what do I have to go to Sydney for?'

'To sit there at the forensics lab in Pemulwuy and make sure they get me the DNA results as fast as possible,' I said. 'Plant yourself in the waiting room and stare at them. Set a timer on your phone for seven minutes, and every time it goes off, go to the counter and ask them how it's going.'

Evan's face pinched. 'You do that? You sit there all day asking them every seven fucking minutes whether they have your test results yet?'

'It works.'

'There's stuff I could be doing on the ground here. You'll be a whole man down if I leave.'

'That's debatable.'

'You're just trying to get me to go away, Russell.'

'*Now* you're catching on.' I tapped my temple and smiled as I headed out the door.

1994

RUSSELL

The banging at the car window came when Rhianna King had her tongue in my mouth, so when she screamed, I felt the sound vibrate through my lips. She was out of my lap so fast she actually slammed into the opposite door of the Chevrolet, her knees up, staring wildly at the window beside me. I knew who it was from the first bang, sat frozen for a good ten seconds with a terror so strong it was all I could do not to piss my pants. I was seventeen.

'Police! Open up!'

My father banged the leather handle of his baton on the glass again. I heard Evan and Kate Englander scrambling in the Ute bed.

'Oh my god! Oh my god! Oh my god!'

'It's okay.' I put a hand on Rhianna. The sweat on her legs, which had been blood-warm a second ago, was ice cold. 'It's just my dad.'

I got out and shut the driver's-side door, and faced him. Arthur stood back and put his hands on his police utility belt, a grim satisfaction making his features a deep, ugly mask in the cabin light from the old vehicle. Evan hopped down from the ute bed and Kate went to Rhianna, the two girls meeting at the hood, voices high and whimpering, discussing whether or not to bolt into the tree line.

'Don't even think about it.' Dad waved the baton at the girls. Kate's bra straps were hanging around her elbows. 'Stand right there, with your hands by your sides.'

'Dad—' Evan started.

'So, you got it going, huh?' Arthur flicked his chin at the car behind me. The Chevrolet was a rusty 1950s beast that sounded like a building collapsing when it started up. 'I had a feeling you two boys were fucking around with one of the cars. You've had axle grease under your nails for about a month, Ev.'

'We're sorry,' my younger brother whined.

'Do me a favour, will you? Don't go into serious crime. You're too dumb.'

'We didn't use any of your petrol, or your oil,' I said. My stomach was hard as a rock. 'We've been mowing the back paddock for the school. They're paying us.'

'You used my tools, though. Right?' Dad said. 'My tools. My shed. My car.'

I felt Evan's eyes on me. Didn't answer.

'And you didn't offer me a *cent* of what you earned on those lawns.' Arthur worked his jaw. 'Here I am, out all night, a single father supporting two young men. Putting my life on the line. Not a *cent*, huh?'

'Can we go?' Rhianna asked. I winced. While Dad's focus was on my brother and me, he might have forgotten about the girls. She'd just reminded him of their existence. 'We have to get home. Our mums are expecting us.'

'What galls me is that you two spend *months* fixing up one of my yard cars in secret,' Arthur went on, his eyes never leaving mine. 'And instead of using the car to blow out of this piece-of-shit town, you go pick up a couple of molls from your school so you can get a bit of a grope in. What a fucking wasted opportunity.'

'Dad, we didn't—'

'Leave it.' I shot Evan a warning look. All we could do here was let the old man have his moment and hope to get out of it without any broken bones. 'We're sorry, Dad. Let us drop the girls home, and we'll talk about this back at the house.'

'Oh, no, no, no.' Arthur put his hands up. His tone lifted. Became dangerously light. 'Please. You two fellas worked hard to get yourselves into this situation. Don't let me interrupt your little smooch-fest.'

'We really need to go home.' Kate's voice was heavy with tears. 'We don't need a ride. We can walk.'

'I'm dropping you home,' Arthur snapped.

I felt all the hairs on my body stand on end at my father's words. Arthur looked at the cowering teen girls as a full-body wave of animalistic instinct came over me. 'That'll be *after* my boys are done with you both, and not a second before.'

'What?' Rhianna squeaked.

'He's joking,' Evan tried.

'The hell I am.'

'That's enough,' I said. 'It's *enough*, Dad.'

'It'll be enough when I say it's enough, my son. Get back in the car. You too, girls. Get in. *Now.* Evan, you and the blonde one, get in the back.'

None of us moved.

'I get to watch.' Arthur folded his arms. His eyes bored into my face. 'What? You're happy enough to do it in front of your brother, but you won't do it in front of me? What *utter* bullshit. I paid for tickets to this little spectacle, with *my* tools, and *my* shed, and *my* car. With the food I put on your plates and the roof I put over your heads. Get in the car, all of you, now.'

Kate started openly sobbing. Rhianna's eyes were huge in the moonlit bush, looking at me for help. *Everyone* was looking at me for help, always.

'We're not doing that,' I said.

'Yes, you are.'

'No, we're not.'

Arthur took a step forward. The cuffs on his belt rattled. His nose was inches from mine. I could taste the ash on my father's breath invading and consuming the taste of Rhianna King's cherry lip gloss on my tongue. 'Your decision, boy. You get back in that car and finish the job with that girl, and let me watch. Otherwise, I'll meet you back at the house, and I'll put on a private show, just for you.'

I knew what that meant. So did Evan. It meant I was going to sit on the steps of the front verandah of our secluded property and watch my father beat the shit out of my little brother, as I had done many, many times before over infractions such as this. I had to make the decision for us all now. Either atrocity was going to be my fault. My natural instinct was to try to minimise the number of victims, protect whoever in the equation was lucky enough not to have Powder family blood in their veins. Contain the poison. Protect the outsiders.

'Girls,' I said. 'Run.'

They didn't need to be told twice. They took off down the dirt road leading back towards the highway. Rhianna was barefoot. Her handbag was still in the car. I opened the driver's-side door to the Chevrolet while Evan hopped obediently into the front passenger seat, his eyes distant, breath fast. Arthur got in the squad car and flicked the high beams on, and rode our bumper all the way back down the mountain towards home.

In the rumbling darkness of the car, Evan was unnaturally still, his eyes on the rear-view. Dad must have been inches from the back of our car.

'He's right,' Evan said. 'We could have taken off.'

'He'd have found us.'

We fell silent. After a while I said, 'Sorry.'

'Nothing you could do.'

He was right. There'd been nothing I could do. All Dad's choices were false choices. Still, that didn't stop me wondering. For years afterwards I would pick over my decision to send the girls running off into the bush, barefoot and terrified and vulnerable to whatever dangers waited for them out there in the night. The intention had been crystal clear in my mind: get them away from Dad at all costs. Whatever that meant for Evan and me. Whatever that meant for them.

EVAN

I stood in the corner of the room, texting Delle, feeling the waves of annoyance roll over me slowly at the past hour and a half spent in my brother's company. The two forensic techs looked tired. They gloved up, gowned up, took to Chloe's body slowly; unzipping the bag and standing, discussing a plan of action for a while in voices full of quiet reverence. I watched as discretely as I could, having witnessed this almost ceremonial procedure only a handful of times in my life. As one of the techs was turning Chloe's head to release part of her ponytail where it was wedged, she murmured, 'Here we go, lovely,' like she was talking to a living being.

The two women started filling ziplock baggies of slides and scrapings and cuttings and combings taken from Chloe, beginning at the top of her body and working down.

All good? I texted my wife.

Just dropped off the second lot, she answered. *They're getting their safety briefing. First lot have gone through and are waiting.*

It hadn't even occurred to me that, because of the number of kids, Delle would have to make two car trips out to the paintball field with the teens, returning two sweaty, reeking, overstimulated carloads of them back again at the end of the day. I sent, *You're a saint.*

Both sets of kids spent the whole trip out there deconstructing Monty Python films, she replied. *BOTH sets of kids, Evan.*

I felt a little sparkle of annoyance at Chris. It was an angry sort of envy at his freedom to be such a weird young man, at his ability to find delight at the idea that he might be genetically seven per cent Norwegian or to see the comic value in Monty Python without (much) judgement or ridicule from his parents. Sure, I rolled my eyes. Delle and I had issued plenty of bewildered and long-suffering sighs over the years, never more so than during Chrissy's amateur taxidermy phase, which was immediately followed by his *Rocky Horror Picture Show* phase. I was envious of all the versions of himself Chris had got to be in his sixteen years. Anime Chris. Medieval-reenactment Chris. Animal-scat-collector Chris. Delle and I had never shamed him, even when things got really odd; we sent him to a therapist when he started collecting his fingernail and toenail clippings when he was nine, but never let on to the anyone outside the household about it. The only version of ourselves that had ever been available to Russell and me was carbon copies of our father, and he would loudly expose us to his cop friends when we stepped outside those bounds: lambasting me in front of an office full of cops once for knowing the words to a Britney Spears song, slapping a novel out of Russell's hands in a supermarket in front of a group of women. The need to be like him had made us both cops and family men. But I wondered who I might have been had I not spent my whole life trying so hard to be Dad, or hating Russell because he was better at it than me.

By the time the forensics team finished up, they had two labelled paper bags full of specimens in tiny containers, and had bagged and tagged Chloe's clothes, watch and handbag and added them to the collection. In all, they told me, there were a hundred and fifty or more evidence items to hand over at the Pemulwuy Forensic Evidence and Technical Services Command.

'I'll drive in convoy with you.' I took my keys from my pocket, tossed and caught them. 'I've got to see the samples in and wait for results.'

'Oh, well, we've actually got to stop at Chatswood on the way back.' The officer was in her forties, with a neck tattoo peeking up above her collar. She gave an apologetic sigh. 'There's a tripod camera in the van we've got to lend to a team there who're covering a gang rape.'

'Why don't they have their own camera?'

'Government-funded police force, sir.'

'Can't you send it with someone else?'

'It's a big piece of kit. Needs the van.'

'Well, I need these samples at the lab now,' I insisted. 'A detour to Chatswood is going to add an hour to the timeline that I don't have. If there's a delay I'll get hammered by the lead detective, and so will you.'

'Yeah, he seems like one scary dude.' She nodded. 'I won't be answering that phone call. If you want to get something to the lab as fast as lightning, give the lab geeks something to get started on, you could maybe take these sets of bio samples and the vic's clothing. But you've got to take official custody, sir. I'm not having that guy blasting me about the protocol.'

'I can do that.'

'You sure?' She raised an eyebrow.

'Let's do it.' I waved her off. 'I'll start loading this stuff into my car.'

We did the transfer in the bright light of the car park, drawing curious glances from patrons who were arriving to the medical centre for their appointments only to hit the sign on the door like cars arriving at a road block. I was handing the chain of custody paperwork back to the officer when Delle called me. The tightness in her voice vibrated down the line. I'd had many a phone call with her like this: a mother trying to keep calm in the face of crisis. 'We're leaving.'

'What?'

'Your son and I,' Delle hissed. She always called Chrissy *my* son when he fucked up. 'He's been kicked out of the paintball centre and banned for two years.'

'*What?*'

'Get in the car, Chris,' Delle shouted, her mouth away from the phone. When she came back, the line crackled with a huffy, angry snort. 'Your son shot one of the girls in the head.'

'What do you mean, Delle?'

'Exactly what I just said. They'd just finished the safety briefing, where they tell you eighteen-fucking-thousand times not to shoot someone from a distance of less than fifteen metres, and your son *immediately* goes and shoots one of the girls point blank in the side of the head before they'd even started the first bloody game.'

My neck was suddenly hot with fury. I slid into my car and turned the ignition, pulling out so fast a few of the sealed paper bags of evidence fell off the back seat and into the footwell. 'Put him on.'

There was a long pause. I wound up the hill through the bush, the engine struggling as I pushed it too hard. 'Chris? *Chris?*'

'Yeah.'

'What the *fuck?*'

'I don't know, Dad.'

'You shot one of the girls in the head?'

'I didn't shoot her. Not on purpose. I, like, put the gun to her head and it . . . it went off. I didn't know it was that sensitive. I hardly touched the trigger at all.'

There was a rumpling sound on the line. Delle came on. 'I stood there and watched you do it, Chris. Evan, he walked up to the girl in the corset, put the gun to her head and said "Die, bitch!", then pulled the trigger. I was standing right there. It was a deliberate act, Chris, and you're not going to try to convince your father that it wasn't.'

Muttered dissent in the background.

'I don't know what in the world you were—'

'Is she okay?' I asked.

'The paintball people are saying he could have killed her if he'd lined it up right. Jesus. *Fuck*. Evan, I'm *so* embarrassed!'

'Delle, try to calm down.'

'*You fucking calm down! My next call has to be to the girl's father!*'

'What condition is the girl in?'

'She turned her head at the last second and the shot glanced off her forehead, but she came up with a huge fucking grapefruit-sized bruise that's as dark as ink, Evan. She didn't have her helmet *or* her safety glasses on. He could have got her in the eye. Can you please come and help me with this?'

'I can't.' I winced. 'Delle, I just can't walk out of the case.'

'Fuck you. Fuck the both of you. Chris, I don't know *what* got into you. That was *in*-sane.'

I heard more muttering in the background; the opening and slamming of car doors. 'I've had to send the girl to the local hospital with one of the paintball techs, for god's sake. I'm taking Chris home and leaving the rest of the kids there.'

'Is that a good idea?'

'They've all paid for their tickets, Evan.'

'But if another one of them gets hurt and you're not there—'

Delle started roasting me, worse than she had thus far, using the last of her furious energy to get out some language I usually only heard around the police station locker rooms, and some I'd never heard before at all. As was her usual mode of operation, she was soon quiet and I felt safe putting the phone back to my ear.

'Why did it have to be us?' She sighed. 'As if people don't talk about us enough already.'

RUSSELL

Five years ago, when Bridie was thirteen, I came home from work and told her mother I was gay. The words had eased out carefully a bunch of times in my fantasies; while we lay together in bed, or sat at a civilised dinner for two, or stood on a clifftop, swept by the winds of change, poetically positioned at the end of the land and the end of what we had known our marriage to be.

In reality, Georgia was in the shower when I told her. I stood beyond the steamy glass, having walked right in and started speaking without the ability to wait a few seconds for her to get out and dry herself. I'd waited years to find the courage. And the courage was suddenly there. I didn't think about the fact that my wife was coming down after a monstrous twelve-hour shift working in sex crimes, standing on one foot, her other foot braced against the tiles, a razor in her hand. I didn't think about the fact that my daughter was right in the middle of the most psychologically impactful years of her childhood. I just walked into the house, dumped my bag, went into the bathroom and ended it all.

There was a lot of yelling and screaming. I took the waves of confusion and humiliation and rage from Georgia right in the chest, eyes open, a man standing in a furious ocean, refusing to bend to the tide. Her surprise, her initial insistence that this was just a midlife crisis, was something I saw coming. Because I'd never given her or anyone even the most minuscule clue that I liked men. My eyes didn't linger on attractive guys I saw in the street or at work or in movies. I didn't have any gay friends. I didn't treat myself to guy-on-guy porn, the kind that might be discovered in a secret folder on the family computer when Georgia was trying to solve a technical problem. My father had raised me as a fighter, a beer drinker, a sports fan, a man who tinkered with cars and knew his way around a gun and a drill and a barbecue. Someone who climbed ladders and killed big spiders and built things and got excited about loud engines and knew all the words to 'Working Class Man'. I didn't keep my nails nice. I knew nothing about fashion. I hadn't cried in my entire adult life. If these clichéd and stereotyped 'clues' to my sexuality weren't enough to sucker Georgia in, I'd also provided her with a storybook romance to solidify her as my 'beard'.

We'd met on the job. Both posted to Newtown after a sudden swell of new drugs in the artsy and alternative suburb had made an overworked area command call for help from surrounding stations. It had been a temporary crisis assignment. Officers crammed in. Sharing desks. Rubbing shoulders. I fell in love with her, wooed her, dated her and married her. If she walked by me naked, I slapped her arse. If she came out of the bathroom wearing new lingerie, I groaned hungrily. I made love to her like I meant it, because I did mean it. I loved her, and I was attracted to her body because that was the body of Georgia, my wife, my best friend. I listened to her and provided for her, gave her every indication possible that this was a relationship that made me happy and that I yearned for nothing else. When we decided to have a child, I wholeheartedly embraced life as a heterosexual married man with a kid. I intended to live that way until I died. I was outlasting and denying the thing inside me that stirred and twisted and demanded to be known. I was winning against it.

Until suddenly I wasn't.

The little voice inside me, the one that had been whispering insistently since I was a pre-teen, started talking gently, and then at full volume. By the time I began to have fantasies about telling Georgia that I wanted to be with men, that voice was a full-bore screaming in my ears. I couldn't eat. I couldn't sleep. I couldn't get through a phone call. I went to a GP, who suggested I go on antidepressants, which I refused to because macho idiots didn't do that. It wasn't the desire to live life as a gay man that was driving me crazy. It was the lying. I was lying to Georgia and Bridie, even when I was saying nothing to them at all. I was lying just by being there.

I tried to tell Georgia on that terrible night that I'd never so much as spoken to a man with sexual intentions. There'd been no emotional affairs, no flirting, no meet-ups, no texting, no cheeky blowjobs in a dark car park somewhere, no secret relationships. But she accused me of all of those things, and worse, stood holding her phone in her shaking hand, howling at me, wanting to know if she should book herself in to be tested for STDs. She asked me if I'd ever loved her at all, and I told her that I always had, that I did still. But I couldn't explain how that was possible *at the same time* as it was possible that I was really someone else entirely to the man she'd known me to be for almost two decades. My inability to explain myself drove her mad. I could explain why there'd never been space in my childhood to come out. I couldn't explain why, after I'd left home, I'd never made that space for myself. Why continuing to swallow down my true sexuality became so vital to my survival. Georgia said a lot of mean shit that night, and she deserved to. But Bridie didn't deserve to sit cowering in her room, listening to it all. That was my fault. I should have picked a better time. I should have sent her to stay at a friend's place. I should have done so many things.

The news ripped through Georgia's family and friends like a chainsaw over the next twenty-four hours, and then it cut through into mine. I wasn't answering my phone. I was just sitting in the house, knee-deep in the ashes of my marriage, trying to be there to answer Georgia's questions, wanting to be there for Bridie if she ever came out of her bedroom again. My father turned up and knocked on the door with a thin veil of shock hanging over his smugness. Things had been steadily deteriorating between the old man and me since Georgia got pregnant, so we were thirteen or fourteen years into what I'd hoped would one day be a peaceful-enough estrangement. I had never taken Georgia or Bridie to the farm in all that time. I didn't answer his calls. My texts were brief, and I never initiated a conversation. I didn't invite him in on that day, instead standing blocking the door, exhausted and twitchy after a night listening to Georgia crying and feeling like I'd just slaughtered something beautiful and worthwhile. My father wanted to know if it was true. When I told him it was, he smirked and shook his head. I heard a floorboard creak behind me, turned and saw Bridie step out, wanting to know if her mother was back from her sister's place, I supposed. Bridie and my father locked eyes. Arthur's pupils were huge and depthless.

'Well, kid, now you know.' The old man shrugged, raised his voice so that it travelled down the hall. 'He doesn't love you. Not as much as he loves a cock in his—'

My father didn't get to finish his sentence. I had punched him as hard as I could in the face, the blow driven from my shoulder and hip, the kind of punch not meant to warn or to teach, but to kill. Arthur flopped like a ragdoll onto my verandah, and Bridie's door slammed as she fled back into her room.

I'd gone inside my house, leaving my shocked neighbours to call an ambulance for my father. I'd called my brother to tell him where to find the old man. At Evan's horror that I'd knocked the old man out, and his suggestions that maybe I shouldn't have done that, I exploded with all the fury at myself that I had left. Evan told me Arthur was still unconscious in the hospital with a fractured skull and a broken jaw. I told Evan that I hoped Arthur died, and if Evan could sympathise at all with the guy after what he'd said to my child, I never wanted to see my brother again.

I told Dodge I'd meet him on a street corner in Wisemans and walked down the hill, thinking about those times, when my child stopped looking me in the eye. Taking out the picture of her again with the lizard and putting her warm, light-filled face and eyes next to the image of the corpse of Chloe Lutz in my mind only added rocks into the pockets of the heavy coat of anger I was wearing. I got myself a takeaway coffee and deliberately didn't get Dodge one. On the drive back, I took and made one phone call after another so that we didn't have time for chitchat, getting more updates from the team on Chloe's apartment and the officers holed up in a room in Maroubra making calls to her student friends, her past work colleagues, anyone who knew her. Dodge parked us at the crime scene, by Chloe's car, which had been forensic-wrapped and covered with a tarp, and was being loaded onto a trailer. Someone had put up a marquee and dragged two picnic tables together, and I recognised a couple of Dodge's people there poring over a laptop. There was an urn, coffee and trays of snacks dotted around. I ended a call and was going to head there to make myself another coffee when my phone rang again. A number I didn't recognise. I stepped away from Dodge.

'Yeah?'

'Is that . . .' The voice on the line was hoarse. Heavy. 'I'm looking for Detective Inspector Gunther Powder.'

'Speaking.'

'This is Larry Lutz.'

I'd known it was Chloe's father, just from the gravel in his throat. The unmistakable raggedness and flatness of voice that comes from losing a child. Many times across my career I'd spoken to these ghosts of people, parents trying to move and speak and breathe in a world irreparably shattered. There's a slowness to them. A shell-shocked lag, like they're waiting for the ground to stop shaking and don't know yet that it never will. I put a hand in my pocket and looked at the river beyond the trees. 'I am so sorry about what's happened, Mr Lutz.'

There was a long silence. Then he cleared his throat wetly and said, 'Right.'

'What do you want to know?' I asked. 'What could I tell you right now that would bring you the most comfort, do you think?'

'Uhhh, well, I don't know exactly.' Larry cleared his throat again. His voice trembled. 'Me and the wife, we're sort of . . . trying to decide whether we want to . . . you know . . . leap in to help you guys or just . . . just . . . just try to get our heads around the idea that she's really gone.'

'Okay.'

'Have you seen her?'

'Yes, I have. And I've seen the crime scene.'

'They're saying her laptop and her phone are missing.'

'That's correct.'

'And can you just tell me . . . They're saying she wasn't raped or beaten up or anything like that. Just that she was killed and her stuff was taken.'

'I believe at this stage that she wasn't sexually assaulted.' I started walking again. 'But an autopsy will tell us more about exactly what happened. She certainly wasn't beaten.'

A sound, strangled and hoarse.

'Larry, your daughter was attacked by someone who wanted her dead very fast. I believe she was specifically targeted—'

'And that's how she died, is it?' Larry cut over me. 'Fast?'

I thought about the blood trail on the carpet in the hotel room. Chloe trying to drag herself towards the window while her attacker searched the room. 'Yes,' I lied. 'It was fast.'

Another silence while Larry took this in. The breeze off the river swept around me. Made the native grass shiver and scratch at my boots, insistent, the land trying to tell me stories, to claw me down and make me answer those agonised fathers who were in line for justice long before Larry.

'Have you got experience with this sort of thing?' Larry asked. 'I mean, you're going to find him, aren't you? You know what you're doing?'

'I'm going to find him, Larry,' I promised. 'I always find them.'

'Okay.' A long breath that rattled the phone line. 'What can I tell you that'll help?'

'Talk me through the last six months with Chloe,' I said. 'Specifically her love-life and her work life.'

'Uh, there hasn't been much of a love-life.' Larry's voice loosened a little. 'Her mother likes to live vicariously through her with the dating. Finds it interesting, the twists and turns. Young people and the stupid stuff they do. They're like sisters, giggling about it, or crying about it, you know, Jill and Chloe. But there hasn't been anything in the past . . . I don't know . . . year?'

'Why was that?'

'Chloe had a major break-up with a boy, and he was cheating on her, maybe. She could never prove it, mind you. But his uptake with another girl afterwards was too quick. I'm talking a week. Chloe was getting texts from her girlfriends saying they were seen out together getting hot and heavy. Like I said: twists and turns and stupid shit.'

'Can you text me the boy's name, and anything you know about him? Car. Employer. Address. Was he ever aggressive with her? Did they fight in your presence?'

'Oh, no, no, nothing like that. And I believe the boy's in Italy right now anyway. The detectives here are onto that and they're telling me he's abroad. But I can text you all that stuff.'

'Tell me his new girl's name, if you have it. Same stuff for her. Address, vehicle, employer. Only if you have it.'

'Okay.'

'Why was Chloe in Redbelly Crossing?' I asked.

'I don't know.' Larry heaved a heavy sigh. 'See, this is the thing I don't understand. She used to keep us updated about all that kind of stuff. While she's been doing her degree, she's been making her way writing all sorts of things. Restaurant reviews, and long pieces about people for the paper and for a handful of websites. And she always shows us that stuff. If she ever has to travel to do it, she says so. She'll say, "Oh, guess what, I'm going to Noosa to review a hotel and they're paying for it."'

'Okay.'

'I have been, um, sceptical from the start that you can make a living anymore as a journalist, you know?' Larry said. 'With all the technology that can do it for you. AI and all that. I wanted her to go into something more secure. Like banking, maybe. We're a family of bankers. But she was never excited about that. So I think since she took up the journalism degree, she's been trying to prove to me that you can actually make a go at it if you work hard. She'd say, "I just got paid three hundred bucks for a fifty-word review of this movie" or whatever. So, if she was out there at Redbelly Crossing writing a story, she would have made sure I knew. Just so I'd know she was making money. Had a job. She definitely would have told me.'

'Unless it was dangerous,' I said.

Larry was silent. My words hung in the air.

'Did you ever discuss how dangerous it could be, to be a journalist?' I asked. 'Had she ever talked about going overseas to be a war correspondent or to cover violence?'

'She knows I would never have allowed that,' Larry said. 'There are other people to do that.'

'Did she cover any dangerous stories that you know of? Did she tell you about them beforehand?'

'I can't . . . Urgh. Christ. I can't think.'

'It's all right.'

'I know what you're saying,' Larry went on. 'She's gone out there, and someone's killed her and taken the laptop. Maybe it's *because* she went out there that she was killed. But she never *said* she wanted to do any dangerous writing or . . . or researching. She was happy writing movie reviews and cooking blogs and stuff.'

I didn't say what I was thinking, which was that if I'd learnt anything at all across my career covering the murders of young people, it was that it was almost impossible for a parent to tell whether their child was truly happy or just faking it. Children know their parents. They know what they want to see.

'What kind of story could be out there that someone would murder her over?'

'People murder each other over all kinds of things, Mr Lutz,' I said. 'She might have just had some information that someone never wanted the world to learn. The nature of that information could be absolutely anything. The possibilities are endless.'

'The pub that she was staying at,' Larry said. 'Maybe she knew something about that pub. It's the pub owner who found her, wasn't it? Or says he was. Should you be looking at him?'

'I'll be looking at everybody, Mr Lutz.'

Silence fell between us. The wind moaned in the pines lining the river.

'I'm gonna let you go,' Larry said. 'My wife is calling me from the other room.'

'Call me, day or night,' I said.

I walked over to Dodge, who was standing with his arms folded, staring at the pub. At those back windows to the hotel rooms, trying to assess the angle a person would have to stand at to see both them and the stairwell, it seemed. He was side-stepping towards me. I had to clear my throat so he wouldn't run right into me.

'Beds,' he said.

'What?'

'We need to talk about them. The day is getting on. You and your daughter: you'll need somewhere to stay while you're on this case. And I suppose you'll want the other three rooms here at the pub shut down for the foreseeable future?'

'Until I can establish what, if any, involvement the other guests had in what's happened here, I want it all closed off,' I said. 'The hallway, the rooms, the stairs. Everything.'

'So would you be staying with your brother, then? In Mangrove Mo—'

'Absolutely not.'

'Right.' Dodge heaved another whole-body sigh; paused to think. 'You guys don't seem to be on the best of terms.'

'You're very observant, aren't you, Dodge? You're like one of those extreme empaths.'

'The thing is, this is the only hotel for fifty k's.' Dodge gestured to the building before us. 'The next one would be Wisemans Ferry. Forty-five minutes if the ferry's running. So that's an hour and a half of driving per day, you coming and going from Redbelly.'

'We'll get an Airbnb.'

'They're all full. I called and checked.'

It was my turn to sigh.

'There is an option,' Dodge said, chancing a sidelong look at me. 'But it's a little . . . eccentric.'

EVAN

My father called as I was steeped in dark considerations about Chris and the man who stood behind Chloe Lutz at the pub, the one who looked just like him. The man who had stabbed a woman to death a mere twelve hours or so before my son, on impulse, shot a female friend in the head with a paintball gun. I was so distracted I had to go around the big roundabout at Dural twice, trying to decide if I wanted to take New Line or Old Northern Road. A truck driver blasted his massive horn at me.

'Yeah.'

'What am I hearing about some big swinging dick from Sydney taking over the case and pushing you lot around?'

I had to laugh. 'You'll never believe who it is.'

'Eh?'

'It's Rus.'

I expected Dad to laugh, too. Or come out with some shockingly homophobic slur. Instead, he was silent. I waited, fighting traffic down the hill towards the city. 'Dad?'

'You need to get rid of him.'

'Look, you're not going to run into him,' I said. 'He'll be head down on the case and won't come up for air. If you're worried, just stay out of Redbelly.'

'I don't care about running into him,' Dad growled. 'I care about him taking the case off you and leaving you—and by way of you, *me*—in the dirt. He would do that. You know what he's like. He's vengeful as all hell.'

'This from the guy who checks the obituaries every week for a funeral notice about someone you had a fight with at work *forty years ago*,' I said.

'Yeah, so what? That prick Bernie Carrera is going to die one of these days, and I'll be right there with my shovel to help them bury him.'

'Uh-huh.'

'If Russell solves this, he'll make sure you don't get any credit. And if he cocks it up he'll blame it on you.'

'He's not going to cock it up. Russell is an absolute weapon these days. The guy listens to a crime scene like a fucking maestro listens to the orchestra, trying to find out which tuba is out of tune.'

'Do you hear yourself? What do you think you are, a poet?'

'I'm not going to try to get him removed. Gail Caplan owes me zero favours, for one thing, and even if I did ask her to pull him off, he'd find out and hammer me into the ground like a tent peg. I'm just going to try to do my best here.'

'Your best isn't going to cut it.'

'Well, what do you want me to do?'

'Tell me what you've got,' he said. 'Maybe I can help you. Although you may be the very definition of "beyond help".'

Russell's voice was in my brain, doing that stupid high-pitched baby impression. *I'm a good little boy, aren't I, Daddy?*

'I'm not going to get an assist from my father on this,' I said. 'You're not a cop anymore, and you're not my mentor, and—'

'Did you just say "I'm not gonna get an assist from my father"?' Now he laughed. Hard.

I wrung the steering wheel. 'I needed your help that *one time*, Dad. Which makes it all the more important that I don't take it now.'

He left an uncomfortable silence, one designed to make me break and back down. When I didn't, he said, 'From what I know, it's a girl stabbed in her room. No sexual assault. Full pub downstairs. That's a snap decision.'

'What did I just say about not wanting your help?'

'A case this simple, you shouldn't need it. The girl's pissed off the local loony and he's gone up there and taught her a lesson.'

'That's exactly what Russell is saying it isn't. He thinks it was a carefully executed, targeted thing.'

'Well, he's wrong. Nobody with any sense of risk or forward planning would do this.'

I thought about Chris, lifting a paintball gun to a girl's head, pulling the trigger. *Die, bitch.*

'What do the traffic cams say?'

'The cams.' I wiped my hands on my trousers. They'd been sweating on the wheel. 'I forgot about those.'

If Chris was at the pub, his car would be on the traffic cams coming and going from town, I thought. Again, a whump of guilt in my stomach, that I didn't believe my own son's word over a grainy image on a cheap pub camera.

'Dodge's people are working on the cams, I think,' I said.

'Why isn't that your job?'

Because Russell sent me to Sydney, I almost said. To keep me out of the way like a troublesome toddler given an iPad to play with so his parents can get through dinner in peace. 'It will be. In ten minutes. I'm just coming into town. I've got to go, Dad.'

I ended the call, used the hands-free in the car to text Dodge. *Who have you got on traffic cams?*

Dodge got back right away. *I was just about to put my guy Knowles on that. He was door-knocking with my other two, but he's completed his grid.*

Leave the cams to me, I said. *I'll want something to do while I'm sitting around at Pemulwuy.*

Righto, Knowlesy can do the phone calls to the past hotel patrons.

I pulled into the car park of Pemulwuy Forensic and Technical Services, a wide, almost empty lot behind a boom gate that was manned by a single security guard, who had to pause whatever he was watching on his phone to lean out the door to see to me. I showed my badge and he waved me through. White, hard sunshine hit my face as I exited my vehicle and walked to the sign-in desk of the lab; a cool, grey, featureless box of a room behind glass doors. The kid at the desk was in his twenties and dressed in a patrol uniform, hammering away at the computer like he was writing the next great Australian novel. He had almost certainly been relegated to fronting the forensics lab's sign-in desk on a weekend for screwing up somehow on the job. We were just two toddlers in timeout, he and I.

'Powder,' I said. 'I've got to hand in some samples.'

Something shot through the young man at the sound of the name. He stood up from his desk chair so fast it kicked out from behind him and rolled away. 'Oh, Detective Powder. We spoke just a moment ago.'

'That would have been my brother.' I put the bags on the counter. 'I'm Senior Sergeant Powder, not Detective Inspector.'

'Right, okay.' The guy, whose name badge said Yang, softened a bit. 'No worries. Well, I've been . . . *advised* . . . about the urgency of getting these samples tested.'

Threatened, I thought.

'So, come in, sir, and we'll get everything started.'

I was buzzed through a security door, led around to the counter and directed to sign in on an electronic panel set into the desktop. A lab tech arrived and walked me through to a receiving area, where we set the bags on a large steel bench. The heavy-set tech took a pair of gloves from his back pocket and upturned the three paper bags onto the counter, one at a time, spilling a stack of plastic vials and packets from one and the ziplocked clothes from the other. He turned the bagged clothes, looking at them from either side, like a pawn-shop owner inspecting old leather wares for hock. He lifted the handbag out and set it on the steel tabletop so that it sat upright, then unzipped it.

'I'll get all this unpacked,' he said gruffly, lumping Chloe's tampons and make-up pieces onto the tabletop with all the ceremony of someone clearing junk out of the bottom of their car. 'Then we'll take a photo of all the items. You can sign off on that, and then you'll be free to go.'

'I've been instructed to wait for the results.'

The tech was lining up the vials and packets, recording the numbers of each on a sheet of paper beside him. 'Oh, Jesus. Don't tell me. Russell Powder sent you.'

I smiled and nodded. He gave an aggrieved sigh. 'There goes my break.'

'That's all it's going to take?' I asked. 'Your usual work break?'

'I can get you something in maybe a couple of hours,' the tech said. 'Get Detective Powder off your back. But it wouldn't be anything complex. You've got two sets of data here.' He gestured to the items before him. 'Stuff that needs extraction, and stuff that's already extracted.'

'You're losing me.'

'These.' He pointed to the little baggies and vials the forensic techs in Wisemans had created. Cotton buds and slides of what they had wiped, peeled and scraped from Chloe Lutz's body. 'These are skin scrapings and fluids. I can put them in solution and run them right away. I don't need to analyse them or do any chemical extractions. The bag and the clothes, though, I'll have to conduct procedures to pull the DNA and skin cells out of those items, so I can isolate them for testing. That could take days.'

'Okay.'

'I'll also start with a simple Y-STR DNA test. It's what we use for female rape kits. Designed to get the male DNA out from where it's surrounded by female DNA. It won't give you a complete genetic picture of this guy but it'll give you something to start with.'

'Having something in just a couple of hours would be really great. I appreciate it.'

'I said *maybe* a couple of hours,' the tech grunted. 'And I'm putting aside every other case in the state of New South Wales to do it, I hope you know.'

'It's a murder,' I said, in case it helped.

'Uh-huh. I could tell that from the amount of blood on the clothes.'

The tech lifted the handbag. Seemed to weigh it. Put it back down. Opened it up again and fiddled with the fabric divider that ran between the two halves of the handbag. 'Oh, here we go. Left something behind.'

I watched in astonishment as he caught the tiny end of a zipper in his big, gloved fingers, one I hadn't noticed when I looked in the handbag at Wisemans. He drew the zipper open, dividing the divider itself in half, reached in and slid out a slim black notebook.

'Holy shit.'

'Looking for this, were you?' He gave a smug laugh, flipping the notebook and looking at the cover. 'Handbags. Full of secret little pockets and flaps and zips. You wouldn't believe how many times I've been pulling apart some good girl's bag and found a neat little side sleeve stuffed with drugs that you coppers have overlooked.'

'Can I see that?'

'They're dark inside, handbags. That's what gets you. Small zips so your keys don't get caught. They actually sell lights on Amazon that you can clip on the—'

'The notebook.' I put my hand out.

'Oh, I can't let you take this one,' the tech said. 'It's part of the evidence submission.'

'Just let me photograph the pages, then.' I gestured for him to spread it on the table. 'It's relevant.'

The tech stood there filling out his evidence submission form while I pulled on gloves, then photographed the pages in Chloe's notebook one by one, flipping and shooting, flipping and shooting. When I was done, the tech pulled down an overhead camera that was mounted on a coil and photographed the whole collection. 'Just sign here, please, sir.'

RUSSELL

We'd been walking for five solid minutes, through the trees at the back of the pub and down a dirt road along the riverbank, when Dodge finally got up the gumption to speak again. He was slightly ahead of me, glancing back as I shot texts to people I knew in the grief team about Chloe's parents. I also googled Chloe Lutz and got a sense of her. The girl I'd seen laid out, cold on a slab at the medical centre, had been big-mouthed and smiley in life, animated in a way the CCTV in the pub hadn't shown her to be. She was showing gums in all her photographs. Always struck a playful pose. Her carefully curated internet life gave me the impression of a happy person who was quick to laugh, who felt at home in cafes with a laptop and a cappuccino. She called herself a smattering of different things across her profiles: Student. Journalist. Student journalist. Writer. Woman of letters. Scribbler. She wrote reviews and profiles for online magazines, and on the weekends when uni was out, she flipped furniture she got cheap or free off Facebook Marketplace for cash.

I kept my eyes on my phone screen as Dodge spoke.

'Would you mind clearing something up for me?'

'What?'

'Just because, you know, I'll be needing to do the paperwork . . .'

'What do you want, Dodge?'

'It's not "Gunther"?' He gripped his hat down by his thigh, flicked the brim with his index finger so that it made a rhythmic snapping sound. 'Because your brother is calling you Russell, and you're calling yourself Russell, but my call sheet said—'

'Russell is my middle name. I go by that,' I said. '"Gunther" can go on the paperwork as and where it needs to.'

We kept walking. Dodge managed to swallow his curiosity for all of about three seconds before it came bubbling up again.

'So why not—'

'Because I might be an incredible prick, Dodge, but I'm not the kind of prick who walks around calling himself "Gun Powder".'

'Ohhh.' Dodge gave an awkward laugh. 'Right! Gunther. Gun. Gun Powder. That's . . . That was Dad's idea, I suppose, was it?'

I didn't answer.

'I'm with you, I'm with you.' He nodded. 'I'm Louis, spelt the French way: L-O-U-I-S. But the amount of times I get "L-E-W-I-S" or "Lois" or "Louise"—mate, I have been sorely tempted to go by my middle name.'

I said nothing.

'Problem is,' he said, 'it's "Shirley".'

I looked up. Dodge laughed hard, pointed at me, pleased with himself that he'd got a reaction. I blew out air and tried to resist the urge to turn off the road and walk straight into the river, hands by my sides and my eyes on the horizon, never to be seen again.

We were turning down an even smaller road between the trees, a foot trail at best, that opened onto a field. The gums and wild bottlebrush parted into a decent strip of land beside the brown, snaking river. Cicadas were zipping loudly in the undergrowth. Dodge stopped beside a broken-down gate, scratched at his thinning blond hair. I looked at what was before me in the field, slipping my phone into my back pocket.

'What the hell is that?'

'So, um.' Dodge turned and stood beside me for once and looked at the giant houseboat. The vessel was sitting in the middle of the wide, unmown field, its port side to the road. 'It's . . . It's just an idea.'

'Why are you showing me a houseboat, and why is that houseboat in the middle of a fucking field, Dodge?'

'It's a long story.'

'Make it short,' I barked. 'Three sentences. Go.'

Dodge thought hard, his brow creasing, still flicking the hat brim in a way that was making my shoulder muscles tighten. 'I own this piece of land, and the houseboat located upon it.'

'One,' I said.

'The boat floated here during some massive floods we had a while back.' Dodge huffed a sigh. '*Annnd* it wasn't sensible, financially, for the original owner to, uh, to recover it from my field and to tow it back to its mooring . . . because it was in a state of disrepair, or, um, semi-disrepair, and so an agreement was made between myself and—'

'Two!'

'And if you were amenable'—Dodge's speed picked up, his face reddening with the effort of not prattling on—'I thought this might suit you and your daughter as temporary accommodation, because it's so central to the town and to the crime scene, and . . . d-d-do you want to just go take a look?'

I glared at Dodge and made to turn back towards town, almost running smack-bang into Bridie. I hadn't even heard the Mustang following us, or the sound of it pulling up.

'What the hell is that?' She pointed.

'That's what he just said.' Dodge smiled.

'Don't tell me that's where we're staying. Is it, Dad?' She grinned at me. 'Look at it! How did it get here? Oh my god. Oh my *god!*'

Bridie walked towards the boat, Dodge at her heels. I followed, low scrub brushing statically against the legs of my jeans. The two-storey, wood-shingled vessel was fifty yards from the edge of river, a thing that was weather-beaten on the outside but showing cutesy signs of life from three large windows on the first level on the port side. Coffee mugs hanging over a stainless-steel sink. A kitchen nook in bright florals. Bridie entered up a gangway at the stern and crossed a barbecue area complete with fairy lights and wind chimes and potted plants, while Dodge blathered on with as many sentences as he damned well pleased.

'My main house is down the road a bit, you see,' he was saying. 'And after her hip replacement, my mother-in-law has been staying there with my wife and me. Patsy is her name. Not my mother-in-law. My wife. Renee is the mother-in-law. Anyway, she'd been living in Weatherill Park, but with her getting older and needing her hip done, we thought she should be closer to us. Turns out inside the house with us is *real* close, if you know what I mean? Not to say we don't love having her there, but we did have this land and this boat, and . . .'

I rubbed my temples, following Bridie and Dodge into the vessel, silently reciting a prayer for Dodge to stop talking.

'It's just that the bed situation itself might be an issue,' Dodge droned. 'In the back there you'll find a dining room set. Two bench seats and a big table. The seats fold down and become two single beds, or you can put a cushion over the tabletop and fold *it* down and the whole thing becomes a king-sized bed. But you'll be wanting to have singles, right? Which is fine, except for the fact that I only have linens for a king.'

'I think everything will work out,' Bridie said with inexplicable optimism. 'We're so grateful that you would put us up, aren't we, Dad?'

'I would rather be literally anywhere but here,' I said. 'If a helicopter came down into that field right now, and a couple of guys got out and said, "Detective Inspector Powder, we need you to leave this houseboat, and this town, and the company of Senior Sergeant Louis Dodge, because we've found a mass grave under a serial killer's house, and we need you to spend an indefinite period knee-and-elbow-deep in the brown decomposing sludge that these bodies have become, picking out teeth and bones and searching for forms of identification, I'd say, "What are we waiting for, chaps?"'

'He's very creative,' Dodge said to Bridie, nodding, appreciating me. 'I could see all that stuff he described just then, in my mind. The brown sludge. The teeth.'

Bridie was looking at me the same way her mother used to when she complained about a headache and I'd tell her to drink more water. 'He's just messing with you, Mr Dodge. We'd be so pleased to stay here, and the boat's really cool.'

Bridie rubbed Dodge's arm as she went to the kitchenette. Actually rubbed his arm, like I'd thrown scalding water on it. 'I'm making coffee. Then I'm going to get the place settled. You guys probably both have work to do.'

* * *

It was Dodge's turn to make himself scarce, telling me he'd go get a status report from his staff. Bridie dug around in the tiny cupboards and found me a plastic go cup, made me a coffee and one for herself with some long-life milk that was there while I simmered in the awkwardness of her having rescued Louis Dodge from my jaws. One minute your kid is crying because the nose fell out of her Bubble-O-Bill, and the next thing you know she's drinking coffee and calling you on your bullshit in front of strangers.

'You could take it easy on that guy,' she said.

'I could, but I could also take up cave diving, and neither of those things sounds safe or enjoyable to me.'

'Dad.'

'It's too risky, Bridie.'

She shifted one of her bags from the little kitchen nook and sat down. 'It's risky to be nice to people?'

'Yes,' I said. 'For me it is.'

'Why?'

'Because it opens the door on it, Bridie.'

'On what?'

'All of it.' I sipped the coffee. 'Dodge is a friendly guy. He's talkative. He offers stuff. About the mother-in-law, for example. About the wife. You let him do that for long enough and suddenly he starts feeling free to pick at *my* life, trying to even things up. And what do I say? Huh? "Oh, yeah, I had a wife too, once. Then I destroyed her life and my daughter's life because I found out at nearly fifty years old that I'm a flaming queer."' Something came over her face at the words. I was too afraid to look closely at it, to see whether it was surprise or anger or sadness. 'How do you think that's going to play out in a town like this, Bridie?' I went on.

'I don't know, Dad. And *you* don't, either. It might be fine.'

'What if it's not?'

She didn't answer.

'If it's not okay with Dodge, I have to then spend the rest of the case riding around in a car with a guy who hates who I am,' I said. 'And he won't keep it a secret. The whole town will know by sunset. We're fifty years behind out here, Birds. The further you get from Sydney, the further back in time you go. There are places in the outback where I'd be dragged into the street and kicked to death.'

'You don't want people to hate you because you're gay,' she said. 'So you make them hate you for being a prick?'

'I can control being a prick.'

Bridie thought about that. She took out her phone and fiddled with it. Put it on the table in front of her, rotated it slowly, so that the screen faced down. 'And, like, is that how you see it?'

'See what?'

'What happened. That it was you "destroying our lives"?' Her voice was very small. 'You said you just "found out" one day. That you were gay. Did you?'

'I can't talk about this right now, Bridie.' I turned around, rubbed my sternum hard with my knuckles, relishing the pain, how it drew me out of the moment. It was a habit I hadn't indulged in since I was a kid. 'I *will*. I will talk about it. It's just . . . At this very second I'm too revved up.'

'It's okay.'

The silence was suffocating. I shifted some things around in the kitchen just to make some noise. 'Listen, I was thinking,' I said eventually. 'You, uh . . . *I've* got a stack of things to do. I've got to make some calls. I've got to hold a briefing. You'll have nothing to do.'

'I was going to borrow the 'Stang again and go do a pouch check about ten minutes from here. It just came up on the app.'

'Oh.' I looked at her. One minute they're dancing around the lounge room because they picked the right shaped window on *Play School*, the next they're borrowing your Mustang to fish around in the pouches of marsupial roadkill. 'Well, if there are any more good rescues, can you, uh, save them to do with me?'

'You can't really "save" them,' she said. 'Not if it's an emergency.'

'True.' I sighed. 'I'm just missing out on spending time with you.'

'There are always rescues, though. Always. Especially out here.'

'Okay.'

'We'll catch up properly later,' she said, with a disbelieving edge to her voice. 'You've got to have dinner some time, right? We'll just, like, make the most of it then.'

'Yeah.' I nodded, enthusiastically. 'And Bridie, you can . . . um . . .'

She waited. I struggled.

'You can ask me anything you want.'

'About what?'

'About anything,' I pressed. Just when I thought it was getting easier with Bridie, it was hard again. 'About the break-up. About . . . what happened that day when Dad and Evan came around the house. And what *had* been happening, in the years before. You know? Anything. I'm going to answer those questions you just had . . . about when I knew and . . . whatever.'

'You don't have to.'

'I know, but I'm going to.'

'Okay.'

'Just say, "I have a question for you," and I'll answer. Whatever it is.'

She'd turned and was facing me now. I felt like I was up against a wall. Rifles trained on my chest. She opened her mouth and I winced, ready for a bullet. But instead, she said, 'You can ask me anything you want about who I am, too.'

A shiver ran through me. Right through my guts. Happiness and hope that were so unfamiliar to me they felt like terror. Neither of us spoke for a while, just standing there in the cold sunshine coming through the kitchen window of the marooned houseboat. Father and daughter moving mountains and making eye contact.

'Is there something you wanted me to be doing?' she asked eventually. 'While you're getting around?'

'Oh. Uh. Well. I mean, you don't *have* to help me. But it's just that you're young, Birds. You're good with computers. You could find me everything you can on Chloe Lutz and what she was working on.'

'I'm not a cop, though. I don't want to get in trouble.'

'The only person you could get in trouble from is me. I'm lead on this.'

'But won't there already be other cops digging around in that stuff? Dodge's people?'

'None of Dodge's people look like they're under thirty. You'll know things about the internet that we don't know.'

'Okay then.' Bridie nodded, energised. 'You got it.'

She got up and refilled her coffee, wiped down the sink, put the teaspoon in the dish rack, her long delicate hands lit by that new, hopeful light.

'I'm really sorry, Bridie,' I said. 'We should be at the Dendy Premium Lounge right now, eating a baked wheel of brie with fig jam and water crackers and watching something foreign.'

She smirked. 'You're the only one around here who's actually sad about that,' she said.

EVAN

I sat in my car in the forensics centre's car park, too annoyed by Officer Yang's typing to hang around in the waiting room. Maybe I was procrastinating logging in to the New South Wales transport authority's Police Control Intranet to view the cams coming in and out of Redbelly, dreading seeing my son there. But I went immediately to the photographs on my phone, of the notebook the tech had found in Chloe Lutz's handbag. I had drafted a message to Russell on the walk back to the car about the discovery, but some childish desire for his approval stopped me from sending it. I wanted to go to him in person and tell him about the find, to be able to brief him on what the book contained, my theories about it. See the look on his face. *I'm a good little cop, aren't I, big brother?* I cringed at myself and went to the pictures.

I opened the first image and zoomed in on the loopy upright handwriting of Chloe Lutz. The first page was titled *FORD CAPRI.*

Initial questions:

What colours do they come in?
Was racing stripe standard?
Were they loud cars? Able to fit muffler? Chase down muffler dealer?
How many ever imported into Australia?

Weird to own one of those in a rural area? Dirt roads?
Similar cars Ford Capri might have been mistaken for?

I sat staring at the words, running over them a couple of times. The list had me thinking, in the beginning, that I was looking at a series of idle questions written by a kid journo who was planning to write an article about a vintage car. The final two questions in the list knocked me a little off that course. Was she planning to write about a specific car? Maybe someone out in Redbelly who owned an old Ford Capri? But what relevance would the 'mistaking' of this person's car for similar cars have? I googled a couple of the phone numbers scribbled at the margin of the page and found one was listed on the webpage of the Vintage Ford Enthusiasts of Australia. The other number I followed to the landline of an administrative assistant at Ford Australia.

On the following page, a vague diagram expanded across one of the notebook's small pages: a house with what looked like two sheds; a road that began and ended with two labels, *Into town* and *Towards city*. There was what appeared to be a stopping bay off the road, shielded from the road proper by little scribbled trees. A box labelled *FC*, which I supposed must be the aforementioned Ford Capri, was parked in the bay. This was good stuff. I didn't know how it was good, but it felt juicy. Like I was holding the key to something, just needing to find myself the right lock. I looked at the diagram of the house and the sheds. The larger-sized building was a basic cartoon of a peaked-roof structure with little square windows. The two smaller buildings had crosshatching across their lower sections. Chicken coops? Dog runs? Garden sheds? I was looking for a house with two smaller structures accompanying it. So, essentially, every house from Dural to Mangrove Mountain.

I reached into the back of the car and grabbed the backpack I'd haphazardly tossed in there that morning when I left the house, abandoning Delle with the gaggle of teens. I drew out my laptop, logged in to the New South Wales transport authority's Police Intranet. With the state having long ago abandoned the laborious process of police officers seeking individual approvals from government-employed traffic authority staff to access motor registrations, I could now search fifty years' worth of car registration history using my own log-in. I put some search terms in, looking for owners of Ford Capri vehicles in the Hawkesbury region.

There were none. No one living local to Redbelly currently owned a Capri, and from what I was seeing, no one ever had. I chewed my lips, went back to the photographs of Chloe's diary. There was a new list on the next page entitled *FB MARKETPLACE CARS*.

Leonard Yi—FC MK1—Bought new by father in Prospect, 1969. Originally and still is pale blue. No muffler.

Donna Hickson—FC MK2—Previous owners from new all within family, sending list. No muffler.

Fred Galloway—FC MK1—Mustard yellow but no racing stripe. No muffler. Asked for prev. owners. No answer. Chase up.

The list went on for a page, random names, descriptions of cars, mentions of whether the cars had a racing stripe or a muffler. There was a determined focus on whether the car was, or had ever been, mustard yellow. Heading to Facebook, and with some difficulty, working out how to open up the marketplace section, I searched for Ford Capris and saw that indeed some of the people on Chloe's list were trying to sell such a vehicle. At some point, Chloe's written list switched to Gumtree, then to Carsales.com.au. Chloe seemed to be searching for a specific car. I went back to the diagram of the house, the sheds or chicken coops or whatever they were, the car parked in the stopping bay. Whose house was this drawing of? And if Chloe knew the house, what relationship did that homeowner have to the missing Ford Capri?

The lists broke off into a stream of words that made no sense to me, and seemed not to be connected to each other, separated as they were by large gaps or slashes with the pen.

Inquest proceedings—Freedom of Information request—Is the requester name made public on the website?

NSW Media Team—Alison Black—mediapolnsw@nsw.police .gov.au

Trove newspaper archives—possible old car ads, buying and selling in months before and after?

'Before and after what?' I asked aloud. I scrolled further through the photos of the notebook. At some point the dread and confusion peaked, and I put the phone down, held my face, took a breath. Only half my brain was focused on Chloe's diary. And that wasn't good. I needed to get it over with. Switching from the registry search to the section of the intranet related to traffic cams, I ran a search for monitoring cams around Redbelly. I selected a camera and set a time period for 3 p.m. the previous day to 9 a.m. this morning, a wide expanse of time with the murder of Chloe Lutz stationed smack-bang in the middle. The screen filled with a list of car registrations and times. I noted Chloe Lutz's Toyota hatchback, recognising her registration number, travelling north into Redbelly at 3.51 p.m., not long before she arrived at the check-in counter at the pub.

I scrolled down the list, not sure exactly what I was looking for. Chris couldn't drive, and the evening before had been like any other, the kid announcing, 'I'm going out, back later!' and neither Delle nor I being bothered to get up from our evening wine at the kitchen counter to look out the front windows of the house and see who he was getting into a car with. We'd done that very thing when he was younger, looked out, noted down numberplates, gone out a few times and spoken to cagey cars full of teens. But the pathetic feeling the surveillance gave us won out, in the end. The sense that we were being helicopter parents, curtain-twitchers and pearl-grabbers. By the time I was sixteen, Russell was out of the house in the police force, and I'd been living as an adult on the farm at Maroota while Dad disappeared for several days at a time without explanation. I drove myself to the shops. I paid the electricity bills. I mowed lawns and did odd jobs for the neighbours to keep myself going.

A thought occurred to me, and I took up my phone, opened Uber and set my location to my house in Mangrove Mountain. I ordered a ride to Redbelly, and waited while the map expanded and contracted and tiny cars puddled around the screen. I saw that there were two Uber drivers currently operating in the town. One of them accepted my job. I opened the notes app on my phone, copied down the numberplate, then cancelled the ride. Waiting a few minutes, I ordered the ride again, and the other Uber driver in Mangrove Mountain accepted it this time, now that I'd probably deeply annoyed the first one by dumping his job. I noted down this numberplate too, and went back to the list on my laptop, my heart in my throat.

There, at 7.54 p.m., was an Uber driver heading south into Redbelly on the night Chloe Lutz was murdered. I scrolled up and toggled the list so that the accompanying images taken by the camera would show the vehicle itself on the road beside the listing.

A silver Mazda. The occupants in the two front seats were clearly visible. The driver, a muscular, shaven-headed guy. And beside him, my son.

Every part of my brain was saying that I was looking at my child. The posture. The thin slice of jaw that I could see under the black ball cap. I was sure I could discern the shape of his hair against the blackness of the seat's headrest. My jaw locked into place, and I slammed the laptop shut and tossed it aside.

'Fuck this,' I said, starting the car and heading out of the lot.

RUSSELL

I sat at the head of the plastic table in the second of two barbecue areas on Louis Dodge's marooned houseboat. This area of the vessel was a lot less loved than the stern with its with fairy lights and potted geraniums. Up here the awning was partly deconstructed, sheets of corrugated iron stacked outside the wheel room through which the area was accessed. Dodge seemed to be in the process of cutting rotted parts out of the frame and replacing them. One by one, his crew of officers arrived; Fry and another man I'd seen smoking outside the pub when I came into town, and two women who nodded a wary hello then set to muttering in the shadows, their arms folded and heads together. Dodge didn't seem to know whether I wanted everyone to sit at the table or not, and I didn't issue any invitations, so he swept a hand over the team when they were all assembled but left them standing.

'Detective Inspector Powder, you know Constable Fry, and this is his partner, Constable Knowles.' Dodge indicated the two male officers, both in their thirties. Knowles was reedy thin and Fry was just a blob in the corner of my vision, because looking directly at him felt like putting a gun to my head.

'And over there we have Constables Kalowski and Lee.'

I nodded. Didn't smile. Beneath me I heard Bridie returning in the 'Stang.

'Knowles and Fry have taken official statements from publican Rob Winter, the guests who were staying at the hotel last night, and a couple of the local tradies who were at the pub in the evening and saw Chloe having dinner,' Dodge said. 'Then I've had Kalowski and Lee hitting the door-knock trail.'

'You two first.' I pointed at Knowles. 'Keep it short and sharp.'

Knowles's Adam's apple bobbed as he looked to his partner; then, seeing no sign Fry was going to take the hit, said, 'We don't have anything on Robbo.'

'On *who*?' I asked.

'Mr Winter.' Knowles reddened considerably. 'We've run a check on the past female guests of the pub's hotel going back six months, like you asked. A lot of them were international. We haven't been able to come up with anyone who says Mr Winter was anything but polite. Maybe a bit aloof. Always busy. His staff, past and present, have all said nice things about him. He remembers birthdays and pays on time. He's sacked a couple of people over the years but has never done it aggressively or without good reason. They saw it coming and felt they deserved it.'

'Is he single?' I asked.

'Yeah.'

'Why?'

Everyone looked at each other. 'We . . . We haven't asked.'

'It's time to ask.' I gave an impatient huff. 'Don't you think? Woman murdered in his pub? All-female staff? Constantly surrounded by intoxicated women? How is this man getting his rocks off? And if he's not getting his rocks off, how does he feel about that?'

'Maybe he's gay.' Lee gave a little smirk.

'Robbo? Robbo's not gay,' Knowles scoffed. 'He was with that woman from the Mountain for a while. The one with the dreadlocks. Plus, he's Catholic.'

'You can be Catholic and gay,' Kalowski reasoned.

'Can you?'

'He usually has an all-female staff, yes,' Dodge said. 'But that's just how it is out here. Young men mow lawns, lay concrete and haul junk. Women clean houses and work at the pub.'

I nodded, thinking.

'Chloe—*Ms Lutz*—was seen to have attended dinner at 8.07 p.m., as you know.' Fry took out a notebook and started flipping through it. He looked at his colleagues. 'We've got her on camera. From the accounts of the locals, she took a seat at a table under the big tree out there after leaving the counter. She was alone for the duration of her dinner and wasn't seen taking any phone calls. One Mr Stephen Branch, a local pest inspector, seems to have been the only person in the beer garden to actually speak to Ms Lutz while she had dinner and worked on her laptop.'

'And what did he say?' I asked.

'He admits to commenting to Ms Lutz as he passed her at the table that she was working hard.'

'She was "working hard"?' Dodge frowned.

'Yeah.' Fry looked at his boss. The drop in formality as Fry spoke to his superior as opposed to me was instant and stark. His country accent thickened and his shoulders lowered. 'It's like, she's been there hammering the keys madly, spewing out words in a document. And Branchy has walked by and said, "Workin' hard, eh?", sort of thing. He said she said, "Ah, yeah," in response and smiled, but didn't really engage. Like, she hardly looked up. Just went back to her work. Branchy reckons she seemed really focused on what she was doing.'

'Was he trying to engage her?' Dodge asked. 'Was it a conversation starter that she rebuffed?'

'It seems that way,' Fry said.

'And these guys have noticed her go back up to the room?' I asked. '*Branchy*, and co?'

'Yes,' Fry said. 'Mr Branch and a couple of his friends have confirmed they saw Ms Lutz go up the external stairs and pass Mr Turth, the electrician, as he came down for dinner. Mr Turth timed his exit from his room by a text message he sent to his girlfriend before he left, so we're talking around nine o'clock.'

'And you showed Branchy and crew a picture of Mr Turth,' I said slowly, 'to confirm it was the same guy?'

Fry and Knowles looked to the female officers for help. None was on offer. 'I mean, we knew it was Turth from their description.' Fry said.

'But you didn't back it up with a photo?'

No answer. I made the kind of sound I make when I sprint out of the shower to answer the phone and the caller hangs up just as I get there.

'They'll go back and confirm it with a photo,' Dodge said.

'Uh-huh.' I sighed. 'So, we've got the text message to give a rough estimate, by Mr Turth's account, of what time Chloe went upstairs.'

'We've also timed Ms Lutz's return to her room,' Kalowski piped up, 'using the cameras over the bar. At the time Ms Lutz was eating dinner, there were two other tables at dinner in the beer garden. A table of eight and a table of four. It's the policy of the bar staff not to clear a table until everyone has finished eating. We can see on the footage that one of the bar girls brings back a single empty plate and a beer glass around quarter past nine.'

'Ms Lutz ordered a schnitzel,' Lee added. 'And a schooner of Tooheys New. We've got her debit card transaction.'

'You know what time Mr Turth sent his text message,' I said. 'And you know what time Ms Lutz's table was cleared. But you don't know what time she went up. Neither of those things are good enough indicators. Both of those times are easily blown out by up to a half an hour. Turth estimates the time it took him to leave the room by the text message. But after he sends the message, he changes his shirt, takes a piss, stares at himself in the bathroom mirror and contemplates what the fuck he's doing with his life: there's fifteen minutes he didn't pay attention to. And the bar staff were, by Mr Winter's account, fucking around all night chatting and giggling. They most likely didn't get to Chloe's table to clear it right away. Maybe we add another fifteen minutes.'

'Does a half an hour really matter that much?' Kalowski jutted her chin at me. I locked eyes with her. Electricity in the space between us.

'Are you genuinely asking me whether a thirty minute over-under for our murder window *really matters*?' The ice in my voice froze Kalowski in her spot.

'They'll narrow down the time further—won't you, team?' Dodge said. 'It'll be priority number one.'

I sat, thinking. Frogs were making a racket in the thick reeds that framed my view of the river. The water was lit purple by an artificial evening created by the walls of the valley. The temperature was down in the teens now, I guessed. Above us, the remaining sheets of corrugated iron on the awning gave a gentle rattle as a breeze drifted through.

'Nobody in the beer garden gives an account of anyone acting strangely towards Ms Lutz?' I asked. 'No one else talking to her? Watching her? Looking over her shoulder? We're trying to lock down a vantage point, here. The back of the pub is the only place where you can see the external stairwell and the windows to the hotel rooms. If it's not Rob Winter going up there and knifing her because he knows which room she's in, it has to have been someone hanging around in that time period, between eight p.m.—or seven-thirty—or nine p.m.—or fucking *eleven-thirty*, for all you chumps know—when she went up to her room, and 12 p.m., when Superman Ears got home.'

'Superman Ears?' Lee squinted at me.

'Guest in the next room. Excellent hearing,' Dodge said. 'Allegedly.'

'There are no reports of suspicious behaviour.' Knowles shook his head. 'Everyone said—'

'Don't give me that,' I barked. 'Half the guys in the beer garden that you've interviewed appear to be your mates. They're not going to report their own suspicious behaviour, or each other's, and your own personal biases are going to water down any weirdness you hear from them anyway. He had to be there, he had to be watching Chloe, and someone had to have seen him doing that. Who's the creep at the bar? The one we saw watching her on the CCTV?'

'We haven't locked him down yet.'

'Why not?'

Kalowski gave an exasperated sigh. 'Because we're human beings, and it takes us time to do shit, sir?' I gave her a warning glare. She carried on defiantly. 'He might be from out of town. We're showing a photo around, but no one is recognising him. He paid cash at the bar and only ordered the two drinks.'

'Two drinks?'

'He came to the counter one time *before* the time we saw him with Chloe,' Fry said. 'Ordered one drink, alone at the bar. Two trips, two drinks. Pays with cash. Never appears on the cameras again.'

'Anyone in the beer garden remember him?'

'No.'

'The girls who served him at the bar?'

'It was the same girl both times. I've taken her statement, but she knows you'll want to speak with her.'

'What was Chloe working on?' I asked. No answer. 'In your door-knocks, did you come across anyone in town who knew she was coming? Anyone who expected to meet with her?'

'No.'

'Where are her laptop and phone?'

'Both the laptop and the phone lost signal at approximately 11.41 p.m.,' Dodge read from his phone.

'Who told you that?' I asked.

'I've been working with Gail Caplan, trying to get into Chloe's accounts,' Dodge said. 'About fifteen minutes ago, she told me Apple sent her through some information. Not all of it. Not everything we want. But they triangulated the phone and laptop when the signal went out, and gave us a time.'

'Where were they located when they blinked out?'

'In Redbelly.'

'You got nothing more specific than that?'

'No,' Dodge said. 'They were only able to pinpoint the signal using one mobile phone tower and one satellite. So it's vague. Looks like he turned both devices off as soon as he killed her.'

'Or she turned them off before she went to sleep,' Lee suggested.

'Young people don't turn things off,' Fry said.

'The accounts,' I asked. 'When do we get access?'

'Superintendent Caplan said she'd let both you and I know "the very millisecond" they come in,' Dodge said. 'Her words.'

I let a long silence fan out. Lee and Kalowski and Knowles and Fry and Dodge were all looking how I wanted them to look: pissed off, under-appreciated and tired.

'Motive,' I said. 'We don't have a motive. That's a problem. Whoever did this wanted Ms Lutz dead. *Ms Lutz* specifically, and no one else. No one more easily available. Because Ms Lutz was hard to get to. She was *in her room*. Okay? You fuckers listening? Chloe Lutz was behind at least two locked doors, and getting to her without being seen going up those external stairs would have taken patience and immaculate timing. We need to understand why it *had* to be *her*. Why the risk was worth the reward.'

No one spoke.

'Whoever did this,' I said, 'they either *knew her* and wanted her dead, or *didn't know her* and wanted her dead. Whether it's the first or the second possibility, the attack was deliberately targeted. So, let's run down the idea that they *didn't* know her. That this was a chance meeting. Her sitting out in the beer garden like that, working. It's a spectacle. You wouldn't look twice at a young woman working on her laptop while she eats dinner at a pub in Sydney. But this is a rural pub. Everyone else there last night was having a good time. And there she is, ignoring everyone, tapping away, in her own little world.'

'That's most likely why the boys noticed her.' Dodge nodded. 'It was an odd sight. And maybe you're right, maybe it was an *upsetting* sight. I can imagine being one of the local labourers from around here: you've spent all day hosing out someone's septic tank or clearing the dead rats out of their horse stables so you can rub a couple of pennies together to buy a beer. Then you have to sit there while you have that beer watching this cute city kid with her book smarts and her laptop.'

'Knowing she's probably earning five times what you do,' Fry added. 'And even when someone's tried to be friendly to her, she's brushed him off. Maybe that annoyed someone. Maybe it annoyed Branchy—Mr Branch, I mean.'

'I'd brush Branchy off.' Kalowski's mouth twisted. 'He gives me the creeps.'

'What?' Lee's voice was high. 'Ole Branchy? You're kidding. He's all right. He played Santa Claus at the Maroota Fair last year.'

'Case in point.' Kalowski shuddered.

'You're crazy.'

'No, there's something there with that guy. Underneath the surface. You can see it in his eyes. Or I can, at least.'

'You've never said anything about it.'

'Why would I? Nobody believes me.'

'That's because we've all met your ex.' Lee smiled. 'We know that judging character is not your special talent.'

Kalowski rolled her eyes. Knowles folded his arms when he saw my face. 'Look, we get it, detective. We get what you're saying about us being familiar with the suspects we have out here, but that's just how it is. Stephen Branch is a friendly figure about town. Well loved. Makes people laugh. He does amazing impressions.'

'That's right.' Lee grinned.

'He does a great Dolly Parton.' Dodge looked at me sheepishly, trying to steer the ship back on course. 'Some of the local boys, they have domestic violence or male-on-female assaults on their records. Not Branch, as far as I'm aware, but I'll check. We can interview them in the morning. Ask for DNA swabs.'

'Run that as a rumour, tonight,' I said. 'Down at the pub. You four, get down there, among the crowd. Just for an hour. Let it be known that we're going to swab everyone who was at the pub last night, and that we'll be door-knocking again and asking for swabs tomorrow morning. That should drum up some panic. Are your out-of-town coppers at the pub yet?'

Dodge nodded, whipping out his phone. 'I've got five officers down there, listening. Two from Cessnock, three from Katoomba.'

'Make sure they all stay until closing.' I turned back to the women at the deck rail. 'Who was on traffic cams?'

'That would be Senior Sergeant Powder,' Dodge said. 'He said he'd bring the list when he arrives back in town.'

'We need to decide how we're going to divide the night up,' Fry said. Knowles glanced achingly at his watch. 'Who takes first shift and who takes relief.'

'No, there'll be no shifts,' I said. 'We push on. No one sleeps.'

I looked out across the barbecue area. Five sets of eyes watching me. Cops who hadn't worked a real murder maybe ever, staring down a cop who had been dealing with one weekly for the past seven or eight years. 'Don't tell me you're surprised.'

'Well—'

'A young woman was just murdered in your town. The sun is about to set and you still don't have a clue who the fucker is. This is a race, and you're all behind. You're falling *further* behind by the second. So, while the killer sleeps tonight, you catch up. Knocking on more doors. Making more phone calls. Walking the scene. You are going to do those interviews, and you are going to take those swabs. But they won't be tomorrow morning. They'll be tonight. I'm not blind. I can see you're tired. Guess what? I don't give a fuck. A couple of nights of lost sleep is the minimum you owe to Chloe Lutz for letting her get stabbed to death on your turf. So, smash a case of Red Bull. Do a line of coke. I don't care. The longer we go on without a solid suspect, the harder and faster you need to work.'

The officers all glanced at each other. I stood, and they seemed to get the message that the meeting was over.

'And stop treating everyone in town like your mate,' I said. 'There are no mates here.'

* * *

I heard some mutterings in the wheelhouse as the officers left. A dread-heavy laugh. Dodge remained at the boat rail, trying to drag that utility belt up, and with it every ounce of his manhood. He gave the resigned sigh of a man who knows he's about to get bitten by the snake he's trying to remove from under a car seat. 'Okay. Look. Detective, we need to have a little chat.'

'What is it, Dodge?' I didn't take my eyes off the text I was typing to Gail.

'I can't have you talking to my staff like that.'

'Like what? Like I'm pissed? Like I expected more of them than they've given me in the past eight hours? Frankly, I'd have expected more from the Scooby-Doo crew than this pack of no-hopers. Apologies for not handing out certificates of appreciation.'

'You don't actually mean any of that.' Dodge was watching me. I put down the phone and looked at him. 'My team's performance has been pretty reasonable, given their limited experience with homicide and the time they've had to work on this case. You're being an A-grade dickhead to them, and to me, because you're trying to maintain some distance.'

'It doesn't seem to be working.'

'You need to dial it *the fuck* down,' Dodge snapped. A tingle of excitement entered my brain. I took a step closer to Dodge. I towered a good foot above him, and most men. But the move had no effect. 'Nobody here wants to get into your business, Detective Inspector Powder. Nobody is trying to be your friend. So you can stop snarling at us. Okay? Because we're already convinced—*well and truly* convinced—that you're not worth the trouble.'

'Is that right?' I asked. 'You've got me worked out, have you, Dodge?'

'More or less,' he said. 'In my experience, dogs don't do this much barking unless they're protecting something. And I'm here to tell you: whatever it is? Nobody's interested.'

He held my eyes for a while. The growing night howled around us, open and dark and speckled with the first of the evening's stars. A peacock cried down at the pub, a sound remarkably similar to a call for help. The silence in its wake felt lonely.

Dodge announced he was going to the pub, and I watched him go.

* * *

When I got downstairs, Bridie was sitting at her laptop at the little kitchen nook, her back rigid and eyes following me in. There were two coffee cups on the table before her. She pointed to one that was full. I felt like a dog being shown its bowl, went and gulped down a big mouthful before I'd even taken a seat. I was mindful as I eased in beside my daughter not to crack my skull on a row of high cabinets above the portholes, cabinets that I knew in my soul I was going to forget were there and bean myself on at some point. The coffee was good. The previous night spent up doing damage control for being a 'punch-happy sack of shit' was catching up with me, along with the heaviness of my responsibilities here in Redbelly Crossing. My promise to Larry Lutz that I always got my man.

'What happened with the roo?' I asked Bridie, resisting the urge to reach over and pull her to me and hold her. 'Any luck?'

'It was male.'

'Oh.'

'I've been here finding out about Chloe.'

'You got anything good?'

'Yeah,' Bridie said. She swivelled her laptop towards me. 'I think she'd pissed off a serial killer.'

2024

EVAN

The car was on Eight Mile Trail at eleven o'clock on a Friday night. Footy night. I sucked air between my teeth when I saw it rumbling through the trees ahead of me, because I knew even before I noticed the wheels kissing the rocky edges of the trail as it drove along that the driver had to be drunk. Circumstances just guaranteed it. Stupid move by me to take the shortcut between Redbelly and Mangrove Mountain, known almost exclusively by locals. Because, although I had officially finished my shift for the night, I was still in the patrol car, having just delivered some files to Dodge and his guys in Wisemans. Policy dictated that when I was in the car and I saw a crime, it was mine to deal with. I watched the big black Jeep Wrangler drift over and narrowly miss clipping a huge lump of sandstone in the bush, and cursed my life. I hit the lights. I'd been on the cusp of five days off after twelve days on, was already emotionally and physically checked out, needing only to return the squad car and sign the station register before entering full-blown holiday mode. Now the finish line had been yanked away just as I put on a last burst of speed. This was going to delay me getting home for dinner, and Delle had texted to say she had homemade pizza in the oven.

Something big crashed through the bush as I exited the squad car. The telltale thumping of kangaroo. With lush bushland hugging us all around, lit blue and red and yellow like an enchanted fairy garden, I approached the driver's side of the Jeep with dread in my heart. Watched the window roll down. A thick forearm lolled out onto the sill. There was a passenger in the front seat, looking over at me, white eyes glittering in the dark. When I recognised the ruddy, sunburnt face of the driver my breath hitched in my chest. This was both good and bad.

'Oh, hey, look who it is,' I said, putting a hand on the top of the car. 'G'day, Blake.'

'Heeeeey.' Blake Sanderson leant back, his mouth shifting awkwardly as his bloodshot eyes wandered across my face. 'There you are.'

'Evan Powder. Chris's dad.'

'Of course!' Blake grinned, putting a hand out. Shaking mine too hard, so that both our hands knocked on the windowsill. 'Of course! I know who you are. Good to see ya, mate! Good to see ya! This is Constable Powder.' Blake turned to his passenger, a similarly built sun-baked brick of a male in a singlet and ball cap. I let the misidentification of my rank slide by as he went on. 'His son goes to school with Jacky.'

'Oh, right. How ya goin'?' The passenger flashed me an open palm, fingers spread wide, the awkward wave of someone caught red-handed.

'Yeah, I'm good. Just noticed you were wobbling a bit.'

'Oh, this bloody thing's acting up.' Blake slapped the steering wheel. 'Just had the alignment done on it the other day and it's still pulling to the left.'

'Are you heading back from footy night at Wisemans?'

'Ah, we stopped in at the RSL for a biiiit . . . ? But we weren't there for long, were we, Trev?'

'Nah. Middy of mid-strength. That was about it.'

'That was about it,' Blake confirmed, turned and grinned at me. His red eyes were full of tense hope. Because, surely he knew how badly he stunk of bourbon. Knew it was permeating the air around us, completely overpowering the acidy, minty taste of the eucalypts. Blake could see that I was struggling with the next few steps. He reached out and touched my arm with his meaty fingers to help me along. 'Your Chris, he's the one with the long hair, yeah?'

'That's him.'

'I've seen him and his mates getting around town, in their hoodies.' Blake smiled. 'With the make-up. Heavy metal kids, are they?'

'Ah, well . . .'

'There were heavy metal kids at my school,' Trev offered. 'I was one of them. And look how I turned out.'

'They're a good lot, though, Evan's son and his crew.' Blake shot his friend a warning look. 'Not like this degenerate here and his band of wannabe satanists.'

'He's a good kid,' I confirmed. 'Going through a phase, that's all. We've all been there.'

'How's he going at school?'

'He's all right,' I lied.

'Listen, when he's done with his heavy metal phase, why don't you see if he wants to come over our place sometime and hang with Jacky and his mates? Jacky could use a couple of friends who aren't such boofheads. A thoughtful little bloke like your Chris might do Jacky good.'

'Maybe.' I felt the devil whispering in my ear. Looked at Blake's big hand on the steering wheel. 'Maybe. Listen, Blake—'

'Sometimes I let the boys take the ute and go off down the paddocks,' Blake cut in. 'You ought to see them when they get back. It's like they're a bunch of five-year-olds again. Grass in their hair and sparkles in their eyes.'

Trevor laughed. I ignored the uncomfortable stirring in my stomach, trying to think of the last time Chrissy had romped back into the house after a day in the wild, grass in his hair and sparkles in his eyes. The last time he'd been outside by choice at all. 'You know, that sounds pretty good, actually.'

'You can sit up on the verandah with me and Melissa and have a barbie, ay? Bring your missus. They can fret about where the kids are and we can sink some schooies.'

'Am I invited?' Trev asked.

'You? Mate, I couldn't be clearer: I'm trying to *cut down* on the number of boofheads coming in and out of my house.'

I laughed now. Feeling a part of something. Feeling the enveloping arms and golden gaze of the in-crowd. Like I was in fucking high school again. Blake rolled his eyes, jerked a thumb towards Trev, conspiratorial. 'This guy, eh?'

'I appreciate the invitation,' I said. 'I'll give it some thought.'

'We're just down here.' Blake pointed at the windshield. 'The one with the red mailbox. Five minutes, tops.'

'Is that all?' I chewed my bottom lip. Teetered on the jagged edge of destiny for a few precious seconds without knowing I was doing it. 'Ah, well. Fine.'

'Good.' Blake smiled.

'I'll let you blokes go,' I said, tapping the car roof. 'Maybe get that wheel alignment done again, huh?'

I got back into the cruiser and followed the Jeep at a respectable distance, leaving that life-changing moment deep in the wilderness behind me. We got to the main road leading back to the Mountain. When Blake Sanderson pulled to the roadside by a big red mailbox, he stuck his huge arm out the window in a wave, and I waved back, feeling worthy.

* * *

The call came four hours later. I was deep under the doona, with a belly drum-tight full of the world's best meatlover's pizza and half a bottle of wine. Climbing up through the layers of consciousness took deliberate effort, akin to pulling myself, hand over hand, up the rugged face of a cliff. Delle sat bolt upright in bed, saw it was my phone and not hers, and slammed back down again like a cartoon vampire. I took three or four tries to slide the electronic button on the screen in the dark.

'Yeah?'

'I need you to listen to me very carefully,' Hayley Twitcher said, in a voice that made my skin grow cold in a sudden, sickening rush. 'And don't say anything until you've heard all of the information I'm about to give you.'

'O . . . kay . . . ?' I shot out of the bed, went to Chris's room, threw the door open. His figure was there in the sheets, twisting, reacting to the light like a bat, all scrambling limbs and squinting eyes.

'What is it?' I said into the phone. 'What's happened?'

'Blake Sanderson just wrapped his car around a fucking tree.'

'What?'

'He had a passenger with him. Trevor Willis. Willis is dead, and they've just taken Sanderson in for surgery. It's not looking good, Evan.'

'What the fuuuu—' I forgot how to breathe, to swallow; coughed and went into the kitchen. I was starting to shake now. 'Are you serious?'

'Yes, I'm serious, Evan. And I'm getting more and more serious by the *second*, because I'm here at the hospital, and I'm seeing it and hearing it. Sanderson just told an emergency room nurse that a local cop pulled him and Trevor over not ten minutes before they crashed and that cop cut them loose again.'

The words wouldn't come. They dissolved before they were half-formed. There was screaming in my head. A long, loud, animalistic wail.

'Was that cop you, Evan?'

'No.'

'Are you sure? Because Acosta was here all night, and Jenny says it wasn't her. Is she lying?'

'No, no, no, no.' I shuddered. Delle was behind me, eyes full of fear. 'No, I mean, I didn't . . . I was there but I didn't . . . pull them over.'

'You just drove by them?'

'No, I mean—'

'Jesus, Evan.' Hayley's voice was shaking. 'Trevor Willis has got two kids. Blake was saying he couldn't feel his legs. This is *not good.*'

'I'm coming there.'

'You better.' She hung up.

Delle grabbed my arm. 'What happened?'

I just shook my head, went to the bedroom. Dragged a T-shirt out of the wardrobe with fingers that were numb and tingling. With my other hand, I dialled my father.

EVAN

Chrissy's door was ajar. The kid was sitting back in his desk chair watching a chat conversation roll up the screen, Metallica blasting. The room smelt of sweat and Lynx body spray. I was so used to coming in and turning the music down I didn't even have to look for the knob, did it by feel as I sat on the bed. I steadfastly avoided looking at the cum stains on the sheets beside me and said, 'Hey, birthday boy.'

'Hey.' The kid didn't look up. Spaced out. He was resting one of our nice crystal tumblers on his belly and sipping from it now and then, something that, from the smell, was probably vodka and Red Bull. The blatant underage drinking was typical Chris. He was in trouble for the paintball shooting. Might as well double down and defiantly drink my stolen vodka in our special glasses right in front of me. 'Mum's pissed at you.'

'Mmm. Well, she'll get over me abandoning her to go to work faster than she'll get over you shooting one of your friends in the face, Chris,' I said. 'She just showed me the photo. That kid's not going to school on Monday.'

'Yeah, so what?'

'So we need to talk about today. And last night.'

Chris shook his head, blew air out through his thin lips. 'Man, this is rich.'

'I know you were in Redbelly last night,' I said.

'No, you don't.' His words were firm and slow. 'Because I wasn't there.'

'There is only one reason I can think of that you'd lie to me about being there,' I said. 'Because you're afraid of being in trouble. For underage drinking, or for being with someone you're not supposed to be with, or for anything else that might have gone down.'

'Dad.'

'Someone who looks exactly like you caught an Uber into Redbelly last night, just before eight, and bought a drink at the bar. They had a good hard look at the murder victim. That person—'

'Jesus, fuck!' Chris suddenly roared, throwing down his drink. The crystal glass thunked loudly on the desktop, sloshing liquid over some papers. There he was: the angry, cornered Chris. The shyest abandoned dog at the shelter, which, if pushed hard enough, could become the most savage creature in the building. He'd always been like that. Bottled up fury. 'Would you *listen to yourself*? I give you an answer to your question and you just keep going at me like I didn't answer at all. Why am I even talking to you?'

'Where did you go, if you didn't go to Redbelly last night?'

'To Liam's.'

'Call Liam on your phone right now,' I said. 'Put it on speaker.'

'No.'

'Open your Uber app and show it to me.'

'Make me, bitch!'

Fury sizzled in me. Because I bottled my rage, too, but over the years the lid that kept it down had become old and degraded. I told myself to loosen my grip on the edge of the bed. 'Do you have any idea what would have happened to me if I'd called my father a "bitch" at your age?'

'Don't start down that road.' He waved a hand at me, eyes back on the screen. 'You think he's a terrible person. I get it. I've been hearing it for years, how terrible Pop was to you and Uncle Rus. I've got news for you: *everyone* thinks their parents are terrible people. It's part of life.'

'Chris.'

'He never burnt you with cigarettes. He never left you to starve.'

I was starting to shake with rage.

'He's never told you that he loves you,' my son went on. 'Too bad. Get over it.'

I blew out a measured breath.

'You've got no empathy for the guy at all,' Chris said. 'His parents died and they put him in a boys' home at *six years old*. Do you know what used to happen to little kids in those homes back in the day?'

I didn't answer.

'What about if you, like, thought about Pop as a guy. As just some guy. You'd see his story is actually really sad, Dad. His wife killed herself and left him with two young sons to raise all alone,' Chris went on. 'Can't you have any forgiveness?'

'I can't believe I'm listening to this,' I murmured.

'You ought to go on TikTok and look up "intergenerational trauma", and, like, see what you think about him after ten fucking minutes of self-education.' Chris shook his head. 'Check out "covert narcissism" while you're at it.'

Empathy. Intergenerational trauma. Covert narcissism. I was biting the inside of my cheek without knowing it, only realised when I tasted the blood. I spotted the ancestry DNA kit box on the edge of the desk, by a pile of tissues and an empty bowl lined with furry mould and old lumps of puffed rice. My pulse quickened as I reached over and plucked it up. 'I'm sitting here wondering if this isn't all connected, Chris. If maybe you went to Redbelly because you were meeting my father there. The Redbelly pub is a weird place for a kid to hang out. It's usually locals and older people there. But it's halfway between Mangrove Mountain and Maroota, and here you are, suddenly a little spokesperson for Arthur Powder.'

'I'm disengaging from this conversation.' Chris sighed.

'You know you're not supposed to be alone with your grandfather.'

'Why?' He looked at me, his eyes big and wild and defiant. 'What happened at the farm was my fault.'

I put the ancestry kit box in my lap so I could hold my head. I had known, deep down inside, that Chris felt that way about an incident that had occurred between him and my father a couple of years earlier. But I'd never actually heard him say it.

It had been the anniversary of Russell's coming out. November. Heading into Christmas. A touchy time for any toxic family. Arthur had been calling me drunk every few nights, ranting about Russell, wanting to know if I'd known, if I'd ever had any hint. Wanting to explain to me that it was our mother's suicide when Russell was eight and I was four that had caused all of this. Because she'd known that shooting herself in one of the back sheds on that particular day, at that particular time, would mean that Russell would be the one to get home from school early and find her, and not Dad. The suicide had warped Russell's mind, caused him to be unable to tolerate having a beautiful, loving, nuclear family. 'He had to find a way to fuck it up,' Dad had rambled. 'This whole gay thing is just the biggest way he could think of to drop the bomb and blow up his family.'

'Dad, I'm pretty sure that's not how homosexuality works,' I'd said dryly. 'At all.'

I couldn't tell, during these calls, whether Arthur was crying or not. His voice sounded husky and thin and worryingly old. When he'd begun asking about Chris, I'd relented and suggested Chris go out there for a day to help him with some mowing. My thinking had been that Arthur was learning something. That he was seeing the error of his ways. That maybe he was feeling some actual human emotions, like remorse, and regret, and sadness, and aching through the great empty silence that Rus had left in his life, the same way I was. It was far too late for Arthur to be a decent father to Russell and me. But maybe there was some way he could heal—and through that, I could heal—by his forming a healthy relationship with Chris.

I'd sent Chris, defying Delle, who had misgivings about the whole thing. A mother's instinct. Chris had lasted at my father's farm for about an hour before calling me, near hysterical, to come pick him up. In a series of breathless confessions, Chris told us that

Arthur had taken him straight to the back sheds almost as soon as I departed after dropping him off. The old man told the boy the lawns could wait, because he wanted help to cull his entire coop full of chickens so he could pluck and gut and freeze them. The old man had just bought a new deep freezer second hand, and he was sick of caring for the birds. As my thirteen-year-old son stood and watched, my father started grabbing and beheading chickens with an axe on an old sawn-down slab of tree stump, tossing the dead birds aside, working through them swiftly. All the while he encouraged Chris to participate, getting steadily angrier and angrier when he wouldn't. Chris's reaction to the scene had sent Arthur into a flaming, spitting rage, and he'd brandished the axe at my kid, bloody and manic. Delle and I sat numbly and listened to the tale in the car on the side of the road not far from my father's house. My biggest concern in sending Chris to his grandfather's to mow the lawn had been the possibility of snakes.

I spent that whole night shifting between Chris's bedroom and mine and Delle's. Delle was in a fury, and I was trying to convince her that hunting and killing animals on farms was a perfectly natural activity, something we'd done an awful lot as kids, and that my father had been well-meaning but deeply mistaken about Chris's ability to witness something like that. In Chris's room, I just held the boy, who shook and cried from sundown to sun-up.

'What happened was not your fault,' I said now. 'But it was a lesson, Chris. That there's nothing for you to gain from looking backwards into our family. Okay? I'd really like it if you didn't do this ancestry kit thing.'

'Nope.'

'I am very happy to replace this gift with something else, Chris.' I told myself not to plead. To hint at the importance of it all. Like showing fear to a dog. 'I'll get you a PS5.'

'Get me a PS5 anyway.' Chris snorted.

'You're opening a door on something very dark.' My voice trembled. 'Okay? This would be very, very dark for me. I don't want to go on a nice long journey into my family's history. I don't want you to do it either. I would consider it a real gift, a real *favour*,

Chrissy, if you just put this away somewhere.' I shook the box. 'Just for a few years, even.'

'Why are *you* the one getting gifts on *my* birthday?'

I had to bite back the rage. Sat, trembling, trying to contain it. 'Okay. Look, if I haven't convinced you, then let's open it.'

'No way.' Chris shook his head. 'I want to do it at Naomi's. She wants to watch, because she's thinking of—'

'I really want to open it now, Chris.' I was right on the edge. My pulse thumping in my jugular. 'I want to read the pamphlet and see what's involved.'

'So go to the website.'

'Open the box.'

'Come on, Dad.'

'Open the fucking box, Chris.'

The boy gave me a look. Reached over, snatched the box out of my hand. Picked weakly at the sticker with a painted fingernail, drawing out the process. I snatched the box back and took my car keys out of my pocket, slashed the sticker, fumbled to open the box. Right under the pamphlet that was resting on the box's contents, I spotted them. Two plastic vials, sitting in vacuum-sealed baggies. I waved the pamphlet at the kid. 'I'm just going to have a little read.'

'Knock yourself out.' Chrissy hammered some words into the chat. Reduced the font size so it was unreadable from where I was sitting. 'I hope it's very informative.'

Heavy silence. Pre-explosion teen anger billowing out into the room, eating up the oxygen. I used the pamphlet as cover to palm the two vials, slip them into my shirtsleeve, shifting on the bedcovers to mask the sound of the crinkling packages they were sealed in. It was a minute or so before I could naturally get my hand to my hip, poke the two vials into my jeans pocket with all the joy and relief of a guy hitting the cash-out button on a jackpotting poker machine. I didn't know exactly why, then, it seemed so important to make the ancestry kit thing impossible for Chris. But his being at Redbelly, me *knowing* he'd been there, had lit a fuse in my brain. When the vials were in my pocket, I had the cold-sweat feeling of someone who'd tripped at the top of a long flight of stairs and caught themselves before the fall. I cleared my throat. 'So, I'm seeing here that there's supposed to be two collection vials.'

Chris didn't answer. I put the pamphlet on the only spare spot on the desk. Made a show of rumpling through the rest of the box. 'I'm not seeing those vials.'

Chris took the box from me. Looked at the pamphlet. Unfolded the instruction sheet so that it was as big as an old-style tourist map. Did the whole routine once more. 'Where are the fucking vials?'

'Maybe they—'

'Stand up.' Chris was out of his chair, waving at me to get off the bed. 'Did you drop them?'

'No.'

Looking under the bed. Going back to the box. Running a finger down the two grooves where the vials had lain. 'So where are they?'

'No idea.'

Chris did one more run-through of the search. Then he stopped, straightened, and looked at me. I met my son's eyes, and I heard a voice deep in my head that was half my own, and half my father's.

Try it, you little shit.

'Did you take them?' Chris asked.

'No,' I said. We held each other's gaze. Then Chris tried it. He lunged at my pocket. I felt an exhilarated, joyful rush crash into the violence already simmering in my chest. The genetic badness. It was all I could do to make the blow to the kid's face a firm but harmless palming and not a slap, as Chrissy came at me and I buffeted him away. His cheeks were immediately beetroot red with humiliation.

'What the *fuck*, Dad!'

'I don't have your vials.'

'Yes you do.'

'I have played nicely with you for as long as I can on this, Chris. But—'

'This is you playing nicely?' His eyes were big and swimming in alcohol. 'Fuck you! You're constantly badmouthing your own father, trying to tell me you're the nice guy in all this. *Fuck* you!'

'Right back at ya, kid.'

'Did you ever wonder whether Pop is the way he is because he's had to deal with *you* his whole life?'

I tried to control the urge to strangle my child. Actually saw myself doing it, a flash behind my eyelids. When I could finally speak, the words came out in a voice that was thick with evil. 'Chris.'

'What?'

'I'm gonna tell you who you're trying to "make a connection" with,' I said carefully. I wanted to scream. The ends of my words pulled upwards, trying to climb, trying to let the rage take over. 'I'm gonna tell you the truth. You wanted it, here it is.'

Delle was in the room suddenly. She put a hand on my arm. I couldn't even feel the weight of it.

'When we were kids, Dad bought Russell and me a dog each,' I said. 'They were border collies. I had the girl. Russell had the boy. We couldn't believe it. We were hysterical with joy. Our mother had just killed herself the year before—'

'Evan, stop,' Delle said.

'Shut up!' I roared at her. She snatched her hand away like my skin was burning hot. I turned back to Chris. 'We figured Arthur was trying to make us happy. Which was something he'd never done in our lives. Not once. He was being weird and giving us these dogs and smiling and letting us sleep with them on the ends of our beds, and we just didn't question it because we were too excited.'

Chrissy was watching me, his mouth pulled downwards, the chat rolling up the laptop screen faster and faster behind him.

'Three months, we had those dogs,' I said. Suddenly it was hard to breathe. 'They went everywhere with us. They would wait at the gate for us to get home from school every day. Then one day Arthur came and told us we couldn't afford to feed them both anymore. We had to get rid of one. And he wasn't just talking about rehoming the dog, Chris, like a normal person would do. He was talking about taking that dog out the back of the property and shooting it.'

Chris's head snapped back hard, the way it had when I'd palmed him off. '*What?*'

'He told us to fight. Me and Russell. The winner got to keep his dog.'

'Why? *Why would he do that?*'

'Because he was teaching us a lesson.'

'*What lesson?*'

'That we should never love anything,' I said.

The night swelled around us. The house was silent but for a clock ticking somewhere. I was trying to stop the words, feeling like my eyes were wild, like I needed to claw the story back out of my son's precious, pure, innocent brain before it was too late. Because it was happening. I was poisoning him. I was letting Arthur's venom get into my son.

'What happened?' Chris asked. His voice was tiny.

'What do you think?' I said. 'Russell and I beat the shit out of each other. I broke his eye socket. He knocked me out cold. Dad took my dog away and shot it dead.'

'Jesus fucking Christ,' Chris said. His voice was a monotone. Delle's mouth was hanging open.

'Russell was so guilty about winning that he ran away with his dog the next morning,' I said. 'He told me years later that he took him all the way up to the Sunshine Coast. Hitchhiked. Wanted to get him into the hands of someone far, far away from Dad.' The breath was finally coming back into me. I was trembling with shame. Rambling. 'I was terrified for those three days that Russell was gone that he'd never come back and I'd be stuck alone with the old man forever. When he got home I was so happy I just . . . you know . . . I couldn't grieve for the dog anymore. I was just so happy.'

My wife and child were silent.

'This person isn't someone who deserves my sympathy, or yours,' I told Chris. 'And you're forbidden from being alone with him. If you were with him last night, you need to tell me right now.'

Chris just shook his head. I waited, but that's all he did: shook his head, sat on the bed shaking it and staring at nothing. I walked out. Went to the bathroom and started stripping, and Delle came right in behind me and closed the door after herself.

'What the *actual fuck*, Evan.'

'He asked. I answered. We're done now. It's over. He wasn't there. There's nothing to worry about.' I pulled my shoes off. 'Now I'm going to shower and change and head back out. I'll be up all night working on this Redbelly thing.'

'We agreed you'd never bring that shit into this house.' Delle's eyes were wild. Wet. 'It stays in the therapy room. It never comes near Chris.'

'There's not enough therapy sessions in the world to contain all that stuff, Delle,' I said. 'And I'm tired of paying thousands of dollars just so I can comfort my therapist about the crazy shit that I tell her. Also, trying to keep the stories out of the house is a little redundant, isn't it? The actual man himself walks right in here whenever he damn well pleases.'

Delle was massaging her brow as I unbuttoned my shirt. 'You never told me that story. About the dogs.'

'Yeah, well, I'm sick of comforting you about it all, too.'

I showered, pulled on fresh clothes and left the house without saying goodbye to anyone. As I pulled away from the kerb, my phone rang, and I answered it on the hands-free.

'I thought you said you were going to wait here for the results?' The tech's voice on the phone was unmistakable, thick and smug.

'You got something?'

'I've got a partial profile,' he said. 'Like I said, it's only a piece. I'll email it to you, you punch it into NCIDD and see if anything lines up.'

I pulled over right there, three streets away from my house, and dragged my laptop out of the backpack. I logged in to the National Criminal Investigation DNA Database and gave the tech my credentials so he could securely send me the coded profile of the DNA taken from Chloe Lutz's body. I thanked him, asked him to deal with me and me alone going forward, and ended the call.

I transferred the code into a new search of a system that contained more than 1.7 million DNA profiles from Australia's criminals, suspects, cops, volunteers, missing persons and unidentified remains. The system started scrolling. I sat the laptop on the passenger seat beside me, pulled back onto the road and continued driving towards Redbelly.

As I crossed the bridge into town, the wooden boards drumming under the car's tyres, I noticed the system had stopped scrolling. Thinking I'd lost internet, I pulled over again with a painful tightness in my chest. I was in sight of the pub where Chloe Lutz had been murdered. Her killer's DNA profile popped up on the screen. Beneath it was a heading that read *Familial link*.

Beneath that heading were two coded profiles. I clicked on the first one.

It was me.

RUSSELL

I slid into the kitchen nook beside Bridie and folded my arms, watched her as she filled in a report on the dead male kangaroo. Nobody had ever taught me to touch-type. It wasn't a thing at my school. So, being a two-finger pecker myself, I always enjoyed seeing the magic of a young person's fingers dancing over the keys. She kept writing as she spoke to me.

'I'll take you through what I've found in just a sec.'

'Great.'

'How was your meeting with your new best friend?'

'I am actually trying really, really hard not to like Senior Sergeant Dodge,' I said. 'But I'm struggling.'

Bridie stopped typing and looked at me, a smile playing about the corners of her mouth. 'Really?'

'He's a good, solid cop.' I nodded. 'Got some backbone to him. He called me an "A-grade dickhead".'

'To your face?'

'Yeah.'

'I love that.' She laughed. 'Imagine how many people in the world are liked by you, without ever knowing it.'

'Hundreds, probably.'

'You could be friends with Dodge if you just loosened up.'

'Friends are for the weak.'

Bridie's fingers stroked the mousepad as she left the kangaroo report and went to Chloe Lutz's Instagram page. What must have been an obligatory shot for all writers—the pretty coffee and a slice of a laptop, a modern cafe filled with light, which Chloe had filtered in sepia. 'Back at it!'. The dead woman I'd just seen laid out on a slab at the Wisemans Ferry medical centre was full of life here, doing things she'd never do again. Smiling. Writing. Wearing sunglasses. Posing for selfies with friends. Patting a dog.

'So I started with her Instagram page,' Bridie said. 'And I went through all her other social accounts. I looked for anything that involved Redbelly Crossing. Because that's what we're really trying to do here, right? Figure out why she came out here and whether it was to meet someone, or whatever. So, some of these photos are geotagged, and some are not. For the ones that have tags, the most rural she gets is Noosa. There are bush-y or forest-y shots sometimes, but nothing that says Redbelly Crossing specifically, or rural pub or anything like that. There's nothing from the hotel room she died in, nothing from the trip out here. Her last post about anything at all was last Tuesday, about how bad the queue was at her local post office.'

'Okay.' I nodded, following the photographs and unplayed videos as they travelled up the screen.

'I started looking at the profiles that commented most frequently on Chloe's posts, and they're all sort of harmless people. Her old boss at a magazine she used to work at is in there a bunch just saying, like, "Wow, pretty" on some of the artsy shots. People say, like, "Great read" about her articles. Her mother, Jill, is there, and a handful of girlfriends. She had a big break-up mid last year, so some posts from before then are missing. And there are a few things around that time, like, "Keep your chin up" and "His loss". Did you know about the break-up?'

'The guy's in Italy, apparently,' I said. I'd fielded a text from Larry Lutz just after my briefing. A screen of details about a kid named Cameron Tosh. I'd seen the Tosh boy standing in Piazza San Marco. Bleached hair and a septum piercing. 'It looks like that might be true.'

'Chloe had accounts on X and Threads.' She showed me each window. Mostly shared content replicated over and over. 'No TikTok, though, and no Facebook, at least not under her own name.

Everything she's got in terms of social media is publicly accessible. Nothing's set to private. And across those sites, there's nothing from her saying, like, "I'm going to Redbelly Crossing," or "I'm working on this or that right now." I guess her phone and email will tell you more. How long until you can get that access?'

I glanced at my watch. 'I've been harassing my boss.'

'It'd be a lot easier if you had her actual devices.'

'A lot of things would make my life easier.' I sighed. 'So, whoever knew Chloe was out here didn't get it off a publicly accessible social media site. That tells me something. But not much. Where are you getting this idea that Chloe pissed off a serial killer? That's a big statement, Birds.'

'Well, so, let me explain my theory.' Bridie kept clicking. 'After I'd checked out everyone who was interacting with Chloe's pages, I started looking at who *she* was interacting with. I looked at what she liked and commented on. And a couple of months ago, her interests took a big swing into true crime. Look at this list of follows . . . here. See? These are in chronological order. Like, she literally followed all these pages one after the other.'

Bridie pulled up a new screen full of listed accounts. Podcasts with titles like *Unsolved*, *Casefile*, *Forgotten*, *Lost*, *Missing*. They were all focused on Australian stories, or produced by Australian companies. I saw images of lighthouses, bushland, outback roads. There were podcast collections by the ABC, *The Age*, the *Herald*, the *Guardian*. Some of them seemed to be covering active court cases. Summaries of trials I knew were unfolding in Sydney at that very moment. I rubbed my eyes. I could see where Bridie was heading with this. 'Okay, so you think she might have been chasing up a true crime mystery out here?'

'Well . . .' Bridie's face twitched. Her confidence faltering. She opened a page full of old newspaper articles. An online library collection. 'There are actually plenty of cases to choose from out here, if that's what she was up to. Look at this. These two guys went into the woods just up the road from here. Like, literally three hundred metres from where we're sitting right now. It was in the 1950s. They were never seen again.'

I read the article, aware that Bridie's eyes were on my face. A real estate agent and a prospective land buyer had met to inspect a property on the edge of town, only to vanish into thin air. The vehicles were found still parked at the roadside. One of the men's jackets was left hanging on a barbed-wire fence. Baffled-looking police officers were pictured in the article, standing on the dirt track leading to the property, heads together, talking. Another was on horseback. The pull quote was from one of the missing men's distraught wife. 'I packed his lunch to take with him. The police said it was still there on the front seat of his car.'

'Creepy, huh?' Bridie asked.

'Sure.'

'What if, like, whoever killed those two guys back then knew, somehow, that Chloe was going to come out here and start poking around about it? And then he came back. He was like, *I'll kill her before she finds anything out.*'

'It's a very creative theory, Bridie,' I said, carefully. 'But whatever happened to those guys in the woods happened seventy years ago. It's not *impossible* that whoever did it is still around. Maybe . . . I dunno. A couple of kids were playing with a rifle on the property. They accidentally shot one of the men, panicked and shot the other one, too. Dragged their bodies into the river. But those kids would have to be eighty-five now? Ninety?'

'Oh. Okay.'

'Yeah.'

'But it is possible . . . ?'

'It's possible, but it's a real stretch.'

'There's plenty more to choose from, though.' Bridie clicked around. 'Look at this one. This is from the seventies. I think this one makes more sense.'

I saw a flash of a headline. *Lone women to lock doors: killer house-caller still at large.* A young woman in a bridal veil. Police on a cottage verandah. I nodded along, trying to open my rigidly closed mind. 'This is more like it.'

I read the articles, got the usual fluttering of anger in my chest at any story about a male predator attacking women in their homes.

Nothing as strong as the fury I felt at whoever had taken Chloe Lutz, but an echo of it. Linda Special had been home alone with her newborn baby in their small house in Redbelly Crossing in July 1973, while her husband worked on an oil rig, trying to get the family set up with a quick burst of high-paying work. She'd been discovered stabbed to death in a hallway inside the house, the baby wailing in the next room, no signs of forced entry. Almost a year later, Marian Richley, a student and bartender living in the flat lands between Wisemans Ferry and Redbelly, had been found the same way. Both women had been sexually assaulted and left to bleed out on the floor.

There was a cup lying smashed on the kitchen floor of Linda's home, just inside the door. The phone in Marian's kitchen had been left hanging off the hook. I thought about the chain on Chloe Lutz's hotel-room door—why she'd taken it off, only to be attacked right there in the doorway. Whoever had committed the atrocities at the rural homes in these articles, presuming they'd at least reached puberty, would be at least in their mid-sixties now. I tossed the theory around a little. Tapped the table and tried to envision it.

'What else have you got here?' I asked, trying to delay expressing my doubts. I clicked over to the last window. Bridie's hands shot forward for the laptop.

'Oh, uh . . .' I looked at the image of my father on the screen. I'd seen the article plenty of times before, but not for twenty years or so. *Hero cop injured in shootout with killer husband.* Bridie was shrivelled up beside me, one leg pulled against her chest, her chin resting on it, eyes restless. 'It just popped up while I was searching.'

'It's okay, Bridie.'

'Sorry. I was curious.'

'Don't be sorry,' I said, as casually as I could. 'You're allowed to be curious,'

'It says Pop went around there to question the guy about his wife's murder,' Bridie said. 'And the dude just shot him?'

'From the way Dad tells it, there were a few shots fired,' I said. 'The wife was missing. Dominique Fine was her name. She'd been gone for a good while. Husband said he was at the pub when she just up and disappeared. Left the back door swinging open and potatoes cooking on the stove. He didn't report her gone until the next morning. Dad went around there maybe six months later. The Wisemans Ferry boys hadn't been able to close the case, so he thought he'd give it a crack.'

Bridie listened, her lips pursed.

'He shouldn't have been there alone,' I said. 'And he should have left when the questioning got heated. But, being who he was, Dad wanted to run a one-man interrogation right there in the guy's house. He got a bullet for his troubles. And so did the husband. Dad survived and the guy didn't.'

'Do you remember it?'

'No. I would only have been three or four.'

'How bad was he injured?'

'Bad enough to remind everybody about it every ten minutes for the next fifty years.' I shifted in my seat, stretched my back. It popped loudly. 'He took it in the meat of the shoulder. Stopped being able to raise his arm all the way. Apparently. He held out for a while, but it got worse as he got older, and they took him off the force and gave him a pension.'

'Wow.' Bridie's eyes wandered over the screen. We sat in silence for a while, Bridie thinking whatever she was thinking, me trying not to say terrible things about my father. Eventually she said, 'So, anyway, going back to this sort of stuff . . .' She clicked away from Dad's picture, back to the murdered women, Linda and Marian. I felt like a collar had been loosened from around my throat. 'What do you think about my theory? There are so many other good cases. I only just started digging. The more I dig, the more I find.'

'It's a very imaginative theory, honey.' I smiled.

'But?'

'But it's just . . . weak,' I said. 'That's all.'

Bridie deflated beside me. Physically slumped a good couple of inches. I felt my stomach sink with her, then turned to her, tried to lighten my tone. 'I mean, it's a good idea! It is, Bridie. It just needs to be so much stronger than this for it to be an avenue worth going down.'

'Why, though?' She shrugged sharply. 'You know she's come out here to write something. Something worth being killed over. What else would you kill someone over?'

'Oh, Bridie,' I said, 'I've seen people kill each other over who gets the last slice of pizza.'

'But they stole her laptop and her phone. So, they must have been trying to cover something up.'

'Where'd you hear that?'

'It's all over town.'

I wasn't surprised. 'Not only that, but he stuck around looking for something else. A notebook, probably.'

'So, my theory makes sense.' Bridie put her hands up. 'It makes perfect sense, Dad.'

'It does, but it's not *strong enough*,' I said. 'I'm not discarding it. I'm just saying we need to make it stronger. A demonstrated interest in true crime, and this town being steeped in true crime cold cases, isn't enough for us to say that's definitely or even *probably* what she was doing here. It's not enough to go rushing off down that path. It just doesn't work like that. We tread carefully and choose our paths with real caution. Because if we pick the wrong one, we'll be wasting time that we just don't have.'

Bridie nodded but she hadn't reinflated yet. I glanced at my watch. Time was on my mind. Wasting it. Cherishing it. Losing it. My daughter sitting here before me, her heartbeat ticking in her neck, and not on a slab in a medical centre waiting to go in the ground.

'Hey, listen,' I said. 'Dodgy Dodge and his Travelling Troop of Ding-Dongs are getting ready to kick things off down at the pub.'

Bridie shook her head, amused and dismayed at the same time.

'I can't attend that right away,' I went on. 'Everybody in town will know who I am by the sight of me. I want things to heat up a little first. So, between now and when I can sidle in, I have fifty more phone calls I have to make. Are there any quick wrangles nearby? Something we could get done in an hour or less?'

She whipped out her phone, slowly reinflating. Her eyes darted down the screen. She nodded. 'Unknown animal in a chimney. Ten minutes from here.'

'You drive.' I grabbed the keys from the edge of the table and slid them over to her.

EVAN

I stared at the results on the screen for a long moment. Then I clicked back out of my profile and clicked the other match, the one below mine. My brother's face, hard and stiff, appeared in greyscale beside his police credentials. Russell's DNA had been entered into the NCIDD database around 2018 when he made detective. I'd gone into the system a year earlier, when I was asked to provide a sample to exclude myself from a bungled crime scene that a colleague had been leading. I called the tech back with shaking hands, misdialling twice. He grunted an answer. 'You get a hit in the system?' he asked.

I didn't know how to reply. For a long moment I sat staring at my laptop screen, the phone to my ear. The beer garden at the pub ahead of me was still roped off. When I looked up, I could just see the edge of the police marquee at the back. But there were people assembling at the front. The tech spoke again, 'Hello? You there?'

'Yes, I . . .' I breathed. 'Yes. Listen, uh, we're in very sensitive territory here. Because there's a suspect in the mix who's in . . . who's maybe in law enforcement. We don't want to tip anyone off.'

'Okay.'

'So just deal with me, and only me, on this.'

'You said that already.'

'I'm saying it again. If anyone else calls, wanting to talk about the results, just refer them to me.'

'I can do that.'

I hung up. Went to Google. Searched *Y-STR DNA test familial link.*

Y-STR DNA analysis can be used to establish familial relationships between males by comparing short tandem repeats (STRs) on the Y chromosome. The tests examine a fixed set of markers known to have high variability on the human Y chromosome. They are an effective way to identify men who share a paternal relative.

I thought about my son. Then about my father. I was dialling Arthur when the urge to vomit rose up in my belly, so swift and hot and fast I had to grab the door beside me and throw it open, retching into the empty space beside the car. Nothing came up. When I shut the door again, Dad was on the line and I was sweating at my hairline in the rear-view mirror.

'Evan?'

'Were you in Redbelly last night?' I asked.

'Me? No.' I heard the unmistakable scratching of the old man's cigarette lighter. 'Don't tell me you're so desperate for witnesses you're just cold-calling everyone you know.'

'I'm pretty sure Chris was there,' I said. 'And I want to know if you were with him.'

'I was not.'

'Where were you?'

'I was here, seeing some arsehole from Maroota about selling the old GT,' Dad said. 'I'm going to have to sell them all. The cars. I can't get under them anymore.'

'You had someone at your house?' I said. 'What time?'

'I don't know. Seven. Eight. You're not honestly asking me for an alibi, are you?'

'I have to go,' I lied. 'Someone else is calling.'

I rang off, stared at the screen before me, the DNA matches. Thought about my father and the gunshot injury to his right arm, the fact that he couldn't even get down on the ground anymore to tinker with his yard cars. He'd been favouring his old gunshot wound when I saw him at my house, clutching the arm against his side, something he'd been doing since I was in my late twenties.

I thought about how much physical fitness it would have taken to pin a woman in her twenties against a wall. I thought about the alibi he'd just given me. Easily provable with the phone calls or messages between my father and the seller, and the account of the seller themselves.

I looked at the screen again. At Russell's face. The presence of Russell as a match to the mystery DNA profile offered me hope for a moment. Russell wasn't in a direct paternal line to Chris. He was Chris's *uncle.* I googled again.

Can Y-STR DNA test link uncles and nephews?

The answer made me sink in my seat.

This testing can be used to establish if two men come from a paternal line, which can include relationships such as siblings, uncle/nephew, cousins and many other possibilities.

There were two possibilities. My father and my son. Arthur had an alibi. Chris didn't. And Chris was on camera.

'Fuck.' I banged my fists against my skull. 'Fuuuuu—'

A horn blast right next to me made my stomach leap into my chest. I turned and looked, saw Bridie's face across the road's centre line, behind the window of Russell's Mustang. She rolled her window down and I rolled mine down, and Russell leant across her to frown at me.

'The hell is wrong with you?' he asked.

I lifted my laptop from my lap, so that it was visible to the two of them. I had to swallow hard before I could form words. 'Technological issues,' I managed.

'You get the swab results yet?'

I couldn't answer, sat breathing and staring at them. Bridie's eyes were wandering over my face, probably taking in the changes since the last time she'd seen me. Five hard years and one of the worst days of my life unfolding right now in real time.

'Because if you haven't yet, you need to get your arse back to where I sent you!' Russell jabbed a finger at me.

'I got them,' I said.

'Well? Was there a match in NCIDD?'

Help, Russell, my brain screamed. *Help me.*

'No,' I said. 'No match.'

Russell gave a disappointed click of his tongue and leant back in his seat. Bridie smiled at me. Her hand was hanging out the window a little. She waved, her fingers out of my brother's sight, and I waved back, and their car pulled away.

RUSSELL

The moon was high by the time we left town. It turned the ghost gums on either side of the road a cold blue. Bridie drove with her eyes hard on the road, leaning forward too far, the way P-platers do. I was glad she took the corners with care as the road ascended quickly out of the valley, not just for the sake of the 'Stang's paintwork but because beyond the guardrail the land dropped off at a sickening angle, sheer walls studded with huge blocks of yellow sandstone. Wallaby country. I reached over and flicked on the high beams for Bridie without saying anything, but she did a little embarrassed wiggle and touched the lever where I'd touched it, as though assuring me she would have done that herself eventually. I settled in and called Gail Caplan, then the guys from Chloe's apartment, then three other people. I was clipped, getting through the calls in mere seconds, disappointed about the lack of a DNA match for Chloe's killer. I reminded myself to ask Evan when I got back to Redbelly just how far the techs were into their testing. Were these prelim Y-STR results, or were they the full shebang? I made a note on my phone.

The headlights flashed on a property with a wrought-iron sign hanging out by the driveway. Grevillea Lodge was perched up another steep embankment, a cantilever house with huge glass walls overlooking the valley. The whole building was lit gold. Bridie parked on a river-stone driveway and yanked the handbrake up in a way that hurt my teeth. 'Okay.' She gave the strained sigh of the anxious performer. 'Let's do this!'

The oversized oak door of the house opened on a spacious entryway, revealing a slender woman in a shapeless cream linen garment I've known rich women to wear; somewhere between a dress and a tunic. Cult-leader chic. Bridie hung to the side with her rescue cage and seemed to want me to introduce myself first, but I didn't. For an agonising few seconds nothing happened, until I gestured for Bridie to take the lead. 'On with the show, kid.'

'Oh, uh, right.' Bridie stepped forward, clutching the cage to her chest. 'Hello. I'm Bridie Powder. I'm here with Wildlife SOS?'

'Well, thank god.' The woman's eyes widened. 'Yes. Hello. Welcome.' She turned and shouted over her shoulder into the house. 'Damien! Damien, they're here! The wildlife people!'

Bridie stepped into the house gingerly, moved to the side again to let me go ahead. I put a hand on the small of her back, pushed her forward. 'What are you doing, Birds?' I murmured. 'You're the wrangler, not me.'

'Oh, I just figured you would want to, uh . . .'

'I don't want to do anything.' We followed the linen-wearing lady through the enormous house. 'This is your gig, Bridie. Go work your magic. I'm just the offsider.'

Bridie seemed taken by some shot of confidence. We walked into a lounge room straight out of *Habitus Living*. Bridie set the cage next to a similarly expensively dressed man: mid-fifties, with the general look of someone gently and expertly dusted off with botox or fillers, the same as the woman. Bridie introduced herself and I hung around with my hands in my pockets, gazing at the view of the violet-dark valley and feeling poor.

'We started hearing the noises around three o'clock this afternoon,' the woman, who'd introduced herself as Myra, told me. She was gesturing to a pot-belly shaped fireplace standing in a corner: a boxy, detached thing with four legs. 'We don't know if it's a bird, or a rat, or a possum, or *what* on earth we're dealing with.'

'What kind of noises did you hear?' Bridie asked. The couple turned to her. They'd both been staring at me, and I was slowly getting the sense that they thought I was the leader of this whole operation, the way Bridie herself had for reasons I couldn't fathom. The couple glanced at each other, then my teenage daughter, who was opening the cage and spreading a towel out on the base.

'Just scratching,' the guy, Damien, said. 'Scratching and clawing. Whatever it is, it seems to get partway up the flue and then falls back down with a thud.'

'Any fluttering or flapping?' Bridie asked. 'Peeping or chirping? Squealing?'

'No, just the scratching.'

Bridie nodded, took a hair tie from around her wrist and put her hair up. With her hair in a high ponytail she looked fifteen, not eighteen, picking her way to the side of the fireplace over the posh rugs and travertine tiles like she was worried about devaluing the property just by being there. She went to the fireplace and peered in through the glass panel at the front, which was clouded with brown smoke-stains. I watched her cup her bare hands around the stainless-steel flue running from the top of the fireplace directly into the ceiling twenty feet above us. Bridie bent and put her nose to the seam where the tubular flue met the black top of the fireplace and sniffed loudly, drawing a deep chestful of air through her nose. She straightened, put her hands on her hips and announced, 'It's an adult male brush-tailed possum.'

The couple looked from Bridie to me and back to Bridie.

'What?' The woman frowned. 'How can you tell that?'

'If it was a bird or a rat it would have been crying out after it fell in, calling for its mate or its pack to come get it,' Bridie said. 'A possum would be silent. It wouldn't want to draw attention to itself. And it's the animal that makes the most sense. Possums climb down people's chimneys all the time. If it rains, sometimes they come in search of shelter, find they can't get back up the flue because it's too smooth inside. Or sometimes a male will chase another male down there in a fight over territory.'

'But how do you know the species? And the gender?' Damien asked. 'You can't smell that, surely.'

'I can. It's definitely male, just from the strength of the odour. But as far as species goes: whatever it is, it's so large it's filling the entire base of the chimney flue.' Bridie cupped the flue again with her hands, which was about the circumference of a bread plate. 'I can feel the warmth of its body through the metal. That says brushie to me, not ringtail.' She turned to Myra. 'Do you want to feel?'

'Not one bit.' Myra clutched at the neck of her linen thing, actually took a step back. 'No, thank you. I won't be coming anywhere near it. I know they can be quite vicious.'

'I wouldn't use that word exactly.' Bridie crouched and eased the lever of the fireplace door down carefully, pried the door open a crack. 'They get pretty scared and put on a performance, but they're not gonna kill you.'

'Wait a minute.' Damien's arms were folded. He nodded at me. 'Isn't now the time for you to get involved, mate? Before it comes flying out?'

'I have nothing to do with this.' I put my hands up again. 'I'm just here for my good looks and sparkling personality.'

'But *you're* not going to remove it.' Myra stepped towards Bridie, her face taut with apprehension, as though she meant to pull the girl back from the fireplace. 'It's—You should—It shouldn't be *her* that does it. It should be you.'

'Why?' I frowned.

'Well, because it's—it's—it's—'

'It's a wild animal!' Damien blurted.

'Yes, so I'll be leaving it to the experts.' I waved at Bridie. I saw a hint of a smile creep onto my child's face, even though she was crouched at the fireplace and turned away from me. Myra and Damien made unconvinced noises as Bridie bent, peering into the area where the flue met the top of the fireplace.

'But, darling,' Myra persisted, 'shouldn't you put some gloves on or something?'

'Look, usually I would.' Bridie shifted something aside at the back of the fireplace. 'But I'm working blind here. I like to feel exactly what part of the animal I'm grabbing hold of.'

'Oh my god.' Myra held her brow.

'What I'm going to do,' Bridie said, 'is shift the plate that separates the flue and the fireplace forward just enough so that I can get a hand in. Then I'm gonna grab his ankles and his tail and pull him out backwards.'

Myra turned away, her hand to her mouth. 'I can't watch, Damien. I just can't. She's going to get savaged.'

'She knows what she's doing,' I said. Bridie looked over her shoulder at me. Even though I could only see her eyes, I saw that they were bright. I jutted my chin, my mind filled with guilt about the lack of confidence I'd shown in my kid in the houseboat for her serial killer theory. 'She's trained, and she's experienced. Just give her some space and let her do her thing.'

Myra, Damien and I watched as Bridie gently manipulated the steel plate from its housing, dealing with the weight of the animal on the plate and rust and ash and grit lodged between the plate and the roof of the fireplace. I had memories of driving Georgia to these kinds of rescues when Bridie was so small she would just sit nearby on the carpet, her eyes locked on her mother and her thumb in her mouth. I'd always encouraged my wife's love of animal rescue volunteering and my daughter's similar fascination with it, because in my own childhood I'd had to accompany my father on hunts, and I felt bad about the psychopathic joy he'd taken in killing and hurting things, and my inability to intervene. Or, early on, my plain childlike ignorance of the pain and suffering of those animals. I felt I owed a debt to animal kind in general.

Bridie lunged suddenly forward and upwards and grabbed something. An almighty moaning, hoarse and wild, echoed up the hollow flue, followed by the frantic scrabbling of claws on steel. Myra had both her hands to her mouth and Damien was by her side, transfixed. Bridie was gently consoling the creature that was doing its best to escape her clutches in the chimney flue. In time she had both hands in the fireplace, twisting and manipulating its limbs, unhooking its claws from holds, as she wrestled it backwards out of the tube.

'Don't be silly, now,' she was cooing. 'Come on. Come on. Come *on*, you big baby.'

The possum Bridie birthed from the chimney and dropped into her rescue cage was twice the size of a house cat, tawny-brown all over with black ears and the iconic bushy black tail. Its huge orange eyes yawned in terror as it did a lap of the cage, throwing itself at the bars, standing on its hind legs and trying to find a way out the top. Bridie clipped the cage closed with all the quiet elegance of a woman who had just plucked a piece of lint from her cashmere cardigan. Her hands were free of scratches and bites. She draped a towel over the cage and stood again, hands on her hips, the mortified rich couple and her unspeakably proud father watching her.

* * *

At the bottom of the driveway leading to Grevillea Lodge, Bridie took the enormous possum out of the cage, swathed its head in a towel and sat it on her lap like a teddy bear facing outwards, doing a series of checks while it groaned and hissed. I supposed she was looking to see if it had been injured while doing its Santa Claus impression. I sat nearby on the sandstone wall, now and then fielding texts about Chloe Lutz and watching as she plucked out the possum's fleshy paws and inspected its sharply clawed toes.

'I think he's fine,' she said, returning the squabbling, hissing creature to the cage and replacing the towel on top. 'But I've got to get approval from the area coordinator before I let him loose.'

She started typing out a text, the gold glow of the 'Stang's cabin lights making the tip of her ponytail look white and aflame. 'Hey, Dad,' she said as she worked.

'Yep?'

'I have a question for you.'

A sparkle of pain in my chest. I took a deep breath. 'Okay. Go ahead.'

Bridie kept tapping. Eyes on her screen. Then she said, 'When did you know?'

The darkness whispered all around me. The forest humming with life. The question came like a slap in the face, even though I'd known it had to be in the works. Had been waiting for it for years.

I'd rehearsed my answer to my daughter about this question ten thousand times. Still, I found myself stalling.

'When did I know I was gay, you mean?'

'Yeah.'

'Like, did I already know when I married your mother?' I said. Struggling, flailing, clutching for wisps of time that dissolved as soon as I had them. 'Was I faking it with her the whole time?'

'Um, yeah.'

I nodded. Folded my arms. Told myself to make eye contact with her. Failed to do so. 'It . . . It's not a simple answer, Bridie. I mean, I . . . I'd had thoughts about other boys when I was a kid. Those thoughts turned sort of . . . sexual . . . when I was a teenager.'

Bridie said nothing. Waiting for more. Leaving me to squirm. I wandered a few feet away from the stone wall. Wandered back. Felt her eyes on me the whole time. Finally, she said, 'We don't have to—'

'No, I want to. I want to try to explain it.' I looked up at the stars. There were no answers up there, but I looked anyway. 'You have to understand that, in my house . . . growing up with Dad. It was like, if you're gay, there's something wrong with you.'

'Okay.'

'Like, anyone who wants to do that kind of stuff with other men has got to have a screw loose. Something went wrong with them in the womb, the gays. That's how they'd explain it to us, Mum and Dad both. So, in the beginning, with me, it was about hiding the fact that there was something wrong with me. From everyone. Especially Dad. Because if you had a weakness, he'd sniff it out and use it. So if there was ever something going on with you, you had to do whatever you could to keep it hidden.'

I glanced over. Bridie nodded.

'And also, I mean, I didn't sort of know that was a possibility. Being gay.'

'You didn't know it existed?'

'I knew it existed, I just didn't know it was *common*. There weren't a lot of gay men on TV in the seventies. I mean, there were gay celebrities. And drag queens. But they weren't real people to me. There were no gay people in our town. None that I knew of. I didn't meet my first real-life gay man until I was in the police academy. So . . . eighteen?'

'Oh, wow.'

'Yeah. And there very much seemed to be something wrong with him. He was a miserable bastard. I mean, more of a bastard than I am, even. Aloof. Withdrawn. He was one of our instructors. Just before my intake class graduated—maybe the week before—he blew his own brains out in his office on campus.'

'Jesus.'

'They said it was a gun-cleaning accident.'

Bridie swallowed. Her mouth was so dry, it seemed, she made a clacking sound with her tongue trying to do it. 'Did you ever have girlfriends?'

'Oh, yeah. I always had girlfriends.' This was getting easier. I couldn't believe it, but it was actually getting *easier* the longer I talked. 'But I wasn't, uh, *attracted to* women. If that makes sense? Like, I didn't go after them. They came after me. They would just pop into my life and we'd end up as boyfriend and girlfriend.'

'But were you were faking it with them?'

'No.' I scratched my stubble. 'No. I've never faked it with anyone, Bridie. Not your mother. Not anyone.'

Bridie shook her head. 'I don't get it, Dad.'

'It's like . . . these women would turn up. And we'd grow close, you know? Become friends. Really deep, sort of . . . *intimate* friends. And then it would turn sexual. I mean, months later. Months and months. Guys used to make fun of me for it. Like, I'd never have a one-night stand. They'd say "Oh, Russell, he needs to meet the parents before he'll get with a chick." But it wasn't that. It was just that I was . . . *growing* an attraction to these women, I guess. Based on who they . . . who they *were*?' I palmed sweat from my hairline. 'Not like . . . them as women. Does that make sense?'

'Maybe.'

'That's how it was with Georgia. When I was with her I was with *her*, I wasn't with *a woman*.'

Bridie was watching me. I eased a breath out slowly.

'So . . . you're not bi?' she asked.

'No.'

'But you were okay to be with these women, though.'

'I wasn't just okay with it. I liked it.'

'So that's bi, Dad. That's bi.' She put her hands up. Let them flop in her lap, exasperated. 'And if you are bi, why did you have to leave Mum?'

'I'm not bisexual, Bridie.'

'But . . .' She sighed. Had no words.

'Bridie, all I can tell you is that when I was ever alone or single or whatever, I thought about men. Only men. And I only want to be with men now. That's how I see things going. From now on. I see myself being with a man permanently one day. Maybe. If I can find someone who will tolerate my never-ending bullshit.'

'But how do you do that for twenty years?' Bridie asked. 'Be with Mum but have this crazy secret hanging around in the background? This future that you're fantasising about with some guy?'

'It wasn't hard in the beginning. It was just a . . . like a voice that I got into the habit of ignoring. It was like living under a flight path. Your brain just sort of blocks out the noise of the planes going over. And I—you've got to understand, Bridie—I wasn't unhappy in my marriage to your mother. I wasn't starved for affection. And I enjoyed making love to her because I was attracted to *her*. To Georgia. Your mother is my best friend, Bridie. I mean, she was. Not anymore, obviously. I'm not hers, that's for sure. But she . . . she's still mine. I don't have a friend in my life who I care about as much as I care about Georgia. And I hope you believe me when I say this, that I wasn't sleeping with your mother and pretending in my mind that she was some random guy. I didn't want to leave her at all, Bridie.'

'What?'

'I didn't *want* to leave her. I had to.'

'Why?'

'Because I was lying to her. And you don't lie to the people you love.'

'Did you ever cheat on her?'

'No.'

'Really?'

'Yes.' I looked her in the eyes. 'Really.'

'Not once in twenty years? Not, like, a kiss.'

'No.'

'Nothing. Not a moment.'

I exhaled, stared at the stars again.

'There was a moment,' I said. 'So I ended it with your mother. Maybe two or three days later.'

'What happened?'

The silhouettes of the forest moved all around me. The gold lights on the hill. I held my face for a moment or two.

'It's so stupid.' I had to laugh.

'Try me.'

I talked myself out of, and then back into, my next words. 'He was a dentist.'

'What?'

I tried to explain. How I'd gone to see my regular dentist in Ryde about grinding my teeth at night, because the sound of it was keeping Georgia awake and I was worried about cracking a molar and having to spend our end-of-year holiday money getting it fixed. Instead of the regular woman who did my teeth, I'd ended up with some big handsome bear-sized guy with a silver-grey buzz cut and dark-rimmed glasses pushed up on top of his head. He'd had a look around in my mouth, listened to my complaints and then asked if he could try to loosen up some of the muscles in my jaw and temples to see what that did to the alignment of my molars. I'd resisted a bunch, of course. Tried to get up. He'd tugged me back down into the chair by my shoulder, and I let him talk me into it. Being the guy that I was pretending to be—the intimidating, ultra-masculine straight guy—the most physically intimate I'd ever been with another man until that point was to begrudgingly accept a hug from Evan once a year at Christmas. And now, here was a guy taking the weight of my head into his hands. Pushing on overworked muscles. Raking his fingers up through my hair. Extracting pleasure and pain in equal parts while I lay there with my eyes closed and let him do it.

Bridie was so rigid as she listened, she didn't even seem to be breathing. Her silhouette was black against the car's interior lights, so I couldn't see her face at all.

'So, a . . .' she began. I was unsure at first, but I thought I heard humour in her voice. Desperately hoped that I did. 'So a *head massage* kind of . . . blew up your entire life?'

I nodded. 'In a sense.'

Bridie was silent for a while. Then she said, 'That's some fucking head massage.'

I blew out a laugh. She laughed, too. Alone in the woods on the edge of nowhere, we laughed together for the first time in years.

A text message interrupted the chuckling. Bridie pulled her phone out and looked at it. She had approval to let the possum go.

I watched her carry the cage to the base of a nearby tree, remove the towel and unclip the top. She lifted the lid off the cage like she was taking the cloche off a fancy dish. The possum gazed around, hunched and slow and wild-eyed. Then it spotted the tree and shot up through the open door of the cage, scaling the trunk in a series of hitching leaps, its limbs hugging the girth, claws embedded, jumping upwards. In less than three seconds it was thirty feet up on a branch and staring down at us.

Bridie waved at it before she walked back to the car.

EVAN

Dodge was standing by the edge of the little marquee at the back of the beer garden, studying the pub in the distance, the sandstone chimneys and the four hotel windows, all dark. All the activity was at the front of the pub. It occurred to me as I approached with my backpack slung over my shoulder that for years to come people were going to crowd into this sprawling, tree-lined place and gaze up at those old windows and talk about the young woman who had been murdered there. As the centuries passed an urban legend would almost certainly develop, about Chloe appearing and waving to punters down below from the shadows, or about the temperature in the room plummeting suddenly, waking any guests who dared to stay in room four. Doors slamming and lace curtains twitching and all that bullshit. I stood beside Dodge for a while and let the fantasies wash over me as a way of staying out of the real world. The awful, awful present. Because I was filled with a numbness now. A careful detachment from what was happening around me. I knew that could break at any second, when it finally hit me; that I was nearly certain about two life-changing, soul-destroying things.

That my son had been there the night Chloe was murdered.

And his DNA had somehow ended up on her body.

'Your brother's right, you know,' Dodge said.

'About what?'

'He really couldn't have watched the windows from the beer garden.' Dodge pointed to the space before us. A fifty-metre-square stretch of cleared grass and picnic tables. 'Not without being seen.'

Dodge beckoned me. I went. We stood so that we were aligned with the stairwell to the hotel rooms, and we could see the windows of the rooms as well. 'You could only really watch from here,' Dodge said. 'Look.'

He beckoned again. I followed, my mind tangled in other things, thinking about DNA and fathers and sons. 'You come back here,' Dodge says. 'See what happens.'

We went into the dark at the roadside. In the shadow of bright and twinkling stars, we crossed the narrow dirt road to arrive beside a barbed-wire fence. There was a house on the hill, maybe a hundred metres up an incline. Almost immediately, two slick black mixed-breed dogs came sprinting down the hill, barking madly as they went, skidding to a halt on the damp grass a stone's throw from the wire. The dogs planted their front paws and dropped their heads low and snarled and snapped at us.

'No watching from here, that's for sure,' Dodge said. We started walking back to the tables and the marquee. 'This is good. It limits our suspect pool considerably. It was either someone *in* the beer garden, or it was Rob. *Or* it was someone she knew, someone she invited to the room. Jesus, I wish we had those bloody phone and email accounts.'

'Okay, but people saw Chloe going up, and the electrician coming down,' I said. 'Why didn't they see the killer going up or coming down?'

'Oh, now, that's an interesting sort of thing, isn't it?' Dodge sighed. 'Because it depends on the moment. People just don't notice things sometimes. Trust me. It's a thing. You can have fifty people at a picnic and somebody walks up and abducts a kid from the edge of the gathering and not one person sees it. That happened. Happened to us, over at Wisemans, couple of years ago. It was the kid's dad in the end who took her, and we got her back safely. But nobody saw the grab. Fifty people there, they all missed it.'

'How?'

'He was super close but just out of sight, waiting for the right moment,' Dodge said. 'The people *here*, they were cutting and handing out pieces of cake.' He demonstrated with his hands, making a cluster in the air. 'Over *here*, you had two kids having an argument and some parents trying to break it up. Over *here* there was a game of cricket going on. Just for a few seconds, everyone was occupied with something else. Broad daylight. He snapped her up like a snake and disappeared into the bush.'

Dodge snatched the air in front of my nose.

We fell into silence, watching the stairwell.

'There's also a thing called "selective attention",' Dodge said. He almost blurted the words, embarrassed, rubbing his eyes. 'If you're . . . uh. If you're interested.'

I turned to him. 'What?'

'Well, my Patsy is a psychologist, you see.' Dodge dropped the hand from his eyes, the gate open and the horses of enthusiasm bolting out. 'And her PhD thesis was on attention. Different types of attention. There's this phenomenon called "selective attention", and . . .'

I stood there watching Dodge, listening to him talking about distractions, intuition, neurological pathways, human habits, the dynamics of attention, and an experiment involving a person dressed in a gorilla suit, for a good ten minutes without taking a pause, regretting my decision to give him free rein so thoroughly that I could barely follow what he was saying. 'Basically,' he said in summation, 'a person walking up and down that stairwell isn't an out-of-place enough stimulus to arouse that part of your brain.'

'Right,' I said.

'Patsy's a genius.' Dodge gave a satisfied sigh. 'I'm very proud of her.'

We looked at the stairwell.

'How'd you go, anyway?' Dodge said eventually. 'At the lab?'

I tried to open my mouth. It seemed glued shut.

'Evan?'

'No match,' I said.

'Ah, nuts. And was there a notebook in the handbag, in the end?'

Not really knowing why, just having the all-body sense that I needed to stop the motion of the investigation until I could catch up, I shook my head.

'Zero from two.' Dodge blew out air. 'What about the traffic cam data?'

'Uh, yes. I . . . I have them on my laptop.'

'Great.' Dodge pointed to the fold-out table beneath the marquee. 'I've gotta go syphon my python. You get set up. I'll be right back.'

I let my backpack slump onto the fold-out table. Watched Dodge march off across the empty beer garden towards the pub's bathrooms. Through the gap between the pub's two main buildings, I could see the crowd out the front of the pub was growing. It was an odd set-up. Cops at the back. Locals at the front. I guessed that had been Russell's plan, for the townspeople to be in view of us, talking about us, passing around their theories and rumours, a swirling pit of speculation. A few were standing in the gap now, arms folded, watching me. I had known cops who would encourage this sort of thing: a curious crowding in at the edges of tragedy. Yes, it was voyeuristic. But once one person put down their shame and bent to their curiosity, everyone tended to follow suit, and a few inconspicuous officers placed within that crowd could sometimes pick up useful whispers.

I opened my laptop, navigated to the list of vehicles that had come in and out of Redbelly the previous evening. I exported the list into a word document. It appeared in a table. I glanced towards the pub, watching a peacock traversing the gravel path between the buildings, giving the people a wide berth, heading for an awning at the back. As I watched, the bird crouched and then leapt up, landing with a clatter on the corrugated iron.

Dodge appeared between the buildings, drying his hands on his trousers and heading towards me. I selected the row of the table that contained the Uber driver's vehicle. The one that had almost certainly carried my son into Redbelly the night before. I deleted the row from the list.

A hand fell on my shoulder. I yelped in surprise.

'Coffee-coffee-coffee-coffee-coffee!' Knowles chanted. 'Can I make you one, sir?'

'Urgh, Jesus. Yes.' I rubbed my eyes hard. 'You trying to give a guy a heart attack, Constable Knowles?'

'Apologies.' Knowles reached past me to grab the sugar canister. 'Anything good on the traffic cams?'

'Dunno yet.' I watched Dodge as he arrived at the table and looked at the list. 'We'll have to match these vehicles up with the punters at the pub.'

'That's Branchy.' Dodge pointed at a vehicle in the list. A white Mitsubishi ute. He stood looking at the list, taking a coffee from Knowles as he finished making it. I felt a strange dread that Dodge could tell somehow that a line was missing from the table. 'That's all I recognise off the top of my head.'

'Hey, where's Grumpy Smurf right now?' Knowles asked.

Dodge nearly spat out the coffee he was drinking. 'Just mind yourself there, Knowlesy. Detective Inspector Powder is Senior Sergeant Powder here's brother. And both are your superiors.'

'He's a "Powder" as well?' Knowles's eyes widened. He turned to me. 'The detective?'

'Yes, Knowles.'

'Oh my god. I've been hearing it all day as "Fowler"!' Knowles clapped a hand to his forehead. 'Christ. Lucky I didn't say it to his face. Huh! How about that, then? Powder and Powder, a crime-fighting super team. You work with your brother often, do you, Sarge?'

'Apologies on Knowlesy's behalf, Evan.' Dodge sighed. 'Too much coffee makes him even chattier than me.'

As though he'd been summoned, Russell's Mustang came rumbling around the corner of the pub and pulled up in the hotel guest parking. He climbed out, and Bridie drove on. I watched the car disappear into the night with a deep longing to talk to my niece, something that hadn't struck me this hard in years. There was also a flicker of jealousy about Russell's beautiful, intelligent, apparently well-behaved daughter and my sullen, weird, girl-shooting son. I was so focused on the pain that Russell's arrival and greeting to Dodge and Knowles was indistinct, like distant thunder. The appearance, then, of a young woman at the table escaped me completely. When I came to my senses I was standing beside my brother and he was snapping his fingers in front of my nose. I couldn't remember if I'd been invited by Russell to speak with the girl or if I'd just inserted myself.

'Wake up, dopey.'

'Sorry.' I slapped my cheeks.

The woman had both hands in the big front pocket of a black apron and was fiddling with pens and bottle openers in there. 'It's Yasmin,' Russell said. 'Have I got that right?'

'Right.' Yasmin had tiny tattoos all over her. Nestled behind her ears, and in the hollows of her collarbones. Thin letters and light little bumble bees and beetles. 'I served the guy. The one you're looking for. Constable Fry was asking me about him this morning, when I was doing my statement. He showed me the footage.'

'Tell the story again.' Russell made an impatient gesture at her. 'You've had twenty-four hours or so to think about it. I want to hear it from your own mouth. And make no mistake, Yasmin: you could have been looking directly at our killer last night. You understand? So, your ability to remember important details about him could be the difference between someone else getting butchered down the road tomorrow night and this guy being locked up before he can do that.'

'Shiiiiit.' Yasmin widened her eyes. 'Are you for real?'

'Unfortunately, he is,' I said.

Yasmin massaged her brow. 'Um, I mean, it was just like you see on the video. The guy was young. Dark hair. Kind of ratty looking in the face, you know? Like, pointy? I think he had a lip piercing?'

I covered my mouth with my hand to hide my reaction.

'You *think* he was young, or he *was* young?' Russell said. 'You *think* he had a lip piercing, or he *had* a lip piercing?'

'I'm not a hundred per cent on the lip piercing. I just have, like, a feeling.'

'How old was this fellow?' Russell pressed.

'Maybe twenty, but just barely?'

'Clothes? Remember any brand names? Something about the cap?'

'No, it's all just blank in my brain. I'm sorry.'

'Don't be sorry,' Russell said. He seemed to catch himself almost being kind and understanding, set his jaw again. 'How did he order? Was he chatty? Quiet?'

'Quiet. Straight to the point. Said "Please".'

'Okay.'

'He came in the two separate times.' Yasmin shifted back and forth on the balls of her feet. 'Pretty close together. Ordered a James Squire the first time and a Tooheys New the second time.'

I glanced at my brother. Realised he was already frowning at me but looking through me, his head cocked.

'Two different drinks,' Russell said.

'Two *very* different drinks.' My mind was racing ahead, but the words were tumbling out before I could stop them. Cop autopilot. 'How far apart were the two orders?'

'Not very. Constable Fry and me, we looked at the footage and we lined it up with the readout from the till. The drinks were ordered seven minutes apart. The first time he came in alone. The second time is when he, like, checked out Chloe's arse or whatever.'

'He was with someone else.' Russell was chewing his lip, thinking. 'Got a drink for himself; friend arrives; he leaves the drink with the friend and goes in to get one for his mate.'

'Why would he do that?' I asked. 'Why not send the friend in for his own drink?'

'The friend is underage,' Russell said. 'You said he was young. He's got a younger friend.'

'Why didn't you card him at the bar?' I asked Yasmin. 'If you're saying he was twenty at a stretch, you should have carded him.'

'Awww, well . . .' Yasmin bobbed her head guiltily. 'It's a country pub, you know? And we don't get a lot of young people here, so

Rob's trying to, like, encourage more to come? We don't want everyone thinking this place is super narky.'

Russell looked back up at the hotel behind Yasmin.

'I know you guys are wondering if he was the guy,' Yasmin continued. 'But—I don't know if this even helps—the guy I served spent his time out the front. And Chloe was out the back in the beer garden. So he wasn't anywhere near her.'

'He was out the front?'

'Yeah, like, near the river, in the dark.' Yasmin turned and pointed. 'If you stand behind the bar, you can see directly out and across the street. Sometimes people go over there to look at the water or whatever.'

'Did you see who he was with?'

'No but he just walked straight out there, across the road,' Yasmin said. 'It's stressful when that happens. Because that's something *else* the bar staff are not really supposed to allow.'

'Why not?'

'Because next thing you know there's fifty schooner glasses in the playground. And if you get caught with punters carrying drinks more than, like, five metres from your property grounds, you'll lose your liquor licence. And without a liquor licence this pub is fucked.'

Russell turned and walked away. I gave Yasmin an apologetic look about the swift, unannounced exit and followed my brother across the beer garden. We entered the crowd at the front of the pub, which was a hundred people strong now. Dogs off leads. Work boots, singlets, sun-bleached hair. There were well-dressed patrons grouped in judgemental huddles drinking white wine, and knots of young people further out, at the edges of the glow cast down from the fairy lights strung along the awning and in the trees. I saw a bucket resting at the base of the sandwich board usually reserved for the pub's menu. Someone had scrawled *For Chloe's Family* on it in chalk. Colourful banknotes lay scattered like autumn leaves at the bottom of the bucket, fifties and hundreds mostly. I guessed there was a couple of grand in there. It felt like every eye watched

Russell and me pass through and cross the road to the playground and the big stretch of grass before the river. There were people out here in the dark, looking at the brightly lit building, which was probably doing its best night of business in years.

Russell stood, and folded his arms. I stood beside him and stared at the bare stone wall of the second floor on the left-hand side, where the hotel was.

'Couldn't have been him,' I said. 'The young guy.'

Russell said nothing, his eyes on the distant pub.

'He could see her go up the stairwell, yes,' I went on. 'But there's no view of the windows. How does he know which room she's in?'

Russell took some side steps, changing the angle. Marched to the end of the playground and back again. I stood still, watching him go back and forth, the maestro listening for the out-of-tune tuba. Eventually he charged back across the road again, into the crowd. I jogged to keep up. We went up the stairs to the hotel section, ducking under five sets of police tape before we reached Chloe's room. Russell took his car keys from his pocket and used one to poke the switch just inside the door to the hallway, illuminating the space. He looked up and around. Chloe's door had been taken off its hinges, the room gaping open into the hall. Russell went into the room, turning this way and that, looking up at the ceiling, down at the floor.

'Turn the light on,' he said to me.

'I can't.' I gestured to the wall beside me. 'Forensics have taken the switch.'

He stood gazing at the lights in the ceiling as though willing them to come on by magic. Russell's enormous shadow stretched up over the closed curtains against the window. Towering legs. A big, boxy skull. Shoulders that encompassed the entire width of the room. Suddenly he waved me over. 'Come here.'

I went. We looked at the lights.

'Why can I see the shape of a bulb in that one,' he pointed, 'but not that one?'

I studied the almost identical circular oyster lights, which were rimmed with glossy white plastic. Russell was right. I could see the distinct shadow of a bulb resting behind the frosted glass of one, but not the other.

'Maybe it's—' I began.

Russell marched off. He was darting into the next room as I arrived at the hall. The lights came on. He stared at the ceiling in the room next to Chloe's. He marched out again so fast he almost knocked me into the wall beside the bathroom. In the next room, and then the next, Russell went in and turned on the lights. I ran after Russell as he ducked out the open doorway onto the stairwell. He moved so fast through the crowd at the front of the pub that he shoulder-barged a drink clean out of a man's hand, and I had to issue apologies before I followed Russell back across the road.

I glanced over my shoulder at the pub. Nothing seemed to have changed. Russell was jogging across the grass next to the playground, heading for a rise in the earth that was crowned with scrubby grass, the lip of sand dunes leading down to the river beach. Russell hit the rise and turned and looked at the pub. He started laughing. He grabbed me by the shoulders as I arrived beside him and swivelled me on the spot.

'Check it out.' He pointed.

I looked. Our position on the rise of the earth gave us a thin view of the very top of the pub's roof. An old-fashioned style, probably designed to accommodate the falling of snow, the roof angled upwards at a sharp angle, then upwards *again* at a much shallower one, meeting at the top at a very slight peak. My mouth fell open as I let my eyes drift over the three brightly lit golden ovals visible along the upper part of the roof's length.

'The second "light" in every room is a skylight.' Russell was breathless. 'You can't see them from close in, near the pub doors. But if you stand back here, you get the right angle. A skylight in every room is leaking light up from inside. Look. There are three. We didn't turn Chloe's on.'

'So he could have watched from here,' I said, trying to hide my horror.

'Probably right here,' Russell said. 'You can see the lights. You can see the stairwell. You're close enough in that you can march up there quickly, when you have the right moment. And out here in the dark, he could have stood watching for as long as he wanted without anyone being suspicious.'

My heart was thumping in my throat.

'I want this young guy,' Russell said. His eyes were on the crowd at the pub. Dodge was there, under the fairy lights, was pushing his way towards us. 'Here comes Dodge. Between the two of you, decide who's the least incompetent, and that person can get the image of the young guy in the cap out to all the locals. Do a region-wide SMS blast of the picture and the description. I'm going to start going through the traffic cams and see if I can spot him in one of the cars.'

'You're not doing that,' Dodge said as he came to a stop before us. 'You're coming with me. We have a problem.'

RUSSELL

Dodge led us to his Hilux. The rural cop was jittery, his eyes a little too wide, the adrenaline pumping. Adrenaline that probably didn't have to do that very often. 'Fry and Lee went out to Branchy's place, and they're calling for backup.'

'Why?'

'I don't know yet. It was Lee calling. She said they're both unhurt, but just to get there quick.' Evan slid into the back seat behind me. I felt a prickle of anger as Dodge started the car.

'Evan, no one invited you. Hold down operations at the pub until I get back.'

'Fuck that.' My brother tapped Dodge on the shoulder, urging him to go. 'I want to be where the action is.'

'It's probably "Fuck that, *sir*," isn't it?' Dodge asked. He started driving reluctantly.

'Tell me what's going on.' I turned back to the front.

'Look, we're getting plenty of gossip from the fishing expedition at the pub.' Dodge made a right at the main intersection of town and passed the darkened cafe, heading for a solid wall of bushland with a dirt road cutting through. 'A lot of it has focused on Branchy. Rumour has been spreading, as you intended it to, that he spoke to her on the night she was killed. So that's caused some . . . other stuff . . . to come to light.'

'What other stuff?'

'Well . . .' Dodge struggled. And I sensed immediately he was trying to back-pedal on the team's obvious affection for 'Branchy' earlier that day. 'I knew he was a little odd. But everyone out here is odd. Okay? That's *why* you live here in the first place. Because your eccentricities don't necessarily slot into suburban life. And as the local cop, people don't always tell me things.'

'Would you just spit it out, Dodge?'

'There's some behaviour that's been talked about,' Dodge said. 'Someone was saying Branchy had the contract to remove a woman's water tank at a property just up the road. He was tasked with installing a new one. But the relationship with the customer went south.'

'I thought he was the local pest inspector.'

'It pays to be multi-talented out here. You go to a property for one job, try to scoop four or five more jobs while you're there.'

'Okay.'

'Anyway, the woman got impatient with him. He kept saying the land was too soft to get the digger in, because of all the rain. It rains here a lot. He kept pushing the job back. Long story short, she's cancelled him and flicked the job to someone else. There's talk down at the pub that once the new guy had the tank up and running for the woman, Branchy's gone and put entrails in it.'

'*Entrails?*' I turned and looked back at Evan.

'Guts,' Evan said.

'I know what entrails are, you fucking numpty!' I barked. 'I was expressing surprise and dismay!'

Evan sighed.

Dodge continued. 'They dunno what animal they came from. But there was enough of them to say, *Oh, this isn't just some creature who's climbed in the outlet pipe and drowned.* A possum or a snake will do that, on occasion, you know. This was . . . there was *an amount*. Enough for the water to taste funny.'

I pinched the bridge of my nose. 'Jesus. And you didn't hear anything about this?'

'Nope. Not my people, either. Not until tonight. Folks like to handle things themselves out here. And with something like that, the woman might have figured she'd make things worse by involving the local jackos.'

'It's the wild west,' I said. 'It really is.'

'There's more,' Dodge said. 'There have also been a couple of snafus with Branchy and women down at the pub. Miscommunications, rebuffed advances, inappropriate jokes. Nothing violent.'

'Kalowski said she thought he was a creep,' I said.

'Yes, well. It might have been more than just one woman's intuition.'

'Any official charges?'

'He was cautioned by my predecessor about showing a pornographic image to a teenager. Said he thought she was older than she actually was.'

'You didn't know about that until now?'

'Oh—I mean, I did,' Dodge said sheepishly. 'But it just slipped my mind. It wasn't an on-the-books thing.'

'What's his charge sheet say?'

'Drugs. A car theft. Nothing recent.'

We rode in silence. Out of town, through the bush, across rolling, moonlit fields and into another dense slab of bushland. The front of the Branch property was a sheer wall of Murraya hedge—twenty feet tall, dense as brick—and as we stopped and I got out of the car I could see the reason for that. Blackberry vine was interwoven throughout the hedge, tumbling out of the structure like a waterfall, lethally thorny, spilling right up to the edge of the road. Fry was sitting on the ground in the light of their cruiser, his knees up, clutching at the throat of his police uniform shirt. It had been only four minutes since Dodge had grabbed me and Evan from the front of the pub in town.

'What happened?' Dodge ran to Lee, who was standing helplessly over her colleague.

'I don't know!' Lee turned terrified eyes on me as I approached. 'We went in through the gates, maybe, you know, fifty metres in? We were on foot—too narrow to get a car in. I turned back, because I'd left my phone in the car. I was only gonna be gone a second! Before I can lock the car up, Fry running comes out like . . . like *this*.'

Lee gestured to Fry. Fry was heaving, trying to suck breath into a closed throat. I knew the symptoms. The gates to the Branch property were just beyond the back of the patrol car and stood cracked open, tall wrought-iron woven with razor wire. I grabbed Fry by the biceps and yanked him to his feet, pointing at Dodge and Lee and Evan with my other hand. 'Move the cars back. Get out of sight.'

The group ran to comply. I marched a gasping and trembling Fry across the road and into the bush. He was sweating so hard it was running down my fingers. I pulled us to a stop where the bush became impassable, but we were hopefully out of view of any cameras affixed to the front of the Branch property.

'Fry,' I said. 'You're having a panic attack, mate.'

He nodded, gripped my arms, mirroring my hold on him. We stood there in the dark, the bush ringing with life all around us.

'You had one before?'

He shook his head. No.

'I'm gonna ask you a question,' I told the younger officer. 'And I want you to focus hard on it. Think it over. Be careful with your answer. Keep your eyes on mine. Hey. Look here, okay? Good. Eyes on me. Only talk when you've got it locked in.'

Fry nodded hard again. I saw glimmers of his huge eyes in the hard moonlight. The whites were robin's-egg blue and wet.

'What's seven times seven?'

Fry drew a huge breath. 'Uh! What? Uh! F-f-f-f—'

'Focus on the question.'

'I can't!'

'Yes, you fucking can.'

'F-f-f-forty-nine.'

'What's six times six?'

'T-t-t-thirty-six.'

'And four times four?'

'Six'—Fry swallowed. Gasped. Swallowed again—'teen.'

'Divide that by two.'

'Uh . . . uh . . . uh . . .' Fry shook his head. His breath was coming back, but the shaking was still there. 'Is it eight?'

'It is.' I let him get off ten breaths, each slower and deeper than the last. When he was okay enough I said, 'What happened in there?'

'Lee l-l-left.' Fry let go of my arms, wiped the sweat from his face onto his palms, then onto the front of his police uniform shirt. Two long handprints that I could see even in the relative darkness. 'I was just standing there. Waiting for her to come back. And I s-s-s-saw him. He was standing in the dark, watching me.'

'Who?'

'Branch,' Fry said. 'He was holding a gun. A rifle.'

'Was he pointing it at you?'

'No but he . . . He was smiling, with his teeth, and . . .'

I waited. Fry struggled.

'What are you telling me, Fry?' I pressed, feeling the hairs on the back of my neck slowly start to stand on end. Goosebumps rushed down my arms as the officer spoke.

'It's him,' Fry shuddered. 'I saw it in his eyes. It's him.'

EVAN

Russell emerged from the bush and walked back towards us, Fry trailing behind him. Fry's head was down and shoulders were up like he'd just been smacked and told to get a hold of himself, which I wouldn't have put it past Russell to do. Dodge and Lee and I were standing between the Hilux and the cruiser, lit by a big, white full moon.

'Where're Kalowski and Knowles right now?' Russell asked Dodge.

'They'll be here in a sec,' Dodge said. 'I told them to go lights and sirens off. What's going on in there?'

Russell explained what Fry had told him. We all stood on the road in silence for a second or two, coming to terms with it.

'He was just standing there in the dark?' I asked.

'Maybe two metres away,' Fry nodded.

'But he didn't point the gun at you.'

'No. But it wasn't . . . he wasn't carrying it down by his side. It was up in his hands. Ready to use.'

'He didn't say anything threatening?' Lee asked.

'His face was not right,' Fry insisted. 'The smile. The eyes.'

'That's not . . .' Dodge began to say.

'He had cammo on,' Fry added.

'You didn't tell me that,' Russell said.

'It's only just coming back to me,' Fry was trembling hard. 'Face paint. Like he was doing a . . . an army operation. I'm telling you that he didn't . . . he didn't come down the road a-a-and say "Hi" like a normal person would. He was off the road. He'd snuck up, and when I spotted him he smiled, and . . .'

Fry's voice trailed off. Russell shot me a conspiratorial look of concern. For a half a second, we were on the same team. Two brothers, trying to discern if our shaken colleague was adding new details into his strange story about a man sneaking around on his own property to justify the terror that had incapacitated him, or if this was a real account we should accept with grave seriousness. I waited for Russell to fire-breathe Fry to ash for being overly dramatic, but he didn't.

'It's him,' Fry said.

'That's a big call,' Dodge said gently.

'I want to get this guy in hand,' Russell said. 'I don't like him. Not the stuff the people are saying about him down the pub, or this weird-arse shit tonight; sneaking up on the local coppers. I want to snatch Branch up and have a proper look at him. What do we know about the property?'

'That's just the thing . . .' Dodge worked the back of his neck, embarrassed, eyes restless. 'I've never been in. And from what Lee's just been telling me—'

'*No one's* been onto the property,' Lee cut in. 'The talk at the pub tonight was that, you know, that's just something about Branchy. He doesn't let people onto his land.'

'Oh, and I wonder why that is?' Russell said. 'Because he likes to run around dressed like he's at war? Is this guy your garden-variety weirdo, or does he have sovereign citizenship delusions, or what?'

'We don't know.'

'So he could have anything going on in there,' Russell said. 'Anything from sex slaves that he's farming to make skin suits, to a cache of weapons he's stocking up for the apocalypse.'

'Nobody knows,' Lee said.

'And it's not their fault that they don't know,' I said. Russell turned his dark eyes on me. The moment we'd been on the same team was a distant memory now.

'You'—he pointed at me—'go back to the pub. Round up the officers that are embedded in the crowd.'

'They'll have been drinking,' I said. 'They're no good to us. The nearest backup we have is in Gosford. That'll be a half hour at least. And you're not sending me off to do busywork, Detective Inspector Powder. I'm the second-most senior officer here.'

'So I've got you lot to work with for a half an hour.' Russell huffed a sigh, the disappointed army captain lumped with the last platoon to go over the trench wall. He turned his fiery eyes on Dodge. 'You know, I just don't get this. You've got a senseless stabbing murder in town, and this guy out here, Branchy—he doesn't spring immediately to mind? Everybody's falling over each other to say what a great guy he is, yet he's been living out here in this Fortress of Solitude'—he jerked his thumb towards the property behind him—'and nobody's blinked at that? Have you seen the hedges? They're twenty foot high!'

'That's not *so* uncommon.' Dodge shook his head. 'Living like that. These guys, they come out here because they like their own space. Branchy has obviously been . . . he's been a certain type of person down at the pub. Friendly and what-not. But out here, he's . . .'

'He's his real self.' Fry's mouth was a thin line. 'And he's just never showed anybody that, I guess. And nobody's gone looking.'

'We've got all types out here,' Dodge went on. 'Religious types. Doomsday preppers. Sometimes guys just don't let people in because they're embarrassed about how hoarded the place is.'

'Lots of hoarders,' Lee confirmed. 'To know a guy for twenty years and never go onto his land is pretty standard.'

'The hedge,' Russell said. 'Does it go all the way around like that?'

'I don't know,' Dodge said.

Russell pointed at me.

'You,' he said. 'Take Lee. Check the boundary that way. I want to know if there are routes in. We're not *going in*, though, Evan. Understand? *We're not going in.* We're scoping out the situation and we're meeting back here to form a plan. Dodge, come with me. We'll take the other side. Fry, stay with the cars and call Gosford for backup.'

RUSSELL

We walked towards the front of the property, past the cracked-open gates. I was almost certain we were walking under the gaze of cameras, but there wasn't much I could do about that. If Stephen Branch was the kind of weirdo who would grow twenty-foot walls of impenetrable hedge laced with razor-sharp blackberry, he was the kind of weirdo who would put cameras not only at his gates but throughout the surrounding bush. Dodge was quiet. I didn't realise I already had my gun out, pulled from the holster at the back of my belt, until Dodge cleared his throat beside me.

'I think I'm gonna pull my gun, too,' he said. I glanced over. He was actually watching me for approval. I guessed I was witnessing a cop pull his weapon for the first time in his career.

We rounded the corner of the property and I saw that same hedge running up the mountain for maybe three acres. The big moon lit the adjacent field. It was still, and wet, and silver. I smelt cow shit and saw black shapes as big as cars lying in the shadow of a tree.

'Let's just walk along here to the corner,' I said. 'See if we can see anything at all before backup gets here. We should have got radios.'

'Should we go back and radio up?'

We were a quarter of the way along the hedge towards the hilltop. 'Yes. We should.'

'Do you reckon we'll end up going in?'

'It's one guy sneaking around his own property wearing army fatigues,' I said. 'That's not a crime. But I trust Fry's intuition about the vibe.'

'You *do*?' Dodge couldn't hide the disbelief in his voice.

'Fry's saying something's not right. He's one of our guys. So until we check him out, we're not leaving,' I said. 'I'm hoping this ends up as a big hoo-ha over nothing.'

'But what is he *doing*?' Dodge's voice was too high, thin. 'Is he alone in there? Is he playing like . . . war games? Why creep up on a cop when you're fucking armed? Are you trying to get shot? Branch, mate, what the fuck?'

'Dodge.' I clapped him on the shoulder. 'It might be time to accept the fact that you don't really know this guy at all.'

Dodge walked on, eyes and pistol pointed at the ground, darkly contemplative. I felt bad for him. He had the rural cop's good heart, the one that liked to believe that the person you knew from playing darts and laughing and sinking schooners down the pub was the same person in their private life. Dodge's was a world in which there were no secrets or lies. A nice world to fantasise about. But city cops came to understand soon enough that the charming businessman could well be a violent paedophile. The doe-eyed mother of four could be a life-destroying fraudster. The guy playing darts and entertaining his mates with impressions was also the guy who would spend his spare time doing . . . whatever the hell we had interrupted Stephen Branch doing tonight. I knew humans were liars by nature. Expected it. I'd hidden the fact of who I really was from my wife for almost two decades.

A hiss stopped us in our tracks. I saw a shape moving through the hedge and raised my weapon, my pulse thumping in my neck. The black shape was crouched low, around three metres from where I was standing, an indistinguishable blob.

'Hey!' The voice was soft and trembling. 'Hey, is someone there?'

'Hello?' Dodge hissed back.

'Oh, Jesus!' The voice rose above a whisper, only barely. 'Hi. I'm here. I'm here! My name is Ashley Wilson. I-I-I'm trapped in here. I'm trying to get out!'

Dodge and I looked at each other.

'Ashley?' Dodge ducked his head, trying to see. 'Is that your name?'

'Yes!'

'You're trapped in there?'

'Do you have a phone?' the girl asked. 'Can you call the cops? Please. I'm not supposed to be here. I can't get out.'

'Who are you?' I demanded, tried to pull Dodge away. He was pressed against the hedge now, already getting himself caught in blackberry vines, trying to tug his sleeve free. 'Are you hurt?'

'I'm okay. I just need to get out of here.' The girl's voice broke into sobs. 'Can you please just call the cops, please, before he comes!'

'Just wait right there.' Dodge's words were fast, frantic. He dropped down, tried to see if he could squeeze beneath the hedge. Must have caught a razor-sharp strip of it against his cheek and reeled back. 'We'll get you out. There must be a gap somewhere.'

'No, no, no.' I tried to grab for my partner, but my fingertips brushed fabric and nothing else. Dodge had already taken off, close to the hedge, looking high and low for a gap. 'Dodge, wait, will you! *Wait! We're not going in!*'

'Ashley? Ashley?'

'I'm here!'

'Follow my voice!'

'Dodge, for fuck's sake! Stop!' I was running now, Dodge's shape moving fast through the moon shadow. My boot caught on a rock. I felt the sandstone cut straight through my jeans into my shin. I went down, was up again fast, barely maintaining a grip on my weapon. 'Dodge, *wait*!'

I looked up and saw Dodge dart through a gap in the hedge. I was seconds behind him, but wasn't there to see the fall. I heard the sickening crunch of a large metallic thing as it snapped shut on something soft. Dodge let out a howl that was stifled by another massive crunching, crashing sound, louder than the first, an explosion of bracken and leaves and the sound of a body thudding onto hard earth. My brain said that a mighty tree had fallen. But I rounded the corner to find Dodge had been swallowed by the ground itself. I came into the gap in the hedge and, through the mottled moonlight, I saw a great hole in the earth and no sign of my partner.

Or anyone. I wanted to call out, to go to the edge of the deep pit, but my training had taught me to go quiet and still in the face of uncertainty. I froze there in the gap, then remembered the silvery, moonlit field behind me and stepped sideways and pressed into the hedge, winced against the pain as a thousand shards of blackberry immediately stabbed at the back of my neck and arms. I knew I was bleeding. The vine gripped every piece of fabric available. I felt it plucking at the back of my shirt as I breathed.

'Oh, fuck.' Dodge huffed a low moan, sounded like he was stifling another howl of pain. 'Russell? Russell?'

'I'm here,' I called, watching the blackness. There was only bushland around the hole Dodge had fallen in. Dense and unmoving. No sign of 'Ashley' or anyone else. 'You hurt?'

'Fucking bear trap,' he huffed. 'It's clamped on my leg. You okay?'

I didn't answer. Thought I saw movement to my right. The darkness was swirling in my vision, ink-black and emerald-green, my eyes struggling to assess depth, failing. Another movement. A twig snapping. I raised my gun and pointed it at the blackness.

'Police!' I barked. 'Put your hands—'

A thunderous noise, like a hundred heavy doors slamming. The bush was set ablaze with white light that exploded into my vision, as painful as a punch, blinding me instantly. The floodlights were attached to trees that stood all around the hole Dodge was in, a dozen shining suns pointing downward, humming with electricity. The lights were on for a second, no more, before they snapped off, and any night vision I'd managed to gain was completely destroyed. Green and red fireworks swirled and billowed before my eyes. I heard the crack of a rifle, felt the breeze of the gunshot passing my right temple, the sonic whine of a bullet that had just missed me. Branch. It took strength to take my hands down from my blinded eyes, to form a plan. My body wanted to freeze. But a thought came to me clearly, panicked and fear-riddled but clear: *Do the unexpected.*

I bolted forward. I knew the blinding lights, the bear trap that had taken Dodge and the mimicked voice that Branch had used to lure Dodge and me onto his property were all carefully planned aspects of some sick game, and, whether I liked it or not, I was now on the game board. I figured I was supposed to run back out the gap, into the moonlit field or down the side of the hedge, where there was no cover, and Branch could fire at me at will.

Instead I ran forward, skirting where I remembered the edge of Dodge's hole was and went onward into the maze. I hit a tree, bounced off it, kept running, hit another, felt blackberry or razor wire slash at my arms and neck and face. The lights came on again with a deafening *ca-thunk*, not exactly around me as they had been the first time, but close enough. I found the nearest tree and put my back to it, slid down, my breath hammering in my chest.

EVAN

A crash, heavy and echoing, like a tree falling over. Then a god-awful thump, like a distant canon booming: a sound I felt in my chest. Lee and I stopped in our tracks, listening for more. We were at the side of the Branch property in the dark, weapons drawn, the bright moon overhead picking out a long, wide strip of mown grass edged on one side by the towering hedges and on the other by sparse, still bushland.

'Sir.' Lee's voice was low. 'What the fuck was that?'

'I know as much as you do right now.'

'Did you hear someone cry out?'

'I only heard the two bangs.'

'Just before the first one. Like a howl.'

I turned back towards the front of the property, started running there with Lee. A feeling like a stretching rubber band was being pulled directly from my chest into the property. I wanted to run through the hedges after my brother. My heart told me he was in there. It was him that Lee had heard cry out. Fry was at the cars, his gun drawn as well. We all ran to the other corner of the property. Looking up along the hedge line, there was no movement. No sign of my brother and Dodge.

'He said we weren't going in!' Lee was out of breath. She swiped at her brow. '*What the fuck*, sir!'

'Stay calm.'

'Oh, Christ, Louis is in there!'

'Yeah, and my brother's in there,' I said. 'We stay calm. We think this through.'

'Someone has to stay with the cars.' Fry put a hand on Lee's shoulder and pushed her gently. 'For when Kalowski and Knowlesy get here. Go, Sandy.'

'But *you* can't go in as well!' Lee begged. 'That's not in the training. First rule of rescue: don't create more casualties. Remember?'

'Fuck the rules,' I said. 'Fry, let's move.'

RUSSELL

The lights stayed on this time: white, humming, blinding. I squinted carefully around, trying to be as still as I could. I knew I was casting shadows. That my breathing wasn't as quiet as I'd have liked. The forest around me was cut through with beaten dirt paths. Stacks of cyclone fencing. A pile of rotting wood. An ancient, rusted tractor. There were wires running from tree to tree, thick and bundled together with cable ties. I saw some huge floodlights that were not lit like the ones in the near distance. I braved a look back the way I'd come, couldn't hear anything above my own heartbeat. Possums in the canopy above me, disturbed by the lights, leapt from one branch to another, shimmying along the wires, trying to get somewhere dark.

I spotted him at the same time as he spotted me. He was dressed neck to knee in camouflage fatigues, gloved up, the chest of the shirt bulging with kevlar. Stephen Branch's face was blacked out with dark green cammo paint, so that when he turned his big eyes on me, and spread his smile wide, his face contorted into a hellish, grinning mask. I was so stunned by what I was seeing, I didn't even think to raise my gun. Branch reached for something beside him, a switch, I guessed, hidden from my view by the trunk of a tree. With his other hand he raised the rifle, prepared to catch its stock and fire at me.

The lights went out. I ran again, hearing the shot smash into a tree to my left, feeling the splinters and smelling the burnt wood. *Do the unexpected.* The world was twisted, my mind was frantic, but the slant of the land under my boots told me which way was downhill, towards the front of the property, where the rest of the police team was. Where my brother was. I didn't head that way. Instead, I turned left, heading uphill, knocking trees with my hands and shoulders as I blundered my way through the blackness.

I felt the earth beneath me give as I stepped on a trap, the hole yawning open to take me beneath a weave of what felt like palm fronds and leaves and sticks. I staggered, almost went down, pushed myself up and carried on. I found something with my hands. Rust, raw metal edges: an old trailer or the hull of a boat left ditched in the dirt. I slid in behind it, waited, minutes passing, grateful for each second that I had Stephen Branch's focus and wanting more time to pass while I kept him away from Dodge and Evan and the others. The snap of a twig behind me somewhere made me turn. I lifted my gun and aimed that way and waited.

A movement in the darkness. I fired twice, heard a cry that was sickeningly familiar. I was so horrified that I stood at full height.

'Evan?'

Lights like another hard blow straight to the eyeballs. Branch was there, behind me, fifteen feet away. I turned to see the rifle pointed directly at my chest. He raised it to fire and a shot came flying past my arm, catching Branch in the hip, below the Kevlar vest, spinning him into the undergrowth. I bolted out of the firing line of the two shooters, seeing Branch lunge for the light switch out of the corner of my eye. Darkness swallowed us all. He was still mobile. I could hear him scrabbling through the bush. I needed to draw him away from Evan. I crashed loudly through the bush, one hand out and one on my pistol, pushing through another thicket of thorny vines, hitting the edge of something hard and horizontal. A verandah. I followed the verandah until it became the familiar slatted side of a weatherboard house.

'Hey!' the girl's voice called. Branch, mimicking a terrified teen girl again. He was somewhere behind me, what sounded like fifty metres, in the bush and coming fast, making no attempt to hide the sound of his footsteps. 'I'm here! I'm here! Please help me!'

'Fuck you!' I shouted back. Because I couldn't help it. Because I was angry, and afraid for Dodge and my brother, and terrified for myself. More gunshots out there in the dark. Pistols popping and the rifle cracking in response. *Do the unexpected.* I started up the stairs, then changed my mind, came down and turned towards the back of the house. I crept along the side of the dwelling with no plan, and no knowledge of what lay inside waiting for me.

Arriving at the back corner of the house, I heard a rifle shot. A window blew out at the front of the house, where I'd just been. The sound of glass spraying on floorboards. That was weird. Why had his aim been so far off? At the back of the building, a soft gold light was spilling from a window. I used the glow to avoid a bear trap lying open and gaping at the foot of a set of wooden stairs, teeth pointed upwards. I dropped and slithered under the house instead of going up the stairs. I lay taking long, shaking, quiet breaths to try to calm my heartbeat.

Silence. Stillness.

Minutes ticked by.

I expected Branch to come around the side of the house. To pursue me the way I had gone. But as I listened, I heard a floorboard creak above me, ten feet or more to my left. I replayed the past minute or so in my mind and realised with shocking clarity that Branch must have been exchanging fire with whoever else was out there in the dark at the same time as I was reaching the house, and he had missed seeing me going back down the steps and around the side of the house. Relief and exhilaration plucked at my insides. That's why he'd fired at the house. Why he'd taken out one of the front windows. He thought I was inside.

I rolled onto my back and listened, blood or sweat trickling down my temples, running in rivulets into my hair and down the back of my neck. In the distance, I could hear sirens, shouting. I closed my eyes, tried to separate the layers of sound. The night, and its creeping, crawling, chittering creatures. The distant growing police presence. And above me, getting closer now, the pad of a boot on floorboards. I knew then, by the sound of that soft footfall, that the person in the house wasn't Evan. Or one of the other cops.

One step after another, Stephen Branch was hunting me inside the house.

An idea formed slowly in my mind. I raised one leg and pushed on the floorboards above me. They gave a satisfying creak. I waited, hearing nothing but silence, then pushed gently again. The sound of Branch's footfall was almost indiscernible. He was probably sticking to the edges of the room, there the boards would be more stable, less prone to creaking. A light came on, glowing dimly through the cracks in the floorboards, not strong enough to be in the room I was directly below, but perhaps a hallway outside that room. I looked around, examined the shape of the joists in the floor, found that the room above me was showing cracks of light in all but one large rectangular space. A cupboard? A wardrobe? I rolled over twice, as silently as I could, pressed my foot against the bottom of that darkened space and eased the pressure on. The floorboard creaked. I heard Branch enter the room, the barest creaking of boards just above where I'd been. I pressed the boards above me a final time.

Rifle shots into the cupboard above me. I bit my lip, raised my weapon and fired at where I guessed Branch must be standing. Five fast, desperate shots, spraying myself with woodchips and dust and cones of golden light.

There was a groan, long and loud and full of pain, let out in Stephen Branch's own voice. Then there came a heavy thud on the floor above me. The sounds told me that I'd hit my mark.

EVAN

'Rus? Rus?'

I went up the verandah steps and stopped outside the front door of the ragged little house in the bush, put my shoulder to the wall. Fry leapt the steps in one bound and arrived beside me. There was shouting in the distance, but beyond the verandah rail all I could see was blackness. I'd heard seven gunshots inside the house, rifle and pistol. Now there was a silence so thick it made my ears ring.

'Russell!'

'Yeah,' my brother said from somewhere at the back of the house. Fry let out a short but heavy sigh of relief. 'He's down. I'm coming in through the back door.'

'We're at the front,' I said. I kept an eye through a glass panel in the front door on what looked to be a kitchen. Garbage bags, plastic tubs filled with items, a dead brown plant sagging over the edges of a pot, dry leaves curled around the rim like witchy fingers. Russell appeared in the doorway, paused, looking through it into another room. He was covered in blood from head to foot, a bright red mask of it, forearms running long streams that dripped off his fingers. The nice white business shirt was filthy with sweat and blood and dirt. I was fairly bloody myself from pushing through the blackberry, but nothing like this. He looked like a horror-movie extra, turning his fierce, adrenaline-pumped eyes on me as he opened the unlocked front door and I came into the house.

'Why *the hell* did you come onto the property?' Russell shook his head at me. 'I thought I must have clipped you when I heard your voice out there.'

'You were pretty close.' I showed him the tear in the shoulder of my T-shirt.

'I thought you were him.' Russell's voice was intensifying. 'I could have—'

'Don't leap down my throat too fast.' I put a hand up. 'You went in long before I did.'

'I was following that pudding-brained, cretinous gastropod Louis Dodge,' Russell said, turning to Fry in a way that made the smaller officer wince. Russell put an arm out and pointed into the dark. 'He's off in that direction, lying in the bottom of a hole with a bear trap on his leg. Go and see if he's all right, Fry. And if he is all right, bring him here so I can strangle him.'

'Yes, sir.'

Fry went off. My brother eyed me for a moment in silence, with blood dripping off his chin onto the front of his shirt, trying to decide, perhaps, whether he should go ahead and re-launch into berating me for coming onto the Branch property anyway. Then he said, 'I'm somewhat pleased that you're not dead right now, Evan.'

I gasped, clutched at my heart, did a little mock stagger back. 'My god.'

'Don't,' he warned. 'I'm not in the mood.'

'That's the nicest thing I think you've ever said to me, Russell.'

'Get in here and look at this place with me.'

'Who is this new, emotionally vulnerable, deeply sensitive Russell Powder?'

'Do it *quietly*,' he snapped.

RUSSELL

The front of the Branch property was a hive in two hours flat. Locals who had heard about the shooting, cops from surrounding jurisdictions there to secure the scene, ambulance crews who had come to tend to the injured. There was talk of bringing in a bomb squad, but I wasn't a part of that. Together, Fry and Evan took over the scene direction, because apparently I was too covered in blood to be worth listening to. Dodge was hauled off on a stretcher, giving prattling protestations that he was fine, that he'd be back before sunrise, that all he needed was a few stitches in his calf. I saw, from my vantage point on the back of a different ambulance, that the left leg of Dodge's jeans was black with blood from the knee down. I guessed there might have been more than simple stitches in his future. I was annoyed at being taken out of the game for the simple crime of bleeding from every surface not covered in fabric. Ambulance people kept approaching me and trying to wipe my face and shine lights in my eyes. I gave a flat-toned and colourless statement to a couple of cops from Gosford, who recorded the whole thing on their body cams, then we all turned to watch as Branch's body was loaded into a third ambulance under a dark blue sheet.

I saw Gail Caplan coming too late. I got up and tried to walk away anyway, but she skewered me in place with a look as she marched angrily from her personal car.

'And here I was thinking my night couldn't get any worse,' I sighed.

'*Your* night?' She pulled up short. 'Oh, that is rich. I've been at the bludgeoning on the waterfront all day. Then I get a message telling me you entered a suspect's property, knowing it was hostile, without backup. Your partner got caught in a bear trap, and you shot the suspect dead.'

'That's about the sum of it.'

'Fuck *me*, Russell!'

'No thanks.'

'In twenty-four hours you've punched a junkie and shot a rural lunatic.' Gail's nostrils were flaring. 'What's next? You gonna harpoon a paedophile?'

'You got one handy?'

'What? A paedophile or a har—Look! Enough! I am beyond tired of your shit. You know that? I was thinking on the way here that I understand completely now why your mother called you Gun. You're a cold, loud, trigger-happy *tool*, and you present a *constant danger* to everyone around you. Whenever you do *anything*, you ruin someone's day!'

I had to smile at the creativity.

'The dead guy,' Gail said. 'Is he the killer, at least?'

'It sure looks good,' I replied, which is something I said when I meant that something had all the right appearances and not much else.

I described what I'd seen on my walk-through of the house with Evan. I'd found Branch breathing his last gurgling breaths in an airless and bare room. The wardrobe was open, and it and Branch and the floor were all full of bullet holes. In the living room, there were cardboard moving boxes and plastic tubs scattered everywhere, maybe twenty of them, full to the brim with women's underwear. I'd stood in the glow of overhead lights that were slick with tobacco tar and cooking grease, and lifted a piece of underwear out of the nearest tub, examining it. Blue polka dots on white, with a lace trim, the elastic a little worn from wear.

'*Twenty* boxes of women's underwear?' Gail gazed at me, her head cocked.

'By my estimation.'

'Is it his underwear? Like, has he been wearing it, or . . . ?'

'I don't know, Gail.'

'Why was it . . .' She shook her head, trying to fathom it. 'Why was it lying around in tubs like that?'

'If I had to guess, I would say he was trying to pack up the household and get out of town before my people came knocking about Chloe,' I said. 'But halfway through, he gave up. Figured it was too big a task. So he decided to go full *Deliverance* on us instead. Enact "Operation Crazyfuck", which it looks like he's been cooking up for some time. That's my theory, anyway. The underwear was being packed into boxes in the living room, but there were other things being packed up elsewhere. The kitchen was half done. The bedroom was full of photographs that had already been loaded into tubs.'

'Photographs?'

'Tens of thousands of them.' I nodded. 'Maybe hundreds of thousands.'

'What were the pictures of?'

'Women in their natural environment.' I wiped at blood that was trickling down my neck. 'I didn't look at too many. But I got the gist. Women photographed through windows or between the slits of curtains. Undressing. Cooking dinner. Sitting around. Putting children to sleep. There were women that were older, and there were kids, too. Always females.'

Gail just stood staring at me, her mouth slightly open.

'He's been creeping around taking pictures of women through their windows at night,' I went on. 'Probably in the cammo. Treating it like a secret operation. From the settings, the furniture in the pictures and the clothes on the women, I'd say he's been doing it for decades. And the underwear, it's all used. It seems to range from big granny knickers to undies for little girls. He's probably spent decades doing that, too: pulling them off clotheslines, or maybe raiding them out of laundromats.'

'Jeeesus fuuu . . .' Gail let her hands slap by her sides, stared off towards the crowd gathering at the police tape. 'So what . . . what . . . *why?*'

'I have no idea, Gail.'

'This is going to totally eclipse the bludgeoning.' She pinched the bridge of her nose. 'A guy who stalks women in their houses with half his spare time, and runs around rigging his property with booby traps with the other half. This is going to go international. The press will be feverish.'

I nodded, studied the blood on my hands, black beneath my fingernails. Cops nearby were describing the scene to newly arrived colleagues, who were gawping just like Gail had been. The officers had marked on a rough drawing that was being handed around where the known bear traps were, and where the house was, and which parts of the property were unexplored. I listened to that for a while, playing with my nails.

'You're quiet,' Gail said. I realised she was looking hard at me.

'I just killed a guy. It makes you contemplative.'

'Go get some sleep.'

'No.' I jumped down from the deck of the ambulance. 'I want my team to get out there and do some DNA swabs. And I'm looking for a young guy who was seen in the pub that I haven't identified yet. And I'm waiting on—'

'But it's over.' Gail gestured to the Branch property gates. 'Are you kidding me? This is your guy right here, Rus. The briefing I got said he was the only person on the ground last night to speak to the victim. And then you come out here and find *this*? Come on!'

'Yeah, maybe.' I shrugged. 'Like I said, it looks good. But I don't like things that look this good. If you look harder—I mean, really stare at it—you start seeing imperfections.'

'Like what?'

'There's no violence,' I said. 'There are no home invasions, no stabbings and no rapes on Stephen Branch's rap sheet. From what I'm seeing of the inside of that house—the undies and the photographs—he seems to be a looker. Not a doer. The worst he's ever done in town is sleaze onto a couple of women at the pub. Aside from that, he's never actually *done* anything of note.'

'He just lured you and your guys into an *Apocalypse Now*-themed death maze!' Gail scoffed.

'Exactly,' I said. 'The *one time* he's ever done anything violent, he appears to have spent several years planning it, and he's perpetuated it against a couple of men. *And* he wasn't very good at it. He took five or six shots at me overall. Nothing hit. He lost sight of me completely at one point. That slip-up cost him the game. What happened to Chloe Lutz was a crime of opportunity. Something squeezed into a very tight window that would only have opened up on the night it happened. It was conducted by someone who was waiting for their moment, and knew what they were doing, and had probably done it before.'

'You're out of your mind.' Gail shook her head.

'I don't think so.'

'You're going to go somewhere and get some sleep.'

'No, I'm not.'

'You're sleeping, and your people are sleeping, too,' Gail snapped. 'I bet you came out here and pulled that "Nobody sleeps!" bullshit like you always do. I'm not having it.'

'Yes, you are.'

Her tone shot up, harder and louder, a ferocity coming into her eyes that I was deeply familiar with. 'Detective Inspector Powder, you just killed a fucking civilian! You're stood down from duty, effective immediately, for a period of at least ninety days! That's protocol! I'm not negotiating this with you!'

'I'm not negotiating this with *you*!' I shot back. Natural instinct. Gail and I having fired shots at each other for years. 'Fuck your "protocol"! I don't need to be signed on to keep chasing this thing! I'll do it on my own time!'

'I'll have my officers watch over you, Rus, if I have to.'

'They'd better be fast on their feet.'

'This is so you,' Gail sneered. 'I have to shove you as hard as I can just to get you to come out here in the first place, and now you're going to give me hell getting you to leave. You're like a fucking toddler who won't take a shower and then throws a tantrum when the water's turned off.'

'Good thing I'm cute then, huh?' I winked. The cops nearby who had been listening to our little exchange of fire snickered. Gail went over to roast them about standing around. I went to my car with a smile.

EVAN

Delle knocked on the shower door and scared the life out of me. It was 2 a.m. I'd parked in the street and snuck into the house the back way, hoping to preserve her and Chris's sleep, and to get the blood and the smell of gunshots rinsed off me before she noticed. But the water at my feet was pink and there was debris in my hair, and she opened the door and looked at it all like she knew exactly how close I'd come to dying that night. The wives of cops just know when you've come close to that ragged edge. You never get away with it. So, I watched her pull her robe off, and she got in under the hot fount with me, and I kissed her and held her and gave her the bare details, while she pulled thorns out of my hair. My murmured voice bounced off the bathroom walls and the mirror clouded up with steam.

'Is he the guy?' she asked.

'He's got to be,' I said, smiling. She smiled back. My wife probably thought the light in my face was relief that a murder investigation had been wrapped up so quickly and neatly, and that the whole ordeal was going to do for my career exactly what we both had hoped it would do. Get us out of Mangrove Mountain, where she couldn't put petrol in the car or stand in the grocery aisle without feeling eyes on her.

Really, it was relief that Chris was out of the lion's den now. No, I didn't know how his DNA had ended up on Chloe Lutz's body. But it seemed safe to assume it was an innocent case of DNA transfer, where he'd brushed up against her or touched something that she'd then touched. I'd seen that happen. Two people grip the same doorknob. Two people brush shoulders in a tight hallway. There'd been a case I'd run into in my early years on the beat. I'd been in court for the day, killing time waiting to give evidence on a traffic case, so I'd sat in. A husband had departed from his mistress, kissing her on the lips, unknowingly then carrying that saliva-based DNA home to his wife, who he then slept with and immediately murdered. Making a case about how the mistress's DNA ended up on the wife's lips and breasts at the crime scene had the mistress's defence lawyer pouring sweat so bad he had to dab his face every few minutes with a towel.

There was a way out. Reasonable doubt. That was enough.

And yes, okay: from what I'd seen in Stephen Branch's house, and what I knew of his criminal history, Branch didn't *exactly* fit the behaviour profile of Chloe's killer. But he was a hell of a lot better as a suspect than my Chris. It all seemed so safe. I'd meant what I said to Delle, in those exact terms: Stephen Branch had to be Chloe's killer. He *had* to be.

I basked in the relief, the quiet, thinking about how I'd probably never have to explain to authorities why Chris had been in Redbelly that night, or why he'd lied about it, or why his DNA was on the dead woman. It would be a footnote in the coroner's court inquiry, which would happen five years from now, and would be so focused on Stephen Branch's weird house, his past behaviours, the shooting, all of that stuff, that Chris would get lost in the wash. He probably wouldn't even be called to appear.

I pushed my wife against the shower wall and slicked her hair over her shoulder and entered her slowly, the way I knew she liked. Thought about something other than murder for a few minutes. The water pooled in the shapes we made, my chest against hers, our bellies together, our lips. When we were finished, I went to bed with her and lay against the pillows and listened to her fall asleep beside me while I stared at the ceiling.

An hour later, I was still staring at the ceiling.

And an hour after that.

I got up and went to the kitchen, sat at the cold marble benchtop and took out my phone. I tapped through the pages in Chloe

Lutz's notebook. After the Ford Capri section, there came a new page entitled *COLD CASE FILES, SERIES FIVE: WANDERER.*

A list ran down the page.

Ep 1: Runaway Bay, setting, Diana's life etc. Crime stats. Leading to morning of.
Ep 2: 'Morning of' timeline. Husband reaction. Neighbour reaction. Initial clues.
Ep 3: Major police theories. Interview lead detective, career profile. Newspaper coverage, including editorials.
Ep 4: Diana-centric episode: major suspects, her behaviour, her diary.
Ep 5: Red herring guy. Intro, then unpicking.

I squinted at the page. Closed the photo app and opened Google. I typed in 'Runaway Bay Cold Case Files Diana'.

The first hit was the website of a podcast called *Cold Case Files.* I opened it up. On the home screen, a black-and-white photograph of a slender woman standing at the edge of what looked like a cropped school photograph. Children at her side, arranged in rows, their faces blurred. I read the text beneath the picture.

The Guardian's award-winning podcast series COLD CASE FILES continues in its fifth season, WANDERER: a deep examination of the unsolved murder of Gold Coast school teacher Diana Summerton. Subscribe now!

I clicked through the show's credits. Chloe wasn't the writer, or any other kind of contributor. I went back to Chloe Lutz's notebook. I scrolled forward through the pages. There was a more detailed breakdown of each of the episodes in the *COLD CASE FILES: WANDERER* series, including topics, the times they were discussed in the episode, and key lines in quotation marks. I scrolled forward through the diary, flipping fast, supposing the detailed deconstruction of an existing podcast must have been a project for university that Chloe was working on. A new podcast series deconstruction began. I googled the show. *MURDER BEHIND THE MIC: SERIES THREE* dealt with the unsolved death of a teenage girl in Picton in Sydney's west. In her notes for episode two Chloe had scribbled in the margin *Real audio from scene/atmosphere—will need good mic.*

Okay. So, she was going to start a podcast, I realised. The understanding clicked into place like gears engaging in my tired brain, a heavy clunk. I flipped back to the first pages of the notebook. The Ford Capri—that car, and the possibility that it was 'mistaken' for another car—must have been a clue Chloe had picked up. I went back to Google and punched in 'Ford Capri clue unsolved Redbelly'. A link came up to a historical news site. A tiny article arose, highlighted in a faded, scanned image of an old-style newspaper. I zoomed out and found that the paper was the now defunct *Hawkesbury Journal*, and the issue was from September 1976.

> *POLICE SEEK WITNESSES IN ATTACK ON MINOR*
> *A fifteen-year-old girl was sexually assaulted in her home in the town of Womerah, north-west of Redbelly Crossing, on Thursday evening, 16 September. Police would like to speak to the owner of a mustard yellow Ford Capri seen parked near the location on the evening of Wednesday 15 September. Members of the public with any information . . .*

Womerah. I knew it, but only from travelling through, seeing the sign, wondering to myself how the cluster of tiny houses could be called a town at all. I guessed in 1976 it would have been smaller still. I rubbed my eyes, causing the text on the screen before me to double. A sound at the front of the house made me jump. I looked up the hall. Waited. Listened. Nothing moved. I needed to go to bed. The jumpiness was becoming exhausting. And I was only tormenting myself now. It didn't matter what Chloe Lutz had been working on. She was dead, and her deadness had nothing to do with me or my family.

I stood, and my phone rang, sending yet another *whump* of fear through my chest. I grabbed the phone and answered just to silence it, glancing at the microwave.

'Do you own a clock?' I asked my father.

'Guess what I'm doing,' he said. I heard a pop in the background of the call. The sloshing of liquid.

'I can't decide if it's appallingly early or appallingly late to be drinking,' I said. 'But I'm guessing you didn't just start, if you're calling to tell me about it.'

'I started an hour ago, when I heard you bagged the Redbelly stabber.'

'Uh-huh.'

'Now I can walk around town with my head held high again.' His words were slightly slurred. 'When will you start packing to leave the region? I'd like to help.'

'You're a few steps ahead of yourself, aren't you?' I said. 'This case might get me out of the red. But it won't put me in the green. And that's if we don't all get smacked on the wrist for entering a hostile scene without backup and killing a man. I think I'll need to behave myself for a couple more years before I'm ready to pack my bags.'

'I'll make some calls tomorrow morning and see what I can arrange.'

'This makes me feel so loved,' I sighed. 'Did you know the guy? Branch?'

'No. I don't hang out up there. The further north you go from Maroota, the fewer teeth people have. And I've only got half a set myself.'

'Hmm. Anyway, I'd better—'

'And that pub's a shithole. Twenty-five bucks for a burger, my arse. I haven't stayed in the hotel rooms, but I hear they're the pits. Tragic place to get poked to death. The girl should have stayed in Sydney and left the past in the past.'

'Yes, well. As much as I'm enjoying this conversation, I'm gonna go now, Dad. It's three in the fucking morning.'

'You answered.'

I hung up, went to the bedroom, put the phone on charger and slipped between the sheets. There was blue light coming from the shutters on the front windows. It fell on Delle's bare shoulder in stripes.

I sat up sharply after only a minute.

RUSSELL

As I stepped down into the houseboat kitchen, Bridie froze in the doorway to the bedroom, the light behind her haloing around her shoulders and making wings of the sleeves of her white pyjama T-shirt. She'd heard me getting dropped off, and took in the image of me with her mouth open wide.

'Daaaaad!'

'I'm okay!' I put my hands up. 'But I really need a shower before I do anything else.'

I went in and stripped my clothes off, showered, came out of the tiny bathroom not sure if I preferred being covered in thousands of tiny, open, dirty scratches or thousands of tiny, clean, rapidly closing ones. Every inch of me itched. My palms were ripped raw and trailing white, dead skin. I looked like I'd gone toe-to-toe with a hundred and fifty cats in a pit full of scalpels. Bridie was sitting on the end of one of the single beds at the back of the vessel, her legs crossed, watching me come in with the towel around my waist, her eyes still bugging and her mouth still open. 'What *happened*?'

'Blackberry bushes,' I said. I pointed to the sheets, the freshly made beds. 'What happened here?'

Bridie looked. 'Oh, a local lady brought them over. They're lovely.' She patted the coverlet beside her. 'I literally think they're washed in lavender laundry liquid. You can smell it. And she made us cupcakes. They're on the kitchen counter.'

'Oh no.' I went into my bag, pulled out my boxers and tugged them on under the towel. 'Old woman.'

'How did you know she was old?'

'The cupcakes. The sheets. The whole gesture. I'm a detective, but it wouldn't have taken one. I don't like old women, Bridie. So if she comes back, you keep her away from me.'

'What are you talking about? Who doesn't like old women?'

'Me.'

'Why?'

'They have incredible gaydars.'

'*What?*'

'Old women have the best gaydars. I can't explain it. It's true. You just have to accept it.'

'I can't accept it. That is not a thing.'

'Yes it is.' I eased myself onto the bed with a chorus of groans. 'They can *smell* it on you. She'll come back here and she'll figure out I'm a queen in five minutes flat, and then she'll insist on organising an unexpected but adorable encounter between me and the local gay and I'll never recover from the awfulness of it, Bridie, I'll *never* recover.'

Bridie shook her head. 'You're insane, Dad.'

'I'm right.'

'No, but you actually need, like, professional help.' She leant back against her pillows and flipped her long legs up. 'And if she does come back around here, you can't yell at her. I'm not going to sit by and watch you make someone's nana cry. You can't act the way you do around people anymore.'

'Why not?'

'Because you're going to end up an angry, lonely old man, that's why not.'

'I won't be lonely. I'll have you.'

'No you won't, unless you clean your act up.'

I felt a chill enter my chest. She was quiet, clearly examining the gravity of her own words, trying to decide whether to withdraw them or not. Silence fell around us. A full minute. Two. I was simultaneously proud of her for not backing down and in a rage at myself, at who I'd become. How right she was about everything. Somebody had to say something, so I said, 'You'd better go back to sleep. The sparrows haven't even got up to do their morning wee yet.'

'No way. I want to know why you decided to roll around in a million blackberry bushes.'

I told her. Didn't leave anything out. She's the kid of two cops.

'Holy crap,' she said when I was done.

'Yeah.'

'So the case is over?'

'No.'

'But you're off it, at least.'

'Also no.'

'I mean, officially, though?'

'Yeah, but that doesn't mean anything.'

'Are you going to sleep?'

'No.' I took my phone from beside me and set an alarm. 'I'm going to have a little lie-down. Forty minutes. Then I've got shit to do.'

Bridie got up, pottered around for a bit, then came back, flicked the lights off and sat against her pillows again, playing with her phone. I didn't realise I was asleep until I woke myself up snoring. She gave a snicker from across the room.

My mind drifted for a while. Then I said, 'Hey.'

'Yeah?'

'I have a question for you.'

'Go for it.'

'Do you . . .' I started. Paused to get my words in order. Heard a sharp sigh from over there. 'What?'

'*Do you have a boyfriend?*' she said. Her voice was tight. 'That's the question, isn't it?'

'No.' I laughed. 'Why would it be?'

'I don't know.' She gave another sigh, like a train trying to get up a hill. 'It just seems like every time I meet a new adult the only two questions I ever get are *How's school?* and *Do you have a boyfriend?*'

I put my head back, shifted position. My knees were giving me hell from all the running. 'I'm not trying to find out about some teenage dirtbag boyfriend, Bridie, I'm trying to find out about you.'

'Oh. Okay,' she said. I could hear her smiling.

'Do you have, like, a . . .' I still couldn't find the right words. 'Like, a . . . *vision* . . . about what you want to do? And how you want to live? In the next . . . I don't know, decade? Or whatever?'

'You mean, like, what do I want to do for a job?'

'I mean everything.' I rubbed my head. 'I'm just trying to say . . . when you imagine yourself in ten years. Twenty years. Are you . . . are you . . . what? A healthcare worker in Nigeria? Are you an airline pilot in Japan? Are you a vet in Sydney? Are you homeless and living under a bridge? What's the plan? Do you think you'll have kids? Do you want to get married?'

'That's a shitload of questions, Dad.'

'Sorry.'

'Did you just decide you were going to ask me every question you've been thinking about for the past five years all at once?'

I laughed. There was so much laughing lately. She was so fun to talk to. 'I didn't realise they were all tied together until I started pulling them out.'

'Well, I think I want to stay nearby, long term,' she said. 'I like Sydney. I don't know if I'll have kids but if I did I would want to be near you and Mum.'

'Okay,' I said gently, careful not to punch the air with joy.

'And something with animals suits me,' she mused.

'Of course.'

'But I don't know about going full-on down the veterinary science route. There's a lot of hard work there. Crazy hours. And so much death. I mean, *so* much *death*!'

'Right. Okay.'

Her voice became light, almost feathery, floating with possibility. 'There are, um, people who manage wild brumbies? In the outback? They trap them, study them, figure out which ones can be domesticated. I've talked to Mum about maybe going and doing that for a while, after the HSC. Managing the brumbies. Maybe I could build up some equine skills and knowledge, before coming back to Sydney and settling down and doing something with horses at home.'

I put my hand on my chest, trying to smother the growing sparkle of terror at the idea of my beautiful teenage daughter surrounded by lonely horse trappers twice her age and huge, feral horses, in a landscape so sparse and desolate it might as well have been outer space. 'That sounds awesome!' I flat-out lied.

'You think so?'

'Yeah.'

'Hmm.'

The silence fell. I was walking the razor blade between sleep and the desire to close the gaping wounds of wonderment in my heart. To know my daughter again. This almost-woman who had once been a tiny girl attached to my side like a limpet on a rock, trembling in the big bed between Georgia and me, having crawled in there during a thunderstorm. 'So I haven't turned you off marriage, then?'

'What?' She laughed. 'Oh, nah.'

'Because what happened between your mum and me, that's not normal. That was my fault.'

'It was and it wasn't,' Bridie said. I gripped onto those words tightly, holding them to my heart, afraid to open my palm and look too closely at them. 'I mean, sure, it was an awful mess,' she went on. 'But I think she's going to be okay. Mum.'

'You do?'

'Yeah,' Bridie said. 'She's dating. She's going to things. She laughs.'

I smiled. 'Good.'

The silence lingered for a while. 'Do you . . .' she began.

'Do I have a boyfriend?' I scoffed. 'Bridie, how *dare* you ask me that?'

The laughter rose and fell and rose again. 'I sometimes go to DejaVu and get a bit worried I'll see you there,' she said.

'Oh, Jesus.' I rubbed my head. 'You wouldn't catch me dead in that place. I can't dance and I can't afford the cover charge.'

'Do you see people, though? Men?'

'Yes, Bridie, I see men.'

'How?'

'I date online,' I said. 'Sporadically. And very privately. I'm not a stand-around-in-a-bar guy. Or a clubber. I tried that, in the beginning. Thought I should go to a gay bar and just present myself as a prospective member of The Gays. Fill in the application form. After a few soul-destroying nights of being avoided like a leper, a helpful little twink came up and told me that the way I was dressed and the way I stood and the way I was looking at people was screaming "cop" so loudly nobody could think straight.'

'Oh my god,' Bridie snickered. 'What did you do?'

'I said, "Honey, this is a gay bar, nobody in here was thinking straight anyway."'

'What! Did you really say that?'

'No.' I sighed. 'I thought of it three weeks later.'

'Oh, man.'

'But I'll have it pre-loaded for next time.'

'Do gays not like cops?'

'Sometimes, but definitely not in that circumstance. In that situation I was so cagey they figured I was undercover wanting to bust people for drugs.'

'Poor you.'

'You live and learn.'

'So, now you date online,' Bridie said.

'Yep.'

'Are you with someone?'

'Oh, no.'

'Why?'

'Urgh. How much time have you got?'

'Plenty.'

'I'm emotionally unavailable.' I started listing on my fingers. 'I don't text. I don't take selfies. I don't hold hands. I'm a socially anxious workaholic with a huge chip on my shoulder, and I could really use a pedicure.'

She laughed. 'Well, at least you're self-aware.'

'I'm not going to end up an angry, lonely old man, though, Birds.' I glanced over. 'So you don't have to worry.'

'Oh?' she said. 'You're not?'

'No. I just decided. When you said those words. I'm not going to be that. I'm going to get you back, and I'm not going to lose you again.'

'So what are you going to do, then?' she asked. She sounded unconvinced. And that hurt so badly I could hardly breathe for a minute.

'I'm going to learn,' I said. 'And I'm going to change.'

She made a little sound. I was too tired and scared to try to figure out if it was an interested, disbelieving or relieved sound. My mind drifted away, led by the call of the creatures out there and the whispering of the nearby river.

EVAN

I turned right at one of the vast nurseries lining the main road, a lot ribbed with river stone walkways, long steel tables of tube stock in both natives and foreign species. Blood-tipped photinia, wet with dew, moved in the night breeze. The road I took wound through slabs of bush that thinned and became farmland, and all the while as I drove my stomach sank further and further, muscle-memory dread from a thousand different awful journeys down this very path. To perform the obligatory Christmas visit, with its traditional drunken afternoon tantrum. Or to bring a girlfriend for my father's inspection, with the ride home inevitably spent comforting her as she cried in horror at something Arthur had done or said. The dirt road to the farm was not marked by a milk-urn letterbox or a cute sign with the property's name but with a pile of junk and lumber and cardboard dark and limp from recent rains. The field leading to the house was a green sea of long grass tossed with rusted car body islands. Broken-down whitegoods, an aviary where Dad had raised and killed ducks for a while before the stink and the upkeep and the rats took the fun away.

I parked where I'd been parking since I got free of the family hellscape at seventeen, and got out. The bullet smashed into the pillar of the sagging car port a foot to the left of my face, showering me with rotting wood, before I even heard the gunshot. I hit the deck as I was trained to do, felt the wet gravel soak my shirt and jeans immediately. Dad was on the verandah, lowering the rifle and laughing. When the panic released its chokehold on my trachea and I was able to breathe and figure out what had just happened, I got to my feet.

'Fucking pussy.'

'Jesus *Christ*!' I wiped mud from my belly with my equally muddy hands. 'Dad, are you out of your mind?'

'This rifle is off.' Arthur slid the bolt forward, popped the casing out of the chamber. 'I was aiming much closer to your head. What? Oh, give it a rest, will you? It's only fun and games. I thought I'd get the mood going. Bit of atmosphere, before you come in and tell me all about the shootout. That's what you're here to do, isn't it?'

The shivers were coming in waves. Clouds at the corners of my vision. Adrenaline dumps. I walked up the stairs to where the old man was standing in the pre-morning gloom. 'Put the fucking gun down. Now.'

'Yeah, yeah. Better get inside. Before the jackass neighbours join you in a chorus of hysteria. Make us coffee, will you?'

Nothing major had changed since the last time I had visited maybe a year earlier. There were pieces of furniture in the main room of the cottage that had been around when I was conceived: a mid-century floor lamp, once a jaunty orange, tobacco-stained now to a beer-bottle brown. A buffet cabinet stuffed with figurines that had been my mother's, the cherub-cheeked girls and boys swimming so deep in dust only their little sticky heads were visible. Tar was everywhere, coating the timber veneer walls, adhering to the light fixtures in the ceiling, making rivulet patterns on the walls of the kitchen where the steam periodically loosened it. I washed the mud off my hands and made the coffee, because doing what I was told here without question was as natural as breathing. The kettle on the stove gave a loud and pained squeal like a thing being strangled. The instant coffee granules leapt off the spoon as my hand shook. I reminded myself that this was far from the first time my father had fired a gun at me.

Arthur took the leather recliner, so I sat on the end of the floral couch. The fabric was glossy in parts with filth. I tried to rinse the tobacco taste off my tongue with the coffee. It didn't work. When I didn't start speaking immediately, Arthur gave me a sharp, impatient shrug.

'Will you get on with it?'

'I will, I will,' I said, my mind racing, fifty steps ahead, wary of the rifle still leaning against the wall beside Dad's chair and the whisky in the greasy glass on the fold-out table beside him. 'I'm . . . I came here to talk to you about the shootout, like I said on the phone. But I'm also on a bit of a side mission. Chris is into this, ah, ancestry stuff. I don't know if he told you, but his friends got him a genealogy kit for his birthday.'

'Weird, all of that.' Arthur shook his head, looked out the grimy windows towards the yard where the sun was trying to rise. 'It's your artist wife that gives him this kooky side that he's got. You know that, don't you?'

'He wants some old photos. I know you have a box lying around somewhere.'

Dad made a throaty sound, thrust his arm towards the back room. I started telling him, yelling over my shoulder, about the shootout. The box I was looking for was at the bottom of a huge pile of junk: folded camp tents, some half-sanded dining room chairs, boxes of machinery parts dripping grease and oil. I brought the box out to the living room, still carrying on with the story. The dread, the sense of foreboding, was creeping up my throat like bile.

There were about a hundred photographs in the box. Old Polaroids of my mother and father, people I didn't recognise; friends of theirs, back when they had friends. The farm was newer and less chaotic in the pictures, the grass mown and the buildings cleanly painted, the water tank freshly installed. My mother's smile began disappearing and her eyes hollowed out, and then she was carrying a roly-poly, frowny-faced baby around with her in the images. I was desperately avoiding looking at Mum, and Dad, and my brother, and the pictures of my tiny self that then began to appear: playing with a kitten on someone's verandah, sitting in the grass sucking my thumb. It was the raw sadness of it all, but also a diverted focus. I wasn't looking at the people. I was looking at the cars.

'Women's underwear?' Dad snorted from somewhere across the room. 'What was he doing with it all? Why was there so much of it?'

I flipped through the photographs faster and faster, specifically searching for shots of the farm. The yard cars. Barely listening to my father. 'Dunno.'

'I arrested a guy like that when I was posted in Campbelltown.' Dad's voice was a muffled buzzing in my ears. 'Early days. Maybe one year in. Still a constable. He'd steal the underwear, take it home, do things with it. Then he'd mail it back to them. What was his name? It's on the tip of my tongue.'

The photo was the second from the last in the stack. It was of my father sitting, lighting a cigarette, on the edge of the verandah, his cheeks sunken in as he sucked at the paper tube. He looked like Russell. Broad. Muscular. Healthy. Over his shoulder, parked by the first barn in the row, sat the back half of a mustard yellow Ford Capri with a black racing stripe.

A cold rush fell over every inch of my skin. It was like being plunged into a winter lake.

'Carlton?'

'Huh?'

'Carlton. I think the guy's name was Carlton.'

'Dad,' I said. He stared at me, his ankle resting on his knee, a jumble of old sticks tossed into the filthy armchair.

'What?'

'When we talked earlier, you said that . . .' My mouth ran dry. I had to gulp my coffee to carry on. The hand that lifted the cup was trembling. 'You said that, um . . . that Chloe Lutz was out here and she . . . she . . .'

'Would you spit out what you're trying to fucking say, Evan?' Dad snapped, taking up his drink.

'You said she should have left the past in the past.'

Dad swallowed, twitched, squinted. 'No, I didn't.'

'Yes, you did.'

'Evan—'

'You did, Dad, you said that. You said, "She should have stayed in Sydney and left the past in the past."'

'Okay? So?' He waggled his head, eyes bulging. 'What the hell are you trying to ask me? You sound like you're the one who's been drinking.'

'I want to know how you knew that's what she was doing out here,' I said. 'Even if you'd heard from local gossip that Chloe was a writer, she could have been out here writing about anything. About the town, or the pub, or . . . or someone local. But you said she was out here digging up the past. How did you know that's what she was doing?'

My father stared at me with his cold, black, hollow eyes. A silent moment passed, in which the air seemed to ring. He looked beyond me, into the wall behind me. Into whatever dark imaginings he had locked up in his evil brain. Then my father sat his drink down on the table again, put both his feet on the floor and gave a little smile.

'All right,' he said. 'I guess it's time.'

RUSSELL

My phone pinging beside me on the bed woke me at 6 a.m. The annoyance at myself, that I'd slept right through the timer I'd set, was quickly consumed by the wave of exhilaration I felt at the sight of the email that was waiting on the screen. I got up and went into the kitchen, sat down carefully at the nook under those deadly cabinets, and pushed open my laptop. I picked up the email, followed the link it contained, and typed in a password. In seconds I was looking down a list of phone calls made by Chloe Lutz in the days before she was murdered.

'Here we go,' I murmured, energy sizzling in my aching fingertips as I scrolled past the numbers themselves to the various accounts they belonged to. The providers were all familiar. Telstra. Vodafone. Optus. Dodo. I shifted the page over and came upon a list of names. Lutz, Jillian. Lutz, Lawrence. Pillner, Cameron. Smith, Warren. Brackett, Saskia.

I opened a new window to begin searching the people listed, who they were, their connection to Chloe. Before I could, I spotted a name that made me freeze in my seat.

Special, John.

The world seemed to hold its breath, a moment of stillness pregnant with possibility. I could almost feel the game board shifting underneath me. New pathways opening up. Understandings that I couldn't grasp yet, waiting on the horizon. I hovered my mouse over the name, highlighted it. Special.

Weird name, like mine. Name that I had noticed before. I went to Google, dropped down my history list and picked up a website I'd accessed less than twenty-four hours earlier.

Lone women to lock doors: killer house-caller still at large.

I scrolled down the article. Found the name.

> *. . . have frightened locals of Redbelly Crossing and surrounds. Police are yet to confirm whether they suspect Marian's murder might have been committed by the same perpetrator who killed Wrights Creek Road mother Linda Special in July last year. Ms Special's husband John was away on . . .*

I tapped and clicked. Fished around. Glanced quickly at articles, at accounts, at Chloe Lutz's phone records and her emails. Another of the names in the sent folder made me do a double take. But not for long. I got just enough to confirm what I was seeing, get a picture of it all, and nothing more. I was too excited to go deep yet. A rope of exhilaration was trying to pull me out of my seat.

'Bridie?' I called. I stood up too fast, finally banged my head on those fucking cabinets. I went up the stairs onto the back deck, wincing and rubbing my skull and looking for my kid. I found her on the little wooden platform at the bottom of the steps to the stern, a pontoon in the grassy sea. When I called her again she shushed me hard, waving me down with an impatient hand.

I crept to where the girl was crouched, barefoot, her hands gripping the knees of her pyjamas. She put a finger to her lips as I squatted beside her, then pointed to a sizeable gap in the old, battered wooden planks beneath her feet. I steadied myself with a palm against the wood and looked down into the dark. Below, on the bare and dusty earth, a thick, midnight-black body was slowly slithering. I recognised the red-bellied black snake's glossy scales immediately, the almost neon purple sheen that came off them as the morning sun slipped through the cracks in the wood and hit the reptile's gently gliding form. The snake was working its way towards the river.

Bridie and I watched it go, until it eased itself peacefully into the long grass at the edge of the platform and disappeared.

'Whoa,' I said.

'Yeah, whoa,' she agreed.

'Birds,' I said. 'I've got something to tell you.'

'Mmm?'

'Chloe Lutz was out here looking for a serial killer,' I said. My daughter, still crouched as I was, stared at me. 'Four days ago she called one of the husbands of the murdered women. John Special. She'd already emailed him maybe two weeks before that to inquire about the cold case. They were due to meet for an interview yesterday. The morning after Chloe was killed.'

'Whoooaaa,' Bridie said.

'Yeah.' I nodded. 'You were right. I shouldn't have doubted you.'

We didn't say anything for a while, either of us. We just watched the river throwing hard white reflections at us. All that morning sparkle, and the long grass, and the fall of the land hid the deadly creature we'd just seen heading that way. The snake was down there now, I knew, at the water's edge, silently winding between the reeds, hunting its first meal of the day.

'Do you think he's still here?' Bridie asked me. 'The killer? Do you think Chloe found him?'

'I think he found her,' I said.

EVAN

'I'm just going to come right out and say it all,' Dad said. He swept his hand over the room, the filthy furnishings and carpet. 'Because the time had to come eventually. I figured if someone hadn't seen me, then there was going to be DNA. And if there wasn't DNA, well, there was going to be the email. The one she sent to me. If it had to happen sometime, it's better now rather than later, so you can do what you have to do.'

'Dad, what are you talking about?'

'I killed the girl. Chloe Lutz.'

All the breath left me at once. The box of photographs on my knees slid onto the floor. I was left holding the picture of my father from 1976, the Ford Capri in the background, a slightly blurry but unmistakable shape. I had to suck air through a closed throat and blow it out as hard as I could to make a sound at all.

'*What?*'

'Now, don't do that,' Arthur said, exhausted with my bullshit already, his eyes languid as they lifted to me. He held up a finger and shook his head. 'Don't sit there saying *what-what-what?* the whole time. I just want to get it out as painlessly as I can. So, you're going to have to shut up and pay attention and get all the details squared away into that meat-filled head of yours, and not get me off track by being all melodramatic about it.'

'You . . . You . . .' I managed.

'She was out here looking into some indiscretions of my past,' Dad said. 'Chloe. She was initially just interested in the two cold cases. Linda Special and Marian Richley. But then she decides to get clever, and in doing that, the silly nosy parker went and joined a couple of dots that no one in the whole Hawkesbury region had ever been smart enough to join before.'

I stared at my father.

'The first I heard about it was through Herman,' he said, taking his cigarettes out of the chest pocket of his flannelette shirt. He lit one up. 'Herman Grey. Old colleague of mine. For the past—oh, god—*fifty years*, I've kept my finger on the pulse of Herman and all the other Wisemans Ferry cops, the ones who worked on the cases back in the day. I go down there, to the RSL, about every six months, and I let it come up naturally. The old cases. The unsolved ones. Because someone's always still bothered by that sort of thing, you know. Mistakes they made during cases. I know I am. I always wait until someone asks the question, or I ask it myself: whether anybody's heard anything. Three months ago, Herman says to me, *Shit, you know what, Artie? There has actually been something. This young girl from Sydney, she emailed me. Wants to know about Special and Richley.* He showed me the email on his phone. Sure enough, there it is. This girl Chloe Lutz wants to come out and interview him. She's got this big grand theory that the same perpetrator of Linda and Marian's killings might have been the rapist who attacked that girl out at Womerah. While there are basically no clues about the Special and Richley killings, there *is* a good clue about the rape. Herman was all set to speak to Chloe. He was a show pony, Herman. Chucked a heart attack before he got the chance. That was maybe two months ago.'

'Wait . . .' I said. Every muscle in my body was rock hard and trembling. 'Who . . . Who were they? Special and Richley?'

My father smoked his cigarette. Took his time.

'Women from out here.' He shrugged eventually.

'And you,' I swallowed. 'You . . . Chloe was looking at mistakes that you had made during those cases? That's what you said. You made mistakes.'

'I sure did.' Dad snorted.

'What did you do?'

My father looked at me.

'I committed them, Evan.'

My mouth was already hanging open. Now a shuddering groan came out of it. Dad just watched me with a disgusted sort of expression on his face, the way he used to watch me when I'd cry as a child.

'You killed those two women? You . . . you . . .' I shook my head. 'No you didn't. That's not what you're saying.'

'Yes, it is.'

'But—'

'I came upon her for the first time riding along with Herman, actually.'

'Who?'

'Linda,' he said. 'Linda Special. She was an accident.'

I couldn't speak.

'I'd dropped over there to the station at Wisemans from my station at Maroota.' It was all just falling out of his mouth now. The door busted down. 'My boss had lent me. Just for the day. The Wisemans Ferry boys needed help clearing out their basement. Evidence stockpile. At lunch time, Herman said, "Why don't we go for a drive?" because he had to see some woman at Redbelly Crossing, and they had nice food at the pub back then.'

I listened, barely breathing.

'Linda was at home alone for a month because hubby had taken a job at an oil rig,' Dad said. 'The idea was that he'd make enough money to come back and pay the house off entirely. With the new baby, they needed the financial footing. But she was scared, being home alone like that every night. It was a remote property. Well out of town. Bushy. And she was young. She was twenty-five, I think.'

I tried to keep up. To accept what I was hearing.

'She'd called the cops because her chickens were disappearing, and she had the idea that a prowler or a neighbour was stealing them,' Dad continued. 'She was a fool. There was a hole in the coop as round as your head. Fox tracks in the dirt. She might have just wanted a cop to put an eye on the place and maybe fix the hole in the coop without her having to pay for it.'

'And you did? You and Grey?'

'We fixed the hole and we gave her home security advice.' Dad waved his cigarette. 'Get a lock on that window there. Put curtains over this bit so no one can see in. Cut down some dowels, put them in the window tracks. I left a hole for myself for later, through the laundry window. In case she didn't accept what I told her at the door to and let me inside. I told her the window was too small to worry about.'

I waited, shivering, telling myself not to throw up. It didn't work. Before my father could start speaking again, I went into the bathroom off the spare room, crouched and vomited into the toilet.

'Jesus.' He shook his head when I returned and fell into my spot on the couch. 'The dramatics.'

'You knew that you were going to come back and . . . and . . . kill her?' I asked.

'You're not real bright, are you, Evan?' Arthur snapped. The fury was always right there, just below the surface. 'I told you it was an accident, what happened to her.'

'But you knew you were going to come back, though. You said it yourself, just now: you left a hole for yourself so you could come back later. Because you knew you would. You were determined to get in whether she let you in or not.'

'Things would have been a lot different if she'd played along. That's all I'm saying.'

'Played along with what?' I asked.

My father just stared at me.

'Oh my god, Dad.' I put my face in my hands. The sobs came, hard and painful: deep ones that ratcheted through my chest, seemed to hammer against the inside of my ribcage. '*Oh my god, Dad. Oh my god.*'

'Oh my god *what*, Evan, you hysterical waste of space?'

'What *are* you?' I dropped my hands. 'Are you . . . Are you . . . Are you a *rapist, Dad*? Is that what you're saying to me? You're a *cold-blooded killer*?'

'It would be just like you to think of me that way.' Arthur nodded, smiling. He looked me over, head to foot. 'You always saw the worst in me.'

I almost laughed. I was so sick, so sad, so unsure if I wanted to go and vomit again or just sit here crying. Arthur went on, 'You have no idea how you got where you are in your life, do you, Evan? You think everything you have was just—just—*bestowed* upon you by god. You think the house, the wife, the son, the career, all these things just came to you out of thin air.'

Arthur waved his cigarette around, his hands raised to the ceiling. Smoke made a coil, whispered away.

'I raised you to be who you are,' Dad sneered. 'I made you *hard*. Me. Nobody else. Your mother bailed out on us all. Her parents left us with nothing. You and Russell, you were like boulders chained to my legs. And what credit do I get for it all? *Everything you have in your life is because of me, Evan.*'

I just shook my head.

'I'm sitting here telling you my deepest, darkest secrets.' He tapped his chest. 'Terrible mistakes that I have made. And your response is to call me the worst of all possible names.'

'Dad—'

'I'm a good man who made a couple of errors of judgement. I'm a *good man*, who raised his sons well. But you forget all that. You learn this one thing about me, and you've just decided I'm a monster.' Arthur tutted hard. 'How long did it take you, just then, to decide it? That I'm unredeemable. Three seconds. You didn't even take a minute to think about it.'

'Did you rape that girl in Womerah?'

'Yes.'

'And Marian Richley?' I gagged. Swallowed. Put a hand to my mouth. Had to speak through it. 'Was she the same?'

'She was a pub girl from Wisemans Ferry. We all used to drink there. I followed her home one night, watched her for a while. Came back a couple of weeks later.'

'Dad.' I heard my own voice. The voice of a child. '*Dad*.'

'The ingratitude that you are showing me right now is staggering, Evan. It really is.'

'No amount of gratitude is going to rub this out.' I broke through my tenuous calm. My voice came up, high and, yes, hysterical. 'Three women are dead! They're dead! *They're dead!*'

The old man nodded. 'Yep.'

'Oh my god.'

'They're dead, and you're going to fix it all for me, Evan.'

'*What?*'

'That's why I brought Chrissy along this time,' Dad said. 'As a failsafe. Because I knew this was all going to come out. As soon as I saw that first email from Lutz, I knew. The clock was ticking. Eventually, no matter how carefully I did it, I was going to need you to pay me back and help me through this. I'm an old man, and times have changed. I knew I wouldn't get it exactly right.'

'You . . .' I breathed. 'You took Chris along?'

'I needed to have someone there to throw to the dogs if it came down to it.'

RUSSELL

Dodge was standing in the steep driveway outside his house, at the open driver's door of his Hilux. He was simultaneously trying to manhandle his phone into his pocket, stop the door closing on him and keep himself upright with a shoulder bag on one arm and an aluminium crutch braced under the other. I pulled up at the roadside and watched for a half a minute, thinking about the time I sat in my patrol car watching a nodding meth addict trying to cut through a bike chain with a pair of barbecue tongs once in broad daylight on King Street in Newtown. Then I got out and walked up. Dodge froze like a boy caught with his hand in his dad's porn stash. I took the bag off his shoulder and shut the driver's door, dealing with two of his problems for him before I'd said a single word. I nodded towards my car. 'I'll drive.'

'I'm not sure I'm supposed to be working.' Dodge turned to me. 'But I'm pretty damn *certain* you're not.'

'Yeah, well, too bad. I want to tell you some things about what Chloe Lutz was working on.'

He started down towards my car, hobbling on that aluminium crutch. A woman who I assumed from her age and nosiness must have been the mother-in-law came out of the front door of the house. I was caught not wanting to walk off on her without saying anything, but not having Dodge there to introduce me. She frowned at me, a little shrivelled person with one of those light bulb–shaped haircuts you can only get at country hair salons, the ones they refuse to give you until you can prove you're over eighty. I nodded a polite hello and she folded her arms and glared up at me.

'Get him back in one piece this time, will you?' she said.

'I will,' I promised, noting silently that I hadn't even said who I was, nor claimed responsibility for the state of her son-in-law.

'We need him here.'

'I'm not surprised by that.' I gave my warmest smile. 'He's a good man. Everyone could do with a Louis Dodge in their life.'

Her eyes narrowed even further at me. 'Not you, though. He's a happily married man, and he's staying that way.'

The little woman went back inside the house. Once I'd picked my jaw up off the floor, I walked down to the car and wished with all my soul that Bridie had been with me for the past fifteen seconds of my life to witness my hypothesis about old women and their gaydars proven.

'I would have thought you'd gone back to Sydney with the kid.' Dodge groaned as he sunk awkwardly into the seat next to me in the Mustang, hauling the injured leg up and in with him.

'I'm about as enthused about running out on this case as you obviously are,' I said. I waved at his trouser leg. 'Show us the damage.'

He pulled up the end of his trousers on the left-hand side. The whole leg was an angry blue and swollen from the knee down, the calf cut through with tightly wrapped bandages where the bear trap had sunk its teeth into the limb. 'The leg's okay. I'm supposed to stay off it, but I don't know if I believe in that. I think it should have movement and blood flow, don't you?'

'No idea.'

'The real annoying thing was all the needles. The bear trap was rusty, so the doctor shot me for everything from tetanus to diphtheria. In the arm I sleep on, of course.'

'Diphtheria?'

'She just emptied her entire arsenal like she was trying to get rid of old stock.' He took the coffee I'd made for him at the houseboat with caution, sipped it like he assumed it was filled with arsenic.

'Listen,' I said. 'Chloe's accounts have come in. There's news.'

I pulled out onto the road and explained what I'd found on Chloe's hard drive. When I pointed, he took up my laptop from the back seat and started fishing around himself where I directed him to, looking at the emails I'd flagged and the calls I'd highlighted. I drove impatiently, glancing over for a reaction. His mouth hardened and he shook his head. 'Awful cases. Special and Richley. The juvenile, too. I know her name from the files but it's escaping me now.'

'Did you know about those cases?'

'Oh, I mean, I looked,' he said. 'Just out of pure curiosity. I grew up past Womerah, so the story of the rape was a thing we all knew about. It seems Chloe thought that might have been connected to these two murders.'

'I can see how cops at the time might not have connected the two,' I said, slowing as I approached a kangaroo and her joey eating grass at the side of the road. We passed without them leaping out. 'Linda and Marian were in their twenties. They were at home alone at night. The coppers were thinking he's come and knocked on the door and talked his way into the houses.'

'Why did they think that?' Dodge clicked around the screen, squinting.

'There was a smashed cup on the floor at Linda's place. Phone off the hook in Marian's kitchen. The thinking was he's knocked and asked for a glass of water. Or to use the phone. They've let him in and he's attacked them. There was no forced entry, and police found every door and window in both houses was shut and locked except for the front one.'

'This article is saying the girl, the minor, was attacked in her bed after she went to sleep.' Dodge's head was down, his nose inches from the screen. 'That's a different MO entirely.'

'Probably why nobody bothered to connect it.'

'Why did Chloe connect it?'

I shook my head. 'I haven't been through all the emails. And there's no notebook. But maybe she was just . . . I don't know. She was winging it. Thinking creatively. Wanting to have some red herrings for her podcast.'

'She was going to do a podcast?'

'There's an email there to a guy named Herman Grey.' I pointed vaguely, my eyes on the road. 'Early on. One of the first emails in her account that mentions the case.'

'Oh, yep. I see it.'

'Grey was an old copper from Wisemans. In the email she says she's thinking about doing a podcast.'

Dodge read. I drove. The valley hugged us as we crossed the bridge and wound up through Redbelly. There were press vans parked by the river. I caught a glimpse of Gail Caplan at the marquee in the pub beer garden. Fry and Knowles in plain clothes, listening to Caplan talk. She had her hands on her hips, and they had the relaxed shoulders and unfurrowed brows of guys who had been stood down from duty.

'Uhhhhh . . .' Dodge scratched his temple.

'What?'

'There's an "Arthur Powder" here.'

'Yeah,' I said. 'I saw. That's my father.'

'What'd she want to talk to him for?'

'She's emailed all the old coppers from the whole region,' I said. 'A copy-and-paste email explaining briefly what she was interested in and asking if they wanted to talk. When one didn't answer, she moved on to the next.'

'He didn't answer.'

'I'm surprised he even has an email address. Or that she found it. She was going to be a good journalist, Chloe Lutz.'

'Should we go speak to him? Your dad? Is he still out here?'

'I want to go to my father's place about as much as I want a battery acid poured on my testicles, Dodge,' I said. 'I'm taking us out to speak to John Special.'

'So you're not on friendly terms with your father?'

'No.'

'Why's that?'

'Because I'm gay and he's not okay with that,' I said. Silence in response. I looked over. Dodge had his eyes locked on my face, quickly snapped his gaze forward to the road. 'That's not the only reason,' I went on. 'It's just the most recent one.'

'I'm sorry . . . You said *you're* gay? Or *he's* gay?'

'*I'm* gay.'

Dodge started to blow out a disbelieving laugh, but swallowed it halfway through. What came out was a kind of breathy croak. 'I would not have picked that!'

'Good.' I nodded. Dodge was blinking hard. He rubbed his face with both hands like he was trying to wake himself up.

'That's what it was, the whole time,' he said. 'That's what you've been so fucking . . . guarded and angry about.'

'I suppose.'

'From the way you've been carrying on, I was sure you'd killed someone.'

'I did,' I said. And he probably thought I meant someone on the job. Or Stephen Branch, the night before. But what I meant was the thousands upon thousands of killings I had to perform whenever I let someone find out who I really was. I'd murdered the man Georgia thought of as her husband. The one Bridie thought was her dad. As we drove, Dodge and I were getting further and further away from the Detective Inspector Russell Powder he'd thought he had a handle on mere moments before, leaving him expiring by the roadside like a hit bird. Now he had to come to terms with this new guy he had sitting beside him and decide whether he accepted him or not.

'Okay, well, fair enough.' Dodge shook the whole episode off, literally shifting in his seat and throwing back his shoulders. 'We can work with that.'

EVAN

My lips peeled apart as though they'd been glued. I rasped the words. 'Chris didn't . . . He didn't . . .'

'Of course he didn't,' Dad rolled his eyes. 'He didn't know anything about it.'

I gripped the arm of the couch I was sitting in.

'The kid nearly dropped dead from terror when I killed a couple of *chickens* in front of him.' Dad shook his head. 'I bet you have to get him six weeks of therapy just to have a nugget in that house.'

'What did you do, Dad?'

'Well, first off I got Steve Venables over to show him that car I told you about,' he said. 'So I'd have an alibi. Venables lives up the road here. By mid-afternoon every day he's staggeringly drunk, so I called him, told him to come round. He won't remember what time he came or how long he stayed for, so he'll go along with what I tell him about the timing. Then I asked Chris down to the pub for a birthday drink,' Arthur said. 'We stood out the front, near the river. He went in both times. He had a fake ID in case they carded him. You know he had that? He showed me. Pretty convincing.'

My throat was burning. The coffee was gone, through my stomach and back out again, into the toilet. I could feel it at the back of my nose, stinging. 'When did you . . .'

'After he left,' Dad said. 'I hung around out there and watched her go up. Made sure I had the room right. You can see the lights from the front. The skylights. I was hoping to get it done some time close to Chris having been there, because I didn't know where he was going afterwards. I didn't want him popping up somewhere else and giving himself an alibi. There was one guest up there. A guy. He left, and Chloe went up, and then Chris left, and I just watched and waited for the right time.'

He puffed on his cigarette. Trails of smoke eased from his nostrils.

'That's half of it,' he said. 'The waiting.'

'Half of what?'

Dad shrugged. I felt more ill than I ever had in my life. Because I knew. I could see it on his face. The waiting was half the pleasure.

'What did you tell her at the door?'

'Oh, I just played the confused old man.' Dad stubbed his cigarette out on the arm of the couch, brushed the embers away. There was a great hole where he'd been doing that for years, blackened foam. '*Deary, I'm looking for my room. Is this number three or number four? Oh, fiddlesticks, I've dropped my card.*'

'That's what you did with Linda and Marian.' I shivered. 'You gave them a story at the door.'

'That was part of it, too,' he said. 'Whether I could get them to let me in or not. Linda recognised me from the week before. I said there'd been an accident down the road a bit, and I needed to call my station. I remember running up to the house so I'd look breathless when I got there. She got me water. Marian . . . Oh, I don't remember. It was years ago. I told her something. Probably the same thing. There was a problem and I needed to use the phone.'

I held my face. Shook my head, made myself dizzy. 'I can't clean this up. You're asking me to . . . to . . . I mean, you murdered them, Dad. If what you're saying is true, you . . .'

He was silent. I was suddenly so afraid to look at him. I stared at my hands.

'You were so sure,' I said.

'Excuse me?'

'Of the game. You were so sure of how you'd do it. How it would work. What you wanted.'

'Don't get into that. Don't make—'

'Were there others?'

'—your own life harder than it needs to be right now, Evan.'

'But this wasn't the first time, was it? With Linda. The killing you've described. It was so . . . escalated. So advanced. People like you, they don't go from zero to ten like this. There must be—'

'The coppers,' Dad cut over me. His eyes, when I braved to look at them, were full of warning. 'They'll have Chris coming into town, Evan. They'll have him on the CCTV at the pub. And they'll have the text message, on my phone *and* his, telling him to come down and meet me. You need to make sure this doesn't become a problem for me, my son. Because if this becomes a problem for me, I'll tell them that I did indeed meet my grandson at the pub at Redbelly that night. That he was talking aggressively about a girl who was inside. That he's a fucked-up little weirdo who has threatened violence before, and that I left because I was starting to feel uncomfortable. I'll say that the last time I saw him, he was heading towards the stairwell.'

'*Your* DNA is on her!' I had to growl the words through the rage that was suddenly so hot and all-consuming it made my teeth lock together. 'They have *your DNA*!'

'Do they?' he asked brightly. Gave an amused snort. 'You know, I asked you to come onto this because I wanted it bungled. But you and your brother have really cut to the chase with the whole thing. I'm actually impressed.'

'I thought the sample was Chrissy's,' I managed. 'It's a familial match to me and Rus. They'll test it further. It'll come back as you. What the hell am I supposed to do about that?'

'I can explain away my DNA transferring from me to Chris, and from Chris onto the dead girl.' Dad waved a dismissive hand. 'I'll have a hell of a lot of an easier time making a jury believe that story than you will making them believe an old, chronically injured hero cop killed that feisty young woman in that room.'

'You're not chronically injured,' I said. 'You can't be. The strength it would have taken—'

'I've been playing up the injury since it happened.' He rotated his shoulder. 'I'm fine.'

I thought about that case. The wife who went missing. The back door of the house open, and the potatoes cooking on the stove. The husband accused. My father shooting him before he could ever be officially pinned down for the crime. I wanted to ask if it had been him. Dad. If he'd killed that woman, too. My thoughts turned to my mother. Dead, slumped, in the back shed, waiting for my brother to come home and find her. I got up and went to the windows. Gripped my hair in two handfuls, tried to make the pain take me away from this moment. It didn't work. The whole world was closing in around me. 'You're talking about my son, Dad! You're talking about my baby!'

'Evan—'

'I can't clean this all up. I'm . . . I'm behind. I'll never catch up. I'm not smart enough.'

'For fuck's sake, Evan.'

'Don't do this.' I hid my face and cried into my hands. 'Please, please, please. Dad, please. Don't take my baby.'

'I warned you,' came his voice from behind me. 'Didn't I? I warned you, a long time ago. Never love anything. That's the safest way to be in life. You never love anything, and you've got nothing to lose.'

He got up and went into the kitchen. I stood at the windows and looked out into the yard, at the rusting car bodies and the broken-down coop and the distant bush. It was as still as death out there. No sound beyond the drumming and thundering and splintering and crashing between my ears, the orchestra of panic and rage that had been silenced far too long. I almost felt my body giving into it. Letting that inky black thing inside billow out and take over, stretch into my fingertips and the soles of my feet. The thrumming in my skull softened, and what took its place was the noise of the screaming of the kettle in the kitchen. The kettle noise masked the sound of me walking over and picking up the rifle by the armchair.

Dad was at the sink. He turned around, going for the coffee canister, and noticed me standing there. He looked at the rifle in my hands, then at my eyes. A disbelieving smile fluttered at the corners of his mouth. It dropped off his face as I ratcheted a bullet into the chamber.

'Evan?' he said.

I shot him in the chest. The rifle kicked hard into the hollow of my shoulder, hit the bone, which sang with pleasure and rightness. My father gripped at the hole in his sternum, went down onto the linoleum. I came into the kitchen, sliding the bolt forward and back again, the shell casing singing as it flew and hit the top of the fridge. Dad tried to slide away from me, his back on the floor, leaving a trail of blood, his legs working. One hand up. Reaching for his child.

'Oh god! Oh god! Oh god!' he cried.

'There's no god where you're going,' I told him.

Then I shot him in the face.

RUSSELL

John James Special was a slight man, silver-goateed and with rich brown eyes that hid behind those spectacle lenses that go dark when they're hit by sun. They were doing just that, hiding his expression, as Dodge and I pulled up on the gravel driveway of his neat little property fifteen minutes outside Redbelly. John was putting a bowl of biscuits out for a scruffy white dog, which lost its damned mind at the sight of us and scrambled down the stairs to meet the car, a hairy tornado of fury. Cockatoos in the nearby gums also started going bananas. I was beginning to feel like it was personal. John silenced the dog with a single word and it went back to his ankle-side, still unconvinced about us and issuing high-pitched whimpers.

'It's my daughter's dog.' John glanced at the creature. His voice was unusually raspy, like he'd been gargling sawdust all that morning before we got there. 'She's away, so I'm dog-sitting it for her. Mongrel thing hates everyone.'

'Mr Special,' I said, 'we're here about the murder of Chloe Lutz.'

The old man's mouth dropped open, and he turned to Dodge for confirmation.

'What?'

'We understand you were due to meet with her yesterday,' Dodge said. 'About your wife's murder.'

'Yes.' John took a tentative step forward. 'It was my *wife* that was murdered, not—'

'Chloe, too.' I nodded, straining my vision hard to see his eyes behind the darkened lenses. 'She was stabbed to death at the pub down in Redbelly on Friday night. The night before she had arranged to come out here and see you. Are you telling us you've heard nothing about it?'

John's mouth turned downward, hard. He looked all around, finally settling on the dog, which he scooped up into his arms. He went inside, saying nothing, just opening the screen door and going in. Dodge and I followed into the shady, cutely decorated little house. There was art hanging on the walls. Seascapes with rocky cliffs, apartment buildings. They reminded me of Maroubra, my usual jurisdiction. For a moment I had to remind myself where I was. 'Surely you must have heard what happened,' I pressed.

'Nope,' he said with obvious bitterness, putting the dog on a couch and shuffling to the kitchen. 'I saw there was commotion down at the pub, yes. When I got back into town this morning. But I didn't go snooping. I just supposed it was a robbery or something.'

He picked up a tea towel from the edge of the sink, threw it down again. I could see his mouth working, chewing on emotions. 'What bloody well happened to her, then?'

'She was stabbed.'

'What for?'

'We don't know, as yet.'

He shook his head, gazed out the windows at the fields.

'But what did you think when Chloe didn't turn up for her meeting?' Dodge asked. 'Her phone records show you didn't call her to check where she was.'

'Oh, I didn't think too much. I never do.' The old man gave an angry, world weary laugh. He started taking down coffee cups from a row of hooks against the kitchen wall, seeming to want something to do with his hands. 'I've been stood up by journalists plenty of times. They come out here about every five years or so. Someone decides they're going to run a story or make a film or something. Then a more interesting or more recent case comes along and off they go after that. I don't bother chasing them. I've made that mistake. Waste of time. And she sounded young, on the phone. Chloe. I just assumed she got a better offer.'

'So you didn't call,' I confirmed.

'I didn't want to hassle her.' He shrugged. 'I was grateful enough that she'd decided to fiddle around with the case. Nobody on the police side has touched it in a couple of decades. I didn't want to rouse on her the moment she stood me up. I was hoping she'd pop up again in a few days and say—oh, sorry, I got called away. Or something.'

'So, were you here that morning?' I asked. 'Sitting around, expecting her?'

'I was. She was due at nine a.m. At about five o'clock that evening, I went to my daughter's place.' John flicked the switch on a kettle, put his fists either side of the sink and stared out at the tree line. The cockatoos were still screaming. 'I'd been getting ready in my mind, since Chloe contacted me, to talk about Linda again. And everything that happened. When she didn't show up, it was sort of . . . upsetting, I guess. I waited all day. So I went there, slept there that night. She's not far away, my daughter. Monica. She's in Colo.'

'So you didn't have to pass the pub,' Dodge said, almost to himself. 'Wouldn't have seen the crime-scene tape.'

'My daughter, she keeps a spare room for me,' John said. 'It was nice to be there, even if she's not.'

Dodge and I were quiet. Thinking.

'It's hard to explain.' John shrugged again. 'But it's full of life, Monny's house. And I felt like being around some life.'

The old man made coffee, placing a safe bet that as cops we wanted some. Dodge and I threw meaningful glances at each other behind John Special's back about the way he moved. Stiff and considered. Wondering to ourselves whether this could have been the man that pinned Chloe Lutz against a wall and stabbed her to death. I knew from experience that adrenaline did wonders for a person's body, and psychopathic murderers made excellent actors.

'You fellas got a suspect, then?'

'We're looking at several people.'

'Do you think it's him?'

John turned towards us. Dodge and I looked at each other, and I felt a coldness come into me as I remembered my beautiful daughter crouched in the morning light.

Do you think he's still here?

'That's one of the theories we're working with,' I answered.

'You coppers.' John gave a gravelly laugh. 'You all sound the same. Anybody ever tell you that? You've been giving me those lines for fifty years. *We're looking at several people. We're working with several theories.* I sure hope you come up with some new ones, so some bastard related to Chloe isn't sitting around in half a century being fed those same lines.'

I thought about Larry Lutz. 'They won't be,' I said. 'We're getting to the pointy end of things now.'

John's eyebrows jolted a little but his eyes, which I could see through those glasses now, were empty. He put a bowl of sugar and a jug of milk onto a tray and carried the coffees into the living room, set them on a very retro coffee table inlaid with burnt-orange tiles. The dog went mental again as we entered and John gave an exasperated sigh. 'It's the same two blokes, for chrissake!'

We sat down. John Special seemed to know the drill. He began taking us through the hellish time of his wife's murder, more than fifty years earlier, a collection of memories as sickeningly vivid in parts as they were vague in others, blurred by time and trauma. Dodge and I listened to him speak of the first moment, while overseeing a crew of men doing safety checks on the railing system of an oil rig off the coast of Newcastle, when an announcement over the PA system told him to report to administration.

'That's the first time I got any inkling that anything was wrong,' John said. 'People say, you know, that sometimes you can feel it in your guts. Something's happened. But I didn't. Not until they called me in. Then it just came over me like a . . . A fever, almost. This sense that I had to get home. Nobody wanted to be the one to tell me why I needed to get back right away. And I wasn't asking, either. It was like I was being pulled home on a string.'

'Who actually found Linda?'

'The postman,' John said. 'She was friendly, Linda. Talked to everyone. Liked to take people on as a pet project sometimes. I think she felt sorry for them. This postman had just been widowed, so she was encouraging him to get back on his feet. He'd got into the habit of coming up to the house to deliver the mail so they could have a chit-chat. He heard Monny screaming inside, and was knocking and getting no response from Linda, so he went in.'

'And he found her deceased?' Dodge asked carefully. 'No signs of life?'

'He told police he didn't try CPR.' John nodded. 'She was that cold. And her eyes . . . he could tell there was no bringing her back.'

Dodge and I fell silent. John sipped his coffee, took a few long breaths. The scruffy white dog glared at me from the end of the couch as though it was imagining what my jugular tasted like.

'By the time I got home, it was chaos here.' John glanced towards the front windows of the house. 'The cars went right down the driveway and around as far as the neighbour's property. Her parents were here. The coppers were here. The journos. There were people who went to high school with her just standing around on the lawn, crying.'

'I assume the postman was looked at pretty hard,' I said.

'Every man and his dog got a proper look, except for me, because my alibi was the best you could come by,' John said. 'That was the only good part of it: that the cops didn't put me on the rack. Because times were different then, and sometimes they did that. Roughed people up. They held the postman—Thompson, was his name, Hugh Thompson—for about two days, I think. Not under official arrest, just being questioned. I saw him later and he had that look like someone had ground him into the dirt like a cigarette butt.'

'So there were no witnesses that night?' I asked. 'Nobody drove past, saw a car? Heard a scream?'

'Nobody heard anything.' John shrugged. 'The neighbours at the back, they're not far away. But they told police that the cockies were going off that night, like they are now.' He pointed towards the back of the house where the birds were still going nuts. 'You wouldn't have heard anything anyway, over that racket.'

'Do they do that a lot?'

'No. Not really,' he mused. 'Especially not at night. They'll make a racket if there's an owl around. We get big ole owls here.'

'Aside from the postman, there were no other major suspects?' Dodge asked.

'Oh, well, after telling me they were "working with several theories" and "looking at several people" for a few months, the cops were quoted in the local newspaper saying they had no leads,' John said. 'And then they were dead silent, at least until Marian Richley, up the road here, almost a year later. They told me flat-out it was the same guy. Because of the way he operated. No forced entry. Made them shower afterwards.'

'He made them shower afterwards?' I looked at Dodge.

'Yuh. So there was never any DNA. They stook stuff. Ran tests at the time for fibres and hairs. This was before DNA. And then when DNA came in, in the eighties, they tested it for that. But they didn't find anything.' John licked his teeth, thumbed the corner of his eye. A phone trilled gently somewhere. 'Let me just get that.'

The old man got up with difficulty and shuffled out. I scratched at the arm of the sofa where I sat, thoughtfully picking at the corduroy. 'Mid-seventies. A bit early for civilians to be thinking about getting rid of trace evidence.'

'If it's the same guy who got the teenager while she was sleeping, we're looking at someone who was smart enough to think not only about trace evidence.' Dodge nodded. 'But also about mixing up his MO to hide his crimes.'

'Mmm. Because why were there only two murders?' I said. 'Why did he stop?'

'Maybe there are others, but they don't look like this. The MO is different.'

'With Chloe he's right back to his original style,' I said. 'Knock at the front door. The knife.'

John came back. Tried to sip his coffee. Found it was empty and set it back down. 'Marian's people moved away, afterwards. Went to Queensland. It was only her parents anyway, and I heard they died promptly after. It puts a good dent in your life expectancy, burying a child. Especially if it's your only one.'

'Why did you stay here?' I asked. I suddenly felt the shape of the house around me. Imagined it dark. The cockatoos had finally quietened, and I could hear cicadas out there in the trees now, and the ticking of the aluminium roof above us.

'Ah, well, it was a financial decision, in the beginning.' John rapped his knuckles against the empty coffee cup. 'I would have had to sell the house at a cut price, because of what had happened in it. And I had to be home to take care of Monny, so the oil rigging work was over with. Then, after a while, I thought: Fuck you.'

I felt a small smile come to my face. Couldn't help it.

'Whoever did this?' John shrugged. 'Fuck you. You're not going to take our house from us too. Linda loved this house. The breeze that comes through it, and the big gum trees out the back. She used to sit out there and look at the sunset on the mountain range. I still do that, and when I do, I feel close to her. If I'd sold the house, all I'd have is a grave somewhere.'

Dodge and I listened.

'He took her,' John said. 'I wasn't going to give him a single other thing.'

I took my phone out of my pocket and stood. 'I just want to make a short phone call.'

Dodge and John continued talking. Their voices lowered to a soft rumble as I made my way back into the hall, up and through the kitchen, passing the spot where I assumed Linda Special's body had been found, judging by descriptions in the newspaper articles I'd read. The floorboards creaked as I stepped through the spot, the very centre of the house, it seemed. The heart. I told myself not to step over the place where she had lain. But I did, anyway, taking a long stride, not sure exactly why the impulse presented itself. Respect, maybe. Superstition. Fear. I went out the back, where there was a little sitting area, the one John had said his wife used to sit in to watch the sunset. I dialled my brother.

EVAN

I went to the verandah, shouldered the screen door open, stood there listening. I was waiting for the approach of Martin Rodger, the neighbour to the east, upon hearing the gunshots. 'Uncle' Rodger, as Arthur had bitterly dubbed him, had been storming over from the direction of his similarly hoarded and unkempt property intermittently since Russell and I were kids, reacting to gunshots, the smell of smoke, loud music or the animalistic whooping of teen boys in the wild strip of forest that separated the two slabs of land. I counted off five minutes, hearing only the sound of distant ride-on mowers, bugs buzzing, dogs barking. Country sounds. Then I went back inside. One of my father's feet was rhythmically twitching, like he was revving an engine in his sleep. Blood was pooling everywhere, black and inky, following the patterns in the linoleum.

I was emotionless. Hard, cold, moving from one action to the next. I went to the bedroom, tugged the comforter from the bed and brought it into the kitchen. The foot-twitching stopped. I rolled the old man onto the comforter, wasn't shocked by the soft, breathy groan that came as air moved around in my dead father's lungs. I tucked the top and bottom of the comforter into the bundle, rolled the man twice more, and then hefted him onto my shoulder.

I took him down through the long, wet grass to the third shed along a winding row of leaning aluminium structures filled with rusting trash. I heaved the bundle onto the ground, pulled up the door and went in, opening the front passenger side of Dad's current main car, a Ford Falcon sedan. In the footwell, I spied what must have been Chloe Lutz's laptop and phone, quiet, still, the batteries removed and lying on the mat beside them. I didn't even move them. I ratcheted back the front passenger seat, loaded the bundled comforter with its swaddled body into position and shut the door.

My breath was coming in short, dry huffs, like I was jogging back to the house, not walking. Working my way through the miles and miles it took to murder a person, a marathon. I was staying focused, talking myself out of the impulse to stop, to give in to the exhaustion. A big, cheerful yellow sun was rising above the eucalypts. Lorikeets tinkling. I went to the house, walked around the blood pool that was left where Arthur had died and into the laundry off the kitchen. I started gathering supplies.

It took a good half an hour to clean up the blood on the linoleum. A garbage bag full of rags, towels, paper towel, sponges. There was blood spray on the kitchen window over the sink. On the cabinets. In their handles and hinges. When I was done cleaning, I went into Dad's bedroom, changed into a set of his clothes, and took an old duffel bag from the shelf, dropping my sopping and bloodied and gunpowder-dusted clothes into it. I zipped up the bag, tucked it under my arm. Taking the garbage bag with the used cleaning supplies and my bloodied clothes in the bag, I went out and walked it back to the car where Dad lay waiting for me.

* * *

Driving beside my father, I gripped the wheel, stared ahead, told myself that the bundle slumped beside me contained bones and flesh and blood and nothing else. Arthur was gone. He was *gone.* I tried to believe it. But the hope always came side by side with the terror of disappointment. They were siblings, those two.

My phone rang in my pocket. I slid it out and answered it, my eyes locked on the road ahead.

'Where are you?' Russell asked. No hello. Nothing.

'Dad's.'

'Good,' he said. 'You're already halfway to Sydney. I have two jobs for you, and one involves going back to Pemulwuy. To evidence holding, this time.'

As I drove my murdered father towards the nearby river, my brother explained what had been found in Chloe Lutz's phone and email accounts. Linda Special, Marian Richley, and the unnamed teenager from Womerah. 'She might have been on the edge of something enormous here,' Russell said. I could hear the excitement in his voice. 'She might have been about to solve a case that's been around twice as long as she was even alive.'

'Maybe,' was all I could say. My jaw was chattering and my fingers were tingling on the steering wheel. Shock finally kicking in.

'I want to keep my feet on the ground about this,' Russell said. 'Not get carried off with the fairies too quickly. Because it's a very long shot. The guy would have to be in his seventies at least.'

I looked over at the bundle beside me.

'So, I'm not dropping the angle with the lanky kid with the cap,' Russell said. 'I want you to get Fry to send you the image from the CCTV, and I want you to organise a region-wide SMS blast. Tell him to get it to the local press. The ones coming into town.'

I managed to breathe the word 'Okay'.

'At Pemulwuy,' he went on, 'get them to tell you what they have in evidence holding for Linda and Marian's cases. Linda's husband says there was never any DNA. But they can run everything again. The technology is better now. We might get something. And if we can link Linda and Marian's guy to Chloe's killer . . .'

Russell trailed off. I held a hand against my mouth so I wouldn't gag.

'Anyway, go do that,' he said. 'Now. Stop rubbing your father's tootsies for him and get back to work, and while you're leaving, tell him I said to do the world a favour and go fuck off and die.'

'He might be about to do just that,' I said.

'What?'

'He's got cancer.' I cleared my throat, adjusted my grip on the wheel. 'Dad. He's got lung cancer. He's packing right now to go up north for a while. Hasn't said exactly where.'

'Oh, Evan,' Russell said, 'I wish you'd saved this news for me for later on today. It's too early to get stuck into the champagne.'

I didn't answer. Russell drew a breath and let it out, long and slow and loud, a huge sigh that crackled the line.

'This'll be great,' Russell said. 'It'll be like The Time He Went, only better.'

I remembered. The time our father disappeared on us for six months, a period known as 'The Time He Went' in Powder Brother lore. Russell had been sitting his HSC, and I had been struggling with a minor weed addiction and a particularly bad bout of teenage acne. We'd woken up to find the old man and his Ford Fairmont gone from the driveway, which wasn't unusual. Dad ran his own schedule. Was sometimes there, sometimes gone. But he hadn't been back when we returned from school. And he wasn't there in the morning. The relief turned to excitement, barely contained. The teenage Russell and me had felt it was safe enough to relax a bit in the third week, to truly celebrate in the fourth. Dad had taken off for a couple of weeks or a month at a time before without explanation, so we figured we'd better start enjoying ourselves, quick, before he popped up again. We'd gone fishing all that weekend, had a big fry-up, stayed up late watching TV, got into the liquor cabinet. We'd carried the guns out into the bush to take pot shots at tin cans. We'd lit fires, talked freely without looking over our shoulder, called people on the house phone, gone visiting with girls. We'd cleaned the house from top to bottom, mowed the lawn, lounged on the verandah steps with beers on our knees and sweat on our necks and watched the bats flying over. Russell took the books he kept hidden under his bed out and started reading them in the living areas of the house and leaving them lying around. I'd started playing music on the speakers in the lounge room and sang loudly along. Selling our services door to door and through friends at school as lawn-mowers, rat-catchers, junk-haulers and fox-hunters, we'd made a good living, kept the fridge full and both put on weight. My acne cleared up, and I'd given up the weed. Russell got taller and started sprouting a beard. It was like, with the old man gone, we were forgotten plants getting their first drink of water and sunlight.

And then he was back.

I drove my dead father through the dark back fields now and remembered that day. Hearing the Fairmont on the gravel drive. The dream dying the way everything died—without warning, without a chance to negotiate, to beg for one more day.

We'd refer to The Time He Went now and then, over the years, Russell and me. Dad would do something horrible, and one of us would say, 'Remember The Time He Went?' and the other would smile.

I knew then that I couldn't give in. That I couldn't let a connection be made between Arthur Powder and Chloe Lutz, or Arthur Powder and Linda Special, or Arthur Powder and Marian Richley. Because then people would come looking for my father. This wasn't just about saving Chris anymore. It was about saving myself. I needed this to be The Time He Went and Never Came Back. Because I deserved that. We all did.

Sever the connection. The one Chloe had made. Then all they had was Chris and Arthur at the pub that night. Dad's DNA was on the girl, yes, but nothing else. No reason for him to be watching her. No motive. No hidden secrets. The past staying in the past, and not becoming *my future.* I'd take Chloe's phone from the footwell now and head back to Redbelly with it, after I'd done what I needed to do at Pemulwuy. I'd put Chloe's phone and laptop in the Branch house somewhere. Wait for them to connect the dots. It was all about connecting the dots, completing the circle, making it neat enough that the truth of it all would be carried away on the current.

I rang off with Russell and disposed of my father's body in an unremarkable spot in the river that snaked through a patch of crown land not far from the old man's house. I was determined to watch, as I rolled the car into the water, pushing from the rear, my dad's shoes on my feet sinking into the mud. With all the windows cracked and the handbrake off, the vehicle slid easily into the deep and started spewing bubbles. I stretched my eyes, took it all in, the roof sinking away, the bubbles still rising and rising until they finally stopped. I was afraid to blink. Expected the man to come bursting through the surface. Like Jaws. Like Godzilla. I saw myself wading out to gather Arthur in my arms, pulling him back towards the shore. Crying my apologies. My promises. Because the tears that were streaking down my face now were coming from a brain screaming in that child's voice, *I'm sorry, Dad, I'm sorry.*

It was an extreme act of willpower to turn and walk away. I managed it. Managed the few kilometres walk back to the house, to my car. I carried Chloe Lutz's phone and laptop in my hands all the way there. I started the engine and pulled out and drove away, heading for Sydney.

RUSSELL

The road outside the Branch property was a zoo. It was a stupid decision to come into town that way, but I was distracted, and so was Dodge, it seemed, because he didn't stop me. The mood in the car was sombre: the kind of embarrassed unease that comes from making promises to the victims of a half-century-old homicide that you'd be the one to finally hold the responsible party to account. I hadn't said as much to John Special, of course, and neither had my partner. But the implication was there. What a claim it was. We were going to do something that probably dozens of officers before us hadn't been able to do. In two days, I'd made that precious kind of promise to two broken-hearted men. The promise of vengeance, and justice. The sheer arrogance of it felt weighty in the air.

I wondered if they'd ever asked my father to take a look at the Special and Richley cases. That's what they'd been doing, when they asked him to turn his hand to the missing woman Dominique Fine, and he'd shot and killed her husband. Had they ever asked him to consult on Linda and Marian, and would that mean I would have to speak to him? The thought filled me with horror. I wondered how bad the cancer was. Maybe it would get to him before I had to. I dared to dream, just for a few seconds, about solving a case that my father had been tasked with and had failed to resolve, and him hearing about that. It being one of the last things he ever heard about before he promptly dropped dead of a terrible, painful disease.

How would I ever celebrate such a thing?

I wondered how much flights to Fiji set you back these days.

Press vans, forensic tech vans, and the private vehicles of journos crowded either side of the road. I stopped the car beyond the crowd and started making a three-point turn. A journalist I recognised jogged up to the car. Tiny blonde with wolf-blue eyes and great fashion sense. Amy Sail. She rapped on my window and I was worried about running over her feet, so I stopped.

'Hey, Rusty!' She grinned at me through the glass, jerked her thumb back towards the Branch property. 'Was it him?'

If it had been anyone else, I'd have spun the wheels in the mud and racked off without saying anything at all. But back in Sydney, Sail had done me a solid once or twice, keeping quiet about homicides until I was ready for them to go public, and she called me 'Rusty' like she didn't know that I regularly put people's heads through walls for lesser infractions, so I locked eyes with her and shrugged and said, 'It sure looks good.'

A frown crossed Amy's features. She knew what that line meant. I drove away.

Dodge had to go home to get his pain meds for his leg, so with promises to reconvene at the houseboat in an hour or so, I dropped him there and drove across the unmown field towards the houseboat, hoping I wasn't running over anything slithery that didn't deserve to have its life end under car tyres. Bridie was sitting at the kitchen nook with a small red ball of fluff bundled into a knitted pouch resting against her belly. She was slowly dribbling water onto the juvenile ringtail possum's lips from a syringe, and the thing was lapping at the liquid with its googly orange-and-black eyes, looking up at my daughter in quiet wonderment. This was a scene I had witnessed many times, something both my wife and my daughter had done over the years: rehydrating possums that had been flung aside by their mothers as they were attacked by cats, or found in the gutter, clinging to a deceased adult's carcass. I sat and folded my arms and watched, and without even greeting each other, my daughter and I enjoyed a quiet lack of awkwardness that had been five years or more in the making.

'Where's that going to go?' I asked after a while, gazing at the little creature in her hands. The thing was holding on to Bridie's pinky with a tiny, hairy paw. Witchy-looking, knobbly clawed fingers.

'I'll drop him to a carer later on today, when she gets home,' she said. 'Just want to get him settled for now.'

'How'd you get it when I had the car?'

'The job was only up the hill, actually, so I walked.' She nodded towards the bow of the houseboat. 'But I might take the 'Stang this time if you're not using it. There's a wallaby caught in a fence not far away.'

I clamped my mouth shut so I didn't say anything about my beloved car and how I knew from long experience that the stink of a wallaby could hang around for days on end. I was also keeping quiet about my precious daughter and how much I worried about her getting kicked or clawed or knocked to the ground by an enormous, frantic wallaby. 'Mmm.'

'You could come if you want.'

'Not this time,' I said. 'I just want to drill down on a couple of things.'

Bridie put her little possum friend away in her rescue cage and left, and I pushed open my laptop and started looking at Linda's and Marian's cases again. Marian was pictured in a crowded bar, pouring a beer, her mouth open as she spoke to a punter who was holding bills pinned against the countertop. The guy screamed 'cop' the way I had been advised that I did, all tight shoulders and rigid back and wary eyes. As I examined the photograph, I saw most of the gathering had the cop vibe. Deep in the background, I spotted a shoulder and a slice of ear and neck and hair that only the son of the owner could recognise. The shape of my father standing there, right at the edge of the frame, turned away from the camera. I looked at the date of the article. 1975.

A deep discomfort unfolded in my chest as I looked around the officers, their smiling, laughing faces, the slice of my father back there among them. When I tried to get my hands around it, this eerie feeling growing in me, I felt that it was a suspicion of these men, which as a cop myself always felt traitorous. But whoever had killed Linda and Marian had been able to talk their way through their front doors while they were home alone at night. And when he'd sexually assaulted them, he'd had them wash his traces from their skin. Dodge hadn't said it outright, probably not wanting to offend me, because my father was a cop in the area. But those two aspects of the crime hinted at someone in law enforcement. When the discomfort wouldn't go away, I reminded myself that knowledge of trace evidence at the time would have been common among most types of career criminal, as well as law enforcement personnel. DNA hadn't come into popular use by cops until the mid-eighties, but garden-variety dirtbags would have known about fingerprints and hair and fibre matching before then. I told myself it was the image of my father there on the screen that was also unsettling me. And the ground-shaking notion that one day soon he would be dead.

An email arrived in my inbox, telling me the ongoing collaborative file related to Chloe Lutz's murder had just been updated. I opened the email and scanned down the long, long list of updates, seeing notifications of entries into the file from Fry, Kalowski, Lee, Dodge and Caplan. There were none from Evan, and none from me. I was without entries because as the lead detective it wasn't my job to make entries, but it was my job to oversee them at the end of each day of the investigation, and I'd neglected to do that, for the simple fact that I'd got mildly distracted by killing a man. But it was weird that there was nothing there from Evan, who I knew to be a paperwork nerd.

I clicked on the latest entry, made by Gail Caplan, which stated that she'd sent out the request for the region-wide SMS blast of the image of the young guy at the pub, appealing for information from the public. Weird. I'd asked Evan to do that, not Gail. Another entry by Gail came through, which said that the forensic evidence lot delivered to the Pemulwuy lab the day before by Evan had been categorised and was undergoing testing. I ran an eye down the itemised list and stopped halfway.

I took out my phone and dialled a number. The phone rang twice before someone picked it up. 'NSW Police Forensic Services, Constable Jane Markwell speaking.'

'This is Detective Inspector Russell Powder,' I said. I squinted at the report in front of me, looked at the name of the tech who'd taken charge of the collection. 'Put me onto technician Ryan Snelling.'

A click, and some silence, while I stared at my screen and ground my molars. When Snelling got on the line his voice was tight. 'Yes, DI Powder?'

'Why in the name of Friedrich Miescher's fucking ghost am I seeing a "notebook" reported in the evidence inventory of my case?'

Snelling had to take a moment to think about that, during which he breathed so heavily into the phone I almost spontaneously combusted with rage where I sat, spraying chunks of myself all over the ceiling and windows. 'Excuse me, sir?'

'I'm looking at the collection that was handed into the lab yesterday for testing,' I said. 'Case number 33481B. Chloe Lutz. Fifth item from the top. Under "tampon packet" it says "notebook". Why does it say that?'

'Well, because . . . because a notebook was submitted with that collection, sir.'

'No, it wasn't.'

'Yes, it was,' Snelling said. 'That particular discovery was actually made here in the lab. The notebook was in a hidden zippered section of the—'

'*Why the fuck wasn't I told about it?*' I thumped the table with my fist, made my laptop do a little dance beside me. 'You make a discovery of an extra item of evidence in a murder case during submission and you don't immediately inform the case detective? Is this your first day on the job?'

'Detective Inspector Powder, your submitting officer was—'

'Photograph the contents of the notebook, right now, and send them to me!' I yelled.

'Sir, your officer—'

'Stop talking! Do what I've asked you to! Before I climb down the phone and make it so that your mother has to view what's left of you on a petri dish through a microscope!'

I hung up and called Evan. He didn't answer. Typing in all caps, I sent a series of separate texts so his phone would ping a bunch of times in rapid succession.

NOTEBOOK DISCOVERED IN LUTZ HANDBAG BY LAB TECH.
WHY DIDN'T YOU SEE IT?
I'M
GOING
TO
KILL
YOU
EVAN.

I got up and went to the fridge, enjoyed the blast of cool air that hit my rage-boiling face as I opened it. The cupcakes from Bridie's helpful friend were there on the top shelf in a Tupperware container. Although I have a phobia of women of a certain vintage, I hadn't eaten in at least 24 hours, so I ate two of them in big, fast bites, chain-feeding them into my mouth and moaning quietly to myself at how good they were, because there was no one there to know about it. Lemon curd with soft centres, so moist they stuck to the roof of my mouth. My phone pinged on the counter, so I shut the fridge and went back and looked at the region-wide SMS blast instigated by Gail.

Do you know this man? New South Wales Police are seeking information on the pictured individual, who may be able to assist with enquiries related to a violent incident at Redbelly

Crossing on Friday, 6 March 2026. The individual is described as . . .

I looked at the screenshot of the kid in the cap at the bar, closed the message with satisfaction. At least someone was doing their job. The phone pinged again just as I was about to set it down. The text was from Bridie. Her name on the preview screen, such a rare sight, sent a prickle of excitement through my chest. I opened the message and expected a picture of a wallaby, but instead saw that it was a pinned location. As I was puzzling over the map she'd sent me, another message from her came through.

It was just one word.

Help.

EVAN

I walked up to the desk at forensic evidence holding and immediately felt the number of cameras that were focused on at me multiply tenfold from those that gazed over the car park. The young male desk officer turned to me, another pimpled young guy lumped with weekend lab-desk duty, not two hundred metres from the one who had been manning the desk at the forensics lab across the street yesterday. This one wasn't writing the next great Australian novel but was toying with his slicked-down hair and watching me walk in with nervous cat energy.

'Powder,' I said in greeting. The officer glanced at my badge as I set it on the counter. 'I need to come around there and look at a couple of boxes.'

'Oh yep, okay, no worries.' The guy took up the computer mouse, glanced at his screen. He was a constable, his name badge read Carras. 'What can I get for you, sir?'

'I don't want you to get anything for me,' I said curtly. 'I want to take a wander. Buzz me through.'

The guy shuffled uncomfortably, swung back and forth in the desk chair, a weathervane blown about by winds of uncertainty. I was relying on the swiftness of my movements, on the self-consciousness the senior sergeant's badge might be inducing in the guy, my unexplained unfriendliness. Channelling my brother. I bashed the steel-meshed door beside the counter with a palm so that the metal roared. 'Today sometime, constable.'

'I'll need you to sign in, sir.'

'No shit,' I said. I was buzzed through. Felt the camera above the counter on my face, red hot laser eye glaring. 'Give me the book.'

I signed in.

'Can I direct you where to go, sir?'

'No. I don't need your help.'

'I'm . . . Well . . . I was just being polite, sir.' The guy actually blushed. 'I will have to accompany you into the stacks.'

'Keep up, then,' I said. I marched ahead. The guy fell into step behind me. We walked through the aisles, east to west, climbing backwards through years of horror and sorrow. Shelves of boxes passed us by, boxes I knew were filled with bloody clothes, knives, ropes, guns and a sundry of other usually innocuous items people chose to kill each other with: blind cords and stockings and coathangers and screwdrivers. The boxes changed style every couple of decades. The most recent boxes were transparent plastic tubs sealed with black clips and taped at the seams. The labels were crowded with information, from the last detective to access the box to the boxes' entire itemised contents. The boxes went to cardboard then, stiff and bright and square, in the nineties, still labelled with computer-printed forms not even yellowed with age yet. I glimpsed names, years, suburbs where the crimes had occurred, collections that were tightly aligned according to date, with barely a week missing in any given month. After a while I was walking past evidence from crimes committed in the eighties, and the labels on the boxes became handwritten or stamped, some in blue ink, some in black or red, the information scrawled on an angle, some labels full of words, some labels scarce and patchy. Now and then I glimpsed an assigned lead detective's name, recognised many who were retired. In the seventies, I started to see the names of dead officers. Here, I slowed, seeing boxes that were squashed and crumpled and stained, sitting on their shelves in nervous huddles, the last animals in the rescue centre. Three boxes for a month, then nothing for an almost six-month period, then a couple more. A box sat lonely on a dusty steel shelf, halfway down a row, and I saw there were few boxes beyond it, heading into the late sixties, before the shelf space became dedicated to the evidence holding facility's fire safety equipment and tubs of office supplies.

The box read *SPECIAL, L. JULY 1973.* I stepped back, glanced up the aisle a year, which was about ten metres, and saw *RICHLEY, M. MARCH 1974.* Once I'd seen that the boxes were there, I let my eyes dart away, focused on other boxes. The box directly across the aisle from Special's was crumpled and old, looked like it had been dropped, the bottom corner soft and wrinkled. *PINKERLY, T. 1972.* The security camera at the end of the aisle was affixed to the wall, dead centre, staring at me.

'Did you need to . . . ?' Constable Carras asked, gesturing to the Pinkerly box, like I wasn't capable of taking the thing down by myself. I knew the process from here. We should, according to protocol, take the box back to the desk together, take out a processing form and complete that form in tandem—me identifying myself and describing my reasons for accessing the evidence box, and Carras signing off on that access. Carras and I would then go to a nearby room, where Carras would slit the unique branded tape that sealed the box and observe me going through the box's contents. Here, at the holding facility, I would be allowed to do little more than observe what was in the box. To note the number and contents of the packages that lay within, which would be wrapped in paper and individually labelled. A whole separate set of forms, a whole new ceremony, would be needed to remove the individual items from their bags and packages. Gloves, a trip to the forensic examination offices across the street with the box and a witnessing officer in tow, to provide chain of custody. I had done this exhaustive dance hundreds of times across my career. Today would be different.

'I don't actually need to access the box's contents,' I said, taking out my phone. I pretended to photograph the Pinkerly box where it sat. 'I just want to know that the box is there. I've got a journalist asking if there's anything on a couple of cold cases. But he'll have to go through command and get approval if he wants to actually get a look inside them.'

'Oh. Right.'

I bit my tongue as I mocked snapping more photographs. As I did, I tapped through my contacts list and found the number for evidence holding, keeping the screen tilted away from Carras. 'Just a couple more pictures,' I said as I dialled.

The phone rang back at the front desk. Carras turned his head that way but didn't move. I swallowed several internal screams, sweat beading on my ribcage, pretending to take my phone close now and read through a list. 'I just need to chase down another case now . . . ah, yep . . . says here . . . 1976 . . .'

The phone rang and rang. Carras shifted his weight on the concrete floor.

'Sir, would you mind accompanying me to the front desk, please?' he said. 'I really should get that. Because it's a Sunday, I'm the only one here.'

'Just go.'

'I can't leave you unattended in the stacks, sir.'

'What am I going to do?' I whirled on the guy, insulted. 'The boxes are sealed. There's a camera right there. You can frisk me on the way out if you need to, constable.'

'It's just protocol, sir.'

'Fuck your protocol. If anyone asks, tell them I said you were to go and answer the damn phone. It could be an emergency.'

The guy thought hard. The phone. Ringing. Ringing. My brain was on fire. I went back to my work. Hoped the young constable couldn't see my hands were shaking. 'I need to see if there's a case here . . . ah, yep, Doyle, H. 1976. I need a picture of that one. Hmm. Who else?'

Carras finally went. I put my phone away, slipped my car keys from my pocket, dragged Linda Special's evidence box down onto the floor and flipped it on its side. I slashed the bottom of the box open with my house key, through the black-and-yellow tape, and slid the contents out. Though I knew footage of what I was doing in those very moments would soon cease to exist, I felt the eye of the camera on me. On my soul. I slid the contents out onto the floor. Parcels wrapped in brown paper. A picture frame. A collection of broken glass or china, crunching shards inside what I guessed was several layers of the brown paper. A long package of what felt and sounded like sections of wood, wrapped tight and rectangular, like Christmas presents. There were folders inside the box. Prints of the crime scene and hand-drawn sketches, probably. I left the paperwork where it was, shoved the flaps of the box shut and lifted it back onto the shelf. I crossed the aisle and drew down the first box my hands fell upon. *DOWNES, A. 1976.* I turned the box on its side, slit open the bottom, and shoved the parcels from the Special case into the Downes case. I replaced the now extremely heavy Downes box on the shelf where it had sat, realigning the corners with the dust marks on the shelf. I stepped back and looked at my work. Halfway there. I went further along the aisle and took Marian Richley's box down. I heard a faint voice in the distance, and the same voice, stronger, on the phone I had tucked into the breast pocket of the flannelette shirt of my murdered father.

'Forensic Evidence Holding, Pemulwuy. This is Constable Carras.'

I whipped the phone out of my pocket and put it to my ear, trying not to look at the camera above me. I let my voice rise a little higher than usual. Smoothed it out. Hoped Carras couldn't hear it reverberating with terror. I looked at the evidence box next to Marian's. 'Hey there. This is Constable . . . Frankston. I'm calling from uh, Parramatta station. My sergeant is wanting to look up a couple of case files and see if you've got anything in holding?'

'Is it urgent? I've just got another officer here and—'

'It's urgent, yes.'

'Oh, okay. Yep. No worries. What's your service number, mate?'

I recited a fake service number, wedging the phone between my ear and shoulder as I took down Richley's box.

'Mate, I'm getting a different officer for that service number,' Carras said. 'Can you give it to me again? I can't do anything for anybody until I've cited a badge or confirmed a service number.'

'Yep, can you just hang on a second, though?' I said. 'My boss is just coming to my desk—'

I heard Carras give a sharp sigh of frustration. I slipped my phone into my pocket, then flipped Marian's box on its side and scraped the contents out. Little brown wrapped packages, just like Linda's. I returned Marian's much lighter box to the shelf, took down the box marked FRANKSTON, R. 1977. I slit the box open and shoved Marian's packages into the Frankston box, hefted it, the base now bowing against my hands, back onto the shelf. It was tipping back towards me, the base pinned shut by the edge of the shelf, when a voice at the end of the aisle sent a bolt of pain through my chest.

'What are you doing?'

I turned, still holding the box at a 45-degree angle up on the shelf. Carras was there, the cordless phone from the desk against his ear. I froze. There was no disguising what I was doing now. No escape. Nowhere to hide. I saw in a flash the rifle in my hands. Felt the stickiness of the linoleum on my father's kitchen floor as I stepped towards the man, who was scrambling, begging, bug-eyed. I felt the rifle kick against my shoulder. I imagined my hands coming around Carras's throat now in the lonely evidence room aisle. You've killed once to protect them. Chrissy. Delle. *Yourself.* You can do it again.

'Are you taking that box down, sir?' Carras let the hand that was holding the cordless phone receiver slowly drift to his side. I felt a quiver of hope in my throat. I swallowed hard, ran the words back over in my mind.

Are you taking it down?

'Ah, yeah.' I pushed the box back into place. 'I was just going to see if there was a label on the back that had . . . uh . . . more information.'

Carras pocketed the handset, marched to my side. 'You can't be handling the boxes, sir. Not without supervision.'

'I wasn't going to *open* it, I just—' I tapped the label on the front of the box. 'I just wanted to see when the box was last accessed. Doesn't say here on the front.'

'A lot of the boxes don't list that.' Carras turned the box around on the shelf. Rotated it, showing all sides. I felt sweat running into the waistband of my trousers, tickling down my belly. I imagined Carras lifting the box. Even just slightly. Tilting it backwards and noticing that the bottom was slit and sagging open. 'They didn't have a protocol, back then, for writing the name of the officer who accessed the box last on the box's exterior. So if there's no one listed on the label on the front, I'd say the box hasn't been opened at all since the original submission date. Which would be . . . ah . . . See here? August 1977.'

'Okay.'

'But, sir, you can't handle the boxes *at all* without me being present. It's bad enough that I left you alone with them.'

'Got it.' I nodded. 'I'm done here.'

We walked back towards the front office. I stopped short by the desk, my phone in my hand. Carras had the cordless receiver back to his ear.

'Listen,' I said. 'Can I just use your PC for a second? I want to print something.'

Carras took his phone away from his ear, frowned at it. I guessed he could hear the echo of my words through the call he was apparently on hold on, with the fictitious Constable Frankston. 'Uh, yeah? Sure thing, sir. Go ahead.'

Carras stood there, an elbow on the desk, watching the screen as I drew up the Gmail log-in page. I punched in my email address, clicked the cursor into the password box, then threw Carras a pointed look. 'Do you mind?'

'Ah, sorry, sir.' Carras turned away for the briefest of moments, huffing and sighing at his empty phone call. Keeping an eye on Carras's reflection in the glass of the counter window in front of me, I logged in to my email, then set it aside, opening the find window to do a search of the device.

'Where *is* that email?' I asked myself quietly. Carras gave up on the phone call and occupied himself at the other end of the counter, taking out his personal mobile, fishing around, looking busy. I knew I didn't have long, if all I was pretending to do was find and then print an email from my account. I searched for the facility's camera system. It wasn't hard to find. The program maximised from a shortcut on the desktop. I went in and opened the program's history, found the recordings were arranged by day. I selected the past four days and hit the delete key.

A password rose on the screen.

'Fuck.'

'Everything okay, sir?' Carras started coming over again. I clicked back to my email in the nick of time.

'Yes, yes, yes.' I waved at him. 'I just. I need to print the . . . the . . . the contents of a notebook. It's from a case. Just . . . It's a sensitive case, Constable. Okay? Unfolding right now. I have to get the images to, uh, unzip . . . Just leave me alone for a bit, will you?'

'Do you really need hard copies of the images, sir? Could you ema—'

'Carras! Fuck!'

'Sorry, sir.'

He backed off again. In plain, panicked despair I stood there staring at the password-protected security system, knowing that if I didn't disable that very system right now it would keep recording me. It would hold on to everything I had just done. I looked around the desk for the Hail Mary of all Hail Marys, a Post-it note with a password on it. No luck. I saw myself hurling the computer across the room. Burning the building down. I went back to my email and saw spam waiting, unclicked, in the unread messages.

Protect your computer from deadly viruses, download our . . .

I opened Google. Punched in something wild and desperate and certain—absolutely *certain*—not to work. *Computer destroying virus instant download.*

The screen filled with an infinite list. The first read *Instantly Downloadable Whole-hard Drive Atomic Wipeout.* That sounded good. The website was so dodgy looking I actually smiled. Black background. Red Times New Roman text in dozens of different sizes. Animated icons. I clicked a link and watched a loading bar slowly filling with blue colour, and thought of venom being dripped into veins.

The screen in front of me blinked out with an audible '*tink*' sound. I felt a surge of joy in my chest.

'What the . . .' I clicked the mouse a dozen times in rapid succession, mock confused. 'What happened?'

Carras stepped over cautiously. Reached for the mouse. Performed the same useless clicking. 'Did you turn it off, sir?'

'No, I didn't turn it off.' Carras punched the power button on the PC's tower. Nothing. Stifling my joy and relief took real effort. 'Did *you* turn it off?'

'No.'

Carras ducked under the desk to look at where the computer was plugged into the wall. He flipped the switch on and off. Tried the power again. 'What happened? Did it just go blank?'

'Yeah. It just died.'

'I mean . . . Maybe there's been a blackout. But there can't have been. The lights are still on.'

'Do you have another computer here that I can access? I really need this thing printed.'

'Ahhh . . .' Carras ran a hand through his hair. 'Not really. There's the desktop computers of the other staff, but they're all password-protected. This is the big daddy here.'

'Looks like you're running blind, then,' I said.

'I can't be, though.' Carras nudged me out of the way, dragging the PC tower forward so that he could inspect the back of the machine. 'This thing controls all the cameras. I have to have an unbroken eye on all the boxes, all the time. Chain of custody, you know?'

'Sucks to be you,' I said, clapping the constable on the shoulder. 'I'm gonna sign out. I'm in a hurry.'

RUSSELL

I didn't call Bridie. Didn't text her back. Because there were a dozen or more scenarios running through my mind, each one of them more horrifying than the last, and none of them were resolved or improved by there being some indication on Bridie's phone that her SOS message had successfully reached me and that I was on my way. I shoved my gun into my waistband and my phone into my pocket, ran out the door of the houseboat and remembered that my daughter had my car. Sprinting across the field, through the gate and along the road into town, my whole body aflame from last night's injuries reawakened, I skidded hard and almost fell in the gravel as I spotted Rob Winter, the publican, driving slowly towards me in a dusty blue Land Cruiser. With bewilderment he pulled over sharply as I waved him down, and actually reeled back in the driver's seat as I yanked open the door.

'Get-out-get-out-get-out!'

He got out. I swung into the driver's seat like a man pulling himself up on a horse and slammed the door closed as I drove away. Rob Winter stood in my dust cloud in the middle of the road, hands by his sides, watching me.

* * *

The first clue that Bridie had stumbled onto a drug lab came when I spotted the gate. It was entangled in a passionfruit vine, rusted and barely hanging on to the rotted wooden post it was attached to.

It had all the appearances of a gate that was never opened, but the groove that the corner of the swinging arm had cut in the mud was nice and deep and spoke of regular use. I passed the gate, parked Rob's car and walked back, ducked under a wire wrapped in the same camouflaging vine. I stepped into the moist, rainforest-like undergrowth. The road became barely visible only a few feet back from the gravel edge, the property's interior disguised, as Stephen Branch's had been, by an entanglement of weeds, vines and scrubby trees. I made my way towards the road leading off the gate, and walked by its side but not on it. It wasn't long before I spotted a pipe running across the road, lazily cut into the dirt and painted a similar sandy colour. Intruders, cops, or lost teenagers here to rescue a wallaby would run over the pipe with their vehicles and set off a silent alarm somewhere up at the lab itself. I drew my gun and walked quickly and quietly, keeping the road in sight but sticking to the thickness of the bush.

The sentry knew something was up. Whether it was because I'd walked under a camera or set off some other hidden alarm, I didn't know. But he was dumb enough to take action not by hiding and waiting for me to arrive, but by going out and standing in the middle of the road, a big unwieldly revolver of some type hanging in his fist. I skirted him by as much as I dared, cut in and came back up the road behind him, walking in the dampness of the sandy clay so my boots wouldn't crunch on the gravel. Despite my efforts, a stone popped under my boot maybe six feet out. The sentry turned, and I raised my gun two-handed, cop-style, looking right down the barrel at him, so he'd know exactly who he was dealing with. Like me, he was pushing fifty and broad. He had salt-and-pepper hair and a badly flattened nose that was covered in deep, dirty pores.

'Well.' He blew out air in a disappointed huff. '*Shit.*'

'Yeah,' I said. I tipped the gun a little, and he dropped his weapon in the sand like a good boy. He stepped to the side and put his hands out, and I went over and felt his pockets and waistband. He even tugged up the thighs of his jeans to show me his boots: someone who had clearly been searched thousands upon thousands of times in their criminal career and knew the routine.

'Where is she?'

'At the house.'

'Get going,' I said. 'Stay ahead of me. You stop to scratch your arse and I'll put another hole in it for you.'

The big guy made an aggrieved sound and started walking. Sweat was making my T-shirt cling to my chest, and my jeans and boots were wet to the thighs from the forest. Intrusive, unhelpful thoughts kept zapping through my brain, carrying horrible visions that I had to fight the urge to succumb to. Bridie tied to a chair. Bridie on a bed. Bridie on the floor. Bridie in a grave. My career had presented me with plenty of dead and tortured and mangled women to draw inspiration from. Staying present, and keeping my breathing steady, was exhausting me.

We came upon a damp, mouldy single-storey house set into the rainforest, an asbestos-clad thing that was peeling and dropping paint and sheets of fibro like a half-dead insect shedding its exo-skeleton. My Mustang was parked at the side. Another big, meat-faced guy stood at the bottom of the steps and watched me come up, escorting my hostage. He didn't look surprised, or worried. Bridie came out of a screen door onto the verandah and a shorter guy emerged behind her, and though he was holding another stupidly big silver revolver I was pleased that he wasn't pointing it at my child, otherwise I would have had to kill everyone right then and there, and I was still hoping for a nonviolent solution to all this. The curtain in the front window fluttered, and I knew I had a fourth man watching me, probably pointing a rifle at my head. Bridie looked bloodless and big-eyed, but she wasn't crying.

'I'm Rick,' the shorter guy said, raising a hand at me in a tired and annoyed and embarrassed kind of way. The wave guys give each other when they step out of their vehicles after a rear-ender that was kind of both their fault. 'This is your kid, is it?'

'Yep,' I said.

'We didn't call her here,' Rick said. He had the hollow cheeks and pink eyes of almost all the junkies I'd ever dealt with, but for some reason I got the sense that the thinness and raggedness of him was due to hard work and self-neglect rather than getting into his own product. He was too calm. 'She's explained it to us all. The property that called her about the wallaby is actually our neighbours next door. Your daughter has mixed up the directions and come onto our land by mistake.'

Rick cast an arm out westwards. I didn't follow the gesture, aware that I might have a fifth guy creeping up on me from behind. I kept my ears pricked for footsteps on gravel and said, 'We can get out of your way and forget this ever happened, right now.'

'That would be so nice,' Rick said. 'But the problem is, she's seen the inside of the house.' Again, he gave an almost apologetic sigh. He indicated to my hostage. 'That idiot took a piss break and let her get all the way up the driveway. And *that* idiot'—he gestured to the man at the bottom of the stairs—'found her at the house and brought her in. She's seen all the product, all the gear, everything. I can't just let you walk away.'

'Yes, you can.'

'Mate, there are people to answer to, okay? People above me. If it comes to your two arses, or mine, I know who I'm going to choose.'

'You're not going to kill her,' I said. 'Or me.'

'I'm not?'

'No,' I said. 'Because, while there's been a whole lot of idiocy around here today, you're not going to let it continue.'

Rick gave a rueful nod, like we were on the same team. Two guys surrounded by morons.

'Right now,' I said, 'your worst-case scenario is having to bail out on your set-up. And that'll be annoying. Because you have found a nice little spot, and it looks like you've been here a while. But if you kill us, you'll have every cop in the state on your tail in five minutes time, and they will chase you to the ends of the earth, I promise you. Try explaining that to your higher-ups.'

'You're a jacko yourself, aren't you?'

'Sure am.'

Rick filled his cheeks with air, let them slowly deflate, as though something like this was just typical of his kind of luck.

'Your bosses will forgive you for bailing on your set-up. They won't forgive you for killing a cop and a teenager and making the national news.'

'This is not what I needed today.' Rick adjusted the grip on his gun.

'Sit us both on the ground,' I said. 'Have your smartest lug-head watch over us. You can have the lab packed up and be on the road in an hour. You have your lone lug-head watch us for another hour while you all burn rubber. You can be in Sydney by then. They'll never find you.'

Rick thought about it. 'It won't take a genius to figure out where she's gone,' he sighed. 'If we do kill her, I mean. She showed us the app with the bloody animal rescue job on it.'

'Right.'

Rick looked at Bridie, fingered the trigger, thinking. I counted my breaths. In, out, in, out. The little drug lord turned to me, let his eyes wander from my gun to my hostage, back to my face. 'You're in town for the murder, are you?'

'Yeah.'

'Girl at the pub.'

I nodded.

'We had nothing to do with that, you know,' Rick said. He looked at Bridie, gestured in her direction with the gun in a way that made my shoulders tighten. Didn't go so far as to raise it to her completely. 'We're not here to hurt people. Especially girls.'

'I believe you,' I said, though I'd been listening to him weighing up whether to kill both my daughter and me for the past five minutes. Drug people have a strange relationship with the truth. 'Listen, this is just a mobile cook-out, yeah?'

'Right.'

I had been on drug squad for six months straight out of the academy. I knew the behaviour. The property we were on wouldn't belong to the crew. It would have been scouted by a member of the overall organisation, identified for the secluded setting, the sense that it was abandoned and unoccupied. The crew would have set up here mere days earlier, with the goal to cook as much meth as they could in a short span of time without raising the kind of suspicions their sounds and smells and foot traffic would raise in a city or suburban or industrial setting.

'You have nothing to lose,' I said. 'Pack up and go.'

Rick tapped the gun against his thigh.

'Okay. Here's what's gonna happen,' he said. He pointed with his gun as he spoke, like it was an extension of his arm. 'Matt, you stay on the copper. Dan, you're gonna go with the girl, and make sure she does her job and doesn't run off. Uri, mate?' He turned to the house, to the window. 'Start packing.'

'Wait, *where* is Bridie going?' I squinted, confused.

'To get the wallaby.' Rick looked at me like I'd just submitted my application to be awarded Moron of the Day. 'That's what she came here for in the first place, mate.'

'But . . .'

'The thing's been caught on a fence between their property and ours since this morning.' Rick tucked his gun into his waistband. 'Got its tail hooked up. We can't just leave it there. That's cruel.'

The drug lord drew a couple of cable ties out of his pocket and held them towards me, put his other palm out like he wanted my gun. I handed the pistol over, slowly, waiting for the punchline. There wasn't one. Rick watched as I zipped a cable tie around one of my wrists, looped the other through and zipped it shut as well. He checked the tightness half-heartedly like he trusted me to have done a good job. Bridie was trembling gently, looking at me for confirmation that we weren't both about to be shot in the back of the head and buried in a hole out here. I met her eyes and nodded.

'You can watch from the verandah,' Rick said, taking my arm and leading me forward. 'Come on.'

* * *

We stood on the rickety verandah running along the side of the house, Rick, his men and me, as Bridie and the one named Dan walked across a field that was waist-high with native grass and triffid-like weeds to the edge of a wall of bush belonging to the next property. Matt, my former hostage, who was supposed to be supervising me, forgot about me completely, his eyes and those of everyone present on the lanky girl and her captor approaching the fence line. I could tell from the animal's black face and considerable size that it wasn't a wallaby, in fact, but a black wallaroo, a significantly larger animal that would have weighed two-thirds what Bridie did. It rose on its hind legs to her shoulder height when it saw her approaching. We looked on in silence as Bridie handed the huge hessian sack she used for wallaby, wallaroo and kangaroo rescues to her captor. Rick, who was standing beside me, folded his arms and shook his head, marvelling at the task ahead of my child, while in the distance Bridie tied her hair up into a ponytail.

'They'll kick ya, those things,' he said.

I said nothing.

'They can kill ya, you know,' he went on. 'Better her than me.'

I wasn't doing very well at being conversational. It was the guns. The hostages. The whole having-my-life-weighed-in-someone-else's-hands thing. My stoicism seemed to be disappointing Rick, who I could feel looking at me. I supposed there was no reason drug kingpins shouldn't enjoy making friends just as much as the law-abiding citizens among us.

Bridie crept as close to the animal as she could before it started panicking and thrashing, making the fence posts on either side of it waggle back and forth. The animal's thick tail seemed to be twisted in two lengths of barbed wire. I saw a strip of raw pink flesh. Twisted, rusty, broken coils. Bridie chose her moment then ran up and threw herself at the animal shoulder-first, taking it to the ground like a rugby tackler, while the nation's most cordial drug crew stood around me and guffawed and cheered and clapped.

They pulled out of the property an hour after that, leaving the house empty, the gate hanging open, and Bridie and me tasked with loading the wallaroo into the back of my Mustang. My former hostage hung around for fifteen minutes before taking off unannounced. The wallaroo had calmed and was lying on its side with the hessian sack encasing its body to the base of its ravaged tail, where a drawstring was pulled tight. Bridie spread an old sheet over the back seat of my car to save the leather from the skin-stripped flesh of the bottom half of the tail. She was quiet and pale and hard-mouthed, and we hadn't spoken in all the time we were held captive while the drug goons packed the house, so after she closed the door on the wallaroo I reached out tentatively and touched her hand. For the first time in five years, she fell into my arms.

'Daaaaad!' she sobbed against my chest.

'It's okay.'

'No, it's not!'

'It wasn't your fault.'

'Yes, it was! They could have killed us both. *They were thinking about killing us both!*'

'Oh, honey. I wouldn't have let them kill us both.'

'I'm an iiiiidiooot . . .'

'No, you're not.'

'Can you not tell Mum?'

'I'll never tell a soul.'

Bridie dried her eyes, sucked in some deep breaths and let them out hard. 'Listen,' she said. 'There's a road back there. I saw it from the edge of the field.'

She pointed out towards the fence where she'd wrestled the wallaroo from its entrapment in the fence. I looked. She went on. 'Should you go look?'

I fished around in my mind for what she was talking about. Came up with nothing. 'What for?'

'Well, these guys are drug cooks, right?' she said. 'They don't want anyone to know they're out here. So they'll be using that front entrance, the one we came through, as little as they can. That road might go somewhere. It might go into town, maybe. Avoiding the traffic cameras.'

'Right.' I nodded. 'And they've got cameras at the front. Maybe—'

'Maybe they had them at the back. It's probably a good idea to check all the secret roads around here, you know? The ones only the locals know about? Because if someone was after Chloe, and it wasn't, like, a spur of the moment thing . . .'

'How long can that animal lie there like that, though?' I pointed to the 'Stang.

'He's okay.' Bridie put a hand on the car door. 'He could use the calm-down time in the dark. I'll stay with him. You just go and don't, like, make a day of it.'

I walked off, feeling a burning in my cheeks, at being told to hustle by my child. At having what could be a major, case-saving avenue of investigation pointed out to me by my child. This was a person whose shoelaces I was still tying for them only a decade and a bit earlier. Why had I been about to leave the property without thinking that there was probably a secret road at the back that led into town? I found myself palming my forehead, told myself not to in case the kid was watching me. The thought occurred to me, with painful clarity, that I wanted Bridie to be a cop. I saw her talent. I *envied* her talent. And that hurt, because my father had raised Evan and me to be cops. It was just a given. There hadn't been a choice. That I could want the same thing as a man I despised so badly left me shaken and confused.

The road was visible from the field not for its shape, but for the absence it created, an interrupted density of trees and bushes. I walked over a part of the barbed-wire fence that was down and started looking at the trees for a wireless camera, spotted it almost immediately, a white thing shaped like an elongated egg cable-tied to a tree branch. With no knife on me, I stood on tiptoe and snapped the thin branch, wrestled the camera off the end of the limb and carried it back across the field to the car.

Bridie was sitting in the back with the animal's swathed head in her lap. The car already stank so much I had to roll down the windows, but I didn't say anything about it.

EVAN

He called as I was heading back through Glenorie, past the big pie. There was some kind of Sunday market on in a field off the main road. Traffic. Kids. A Mr Whippy van. Normal people carrying on their lives, while I weaved in between them like a hideous black eel passing between pretty fish, making my way back out into the bush to continue covering up a series of murders. The horror of it all was a handful of rocks rolling around the bottom of my lungs, making everything rattle, making it painful to breathe. There'd been missed calls and messages from Russell on my phone as I left Pemulwuy. He would have to be answered eventually. Everything would have to be answered: why I'd neglected to mention the notebook, what was in it, how that connected to the cold cases. In time, they were going to get a full DNA profile of Chloe's attacker, and that profile was going to link to Russell and me. It would all be pinned down: that Chris was there that night, that Arthur was there with him, that it was Arthur's DNA that was on the girl.

But as a killer, and the son of a killer, my best friend was time. I still had some. Establishing that Arthur and Chris had been at the pub would take days. Days in which my father's body rotted in the car in the river, and his house yawned, empty and still, and where he had gone and how and when he had left and what had happened to him became more and more difficult to pinpoint. Maybe he would stay hidden long enough that the fish and turtles and other aquatic life came for his body and his bones, and establishing his cause of death would be impossible. I could hope.

There was time, still, to find a reason to get onto Stephen Branch's property, and plant Chloe's phone and laptop there somewhere, and do what I could to direct the efforts of those around me towards sewing this all up neatly as being a spur-of-the-moment thing perpetrated by a clear and obvious madman. Time, ticking away steadily, climbing up and up and up, lengthening the case, drawing it out, so that it became a matter of memory exactly who had handled the traffic camera data, and why Chris's Uber ride had been deleted from it, if that was ever discovered at all. Maybe it was Fry who'd handled that. Maybe it was Lee. Maybe it was just a case of a weird file conversion, and my son had fallen off the list by accident; who knew? Who cared?

All that mattered now was that no one connected my father to Chloe's cases. The ones she was investigating. Linda, Marian, the girl in Womerah. That connection *could not happen*. Because if they did, there'd be motive. There'd be questions. They'd come looking for Dad, and they wouldn't accept that they couldn't find him. If he was just an awful old man who'd been in the wrong place on the wrong night, a loose but unimportant thread left hanging, he'd be allowed to quietly disappear without there being panic and urgency to find him.

But if he was a serial killer, they'd look and they'd look and they'd never stop.

And if they found him too early, it was over. They'd get me somehow. I knew they would. Because it would be Russell leading them. Russell wanting to know.

And Russell always got his man.

Blood ties wouldn't matter to him.

I was at the top of the mountain, coming down the winding, sunbaked and truck-scraped road towards the ferry, when Russell called again, and I relented and pulled off and answered.

'Yeah.'

'Tell me you went over to the lab after you were done at evidence holding,' he said. His voice was like acid. 'Tell me you photographed the pages of that notebook.'

'I did,' I said, putting him on speaker and navigating to my pictures. 'I'll send them to you now.'

'I could strangle you for not spotting that notebook in the handbag at the Wisemans Medical Centre, Evan, I really could,' my brother said. 'We could have kept it back from the lab and had it in hand to refer to. A *tech* found it! A *tech*! Honestly, who did you have to fuck to get your policing badge?'

'Yeah, yeah.'

'Why didn't you tell me about it immediately?'

'I wasn't there. I'd left, and the tech found it, and I had to go back.'

'What's in it? Did you even look?'

'A bunch of indecipherable stuff about podcasts,' I said. I selected all the notebook pages I'd photographed, except the one that mentioned the Ford Capri. 'Okay, they're sent.'

'What did you find in the Special and Richley boxes?'

'Nothing.'

'*Nothing?*'

'You know how it goes,' I said. 'The cases are fifty years old. Somebody retires from the force and decides they'll take a box of evidence home to fiddle around with between games of lawn bowls and wanders in the garden. They die and their kid throws it out with all the rest of their personal junk.'

'*Both* cases, though?'

'The boxes were empty, Rus, I don't know what to tell you.'

'Fuck,' Russell seethed. '*Fuuuuuck.*'

'I know.'

'If they're empty, why are they still there?' my brother groaned. 'Who signed them out last? What do the books say? Were the seals still on or were they tampered with?'

'I didn't look that hard. Do you want me to go back?'

'Urgh. No.'

'You were barking up the wrong tree anyway,' I said. 'It's Branch. He's our guy. I know it would just make your day if you could single-handedly wrap up Chloe's murder *and* a couple of cold cases that have been sitting around since you were still in a nappy, Russell. But you've annoyed everyone enough already without getting Cop of the Year for catching a serial killer while you're at it.'

'I have a feeling about this.'

'Your feeling is wrong.'

'It's never wrong,' he said, and I struggled not to groan, because he was acting like fucking Sherlock Holmes or Batman or something. Instead, the arrogance made me facepalm myself so hard it made an audible slapping sound. 'I'm going to go back and speak to John Special, the husband of one of the women,' he went on. 'Maybe he can tell me what the police took, at least. What they *had* in evidence.'

'Okay. You keep wasting your time. I'm going to check in at the Branch property, see what's happening there.'

'Tell me if you can see anything of Chloe's there, will you?' Russell said. 'The place is crawling with coppers, but they're all from out-of-area. Half of them will just be wanting to get a sound bite onto the nightly news and they won't be paying attention.'

'Your unshakeable faith in your fellow police officer is always so heartwarming.'

'They weren't there in the hotel room. They don't know what Chloe's stuff looks like. We're supposed to be on the lookout for a phone and a laptop, but there might be something else.'

'Something else like what?' I said. I started driving again towards the ferry stop. 'There must be eight million pairs of women's panties in that place. You think Chloe Lutz wrote her name on hers with a laundry marker?'

'We might get lucky. There might be something else that just catches your eye.' Russell sighed. 'It's worth trying, Evan. Although—Jesus, you're right. I don't know why I'm asking you of all people. You didn't spot that footprint in the blood. And you couldn't spot a *notebook inside a handbag*. How are you going to spot a serial killer trophy on semi-hoarded, twenty-acre property?'

Something sparked in my brain. I took my foot off the accelerator, felt the car slow.

'Tell me what happens,' Russell said and hung up. I pulled to the side of the road, hoarded properties, serial killers and trophies on my mind. The ferry operator tried to wave me down to the waiting vessel. Instead, I turned around and headed back the way I'd come.

RUSSELL

I had Bridie drop me off at the back of the pub, marched in and tossed Rob Winter's car keys at the first constable I encountered. Told him to go get the vehicle and bring it back. I could see the burning curiosity in his eyes. Probably half the town knew by now that a couple of hours earlier I'd carjacked Winter and driven off in a mad hurry. But he didn't ask. I found Fry hanging around by the operational marquee, overseeing a guy on a laptop, probably as determined as I was to still linger in the case even though he'd been officially stood down. I kept well back so he didn't smell wallaroo on me and held out the camera I'd taken from the back of the drug house.

'You're the tech genius,' I said. 'Can you get any footage from that?'

'Probably not,' he said, before he'd even taken the device from my hand. I heard years of disappointment in his tone, the tendency for tech never to be as useful to an investigation as fiction would have you believe. He took it finally, turned it in his hands. 'I'm not familiar with this brand or model, but most of the time, something like this only works if it's connected to wi-fi and sending its data to a computer. Do you have the computer?'

'No.'

'It *might* have its own drive.' He started picking at a compartment into the back of the device. 'But I doubt it. I'll give it a crack anyway.'

'Thanks.'

The constable at the laptop swivelled sharply in his chair at the sound of my thanks, surprised and confused, like I'd just farted aloud. My reputation continued. I started marching away again and stopped when I realised Fry had followed.

'Something you needed?' I asked, still keeping out of wallaroo stink range.

'Ah, listen,' Fry was still picking at the door to the camera. 'Last night. In the bush. The panic attack. I don't usually, uh . . .'

'I'm not sure what you're referring to, Constable Fry,' I said. 'I killed a man last night. My recollection of the events beforehand is hazy at best.'

'Well, I'll remind you then,' Fry lifted his gaze to mine, determined. 'I had a panic attack, and you got me through it, and I'm telling you right now that I don't usually have those.'

'At what point did I ask you for an exhaustive breakdown of your medical and psychological history?'

'None,' Fry gave an exhausted exhalation at me, at all the rigid dickheads like me he'd obviously encountered before.

'Just as I thought,' I nodded. 'If you're done, I'll be off.'

'You're going to accept my thanks, Detective.'

'Am I?'

'Yes.'

I shook my head, thought about Bridie and my promise, felt vicious words rush up my throat and meet my lips and dissolve before they were spoken. 'Good,' I finally blurted. 'Great. Thanks accepted, Fry. Thanks accepted. You happy now?'

Fry smirked and walked away.

* * *

Dodge picked me up at the roadside, and we drove to the Special house. The cockatoos in the gumtrees around the property started screaming their heads off as soon as I stepped out of the car.

Dodge hobbled up the verandah steps, and I waited for him at the door. He had just learnt from me that there was no physical evidence to speak of in Linda Special's and Marian Richley's cases, which, as my brother had pointed out, wasn't an unusual occurrence for such old cases. Retired coppers taking home case materials or files as a hobby or a souvenir had been standard practice for many years, as well as boxes being lost to floods or fires, or pilfered from evidence holding by corrupt officers on the request of scumbags. That was the reason for the tight security at the forensics holding facility today. Cameras, supervised access to the boxes, sign-ins.

John Special let us in, and I stood there dejectedly in his inner doorway being hysterically shouted at by his daughter's dog while I tried to get a grip on what to do next. I noted that what I was experiencing wasn't just disappointment, but an off-balance feeling I recognised as being tied to this place. It had started the first time we'd come here. When the cockatoos started screaming at me.

At *me*? Yes, I realised: that's how it felt. But that didn't make any sense. Why did I think that?

'You two look like someone's stolen your last zac,' John commented, nudging the dog out of the way with a slippered foot. 'More coffee, I suppose?'

'That'd be nice,' Dodge said. To me he murmured, 'What if we could give them something new?'

I almost laughed. A sad, angry laugh welled up in my throat, at the idea that someone could tamper with or accidentally lose evidence in murders as vicious and callous as this. At the idea that there was still a chance the killer had left his mark here, on the house, half a century later. I shook my head again, deliberately tried to knock that purely insane thought out of my skull. It made no sense. 'What the hell could we possibly give them, *fifty years* later?'

'We could do an exhumation.' Dodge shrugged. 'See what's under her fingernails.'

'That'll take a year to get approved, and she'd have been scrubbed clean for redressing and burial.'

'Uh, Mr Special?'

'Don't tell him.' I grabbed Dodge's forearm.

'I'm just thinking'—Dodge nodded, following the old man into the kitchen—'Do you remember what police took at the time of your wife's murder? The original investigating officers?'

'They took a bunch of stuff.' John shook his head. 'A doorknob. The broken glass. Bits of the shower drain. Her clothes. Some floorboards.'

'They lifted up the floor?' I asked.

'Yup. Took three sections from the hall there.' He pointed. The little dog followed his owner's finger, sniffed the floor and looked suspiciously at me. 'Linda was lying right there when she was found. Bled right through the floor. They didn't exactly know why they were taking the floor, the original guys. They just felt like it made sense. I think maybe they knew something like DNA was coming, in the future. They were right. They tested the boards in the mid-eighties. Didn't get anything, though.'

'Would they have been looking for his blood?' Dodge wondered aloud. 'Did they think he'd probably cut himself while he stabbed her?'

'More likely sweat,' I said. 'Sweaty business, killing someone, in my experience.' I felt both men staring at me. Scratched my brow to hide my eyes. 'I don't mean in my experience of *doing it*, I mean of working murders.'

'Although, last ni—' Dodge started.

'Shut up, Dodge,' I finished for him.

I looked at the spot on the floor between me, in the front entryway, and the men in the kitchen. I went there. The dog moved aside for me. Dodge stayed in the kitchen, talking to John. 'So they replaced those three floorboards, obviously.'

'Yup.'

I bounced on the floorboards in the hall. Heard them creak. Had a flash of being under the floor at Stephen Branch's house, the dirt at my back, pressing upwards with the sole of my boot and hearing those boards groan. I remembered the boards pulling against their nails. Dry, steel nails embedded deep in the joists and reluctant to shift.

'John?' I called.

'Yeah.'

'Do you have a saw?'

EVAN

I went into Dad's bedroom first. There was a tobacco stain on the ceiling, billowing out in a big brown-and-yellow cloud from the top of the bed like a portal to somewhere outside this world. The curtains above the reeking, thin pillows hadn't been shifted in years, it seemed. I opened the bedside drawers, had to heave them back sharply to get them to shift. Water swelling in the chipboard. There were cigarettes, paperwork, socks, junk. An old picture of Mum with a big crack in the glass, buried under packets of various medicines for sinuses and funguses and headaches. I opened the chest of drawers, pushed clothes around, my heart heavy and my body jumpy. Because I didn't want this to be it: this spiral-bound notebook flopped in the corner of the shoe cupboard. Or this: this shoebox crumpled under a laundry basket in the hallway outside the bedroom. I didn't want to find Dad's trophies. I didn't want there to *be* any trophies. I wanted my father to be what he'd said he was: a good man who made a couple of terrible, terrible mistakes. One of them an accident, even. All of them things he deeply regretted.

But I knew, deep down in my soul, that wasn't the case.

So I kept looking.

I went through Russell's childhood bedroom, which was full now of steel shelves and machinery parts and tools and screws and boxes. Moved on to the junk room where I'd found the photographs, the room I'd grown up in, the room with the mouldy chairs. In the laundry, under the rusty sink, stood a row of cleaning chemicals, which were leaking and sticky from disuse. Some had probably been originally purchased by my dead mother, they looked so old, their labels faded completely. I almost disregarded the pink plastic box shoved behind the bottles, exhaustion making me careless. When I drew it out, I knew what I'd found. My body sensed it. I sat in the grease and muck and hair on the laundry floor and pried open the box.

A jade bracelet was the first thing I picked up. It came untangled from the pile neatly, round beads like strung garden peas, glossy and fat. In the tangled lump of jewellery, I saw necklaces. A locket, which I picked open with shaking hands: a tiny oval-shaped window that revealed to me a girl with a slick black bob and chubby cheeks. A ring slid away from the pile of jewellery and clattered into the corner of the box. The letter 'J' was engraved in a little gold heart with a blue stone. I pulled a ribbon out of the pile. Then a hairclip. Then a set of plastic dental retainers.

I put the box down and cried. My phone rang. It was Delle. I had to wait until she'd called and I'd not answered twice, sixteen full rings, before I had the composure to call her back.

'Yeah.'

'Evan, Chrissy is freaking out,' Delle said. 'Have you seen the SMS?'

'Which one?'

'The police have sent one. It's gone out to every phone in the area. Chris and I both got it. It's on the local news, as well. They're looking for a guy who was at the pub on—'

'Okay. Yep. I knew that was coming. And I know that it was Chris,' I said, rubbing my nose. 'Tell him not to worry. I'm going to fix it.'

'He says he was there with your father.'

'I know.'

'Should he go into Redbelly? Can you—I don't know—smooth it over with your people? He's telling me he didn't see anything that night. But he's worried they're going to hang him out to dry because he didn't come clean about being there in the first place.'

'Delle,' I told her, 'everything's going to be okay. I'm fixing it.'

'If you come home, maybe just go easy on him.' Her voice softened. 'He's really worried. We can take him to task for being alone with your lunatic of a father some other time. Right now he's asking me what he's going to do if he's arrested, Evan.'

'Just tell him that he's not going to get arrested,' I said. 'And tell him that I love him, Delle.'

I rang off and sat looking at the jewellery in the box on the floor between my legs, trying to guess how many lives the pieces here represented. How many families. How many people. How many years of sleepless nights and horrific wonderings by parents, siblings, friends. I picked up a small gold pin and turned it in the light from the grimy window. It was a cassowary under a banner that read *Welcome to Cairns Airport.*

A box of ended lives. A wedding ring on a leather string made me look to my own gold band, dull and scratched, sitting against my knuckle. I thought about taking the ring off and adding it to the box. Because my life was over now, too. I couldn't hide this. I couldn't bury this box of lives. The right and good thing to do was to come clean, to end the suffering of these people and their families. And in doing so, I would turn the world's attention to my father. And his whereabouts. They'd find him. And then they'd turn on me.

He had killed me.

My fists balled and I dropped the box.

'You *fucking killed me, too!*'

I could almost hear him laughing from the water not far away. Sitting there, rotting and laughing and being eaten by fish. The rage was suffocating. I threw the box of jewellery against the wall and stood and kicked a hole in the laundry door, kept kicking it until it burst open.

Then the thing stirred in me again. The sharp, black, slithering thing, the thing whose approach was heralded by thunderous noise that blanked out all reason, all goodness and rightness. The thing that had made me murder him. These lives were gone. Mine was in the balance. I'd been willing to bury three girls to save myself and my family. What did ten more matter? What did fifty? Locking me up was not going to give them what they wanted. They wanted Arthur. And he was gone. I had no justice to offer anyone. No closure. It was a waste to give them myself. It was just a waste of a life.

In a state of cold, liquid defiance, I started gathering all the jewellery up. Piece by piece. Putting it back in the box. Signing my soul away.

RUSSELL

Dodge was quiet for a long while, leaning in the doorway, watching me work, because there really wasn't room for the two of us down on the floor. I pried up a second long hardwood plank using the claw hammer John had brought us. The wood was dry, creaky, wanting to crack as it popped sideways out of the tongue-and-groove system keeping it locked in. The nails were almost musical, squeaking and groaning as they surrendered and came out of the joists, bent like talons. I glimpsed bare dirt under the house. Ants. John Special was in the kitchen, sitting with the dog at his feet, watching me sweat and eating Tim Tams.

'Is this a good time to admit I don't know what we're doing?' Dodge asked.

'That makes two of us,' John added.

'I want to get these planks off the floor,' I said. 'And get down to the joist underneath.'

'Why?' Dodge asked.

'Because the officers working this case back in 1977 took away the planks of wood that ran through here,' I said, fitting the claw hammer under a third plank. 'The ones Linda bled onto. I'm hoping she might have bled right through those planks and onto the joist underneath. Maybe her blood followed down and pooled in the old nail holes in the wood. And maybe there's something of her killer's DNA in there, with that blood. Maybe his blood, or sweat, or whatever. I don't know. It's a shot in the dark, but that's what this case is going to take, I think.'

'Why do you need anything further from the floor, if the police have already got three planks worth?' John asked. I put the hammer down, ripped the plank up by hand and slid it into the space beside me, pushing it further down the hall. Sweat was running into the blackberry scratches in my hairline, making them sting. I wiped my hands on my shirt and heaved a sigh, wanting to bark my way out of the corner I was in but knowing that wasn't an option anymore.

'Mr Special'—I looked at him—'my brother is working on this case with us. He's just come from forensic evidence holding down in Sydney. The boxes of evidence relating to your wife's case have been . . . Well, we don't know what's happened. But the evidence is not there.'

John leant forward in his chair, put a withered hand on the green Formica table beside him. 'What did you say?'

'The physical evidence is missing,' Dodge said. I was grateful for the help. 'It's gone.'

'Gone?'

'We don't know that it's *gone* gone,' I said, my voice filled with an optimism that wasn't part of my character at all. 'It's just looking like the boxes it was stored in do not . . . contain it, at the present time.'

'You've got to be fucking kidding me.' John rose to his feet. The dog, sensing his anguish, rose as well and started snarling at Dodge like this was all his fault. '"The boxes it was stored in do not contain it at this present time"? Are you guys having me on?'

'I'm sorry.' I got to my feet. 'I'm sorry. That was . . . that was cop speak. I shouldn't have said it like that.'

'You're telling me that my wife's evidence is . . .'

Dodge came towards the old man, his hands up, placating. The little dog lunged at his bad leg. Louis Dodge, seemingly in possession of more restraint than anyone I'd ever witnessed in my career, bit down on the pain and bent over carefully, taking the dog gently by the collar and pulling it away from his damaged limb until the old man could get a hold of it.

'Just let's take a minute to get some air,' Dodge was saying, gesturing to the doorway to the back patio, his face purple with swallowed screams. 'John, let's sit out here and just talk it through, huh?'

I kept ripping up the floor, trying to understand why I'd lost the ability to speak like a normal person. I didn't seem to know what to say, or how to say it, in this shiny new life where I didn't just snap at people to get what I wanted. I was falling into cop speak, a language I despised. With five planks out of the floor, I took my phone out, turned the torch on, and looked at the joist running across the hallway from left to right. The wood was extremely dark. Ancient, treated hardwood, ironbark or gum by the smell. I couldn't tell if it was stained with blood or not. I shone the light over the old, original nail holes, which sat just millimetres to the left of the new set that had been made when the floorboards were replaced.

Dodge stepped back into the doorway as I picked up the handsaw from beside the skirting board at my elbow. I dropped down into the hole I'd made and set the saw against the joist.

'How is he?' I asked.

'Pissed.'

'That makes two of us.'

'Three,' Dodge sighed. 'The truly sad thing is how often I've heard it. That a box is missing or messed with. This must be about my fourth time.'

'Hmm.'

'If we had those original planks, we could have just re-run them. The tech is better now. We might have got DNA they missed the first time.'

'Mmm-hmm.'

'You're not gonna cut through that whole joist.' Dodge smirked as I started sawing. 'The whole house'll cave in.'

'I'm going to go down a couple of inches and pop a slab off the top. As deep as a flooring nail. That's all I need.'

'That'll be treated hardwood.'

'Yep.'

'You'll have to cut it into sections and knock them through with a hammer. That space is too small for a circ-saw or a chainsaw.'

'Uh-huh.'

'It'll take you all day.'

'Well, Louis, I sure am hoping not to have to do it all myself while someone prattles on at me,' I said, raising my voice, and one eyebrow, at him. He got the hint and beckoned for the saw. I handed it to him and climbed out of the hole.

* * *

The mountain behind the house was quiet as we packed up the Hilux. In all, I took two A4 evidence bags of wooden blocks from the joist under John Special's house. I bagged, sealed and labelled them as Dodge took photos of the handling. John came in from the back of the house as I was nailing the boards I'd lifted back down into a temporary bit of pine Dodge had found in a woodshed. I'd cut the pine to size, filled the hole in the joist and returned everything to where it belonged. The old man watched me work with a distant look in his eyes, like this was just one in a long series of mistakes and mishandlings that had opened a crevasse between him and the New South Wales Police.

I wanted to tell him so many things. That I didn't know the police who'd handled Linda's murder back in 1974—this Herman Grey and his men—but I could assume with good authority that they'd been rural cops in over their heads with this kind of thing, the same way Dodge and his crew were now, and all their good intentions couldn't make up for a lack of training, support and technology that would have made this case easier to solve. I wanted to tell Mr Special that I was sorry about whoever had lost or hidden his wife's evidence, whether they'd deliberately done so or had been taking a shortcut by slitting the box open to retrieve the evidence and hadn't returned the items to their proper place. I wanted to apologise on behalf of whomever had been kicking around this case across the past fifty years, which was almost certainly a series of half-invested, over-worked and under-appreciated homicide cops with crumbling marriages and pent-up trauma. Detectives who had ten to fifteen more urgent, more contemporary cases on their hands at any one time, and who were expected to chase down Linda's killer on their lunch hours or weekends. I wanted to say I was sorry that another young woman had had to die just so someone would look into his wife's death with any real interest or optimism again. But the truth is, I didn't have the guts to say all that. I was just too ashamed. So I said nothing at all as I swept up the dust and wood splinters in the hall with a dustpan and brush I found under the sink.

Dodge and I drove back towards town in silence, the rumble of the road and the mid-afternoon light flicking across the bonnet. I'd offered to drive, but Dodge said he wanted to work the leg. My phone started ringing, and I looked at the number and felt a whump of fear in my stomach that made me groan out loud. I almost asked Dodge to pull over so I could take the call in private, but was so nervous to answer I didn't have time.

'Georgia,' I said. 'Hi.'

It was the first time we'd communicated verbally in a year and a half.

'Why *the fuck* am I seeing your face on the national news?' she snarled.

'Urgh.' I rubbed my brow, glanced at Dodge, who was steadfastly watching the road. 'It's a long story. I caught a murder maybe an hour before I was supposed to pick Bridie up.'

'No, you didn't,' Georgia snapped. 'No, you didn't, Rus. What you did was you smacked a junkie and got sent out of town on a wild goose chase so Gail Caplan could enjoy a break from you and your bullshit. I've spoken to the boys at Maroubra Station.'

'I did say it was a long story.'

'Return our child to Sydney *at once*.'

'Look,' I said carefully, 'Bridie is a legal adult. And she made the decision to come out here with me.'

'I don't give a deep-fried, coconut-encrusted *rat's arse* what she decided! The whole point of you being together this week was so you could reconnect—not so you could chase murderers and she could sit alone in a hotel room!'

'Bridie and I have actually been communicating really well,' I said. 'We've answered some really hard questions for each other.'

'She's not riding along with you on this, is she?'

'I'm talking about the downtime. Which—I mean, there hasn't been as much as there could have been—but it's been good.'

'How nice,' she said. I remembered Georgia's expression when she used to say these words, 'How nice', which she did with a kind of iciness that could freeze your balls clean off your body, make them hit the ground and shatter into a million pieces. Times when I'd come home after big nights out with the boys when we were newly married: 3 a.m., stinking of bourbon. *Oh, you're home finally. How nice.*

'She's in danger there, Rus. There's a fucking madman running around that tiny town killing young women. And if he's not the undies-stealing freak that you killed—which I'm guessing he isn't, because you're still there—then there's a whole separate fucking maniac on the loose! What *is* this place? I cannot *believe* you would take her to this backwater hellhole!'

I chewed my tongue and thought about telling Georgia that, undies-stealing weirdos aside, far more young women were murdered in the safety of their own homes by madmen or, more often, by their boyfriends and husbands, in perfectly large and populated cities. But because I don't have a death wish, I said, 'I'm sorry, Georgia.'

'Fuck your sorries.'

'To be honest, I wish Bridie had been riding along with me on this the whole time,' I ventured. 'She flagged something super early that I think might actually pan out.'

'If you convince that child to become a cop, Russell, I will turn you into liquid fertiliser and hose you all over my lawn.'

'Fair enough.'

'Send. Her. Home.'

Georgia hung up. I slid the phone back into my pocket. Dodge and I met eyes for the briefest of seconds.

'Ex-wife,' I said.

'Ex . . . *wife*?'

'It's another long story,' I said. Now it was Dodge's turn to take a phone call. He answered by picking up the mobile rather than putting it on hands free, which vaguely annoyed me. He listened for a few seconds, then glanced at me.

'Sorry,' he said, pulling off the road. I guessed it was the wife, couldn't think of anything he was trying to keep private from me specifically. He got out and went to the edge of a sprawling green field. A horse got curious about him and walked over. Dodge listened to the call, head down, patting the horse's nose absent-mindedly. He seemed nervous when he came back. Looked through me, like he was trying to figure out how to soften the blow of bad news.

'What is it, Dodge?'

'There's a . . .' He gripped the wheel. 'There's a couple of awkward questions that need answering.'

EVAN

I patted the dirt down with the shovel, making a nice, smooth mound of earth where I'd buried the box of my father's trophies. The spot I'd chosen was between two of the aluminium sheds, an indistinct patch of weeds where the soil was soft and mossy from lack of sun. My phone rang as I was heading back to the house, dusting my hands off on the legs of my jeans.

'I want to ask you a few uncomfortable questions,' Russell said.

Immediately, the hairs on the back of my neck began to rise. Russell didn't have any problems asking uncomfortable questions. In fact, saying the wrong thing and making people around him uncomfortable were some of his favourite hobbies. I stopped beside a rusty body of a Landau that had grass growing across its entire windscreen, blocking out view of the interior. 'What's happened?'

'Well,' Russell said. 'What's happened is that Dodge's entire team has been stood down from duty by Gail Caplan. During that process, Knowles has been doing his handover to his counterpart on Gail's team, and he's started telling the guy about the traffic cameras. The ones he's been working through, one at a time, interviewing all the drivers who came in and out of Redbelly that night.'

I put my head down and kept walking.

'Knowles has tried to find the printout that you had at the beer garden,' Russell said. 'But he can't find it. Because Dodge has it. So Knowles figures he'll just make his own printout directly from the traffic cam database. Only, he notices that there's an extra car on there now.'

'Okay.' I drew a long breath. 'Okay, Russell.'

'That car belongs to an Uber driver. Knowles calls the Uber driver, and what does he say?'

'He says he drove a guy named Christopher Powder into Redbelly on the night Chloe was murdered,' I said.

'Are you *shitting me*, Evan?'

'No,' I breathed. 'No. I'm not. I covered up the fact that Chris was in Redbelly at the time of the murder. He's the young guy at the pub. The one that was on the CCTV.'

'I'm going to fucking kill you!'

'It's not a big problem.'

'"It's not a big problem"?!'

'I'll admit to it.' I went to the house, pulled the door shut. 'It won't blow back on you. I'll say my son was there, engaged in underage drinking, and I panicked and covered it up.'

'How could you do that? How could—With your history—What were you—'

'Could you take a minute and breathe, and complete a sentence?' I said. There was silence on the line. 'You're not completing any of your sentences, Russell.'

More silence. I went to my car and slipped into it, sat in the sun-warmed stillness.

'Listen, Evan.' Russell paused. I got the feeling there was someone else there, inhibiting him. I could hear the airy roar of a car in the background. 'I'm catching a weird vibe off you.'

'Okay.'

'I don't know. Maybe it's just . . . not having seen you for a while. And the past few days. Are you and Delle okay? Is Chrissy okay?'

I bit down hard on my lips, wiped tears from my face. 'Yeah? We're fine. Everybody's fine. I just, uh . . . I did something dumb. Again. I'm embarrassed. There's nothing more to it.'

'Mmm.' Russell was quiet again for a long while. Uncharacteristically quiet. 'I want to see you. Where are you right now?'

'I stopped at Dad's.'

'Okay, stay there. I'm heading to Pemulwuy, so I'll have to drive right past. I'll meet you at the end of the road.'

'Why are you going to Pemulwuy?'

'I've got evidence to hand in. On Linda Special's case. I'm hoping for DNA.'

'What?' I put my head against the steering wheel. Pressed the phone hard against my ear. 'Are you kidding me? You've got something new? How? It's been fifty years!'

'I'll explain later. I'll drop in what I have, rustle them up to move on it straight away, and see if we can't get a DNA profile for this fucker. If he's the same guy who killed Chloe, this whole thing is going to explode.'

I covered my eyes.

'I'm supposed to bring Bridie home,' Russell went on. 'Georgia just ripped my dick off about her being here in the middle of all this. So, I'll drop off Bridie, drop off the samples for testing, go back and smooth it over with Georgia while I'm waiting for the results. I'll hit the lab just before it closes. I'll tell the techs they're not going home until I get my results. I'll lock the doors if I have to.'

A plan was forming. I wrung the steering wheel with one hand, squeezing my phone with the other. 'Georgia can wait until tomorrow, can't she? It's getting late. If you leave Bridie at Redbelly, I could drop her home in the morning.'

'No. It's okay. I'll see if Georgia will go face to face with me,' Russell said. 'I'm trying to be . . . Um. I'm trying to be a bit . . . different. Trying to make things better for Birds. Life would be a lot easier for that kid if I got on the same playing field as her mother.'

'Sounds like those therapists have been getting into your head.'

'They'll do that.'

'If it was me, I'd go see Georgia by myself,' I said. 'Leave Bridie in Redbelly Crossing. You don't want to be facing off with Georgia with Bridie standing right there.'

'Maybe. You might be right.'

'I think that's the way to go.' I eased a long, unsteady breath. 'You, um. You're going to take the 'Stang?'

'What else would I take?'

'Oh, I just wondered if you'd take someone's country car,' I said quickly. 'Aren't you worried about the Mustang's paint job?'

'I want to go pedal to the metal. I'll put the paint touch-up on an invoice to the New South Wales Police. Along with the floor I just pulled up and twenty-seven cold beers I intend to have the night we close this.'

My tears were flowing freely now. I looked like shit in the rear-view mirror. 'You going to leave there soon, then?'

'Soon as I can. Wait for me at the end of the road. I don't want to go anywhere near the farm.'

'Okay. Drive safe, mate. See you soon.'

'Yeah. See you soon,' Russell said.

RUSSELL

She was on the top deck, leaning against the railing outside the bridge where I'd held my meeting with Dodge's crew, her hands clasped and her head turned into the breeze. My daughter watched us approach the property on foot; straightened and gave a little inhibited wave. She reminded me of Georgia in the early days, when she'd still smile at the sight of me. Same smile. Same wave. She was down through the vessel and waiting for us at the door to the kitchenette as Dodge and I arrived at the stern. Dodge paused to take a phone call on the deck, and I went in.

'We've got to go, Birds.' I couldn't look at her. Georgia's anger was still thumping through my body, awakening those old memories. Of that night. Her horror, her humiliation. 'Your mum wants you back home.'

'Oh, Jesus.' Bridie clapped a hand to her brow. 'She found out.'

'Yep.'

'I didn't tell her, Dad.'

'I know. She saw it on the news.' I slipped past her, went down the stairs and into the kitchenette, started collecting up her belongings and placing them on the nook table for her. 'And you shouldn't have had to keep that secret. It's my fault.'

'Let me talk to her. I'll tell her I want to stay here.'

'I wouldn't, if I were you.'

'Is she pissed?'

'Oh yeah.'

'For *fuck's* sake!' Bridie flashed teeth, a rare slipping of her youthful gentility. 'It's not like I'm running around beside you, chasing suspects and shooting at people. I've been here at the boat. I've been on rescues. I got into a fix *one time*, but we handled it.'

'Georgia's got good reason to have a zero-tolerance attitude to my lies,' I said.

'You didn't lie to her.'

'I lied by omission.'

'Come home with me.' She watched Dodge come into the kitchenette, didn't even acknowledge him, her arms folded and her jaw set. 'You can both come and tell her I've been taking care of myself and she should leave me alone.'

'I'm out.' Dodge put his hands up. 'I've spent two days with this guy, now. I don't have the emotional energy to meet the nutjob who was crazy enough to marry him.'

I didn't respond. Neither did Bridie. I didn't realise she was following me until I was in the bedroom pulling the sheets back up on her unmade bed. 'Are you okay?' she asked.

'I'm fine. Help me pack, Bridie.'

'You're quiet.'

'Busy brain, that's all.'

I picked up her backpack and handed it to her. 'And . . . you know. I don't like to annoy your mother.'

She took her backpack from me and started packing. In the silence, we removed all her things from the room. Her headphones, clothes, water bottle, a smattering of books. I lifted the cage from the end of her bed and set it on the coverlet and pushed back the towel draped over the top to check on the possum. The lined, knitted pouch was lying in one corner, with a thin, furry tail protruding from it. At the tip of the tail, the fur changed from brown to white.

I put the towel back in place and turned and Bridie pushed her way into my arms. The feel of her shuddering against me threatened to set off a sympathetic wave of tears. I held strong, hugged her and stroked her hair. 'Hey, hey, hey. Come on.'

'I was having fun,' Bridie sniffed. I had to laugh at that.

'What was the most fun? Almost being killed by drug dealers, or being ignored while I ran around after a murderer?'

'I wasn't being ignored.' She stepped back from me. Looked me in the eyes. 'You've . . . you've come closer to me in the past two days than you have in the past five years.'

Oof. That hurt. The way she described it, the time we'd spent together, as me 'coming closer' to her. It made me sound like a wild fox being beckoned from the edge of the woods by a human, getting spooked and darting away between the trees by any sudden movement. It ached so badly to think of her that way, to know she was *thinking of herself* that way: as someone who had to be still, and silent, and constantly offering lures, just so I'd come within a reasonable distance. I was so sorry for it all, suddenly. Exhaustingly and agonisingly sorry. 'Next weekend,' I said. 'My place. We'll do it. I promise, Bridie. Okay? I promise.'

'You might still be out here.'

'I'll hand this whole thing over and come back. I'll have to, anyway. I killed a guy. Gail won't let me stay on it for too long.'

'Mum won't be happy.'

'I'll make it work, Birds,' I told her. 'You can trust me.'

She chewed her lips, tears falling freely. We stood in the tiny room together, between the beds, her little sniffles and breaths actively scoring the surface of my heart with cuts I knew I'd never heal. 'Did you speak to the carer for the possum?'

'Yeah, it's in Leets Vale.'

'Okay, change of plans, then,' I said. 'You take the 'Stang. I've got to get some stuff to the lab, so I'll go with Dodge. When you've got the animal where it needs to go, you head straight to your mum's. I'll meet you there to get the car back.'

'Will you speak to her?'

'Maybe.'

'*Dad.*'

'How about this,' I said. 'I'll text you on approach, and you can tell me if she's waiting behind the front door with a baseball bat. If she's unarmed, I'll come in and talk.'

Bridie braved a tiny smile, and I held her again. 'Go easy on the windy roads, Birds.'

'I will,' she said.

* * *

I watched Bridie pull out of the property gates with emotion so heavy and suffocating, I couldn't have discerned it as foreboding, fatherly instinct, a subliminal knowledge of what was about to happen. Dodge was in the passenger seat, his head resting against the headrest, rubbing his eyes hard. I slipped into the driver's seat beside him and tossed a muesli bar I'd taken from the kitchen into his lap. Before unwrapping one for myself, I took my gun from the back of my belt and handed it to him.

'What's this for?' he asked.

'I just don't want to have a gun on me right now,' I said. I unwrapped the snack and bit a hunk off as I pulled out of the property. 'I want to stop and talk to Evan at the end of the road leading to my father's house. The temptation to go there and put a bullet in his head will be overpowering. You may have to handcuff me to something.'

'Noted.'

'I'm going to call the lab,' I said. 'And tell them to get ready for us. I want to be top of the queue.'

Bridie was ahead of us on the road past the pub. I glanced at the activity there as someone picked up at the lab.

'It's Detective Inspector Russell Powder,' I said. 'I want—'

'Urgh!' the lab tech, Snelling, made a disgusted noise. I could tell it was him immediately from the huskiness and breathiness down the line. '*You* again!'

I was so stunned by his sudden brazenness that for a moment I was silent. 'Uh, yes. I want—'

'You know, Detective Inspector Powder, I'm getting a little tired of hearing about what *you* need, and about what *you* want,' Snelling barked. 'This phone line is for officers to use to make polite and reasonable enquiries about the samples they've submitted and their place in the queue. It's not your personal hotline for harassing and bullying the staff of this facility into skipping that queue entirely, like you're King Shit of Turd Island!'

'Well—'

'I was trying to say something important to you this morning, Detective Inspector Powder, and you cut me off,' Snelling blasted. 'It's *incredibly rude* to cut people off. Did you know that, sir? Is that something anyone has ever enlightened you on?'

'I—'

'*When* you cut me off'—Snelling paused to delight in his manoeuvre, which I'd fallen for, hook, line and sinker—'you denied me the chance to tell you that your completely inappropriate verbal spray was directed in *entirely* the wrong direction. Because your submitting officer, one Senior Sergeant '*Evan* Powder, was here when the discovery of the notebook was made. So *he* should have told you about the notebook, and it was quite reasonable for me to assume that he *would* tell you about the notebook, so abusing me because I didn't tell—'

'Wait a minute.'

'*Did you just cut me off?*'

'I'm sorry,' I said. The words felt like rocks in my mouth. 'I'm sorry, Snelling. I'm an arsehole. Just go back for a minute for me, would you? You said Evan was *there* when you made the discovery of the notebook?'

'Yes.'

'In the room with you?'

'Yes!' Snelling yelled. 'Are you deaf?'

'He was standing in the room with you. And you pulled out a notebook from the handbag. And he saw that.'

'That's what I said, Detective Inspector Powder.'

I hung up on Snelling. Which probably sent him into a murderous rage somewhere south-east of where I was driving, but it wasn't yet another intentional insult to the man. My mind was whirring. That same eerie discomfort, the one that had begun at John Special's house and continued to build, brick by brick, was becoming so weighty I couldn't focus on the phone or the road.

I pulled over, and Dodge seemed to know to just sit there quietly and let me think, based on the content of the phone call and the look on my face. I hung on to the steering wheel and stared at the road. Then I plucked up my phone again and called Snelling back. He must have seen my phone number in the phone's incoming call screen, because he was already spewing abuse when the line connected. I had to cut him off to get a word in.

'Evan took the preliminary DNA results from you, and he said there wasn't a match in NCIDD,' I said. 'Is that true?'

'I provide the profiles; I don't do the matching, you *gigantic ignoramus!*'

'Can you send me that profile again?' I said.

Snelling grumbled something fast and incomprehensible, and then he hung up. I got out of the car and stood by the field, looking at a distant row of trees that were frosted all over with cockatoos. Dodge got out of the car and stood by me. His hard, downturned mouth told me he was probably thinking exactly what I was thinking. Knew, before I spoke, what I might be about to say.

'Listen,' I said. The words started tumbling out, freefalling, my mind barely planning them or following their implications. 'My father was a cop in Maroota in the 1970s. That's, what—half an hour from here? Chloe emailed him, saying she wanted to come out and talk about the murders. Now I've got Evan hiding the fact that his son was at the pub. *And* hiding the fact that Chloe had a notebook.'

'He couldn't have hidden the fact that the notebook was there,' Dodge said. 'Not forever. All he could do was delay you finding out about it. And maybe that was by accident, sir. Maybe he was tired and distracted and—'

'No. No. It's not that. I feel like there's something here.' I could hear the horror in my voice. The knowing. 'Jesus Christ, Dodge, I can feel it.'

'We could check the police reports for that time, I guess,' Dodge said. 'But . . . I mean, mate. Are you really accusing your own father of . . . of something like *that*?'

'I don't know.' I thought of Evan. Of the weirdness. The fact that he was the one to tell me that Linda and Marian's evidence boxes were empty. Were they really empty? Had he found them empty? Had anyone seen it? I tried to push the thoughts away. But they kept coming back. 'Dodge—my nephew, Chris, was at the Redbelly pub with someone. He came back for two drinks. Two very different drinks.'

'Sir.'

'My father drinks Tooheys New.'

'Mate, I know Evan's work on this case has been a bit, sort of . . . inefficient,' Dodge said. 'And him admitting to covering for Chris . . . Hearing that your brother did that in a police investigation would shake anybody up. But you're making some mighty leaps here.'

'Someone knocks on your door in the middle of the night,' I said. 'You're a woman. You're home alone. They say they're a cop. Or—better yet—*you know them to be* a cop. You'd let them in, right?'

'Yes, but—'

'A cop attended Linda Special's house a week before she died. A *week*!'

'But that would have been a cop from Wisemans. Not from Maroota.'

'I just don't feel good about this.' I put my hands on my knees, bent forward, blew out air. My head was spinning. Thoughts crashing. 'I've got a real fucking *bad* feeling, Dodge. About all of this. The birds.'

'What birds?'

'The cockatoos. They were screaming at me at John Special's house. You were there. You heard them. They were doing it that night, too. The night she was killed. It's like they knew who I was, or . . . or who I'm related to. Maybe they think I'm him.'

'Oh, Jesus.' Dodge took my arm and pulled me upright. 'You can't go letting the local wildlife tell you who's a serial killer and who's not.'

'They can live to be eighty. Cockatoos. Bridie told me that once. I look just like my father. Maybe they saw me walking up to the house and—'

'Let's go and just speak to Evan.' Dodge helped me walk back to the car. 'If you want to run down this crazy idea about your father, the quickest way to do it would be to get our stuff to the lab. Get it tested. Run it against your DNA. The guy said he's sending you the results of the Chloe stuff. We can see what that's about, too. I'm sure Evan wasn't lying about there being no match. I'm sure of it, Russell.'

'Yeah.' I walked on. 'We'll do that. We'll get moving. Get some answers. Let's go. Get in. We've got to catch up to Bridie.'

'It won't be him,' Dodge said, hobbling along beside me. 'You can't have been raised by a serial killer. You'd know. A person would have to know, deep down in their guts.'

I slid into the driver's seat, not answering. Wondering what I did and didn't know.

EVAN

It was easier than I had expected. To let go. I had found the spot I wanted, turned the car around, and backed it painstakingly up the incline as far as it would go, knocking down struggling baby gums and grevilleas, crackling my way over the dry leaves and sticks until I was hidden in the undergrowth by the side of the road. I was pointed downward at a good, steep angle, and could see through the trees to a spot in the road maybe a hundred metres north. I sat there, a coiled spring, watching the road. Sweating, the engine running but the air conditioner shot to shit by someone in the twenty years the car had been rolling around the earth. It was an old Falcon I had chosen, in the end. Wide. Heavy. Ready to jump when I put my foot down, and an easy pick from the bucket of car keys Arthur had kept by the front door. I had found the car by clicking the fob and listening. Saw there was air in the tyres. Good to go.

I wiped my face, whispered reassurances and encouragements to myself, relenting sometimes to a string of verbal hatred for Dad and for myself that threatened to tip me over the edge into delirium. Now and then, a car appeared. A Fiat. A Toyota. A moving van. Once, a black Mazda, with me so ready for Russell's black Mustang to appear that I took my foot off the brake and shunted forward half a metre before slamming it on again. I caught one curious glance from the occupants of a car passing down on the road, heading south. Other than that, no one took notice of me. I watched, and I waited, and I sweated.

Beyond the line of trees on the other side of the road, the river slid past like an ancient brown snake. Silent, lethal.

The plan was just to knock Russell's car into the guardrail. To hit the back quarter, smash it hard, the force of the impact shunting the car sideways, maybe causing it to spin and hit the incline where I now waited with relatively little carnage. I could see it happening. See Russell's body whumping into the driver's-side window of the 'Stang, bouncing off the steering wheel, coming to a bloody and glass-showered halt in the middle of the sun-scorched asphalt. He wouldn't die. *Couldn't* die. Yes, there was always the risk of serious, life-changing injury. But wasn't that fair? Wasn't that justice? If I was going to survive this, I'd have to do it with mental scars that would eat up the rest of my life, slowly and steadily, like a cancer. My family would never be the same again. Delle. Chrissy. Russell would have a shattered leg, a broken shoulder, a fractured skull, maybe, to even things out. Too bad. And Dodge—okay. That part was unfair. But I could feel bad about that later. There wasn't time now. I saw myself exiting my car before the men could recover from the crash, clambering out from behind the airbag, if indeed that was still operating. I saw myself, hood up, cap down, getting to Russell's Mustang while Russell and Dodge came to their senses. I saw myself snatching up the evidence bags from the back seat and stealing away.

When the Mustang finally came, I figured the hardest part would be lifting my foot off the brake. But I was so ready. So *willing*. I hit the accelerator, watching the car through the trees, as our two vehicles came together. I rumbled down the hill. The Mustang sailed along the road. It was a split-second before impact that I saw that it was Bridie behind the wheel. I'd had my eyes on the figure sitting there from a hundred metres out. But she had Russell's height. His big hands on the wheel. His dark hair. Seeing it was her, and hearing my own scream of regret, might have been what caused me to slam my boot down on the brake at that last fraction of a second, so that my car clipped the back edge of the Mustang and didn't smash into the last quarter, as I'd intended. The impact was just at the right angle to send the Mustang into a full spin that Bridie tried to correct with wild steering. My bumper walloped into the guard rail, glass raining everywhere, all the bones in my chest and shoulders and arms and face crunching as the airbag ballooned into me.

I recovered in time to see the Mustang come out of its spin, fishtail off the road completely and go sailing down the embankment just beyond the guardrail.

I watched in horror as the car, with my niece in it, hit the river at a hellish angle, spraying whitewash. The whole front half had disappeared before I could even pop my door.

RUSSELL

I saw the Mustang go into the river.

It happened out of the corner of my eye, the embankment visible around the corner from where I was on a long stretch of road lined by houses up on stilts. It was the movement of the trees that caught my gaze. A hole in the tree line busted through, the car appearing, then disappearing, then the spray. Dodge must have seen the impact at the same time as me. He shot upwards in his seat, grabbing the dashboard. 'Whoa-whoa-whoa-whoa!'

'Bridie!' I howled.

'Go.' Dodge gripped my arm. 'Go!'

I slammed my foot on the accelerator, my eyes on the curve of the river. Dodge had his window down. Was unbuckling his seatbelt. 'Fuck! Fuck!'

'Oh, Jesus! Bridie!'

'We'll get there. Careful of the corner. Careful-careful-careful-care—'

I took the corner too fast, skidded on the road in the Hilux, fishtailed so hard I hit my head on the window beside me. I recovered and approached the straight in the road leading to where my daughter's car had left the asphalt at drag-racing speed. There was a car in the road already, at ninety-degrees to the guardrail. An old Falcon, the airbag deployed. No sign of the driver. I didn't even park the Hilux. Just got to the scene and leapt out. I heard Dodge yell with surprise, struggling to pull the handbrake up as I ran towards the edge of the road, sprinting down the incline, my stride leaping blocks of sandstone and fallen logs, following the path of broken bushes and trees. I hit the water at full pelt, my pace finally slowing, the brown muck and mud and water embracing me with open arms. There was already a guy in the water, the Falcon driver, I assumed, wading out, wearing a hoodie and cap. I ignored him, shoved past and dove in, heading for the rows of bubbles making a slow march across the gently moving tide.

The water was cold, the colour and opacity of milky tea. I dove down and reached out, scooped mud with my hands, no idea how far down I was. The water got black so quickly. Maybe two metres from the surface. I came back up, guessing the car must be further out, my gasps for air punctuated by a panicked whimpering I was unfamiliar with, the sound of a desperate father, the cries of an animal. I shouted for her. Tried to gauge where the car went in and which way the tide was pulling me. I turned, tried to see the bubbles again. I went down. Pulled myself towards the bottom. Gripped dirt and weeds. Came up. Went down.

I was on my fifth trip back from the bottom of the river, rising through the darkness, when I copped a blow to the face. The distinctly curved, rubbery heel of a shoe. Bridie must have been just ahead of me, on her way to the surface as well, when she kicked down and got me right beside the nose. I pulled upwards, kicked hard, burst to the surface of the water right beside her, at the same time. She came up screaming, grabbing me by the shoulders, her hair plastered over her face and her thin arms swinging around my neck.

'Dad! Dad!'

'Oh my god! My baby!' I raked her hair back, held her face, our legs tangling as we fought to stay above water. 'Baby! Baby! Baby!'

'I'm okay!' She coughed up a mouthful of water, drew a shuddering breath. 'I'm okay!'

We were crying. For a few precious, horrifying, exhilarating seconds we swam together and held each other, and I cried for how close I'd come to the nightmare of all nightmares. Then Bridie said,

'Just a sec!' and slipped from my arms and was gone. She didn't wait for me to say anything. She just went.

I grabbed at the water and turned and twisted around, shuddering gulps of horror coming out of me. Screaming her name. I heard my voice ripple off the steep forest walls. She didn't answer, and I wondered whether in a terrified dream I'd imagined holding her in my arms at all. The world careened around me. I took a deep breath and prepared to go back down.

She appeared again, a few metres away, blowing out air and gripping a soaked knitted bundle high above her head with one arm as she swam towards me with the other.

'You went back for the—' I breathed. The fury took me quickly, my words thickening to a growl. 'Bridie! *Bridie!* You went back for the *fucking possum!? Are you out of your mind!?*'

She didn't answer. I didn't realise Dodge was in the water too until he popped up beside me. He saw Bridie and me and started turning back towards the shore. 'Oh, hell. That was close. Is she okay?'

I didn't know if Bridie was okay or not. She got to the shore, sat heavily on her butt on the sand and began frantically unpeeling the knitted bundle. She pulled a sopping handful of blackened fur from the bundle and examined it closely, patting back spikes of matted hair from a tiny face. Meanwhile blood was pouring down her face in dark rivulets from a cut in her hairline. She didn't even seem to notice.

'She's okay,' Bridie reported, holding the little struggling animal to her chest. Heaving a sigh of relief. 'She's still breathing.'

I knelt before my child and looked at the gash in her head. There were cuts all over her arms and chest. Safety-glass rash. Her total and utter lack of concern for anything other than the infant possum made me wonder if she was concussed. Dodge hobbled towards me and sat down, handed me a cloth handkerchief, offered from his pocket and soaking wet, and I pressed it against the cut in Bridie's head. I could see more cars up on the road. Bystanders stopping. The guy in the hoody had disappeared. 'Birds, what happened?'

'It was Uncle Evan,' Bridie said.

EVAN

It was over. Darkness was approaching. I walked the edge of the river, leaving footprints in the sand, mentally envisioning my death. Seeing myself twisting and writhing in the pits of hell.

Burn, burn, burn.

I wasn't entirely sure if it was pure fantasy, panic, or exhaustion-induced delirium. But some part of me remembered Bridie turning towards me at the last second before impact, her hands on the steering wheel and her eyes wide, and I thought I saw recognition in her face. If Bridie had indeed seen me, recognised my face under the ball cap, it didn't matter. Any of it. Dad's DNA. Chloe's murder. The old cases, those women, the women and girls whose pieces of jewellery I had found at Dad's house. The CCTV didn't matter. Chris being at the pub didn't matter. If Bridie had seen me, then Russell would know I had been the one to harm his child, intentionally or not.

And Russell would kill me.

It was over. But that didn't mean I was going to go out on my knees. I was going to give it everything I had, if only to spare Russell having to deliver the deadly blow. I'd run. Because I was a coward, and cowards always ran, and there was something wholesome-sounding about being shot in a hotel room somewhere, thousands of miles from here, by some random outback cop while I tried to cross the country and get away from what I'd done. Something romantic.

I had turned away from the river and was pushing through reeds towards the mudflats bordering a wide, grassy field when I saw the reptile lying like a shiny black stick across my path. I looked down and spotted the animal mid-step, too late to adjust my stance. I stepped on the snake, yelped in shock, tried to tip backwards before my whole weight came down on the creature. I slid in the mud, toppled backwards instead and fell on my butt.

The snake made an imprint in the soft earth. A belly, ridged and curved. It darted forward, shocked by being stepped on, trying to escape, found itself blocked by a lump of sandstone, turned back and found itself hedged in by my leg. I tried to scramble backwards. Put my hand down. The snake struck at my wrist. Just one bite, swift, fleeting, hardly leaving a mark. The impact was barely more painful than a pinch.

The snake made a getaway up over my lap and into the long grass, gone without making a sound.

I lay back and gripped my wrist, my head in the mud, the wild blue sky beyond the trees above me starting to twist and shimmer as my raging heartbeat coursed blood through my veins, carrying the venom along, a sweeping river. I looked at the site of the bite. There wasn't even any blood. Just two holes, slowly darkening lumps, at the wrist joint.

I got up and went on, moving more slowly through the reeds.

RUSSELL

As a cop, you spend a lot of time in emergency rooms. Basically your first two years are spent there, getting statements off assault victims, chasing up the fate of car crash victims, delivering wild, thrashing, often naked junkies there to be strapped down and sedated. It was odd to be sitting beside Bridie's bed in plain, wet clothes, listening to the stories of the patients around me with no investment in their circumstances, no need to catalogue the facts. The bed to our right contained a woman whose partner had broken her nose during a game of pickleball, whatever that was. The partner was deeply, loudly, apologetic. To the left of us, an older woman was sleeping, having been brought in with chest pains, and her husband was reading a newspaper and eating Twisties. Something mysterious had happened to a guy across the room from us, who was unconscious and swaddled in bandages and whose feet were smeared with blue paint.

Bridie was furiously sending texts, her head mended and bandaged. We were waiting to hear the results of her CT scan. Dodge was trying to get the lay of the land, appearing at the end of the room now and then and watching me from the hall while he talked on the phone and paced and chewed his nails.

When Georgia came in, I felt a wave of pre-embarrassment in anticipation of being slapped in front of room full of people. I rose from my plastic chair and prepared to accept my fate. Because I probably would have slapped me, if I was her, for all of this. She was leaner and harder and more sculpted than the last time I'd seen her, still wearing the Inner West detective's usual garb of immaculately tailored grey slacks and black collared shirt, sleeves rolled back over her forearms. She ran in and brushed right past me, swept Bridie's face into her hands, started kissing her.

'Oh my god, my honey. My little honey!'

'I'm okay.' Bridie let her phone drop into her lap and she closed her eyes for the assault of kisses. 'I really am, Mum.'

I wandered away and left them to talk. Didn't go too far. Because I knew the longer I delayed the slap or the kick in the nuts or whatever I was about to get, the worse it would seem. Anticipation is half the pain. I found a spot and leant against the wall beside a big poster about domestic violence towards men, and waited. Georgia came over before long, and I was surprised that she didn't go right in for the blow.

In fact, she said, 'Are you okay?'

'*Me?*'

'Yes, you, Russell.' She looked at my eyes. 'I've been speaking to your partner Dodge for the past ten minutes. He called me on the ride here. Gave me an overview.'

I looked down the room towards Dodge, who was still on the phone. It hadn't occurred to me that he'd been debriefing my ex-wife before her arrival, maybe hoping to soften her perspective towards me, while he paced back there and talked. It was such an unspeakably nice thing to do that for a moment I just stood there, dumbstruck, wondering how the hell he'd even got her number. Georgia was still watching me with her keen brown eyes, and I shrugged. 'Ah, I'm . . . I'm sort of numb.'

'Do you think it's real?' Georgia asked. 'I mean . . . yeah, your dad's a psycho. But *this*, Rus?'

I fell into thinking. I kept doing that, unable to pull myself out, knowing people wanted answers from me but being powerless to give them. The memories were thick, dragging, like sludge. I saw Evan and me in an old car we'd done up on the sly. A Chevrolet, maybe. Two girls. Dad busting us, telling the girls he wanted to watch.

There were other memories. Him arriving home in the wee hours, washing his hands in the tap outside by the water tank. Selling the main family car suddenly, for dirt cheap, having spent far too long cleaning it. Disappearing for weeks or months at a time, or having unexplainable scratches on his face.

'Rus?'

'We could know for sure, in a few hours,' I said. 'The samples got to the lab. Gail got some of her ground crew to take them the rest of the way.'

'But what do you think?'

'I don't know what I think,' I said. 'I'm . . . I'm not as desperate to know if Dad would rape and murder young women as I am to know if Evan would cover it up. Because if that's the case, I've got two monsters on my hands, not just one.'

'There's a Keep A Look Out For order on Evan,' Georgia said.

'Is there?'

'Yeah.'

The world was upside down. I took out my phone and called him.

'He won't answer,' Georgia said, looking at my screen.

'Maybe not to them, but he'll answer to me.'

'No, I mean, he doesn't have his phone.' Georgia put a hand on my arm. 'They found it in the car that hit Bridie.'

I felt my jaw tighten. I looked at my ex-wife and she must have seen the blackness in my eyes, because she took a step back.

'Bridie said it was Evan who hit her,' I said. 'But I thought she was crazy. Shaken up from the crash. She dove back down to the sunken car for that fucking possum.'

Georgia didn't say anything. I remembered the last time I'd spoken to Evan.

You, um. You're going to take the 'Stang?

'He'd tried to get me to leave her there,' I said, almost to myself.

'Who?'

'Evan.' I was trembling with rage now. 'Evan told me to leave Bridie in Redbelly. He asked if I was taking the Mustang. He was trying to figure out what car I'd be driving. I told him when I'd be leaving, and that I was going to be ferrying evidence back.'

Georgia watched my face, a mixture of hardness and understanding behind her eyes in equal measures. The eyes of a sex crimes cop. Of a betrayed wife. I turned to leave and she grabbed my arm. 'Russell.'

I yanked my arm away and walked off.

* * *

The stale white-and-blue fluorescent light of the hospital car park. Then, the vibrant green and red and yellow of the streets around the Hawkesbury District Hospital, traffic lights on the roads wet with misty rain. Black of the bush-lined streets, gold windows of houses and farms. Dodge called me maybe ten minutes after I hit the dark road heading back north. I turned the phone on silent and tossed it into the back seat. I wanted to let my mind drift. Let the anger build, until it was no longer hot but cold and calm and rigid, a vibration in my very bones and a mission in my heart. The moon was hard and white above the tree line. I approached the turn-off to the farm at Maroota doing the speed limit, glided in, and let the two women manning the checkpoint there look at my ID with my face passive and my eyes on the windscreen. They reported who I was to the ground team, and I was let through.

Squad cars were parked on either side of the road, four of them, right outside the gates. A command vehicle further on. A grey cat was sitting by the wheel of one of the cars, its eyes flashing red as I passed and drove up the driveway. My approach had been announced. A stocky guy with a round face was leading the scene, came over, made sure he had a constable with a body cam in tow. I showed my ID silently, afraid that if I tried to speak I'd firebreathe someone's head off their shoulders the second I opened my mouth. I wasn't there to give answers, or be arrested, or make a fuss. I just had to see with my own eyes.

The scene leader, who introduced himself as Tailor, looked me over as I watched the activity up at the house.

'I'm new to the case,' Tailor said, putting his hands up. 'I'm still catching up. But I've been told your brother, Evan Powder, is wanted for leaving the scene of a serious accident earlier today. An officer came here looking for him, as they have been unable to make contact with him at his home address.'

I said nothing.

'When that officer arrived here, they found that your father, Arthur Powder, was not at the residence. But the place was unlocked, and his phone and wallet were inside. There's a vehicle registered to Evan Powder in the carport.'

'Have you actually got a question for me?' I asked.

'Do you know the whereabouts of Evan Powder, or Arthur Powder, Detective Inspector Powder?'

'No, I don't.'

'We have grave concerns for the both of them,' Tailor said. 'Evan especially.'

'Can I go up to the house and look?' I asked. 'Maybe I can see something that'll help.'

'Go ahead.' Tailor nodded, after thinking about it.

I went up. Heard another detective address Tailor behind me. 'You don't want to lock him down?'

'He's not the one I'm after,' Tailor replied.

I walked up to the house and turned off the cracked, weed-riddled path. Noticed a fresh bullet hole in the carport awning, which some officers were examining with torches. I went to Evan's car and looked in the window. The officers hadn't unlocked it yet, were pointing their torches at a phone and laptop that were sitting on the front passenger seat. I went to the house. The living room and kitchen were as I remembered them. Filthy, old, damp and sad. I saw the bucket of car keys sitting by the back door. I crouched down, shifted some of the keys around. There must have been fifty sets in the bucket. I walked out the laundry door, into the darkened field, and made my way between the cars, looking for fresh tyre tracks in the grass. I found them, and realised Evan's plan.

* * *

Making sure I wasn't followed, I drove towards the river, joining Singleton Road, following the curves and straights between the lonely fields. I knew where Evan was. Psychics and moon-and-stars weirdos would call it symbiosis or brotherly mind-meld or whatever, but to me it just made plain sense. Evan would have taken a car from Dad's lot, an unregistered, heavy and untraceable thing, with the hopes of using it to smash into my Mustang and relieve me of the evidence I'd been ferrying to forensic holding at Pemulwuy. With the borrowed car totalled, Evan would have planned to bush-bash back to his own car at the farm. He would have known he'd be exhausted, and possibly injured from the impact of his car into mine, so he'd be looking for the flattest, most hidden and safe route back. Evan would have to bet going back for his car at the farm wasn't safe now. But there was another possibility on the same route home—the neighbour at the back, Rodger, who had yard cars the same as Dad.

I knew where Evan would be now. He'd be down along the old route we took as kids, where we rode our bikes, creek-hopped, stayed out as long as we could away from home. I had to get to Evan before the cops did. I sped up and followed the river through the night.

EVAN

The laughter came in little bursts. A giggle here. A chuckle there. I was never ready for it, that same thought that kept popping up. But whenever I hit a stretch of smooth land alongside the river, and my path was lit by moonlight and the sand was flat and stable, I thought about it again. About how my father had murdered women. Hit and raped and stabbed and strangled women, stolen their fucking lives from them, and here *I* was: here *I* was, wounded and hobbling and running from the law. *My* name would be on the radio channels by morning. *My* face would be on the squad-car laptops right now; my description, my badge number, my car registration. I was going to have to take one of the neighbour's yard cars, then swap cars again once I'd got out of town. Steal something from someone's driveway like a fucking criminal. It was hilarious, really. I had spent my entire life trying to do the right thing. Be a loving father. A loyal husband. I'd left work to sit in stifling school halls to listen to parent information evenings. I'd researched hotel restaurant menus for Delle's fucking birthday getaway. Now I was stopping dead in my tracks and watching the ridge line, trying to pick out the shape of men up there, Russell, maybe, coming to kill me.

This was just amazing.

All of it, incomprehensible.

My whole hand was numb. Wrist, forearm, everything. Numb but throbbing, tingling, not working properly, the fingers swollen twice their usual size. My mouth was dry. My brain screaming at me to take my shirt off and compression wrap the injury. To drink from the river. To give up.

A boat went by, following the river. The noise that had stopped me seemed to come again. Up on the ridge. A roo? I walked on, clambering over rocks, the stink of dead fish on the wind.

I'd reached an impasse on the beach and was heading back into the bush when a set of hands big enough to crush my skull seized on my shirt, and Russell was there, dragging me forward and slamming me into the trunk of a gumtree.

'You *fucking bastard*!'

'Oh, shit!'

Russell wasted no time. The hands let go of my shirt and came around my throat. I allowed myself be forced to the ground. My brother didn't seem to know whether to strangle me or punch my head in, tried a bit of both. I felt my cheek split over the bone. This was achingly familiar: Russell straddling my chest, raining blows. It was the same mistake that had cost me the dog. Letting Russell get on top of me. My bigger brother had always been my bigger brother, fuller in the chest, longer in the arms. My brain was filled with horror. Dad straddling those women. Strangling them. Raining blows on *their* faces. I decided I deserved to die like this, beaten into the ground. I hoped Russell would drag me into the river. I could be beside Dad, where I belonged.

'I'm going to fucking *murder you, Evan!*'

'Do it,' I begged. My mouth was full of blood. Russell got off me, and I coughed it onto the ground. I waited for a devastating punch to the back of the skull. Pleaded for it to come. It didn't. I was lying on my snake-bit arm, and it was prickling and pulsing now, right to the shoulder. 'Russell, please.'

'How *could* you?' Russell dropped down beside me. I heard tears in the man's voice. 'I don't understand it. You . . . you asked me if Bridie was coming with me!'

'I'm sorry.'

'You could have killed her!'

'I'm sorry.'

'Don't say you're fucking sorry!' Russell had a handful of my hair, was grinding my face into the dirt, spittle on the rim of my ear as he roared down at me. 'Don't say that! *You were covering for him, Evan!* I know you were covering for him!'

'He was going to come after Chris.' I swallowed. 'He said he'd take Chris down with him. That's why he was there. That night.'

'Did Chris do it?'

'No.' I tried to get up.

'Did he help at all? Did he see it?'

'No.'

'Where is he? The old man. Did he run?'

'He . . .'

Russell waited. I drew a few long breaths, let them out slowly. 'He was going to take Chris from me. He told me so. I couldn't . . .'

'Evan,' Russell said. 'Evan . . . what did you do?'

I couldn't speak.

'Evan, did you kill Dad?'

I lay in the dirt and cried. Another boat went by. In the white, stuttering light from its search beams, rolling over the other side of the river, I saw Russell hiding his face in his hands, gripping his skull.

'He told me what he did, and he threatened my son,' I said. 'And I . . . I . . . I just lost it.'

'How many were there?' Russell asked. 'The girls. How many. Did he tell you?'

'I never gave him the chance.'

'Oh my god.'

'I know.'

Russell watched the water, restless, his eyes searching the black surface. We fell into silence, trying to catch our breath.

'You're not going to get out from underneath this,' Russell said. The fire was slowly leaving him. 'You can tell the cops whatever you want, Evan. Tell them you were afraid of Dad. That he threatened you, or Delle, or Chris. It won't matter. You'll do jail time. You'll just . . . you'll have to. They'll make an example out of you for trying to cover it up. Those families have been waiting for fifty fucking years. Fifty *years.* Linda Special had just had a fucking baby. Marian was right on the verge of really starting her life. And Chloe . . . You saw her, Evan. She was a *kid*, and so is Bridie, and I'm so . . . *I'm so angry at you right now!*'

'I know.'

'You deserve to go to jail, Evan. And to have everyone see you go.'

'I know.'

'Where's the body?'

'Dad's?'

'Yes, Dad's.'

'In the river,' I said. Russell had released me. I pushed myself upright, so the two of us were sitting now, side by side, facing the water. How many hours had we spent just like this as kids? Watching the water. Quiet and numb, broken and trying to mend ourselves in the aftermath of something Dad had done. Russell raked his hands through his hair. Dragged his fingernails down his stubble. I could hear it. It was so quiet, now. It was like the bush was listening.

'Why didn't you come to me?' Russell said.

'Because I didn't want to poison you with it, too.'

'Oh, what bullshit,' Russell moaned into his palms. 'It has always been us against him! The two of us, together! Why would it have been any different this time?'

I said nothing. My throat was dry as bone. An engine hummed. Somewhere up there, beyond the ridge line. I turned and saw the flashing of blue and red lights against the silhouettes of gums. The lights moved on, but not completely. They were close. 'Are you hurt?' Russell asked.

I thought about it. About everything he'd just said. The women. Linda, Marian, Chloe, and all the others. I made a decision. I folded my arm carefully against my body. Slowly. So as not to be obvious. 'No.'

We sat for a while longer. Russell trying to take it all in, I supposed. Trying to come to terms with the fact that his brother and his father were going to make national news the following day as cold-blooded killers. No news outlet in the country was going to leave out the fact that Russell had killed a man himself on duty that weekend. They were going to show his face while they showed footage of my father's car being dragged from the river with his body in the front passenger seat. Nothing was going to be the same for Russell ever again. He'd hated the attention he got for coming out of the closet five years earlier. This was going to be a nuclear bomb dropped on his world. He had the jittery look now of a shell-shock victim as he turned his distant eyes on me.

'Hey, listen,' I said.

'What?'

'You and I are probably not going to get to talk for a while.'

'At least not without a recording device being present,' Russell grunted.

'I want to say . . .' I gripped my throbbing arm. The hotness and sickness was in my neck and throat now. 'I want to . . .'

'Jesus. Really, Evan? Now?'

'I saw you . . .' I managed. I cleared my throat, which seemed to help. 'After the big fight. After you came out, and you clocked Dad. We hadn't spoken for . . . I don't know. Two years?'

I told him about the encounter. About how I'd been in the Sydney CBD with Delle, catching dinner and a show to celebrate her birthday. We'd been in an Uber on Macquarie Street, and I'd turned and looked out and spotted my brother sitting on a bench at the top of Martin Place, a concrete and sandstone wonderland behind him, the gold lights of fancy restaurants and cafes, legal people leaving their offices and running for the train. I almost hadn't recognised him. He looked smart. Stylish. He looked like a man killing time before a date. All dressed up, somewhere to go. What had fallen most uneasily into place in my mind hadn't been the nice outfit but the smile on his face. He'd been talking on the phone, an almost conspiratorial smile crossing his features, his eyes bright and full of mischief as he listened to the response and then cracked into a laugh.

'You looked happy,' I said now. 'It was weird to see that.'

Russell was quiet.

'I felt happy, seeing you,' I said. 'And surprised. And what a sad thing that was. Because it shouldn't have been weird or surprising to see you like that.'

'You should have stopped and got out and said hello.'

'Next time,' I said.

The sound of voices up on the hill seemed closer now.

'Okay,' my brother said. He took a deep breath. 'I'm going to go up there and talk to the cops. If they lay eyes on you, they'll probably shoot you. They'll all be onto it by now, Evan. Dodge would have told them. It'll be spreading like wildfire. They'll know you did this because Dad was the one. Because you were covering for him. Now he's missing, and they will be thinking that you're armed. They're going to be champing at the bit to be the person to bring you in. But I'll tell them you're going to cooperate.'

I nodded. With my good hand, I took my gun from the back of my jeans and handed it to my brother.

'You didn't call me in to help you before,' Russell said. He groaned as he got up. 'But I'm here now, Evan. Okay? It's all going to be all right.'

'Yeah,' I said. I felt Russell's hand on the top of my head. Reached up and touched it. Tried to stay upright, though that gentle pressure of the palm on the top of my skull threatened to collapse me completely. The waves of dizziness had started. The blood was slowing in my system. 'Thanks, Rus.'

Russell moved off. I listened to him climbing up the embankment. When he was far enough away, I lay down and asked the venom to take me away.

After a few shallow, dry breaths, it did.

ROB

He came in just as the rain eased up and the sun started setting, lighting puddles in the gravel beyond the pub door a blazing gold. Rob looked up from behind the bar, where he was checking off the stock list before the afternoon crowd of locals was joined by the evening gaggle of out-of-towners. He felt a whump of terror hit his sternum, sharp and painful, like a thrown rock. Russell Powder wiped his boots off on the rug Rob placed there when it was wet, and came in.

He was wearing a navy-blue collared shirt with the cuffs turned up, and seeing the dressy sort of shirt gave Rob the first uneasy inkling that he wasn't, in fact, about to be roasted alive again by the enormous detective. And if *that* wasn't going to happen, Rob didn't know what *was*. He glanced sideways, towards the kitchen, wondering if it was too late to simply walk away and get one of the girls to deal with Detective Inspector Powder. But Millie was frying chips and Yasmin was in the dining room, and he was on his own to face the devil at the door.

'Mr Winter,' Powder said with a nod, and Rob swallowed, hoping the next words weren't going to be *You are under arrest on the suspicion of . . .*

He couldn't imagine what. But that didn't matter.

Rob nodded back, gripped the beer taps for dear life, tried to say 'Good evening' and 'Hello' at the same time and instead said, 'Good-o.'

Powder sat down at the end of the bar, only two metres or so to Rob's right. Uncomfortably close. Although, in this situation, Rob pondered, several hundred kilometres was also uncomfortably close. 'Can I get a schooner of the lager?'

'Yes.' Rob numbly took a glass from the rack. 'Of course. Yes.'

'And what's your most expensive whisky?'

Rob baulked. Looked for tricks and traps within the question. Couldn't see any. 'Uh . . . my most *expensive*?'

'Yes.'

'Oh, uh, well, uh, I actually . . . I have a bottle of Glenfiddich Grande Couronne under the counter somewhere. Twenty-six years old. But that'd be . . . It'd be a hundred bucks a shot, sir.'

Powder pulled his wallet from his back pocket. Rob took the bottle of whisky out, trying not to tremble, and poured a generous shot in a nice tumbler he dug up and dusted off. The detective paid for the drinks, took them and sat sipping, looking out at the puddles and the park and the river beyond, a big arm on the counter. Rob shifted around the bar, doing busywork, trying to decide when this was going to turn into whatever it was going to turn into. An ambush. A nasty prank. A campaign of intimidation. Twenty minutes passed like twenty years. The detective drank the beer and nursed the expensive whisky. People came and ordered their drinks, and nodded in acknowledgement to the man at the end of the bar without trying to engage him in conversation or stepping too close. Everyone knew who he was. The entire nation did. The son of what was being reported as one of the country's worst serial killers had been all over the news for a solid week in the aftermath of what happened. As had his dead brother, the disgraced Evan Powder, who the papers were saying had gone a significant way towards covering up for his father's crimes before he snapped and murdered the old man.

Rob found himself thinking, as his heart rate slowed, that, actually, it was sort of a big move for Detective Inspector Russell Powder to show up like this. To sit at this bar. To show his face to these people. A man who seemed to have slithered, from birth, from a viper's nest and into the world. Because surely it was humiliating, all of it. Some of the less classy papers had noted that Russell Powder was a gay man hailing from Newtown, in Sydney. (Rob was so affixed to the story that, like most people, he'd read all that was written about the case, whether classily written or not.) What was Russell Powder doing here, now? In the open, and far from home. Where he was just as likely to be attacked for the homosexuality as he was to have to explain that he hadn't known about either his father's or his brother's dirty secrets?

But was that, in fact, what this was all *about*? Coming here, of all places. Showing his face. Sitting politely and quietly at the end of the bar, drinking hundred-dollar-a-glass whisky and passing the minutes—a decent number of them, now—without issuing a threat or insult or snide remark to Rob Winter? Was this . . . a gesture of *apology*? Rob told himself to get real. He watched the detective from the corner of his eye as he finished up his drink, gazing now through the glass doors to the dining room, where Rob knew one of Dodge's people was with his mates. Nathan Fry. Rob expected the detective to go in there, join the group, order dinner maybe. But instead, he pushed his glasses back towards Rob and smiled as he turned to leave. 'Thanks. See you.'

'Yeah, see ya, mate,' Rob said. He watched the detective go, and felt the band of fearfulness that had been around his chest snap free.

RUSSELL

The sound of the apartment building buzzer reached me where I was sitting on the balcony, warming my ungroomed feet in the sunshine. Instinctively I stood, leant out over the rail, but there was an awning between me and whoever was standing on the steps of my little blue apartment block in Newtown. I went in and clicked the button on the panel without asking who it was, figuring it was one of the backpackers in the apartment next to mine who had forgotten their keys, something that happened almost daily. Then I came back out and sat in the sun again.

I'd been doing that a lot, especially in the early mornings when I couldn't sleep. Sitting in the light, to get away from the darkness. Sometimes my brain was knotted with memories. Of diving down for Bridie in the river. Or running through the dark of Stephen Branch's property. Or standing, watching the pair of officers come back up from the bushland beside the river, where they'd gone down to arrest my brother. One of them giving a subtle head-shake to his superior. The other, less subtle, looking to me for an explanation.

'He's dead.'

The guy had put out his arms, palms up, like it was some prank I'd set up.

The weeks since my time at Redbelly Crossing had been spent running from things like that. Memories and explanations. The news was so saturated with pictures of my father and my brother and Chloe Lutz and myself, that for a couple of days I left and went back to Redbelly, where there weren't TVs in windows and ads on phones and people sitting on the train with newspapers in their hands, the front pages thrust out, waiting for me to see them. The journos came looking for me at my apartment, and the old woman who owned the ground floor flat got so sick of it she threw a bucket of water at them. I stayed in the houseboat, in the last place anybody would look for me, with my phone off, waking early to work on the awning over the top deck. Dodge came some days to sit at the table with his injured leg up and annoy me with pointers and tips about my building work, and stories about the awning and the houseboat and the town and his mother-in-law and his genius psychologist wife and everything else a person could possibly think to talk about. I was better with cars than I was with wood, but I did get the awning up, in the end, and I listened to Dodge without ever once telling him to shut up, or looking at him like anything other than a friend.

While I was out in Redbelly, I visited John Special, and I told him that a male DNA profile had indeed been extracted from the sections of ancient floor joist that Dodge and I had cut from his house. I told him that that profile had been a match to my father. I showed him footage Nathan Fry had expertly pulled from the camera I'd taken from the secret road behind the drug cook's house. How it showed my father's Ford Falcon coming into town, and then leaving again, on the night he killed Chloe Lutz. The old man listened carefully to what I had to say, sitting in his little kitchen, uneaten Tim Tams on the table between us and his daughter's dog glaring at me from its bed in the corner of the room. I told John that he'd never be able to look his wife's killer in the face, or tell him how he felt about what he'd done. That my own brother had stolen that chance away from him forever. I don't know if it helped Mr Special to know that my father had died in terror and agony, the way all his victims had. Or what he felt about me, connected as I was by flesh and blood to the two men who had caused him the most pain in his life. But as I was walking out the front door, he offered his palm, and we shook hands. So that was something.

As I left the property, preparing to make a phone call to Larry Lutz and tell him the same things I told John Special, I passed a beautiful woman in a car coming up the long driveway. She smiled and waved at me as I passed, and she looked so much like Linda Special that I wondered if I'd just seen her ghost finally coming home.

I went looking for more ghosts, stopping by the house where Marian Richley had been murdered, which was a broken-down shell of construction on an overgrown slab of land to the west of the Special house. While nothing belonging to Linda Special had been found among Dad's kill trophies, there'd been a brooch that was identified as having gone missing the night Marian died discovered among the collection. I knew, 'in my guts', as Dodge had phrased it, that my father had murdered that innocent young woman. The brooch was hard, physical evidence of that. But nothing drove the truth home to me more than the fact that as I wandered the ruins of the home where she'd died, the cockatoos screamed relentlessly at me. Dodge would have said I was crazy, so I didn't bother telling him about it.

I sat in the ruins of the Richley house and thought about Marian, and the life she'd been living, and the future that was stolen from her and the people around her. I found little traces of her parents, or her, I didn't know. A smashed plate. The cover of a paperback novel. A screwdriver. A bright floral curtain, faded with age and rain. Marian's former home had been obliterated by neglect and exposure to the elements. But it had really been torn down, and folded in, by the hands of hopelessness. A lost hope her parents surely had, as the days and years ticked by after her murder, of ever finding peace. A wretchedness hung around me then, knowing that the man who made this altar of pain on the hill had also made me. I don't usually talk to the dead, but I whispered to Marian and to her parents everything I'd told John and Larry, knowing they couldn't hear me, but wishing that they could.

I'd been home at my apartment for two days now, no closer to understanding how I felt about Evan, or about Dad. The obvious way to feel about my brother was miserable, and the obvious way to feel about Dad was angry, but I might have been in a place that was beyond both of those, or still too shocked to really feel either. A lot of confusing things were going on. There seemed no way to get my balance. Georgia had invited me to dinner at the house one night, which knocked me right off the rails. Bridie sent me a picture of a pelican she'd rescued that was tied up in fishing line, and that had put me right back on the rails again. I had the urge, one night, to text Delle, so I did. She didn't answer.

A soft knock came at my apartment door. I got up and went and opened it, and Bridie looked at my fluffy, peach-coloured robe and gave a little laugh. I don't know what she expected me to be wearing at seven o'clock in the morning in my own home, but I guessed it wasn't that. The exhilaration of seeing her there in the hallway made me laugh, too. Because this was how I'd dared to envision it, sometimes. Before all the horror. Bridie coming here and seeing my apartment. The two of us pretending to be a normal dad and daughter, for as long as we had to, with the hopes that one day it might become real. Once we'd stopped laughing, we hugged in the doorway.

'Just thought I'd check in.' She gave a noncommittal shrug, like it was no big deal. She brandished two takeaway cups from the cafe up on the corner of King Street in a cardboard carrier in one hand. 'See how you were.'

I invited her in. Took her straight to the guest bedroom I'd done up for her, and she did all the things I'd dreamt of her doing: cooing and gasping and commenting on the wainscotting, which I'd done myself, and the sunset lamp, which I'd bought because I knew young people liked those. After a while, we went to the balcony. She sat in the wrought-iron chair there, kicked off her sandals and put her feet in the slice of sunshine that was crossing the tiles like she knew that was the good thing to do out here: warm your feet, look at the people in the street, smell the jasmine across the way.

Through the balcony doors, behind Bridie's back, I saw Nathan Fry slip silently from my bedroom, dressed in jeans and a T-shirt, his feet bare and boots hanging from his fingers. He gave me a cautious look, his eyes flicking to Bridie. I hung an arm over the back of my chair, lifted the palm, making a motion that said that he was welcome to stay if he wanted to, to join us out on the balcony. He shook his head. Made his hand into the shape of a phone and put it to his ear. I gave him the thumbs up. He left without Bridie even knowing he'd been there.

'Have you seen the news today?' Bridie asked.

'No.'

'They've got another one,' she said. I knew what she was talking about. My father's DNA, extracted from the floorboards, from Chloe Lutz's body, and from his own rotting corpse in the car in the river where Evan had put him, was being run against a series of cold cases, one by one. Photographs of the box of old jewellery that had been discovered freshly buried at his house were being circulated around the families of missing people nationwide, to see if anyone recognised anything. The number of murder victims in New South Wales was up to seven. Queensland had two cases. None of the other states had linked any cases yet. But there was 'hope', the papers were saying. I liked that word. Their use of it. In all the darkness, the victims' families were holding out 'hope' for answers. For an end to decades of thinking, praying, fighting, wondering. An end to hoping. Bridie was smiling sadly at the sun on her toes. I wondered what she felt every time a new match popped up. Probably the same as I did. A mixture of shame and gratitude.

'Have they called you in for an interview yet?' she asked. 'About what you remember? There must have been, like . . . things that make sense now. Times he was away.'

'I did an initial interview,' I said. 'But since then, I've remembered more. It's hard to go back, that's all. I spent so long blocking all that stuff out.'

She nodded, looked at my eyes. 'Do you think they'll match all the jewellery and stuff?'

'It'll be a hard slog,' I said. 'Cold cases are always hard. People die. Memories fade.' I watched her face, trying to sense what she was getting at. When I thought I knew, I said, 'I'm sure they'd be grateful for any help that was offered, Birds. I could get you pictures of the items.'

'Oh, I couldn't.' Bridie waved at me. 'I mean, Mum has told me what she'd do to me if I ever joined the coppers. And I can only imagine what she'd do to *you*, if you inspired me to.'

'I'm not afraid of that woman.'

'You should be.'

'They have dogs, you know,' I said. 'The cops. They have horses. You could skip the whole bit at the academy where they teach you how to rush up and crash tackle someone twice your size. You already know how to do that.'

Bridie's lip twitched mischievously, and I started forming new dreams, about my daughter giving me access to that quick and daring and courageous mind of hers, the one that had gone right out on a limb and decided that Chloe Lutz had pissed off a serial killer. The one that told me to look at the road at the back of the drug cookhouse. The one that had been *dead right* on both counts. Bridie would make an excellent cop. I knew that in my bones. But, again, the shame of wanting something that my father had also wanted prickled in me. I told myself to step back from influencing her, or pressuring her, which I knew I could do without even meaning to. I shrugged and looked at the jasmine across the way. 'Whatever you decide.'

Someone down on the street slammed a door, clopped toward the main road in heels. In the distance, a siren wailed and the city hummed.

'What did you have planned for today?' my daughter asked me, after we'd sat in silence for a bit.

I glanced at my phone on the little table next to me. 'I'm in the market for a new Mustang. I've almost finished grieving the last one.'

'Ooh, let me see,' she took up my phone, turned it toward me so that my face unlocked the screen. 'Where were you looking? Facebook Marketplace?'

'Yep.'

She opened it up and started scrolling, and I watched her window shop for a while, counting down the seconds until she did what I knew she would do: sat bolt upright in her chair, having spotted something I'd seen an hour earlier.

'I've found it!' she said. She showed me the screen. A baby-shit-green 1965 Shelby that looked like it had been left in a field for half a century and periodically beaten with a cricket bat. 'Look at this!'

'I knew you'd pick that one,' I nodded.

'Did you? Why?'

'Because there are so many nice 'Stangs on there, loved and preserved by their owners, and that's the one that isn't. That car you're looking at would take extreme levels of passion and commitment to even extract from where it's lain down to die and get to somewhere it has a chance of being rescued. A madman would pay more than a dollar for it. If I turn the key in the ignition and it actually starts, and a bunch of rats don't go leaping out from under the hood, I'll eat my hat.'

'I love it.'

'Of course you do. It's a rusty hunk of crap that no one else wants. You've looked down that list and found your own father in car form, Bridie.'

'Oh my god,' Bridie laughed. 'You may be right.'

'Uh huh.'

'When can we go get it?'

I took in her puppy dog eyes, and let a huge sigh ease out of my nose, just so she wouldn't get the idea that I was as keen on the car as she was. So that she'd think that as we spent the next few months to a year fixing up the old car together, it was a bit of a hardship on me, and not the best thing that had happened in ages.

I flicked my head toward the door, and she leaped up, and we got going.

Author's note

Dear Reader,

This is the part of the book where I would usually include an acknowledgements page thanking everyone who worked on this novel with me. I hope I'm forgiven by those many wonderful people, because I am instead going to use this space to make a direct appeal to you.

The writing of the novel you've just read, *Redbelly Crossing*, was fuelled in part by research into a true crime. Knowledge of the real-life murders of two young women in Sydney in 1973 and 1974 respectively intersected with my own life in an unusual way. I will explain how I came upon these true crime cases, and my connection with them, in a moment. But first, I want to make it clear that the book you just read is not a fictionalised account of what happened in those cases. You will need to forget everything about the murder victims Chloe Lutz, Linda Special and Marian Richley and what happened to them. You will need to forget about Russell, Evan, Bridie and Arthur Powder. The township of Redbelly Crossing does not exist. It is very loosely inspired by a real town, where there is a bridge, a pub, a river and a hell of a lot of snakes. This real town is, in my experience, full of lovely people. They have a great pub, and a capable and trustworthy police force. There are not, to my knowledge at least, any murderous lunatics running around there.

I learned about the real-life murders of Lynette White and Maria Smith on a random afternoon in early 2021. I was watching my daughter, Violet, who was one and a half years old at the time, toddling around the house wearing nothing but a nappy and a pink top hat, carrying a toy briefcase. I remarked to my husband, who was sitting nearby, that she looked like a little door-to-door salesman. As I said the words, I felt a sensation like a drawer popping open in my mind. A vague memory presented itself: of my mother giving ten-year-old me a safety briefing before she left me at home alone for the first time. She was warning me not to open the front door to the house if anyone knocked. She backed up the warning with a story. She explained that she had answered the door herself once, as a teenager, when she was home alone. The stranger who had come knocking had turned out to be a killer.

Voicing the memory I'd just had to my husband, I found that he was not surprised, or alarmed. Anyone who knows anything about my mother (including my regular readers) understands that she is . . . unique. Insisting that she once had a real-life encounter with a serial killer is perfectly on brand for her. I began texting her anyway, wanting to know more. Was that just a story she had made up at the time, to reinforce the dangers of opening the door to strangers when home alone? No, she replied, the account was real. *Who was the killer?* I asked. *Who were the victims?* I called, and she told me the story.

My mother, whose name at the time was Elizabeth Ann Whiteside, lived on St Luke Street, Randwick. She recalled that in late April 1974, when she was seventeen, she was at home alone studying for her HSC when there came a knock at the front door of the house. Opening the heavy wooden door, she found a man who was approximately twenty years old standing there. He had 'dark, maybe auburn hair' that was 'curly or wavy' and 'fell to his jawline'. He was wearing a brown zip-up jacket and tan-coloured trousers. She described him as being white and having an Australian accent. The man told her that he was going door to door selling encyclopedias. While they chatted in a friendly manner through the locked screen door of the house, my mother described being overcome with a strange feeling of alarm. For an apparent encyclopedia salesman, this man was very casually dressed, in fact was bordering on 'dishevelled'. He was also not carrying anything—no briefcase, no sales pamphlets, no encyclopedias. My mother recalled that the feeling of alarm was so strong—making all the hair on her body stand on end—that when the man asked if he could come in, she pretended that she would have to ask permission from father, who she said was home. Her father had, in fact, died only a week or so earlier. At the mention of her father being home, the stranger at the door turned quickly and walked away without speaking another word.

* * *

Less than one kilometre away from my mother's house, twenty-year-old Maria Smith was murdered in the bedroom of the apartment she shared with her new husband Stephen in the block spanning 14–20 St Marks Road, Randwick. This crime occurred on the morning of 22 April, 1974, only days before my mother says she had her encounter. Maria worked as a student teacher at the Brigidine College, Randwick, where my mother was a student. The school community reeled from the murder of the bright, friendly, newly wedded woman, who had been found on the bed she shared with her husband, bound, sexually assaulted and strangled with her own pantyhose. Maria's husband of only eight weeks, Stephen, had left for work just after 7.30 a.m., and Maria had planned to leave about an hour after him to head to her job. She never made it there. Stephen found her body when he arrived home from work.

Maria's case had similarities to the murder ten months earlier of 26-year-old Lynette White, who lived less than three kilometres from Maria and Stephen, with her husband, Paul, and her 11-week-old son. Paul and Lynette lived at 26 Beach Street, Coogee.

Both women were attacked while home alone, while their husbands were at work. A smashed cup found on the floor of Lynette's home suggested to police that her attacker might have begged his way in asking for water. Evidence at the crime scene showed that

Lynette's attacker had forced her to undress at knifepoint and fold her clothes into a neat pile. The arrival of a delivery of cloth nappies at the couple's apartment may have interrupted the ordeal unfolding inside the apartment. Lynette fought her attacker valiantly, but was stabbed multiple times and died in the doorway to a bedroom where her unharmed infant was sleeping. Paul found his wife lifeless, lying in a pool of blood, upon returning from work that evening. Neither Paul White, nor Stephen Smith, are considered suspects in the murders of their wives.

The cases of both Maria Smith and Lynette White faced extreme challenges in finding resolution, some of which were posed by police actions at the time of the murders. These police were working without the benefit of DNA testing, which would come into use in Australia in the mid-1980s. Lynette White's crime scene was gravely mishandled by police, with dozens of officers traversing the scene and evidence being lost. All of the original physical evidence, in fact, in both Lynette and Maria's cases has been lost by New South Wales Police. This lost evidence included the knives used in each attack, Maria's rape kit, and a bloody nappy at Lynette's crime scene that police believe the killer used to wipe his hands.

Police have also, however, made enormous, sustained efforts to find the killer or killers of Lynette White and Maria Smith. For forty years, police believed the two murders were linked and that they were looking for one suspect. Investigations were conducted into obscene phone calls Lynette received at her home in the days prior to her murder. Leads were pursued in connection to her role as a hairdresser at her salon in Vaucluse, and as a dancer in a Hawaiian-themed hula group, The Alohas, who performed across Sydney's Eastern Suburbs. An obsessed fan of her dancing was questioned. A local man who presented with a hand injury in the days following the attack was questioned, as were suspects in sexual assaults and attacks on women in and around the Eastern Beaches in the time before and after the murders. A man was questioned who had made advances toward Lynette at a cleaning company called Swipe, which she and Paul distributed products for. A composite image of a man with red hair, a red beard and thin legs who had been seen leaving the Whites' apartment block was also distributed.

In Maria's case, police homed in on an encounter Maria had had at a party at the Malabar RSL the Friday before her death. After the RSL, the party had moved to a pub in Randwick, then back to Maria and Stephen's apartment. Stephen had been away that night at an event related to his study to become an engineer. Police say a man at that party made advances toward Maria and was firmly rejected. Investigations continued into people Maria worked with at her job at the Malabar RSL Club. Police pondered how the attacker could have accessed Maria's apartment, and whether he might have climbed onto the balcony.

There have been movements on the case in recent decades, brought about by the creativity and ingenuity of fresh investigators. In 2016, detectives returned to Paul and Lynette's apartment in Coogee and peeled back the carpet to reveal a bloodstain. Police tested the blood in the hopes of obtaining the killer's DNA, presuming he would have suffered some injuries himself during the frenzied attack. They obtained a male DNA profile. Police announced AU$1 million rewards for both Maria and Lynette's cases in 2018. A review of the cases led police to make the decision in 2018 that the two cases should be handled under separate investigations. While they were 'keeping an open mind', they felt that the links between the two cases were not strong enough to definitively say that the same killer was involved in both. They are currently eager to speak to anyone who lived in the unit blocks where Lynette and Maria lived, regardless of whether they have previously been interviewed. Information into a potential new lead—relating to a mustard-coloured Ford Capri with a black racing stripe that was seen near Maria's apartment on the day of the murder—is also of interest to police.

* * *

Diving into the real-life cases of Lynette White and Maria Smith in the days after my mother's revelation, I was dumbstruck. There came upon me a horror and dismay at what these women had endured, and the unfathomable brutality of their killer or killers. I, like Lynette, was a new mother. Like both women, I was happily married. Lynette and Maria never got the chance to really enjoy their young family lives. I felt a deep, dark rage at whoever had killed them. Lynette and Maria had not only been snatched out of their own existences, but they had been stolen away from the roles they would have played in the lives of their family members and friends. And for what? For the temporary, sick, twisted sexual and murderous fantasy of a psychopath. The selfishness of the killer's act boggled my mind. The fact wasn't lost on me that if indeed my mother had experienced an encounter with this man, there had been only a screen door and my mother's animal instincts between him and his desire to visit this hell upon my own family.

I don't know if the man who knocked on my mother's door in 1974 was Lynette's or Maria's killer. I *can't* know that. I don't know if, in the past 51 years, my mother's memory of the incident has changed, adapted or been embellished in some way. While of course I have assisted my mother in passing details of the encounter on to police, I do not know at this time if they have aided the investigations. What I do know is that there may be other women out there who experienced something related to the murders of Lynette or Maria who, like my mother, kept those experiences a secret at the time. My mother claimed, when I questioned her in 2021, that she had never told anyone what happened. 'Just you kids,' she said. When asked why, she said that she had been warned by her mother never to answer the door while she was home alone. She feared being reprimanded for doing so. She also wondered whether she would be believed, by either her mother or the police, about what happened.

Immediately after learning of these cases and my mother's encounter, I tried to get a podcast started about the cold cases. For a couple of years, and with the help of my agent, a true crime writing friend and a producer friend, I pursued that. While I was unsuccessful in that attempt, I could not leave the story alone.

That's when I began toying with the idea of the Powder family. What kind of person might have committed acts of such depravity? What would that man have been like as a father, as a friend, as a colleague? I constructed the concept of Arthur Powder, then I gave him a family. But writing a fictionalised or a reimagined version of what happened to these real-life women and their families seemed ghoulish. Regardless, the story kept turning in my brain, around and around. Suddenly Arthur had victims, both old and new. He had sons. He had a home and a history. Taking the emotions I'd experienced when learning about a true crime and turning them into art was not a practice that was new to me. Most crime fiction authors draw their ideas from true crimes. But somehow, I felt too close to this case to treat it as fiction. And what if Paul or Stephen ever read or heard about the book and saw the memory of their lost wives within the folds of my story? The idea that these men, or someone else who had experienced the loss of Lynette and Maria firsthand, might have their pain deepened by my actions was horrifying to me. So I wrote other books instead. I told myself to leave the story alone.

Then, in 2024, I snapped.

I tracked Paul White down and explained that I wanted to write a novel that in some way used fiction to explore the horror of his wife's case. And I wanted to use the promotional activities related to that novel, and an afterword in the book itself, to add to his already substantial efforts to make his wife's case widely known and to search for answers. I was terrified to meet Paul. I was prepared for him to accuse me of exploiting his wife's murder, and his family's pain, for profit. I knew there was a good chance he would see me as a vulture or a ghoul—a grief tourist mining his suffering. Instead, he saw me for what I am. Someone who is deeply disturbed, and so very, very sorry, about what happened to Lynette. He was on board with me writing the book and speaking about his wife's case in public.

Through Paul, I got an introduction to Stephen, and his lovely wife Rhonda. I told Paul and Stephen that if at any time what I had written, or what I was doing, was likely to cause them emotional harm, they needed only to tell me. I would never speak their wives' names again, and I would adjust the book accordingly. Through them, I made sure that Paul's and Stephen's extended families had no problem with what I was doing, including Lynette's son and his family, and Maria's brother.

It might be confusing why, with such a close connection to the real-life cases, I made decisions in the novel to actively distance Linda's and Marian's cases from Lynette's and Maria's ones. I did that in some circumstances to try to create a separation between the real-life versions of what happened and the fictional occurrences in the book. Setting the book in Coogee, for example, would have created too much confusion between the two sets of cases for readers trying to access their own memories of that place and time. I didn't want anyone thinking that, since I had mace the setting the same, some of the people I featured in the book were the same as those who had worked on or been effected by the real-life case. For the sake of plot, I made other changes. I gave Linda's husband John a solid and unquestionable alibi, so that, for pacing reasons, readers didn't spend too much time questioning his guilt. Changes like this one in particular, had me steeped in discomfort as a fiction writer dealing with the real-life true crime survivors, because I had essentially deleted the unimaginable pain Paul and Stephen each experienced in being the person to find their wife's body. Similarly, I made it so that Maria was single, to avoid the necessity of having two husbands in the novel (and two alibis, and two separate visits by Russell to interview the men). In this way, I've had to roll Stephen and Paul's character into one. That might be something that is routinely done in the media, the careless association of the two men due to the similarity of their circumstances. But Paul and Stephen are completely different human beings, and so were the wives they lost. Their separate tragedies were uniquely felt. This is the risk I face, when trying to use fiction to try to encompass some of that real-life pain. For the sake of the artform's limitations, some of the uniqueness and depth of the victim's pain hurt has been thrown aside. As I write this, I'm still uncomfortable with how futile it seems to even hold a candle to the hurt of these families using the device of fiction.

In my novel, John Special defiantly states that he refused to leave the home he shared with his wife, because he didn't want to let the killer take place that from him. In reality, Paul and Stephen had to leave those apartments where their wives were killed because they were young renters. In a sense, the fictional character of John Special has a freedom that Paul and Stephen never had. I set out to write this book hoping that I could get down some semblance of the pain these men and their families had endured, without softening or diluting that pain in any way. But I soon realised that was impossible. In the end, true to crime fictions conventions and expectations, we meet the killer. He gets what he deserves. There are answers, and there is closure. At the time of the writing of this afterword, none of those things have been available to Paul and Stephen, and everyone who lost Lynette and Maria. I will never be able to write a book of fiction that completely encompasses the tragedy of experiencing murder in real life. I don't believe that anyone can.

* * *

So, now, reading everything you have just read about these cases and how I came to know about them, and what I have set out to do with this book, I wonder if you could help me. You, the reader, who have been lured deliberately to this very spot by what I hope was a compelling novel. I want to ask you: do you know anything about the murders of Lynette White or Maria Smith? Did you, or someone you know, live at 14–20 St Marks Road, Randwick, or 26 Beach Street, Coogee, in and around the period of 1971 to 1975? Did you, or someone you know, own a mustard-coloured Ford Capri during this time? Do you have any knowledge that might be useful to the investigations of these crimes, no matter how small or insignificant seeming? You might hold the key to unlocking this mystery. You, holding this book in your hands now, or listening to it as an audiobook. You might be the person that Paul White and Stephen Smith have been waiting to hear from all these years. If you think that might be the case, please act now. Go to the police and tell them what you know.

Thank you for reading both *Redbelly Crossing* and this afterword. May Lynette's and Maria's families one day find peace. They certainly deserve it.

And if their killer or killers are still out there: I hope you've lived in unrelenting dread and terror all these years waiting for justice to arrive at your front door. I hope, someday soon, you'll hear it knocking.